418

I AM A TEAPOT

EDGAR SCOTT

Saevitia
Publications

Content Editor: Gerald Everett Jones
Line Editor: Daniel Griffin Smith
Copy Editor: Mike Robinson
Cover Design: Raffaello Zucco
Interior Design: Jennifer Thomas

Saevitia Publications
20423 SR 7 Ste. F6 - 418
Boca Raton, FL 33498

Names: Scott, Edgar, author.

Title: 418 : I am a teapot / by Edgar Scott.

Description: First Edition. | Boca Raton, FL : Saevitia Publications, 2021: Summary: In a dystopian world where the working class's minds are separated from their bodies, one man tries to escape his fate.

Subjects: LCSH Dystopias—Fiction. | Science fiction—Fiction. | BISAC FICTION / Science Fiction / General | FICTION / Science Fiction / Hard Science Fiction | FICTION / Science Fiction / Genetic Engineering

Print ISBN: 9780981819716
E-Book ISBN: 9780981819723
LCCN: 2021903412

First Edition March 2021

Printed in the United States of America

For my brother Peter, Professional Engineer.

Who shared his love of technology, science
and its implicit creative power.

May your dreams be electric, pure information;
I only see shadows of ideas too big to comprehend,
which you never got to see, but you now understand.

Thank you for teaching me Arithmetic.

PREFACE

Let's make no mistake about this: 418 is an error!

Originally an April Fool's joke, 418 (four eighteen) is a response code given when a request to brew coffee is made to a web service that actually happens to be a teapot. As we all know, teapots can't make coffee, to ask a teapot to do the impossible is an error.

However, since most internet browsers ignore 418, this has created an opportunity for enterprising network engineers to use it to flag situations where something isn't right but hasn't really gone wrong.

Imagine you are trying to find the results of a bug or security issue within the weblogs of your commercial web cluster. Those weblogs are gushing torrents of text, you can read them, but it would be impossible to keep up. By the time you found what you were looking for, the information is of no use, stale and obsolete. Here is where four eighteen comes to the rescue! With a little server configuration, we can have certain events trigger a 418 response. Now we can pluck those responses from the endless plumes of data exhaust. We have an opportunity to analyze the system state, client state, data and even bits of code being executed; a chance to prevent something that would be unpleasant, without grinding the system to a halt.

So here I present to you, 418. Just to let you know that something isn't right, hasn't really gone wrong; but you might want to look at this and give it some thought before something awful happens.

For further reading:

https://en.wikipedia.org/wiki/Hyper_Text_Coffee_Pot_Control_Protocol
https://tools.ietf.org/html/rfc2324
https://www.google.com/teapot click the teapot!

Please enjoy the story,
Edgar Scott

I am a teapot!

1

EXCEPTION!

20XX-03-02T12:34:00+00:00 EXCEPTION: SIGABRT 686381KAA418

20XX-03-02T12:58:18+00:00 686381KAA418 RESOURCE REDIRECT: CLINIC 14

7:34 and there it was, a message that one of Brian Agarwal's staff, 686381KAA418, had been involved in an exception. Brian looked at the message. An *exception*? Brian loved these concise explanations. SIGABRT simply meant that the programming inside the unit stopped. "Exception" usually meant something messy. Hopefully it was something fixable like a broken bone, cut or sprain; but since it was offline, probably not.

Brian turned to his computer, logged into the Popular Insurance Company's website. A few clicks—clear away a popup or two about some fantastic deal he didn't want—the site said there was a pending case under review, but it didn't have any details. The case had been opened this morning by the billing department at clinic 14. It annoyed him that he'd have to go down to the clinic and see what this particular *exception* was about, but he didn't have much else to do today. Quietly, Brian got up from his desk, stepped into the hallway and locked the door behind him.

Walking away from his office, he sighed. *Well, this is more interesting than sitting around playing solitaire all day.* But it bugged him, the lost wages. He wished he'd noticed the message sooner, before he'd made it to the office. Hopefully no one would notice if his staff didn't pick up the garbage today. He really did need the money.

It was the first time I had ever been, for real, punched. Like all good punches, I didn't see it coming. It took me by surprise, and I don't remember—my face, bones being crushed, flesh tearing. Why had I been punched? I'd never been punched. What did it mean and was it going to happen again?

I was talking to my friends. We were going to meet up at Dr. Pong's that night and hang out. Why had I been punched, though? It didn't make sense! How could it happen? It's true, someone could punch my avatar, but not me directly. My head hurt and the world was going dark. Couldn't keep my eyes open. And I really should be going to work.

Things had started to go fuzzy; images became chunky. My friend—*what's his name, with the soul patch, I just can't think right now*—his mouth stuck open, but he was still talking. His jaw snapped shut, he didn't seem to be in sync with his words. Everything froze, mid-syllable. I felt a tremendous crack from the left side, and something seemed to go snap in my shoulder. A wall collapsed into me, breaking bones, left ear melting, warm waves of color washing over me. The lights went out. My friends were no longer speaking, I was neither awake nor online. I didn't know it was 7:34. I didn't know anything.

At 7:34, the ceiling of Brian's bedroom lit with a soft green glow. Slowly the glow faded, the ceiling returned to darkness, and Brian and his wife Imelda continued to sleep. Yet another message to be ignored until the time he woke and wanted to decide what was important and what should be discarded. Neither Brian nor Imelda ever woke before 8 a.m., and the message would have to wait until then. But the message, having been sent, fulfilled the requirements that the message should be sent, and so everything was as it should be.

At 8 o'clock, the mobile started to make some actual noise, an ascending chime, which caused Brian to roll over and stab at the little computer. Nine more minutes would be ideal. He would get up and make breakfast for his son, Prince, and get himself off to work.

Nine minutes later, Brian groaned at the sound that was coming out of his mobile. He'd slept well but didn't want to get up, another day like every other day. Brian's feet hit the floor, a good solid floor, with a throw rug. His toes squeezed the pile before he put any real weight on his feet—he did this every day—and he was up. Staggered just a bit as the blood rushed down to his legs and bounced back again. He wiped the sleep from his eyes and wandered to the door, leaving his wife snoozing in bed.

In the kitchen, Brian noticed he had his mobile in his hand. He didn't remember picking it up—an extension of his hand— and looked at it. It was happily displaying facts about how many messages he had missed. No doubt some coupons, a message or two of some great importance to no one at all, and the number of emails that he had received, which he would take care of when he got to work. Brian cleared them all in one swoop. He looked at the mobile. All he saw was the time, and a moving picture of his wife Imelda holding their smiling son, Prince. "Now that's how a mobile should look," he smiled.

Prince had heard Brian wander into the kitchen. Perhaps it was a clang of a pot, or the squeak of the refrigerator door. Whatever it was, Prince was up and bounding toward the kitchen. He came busting around the corner, slid on the kitchen tile, bounced off the island and went skittering into Daddy!

"Daddy, Daddy, can we have pancakes today?"

Brian looked down at Prince, at the real excitement in the deep brown of his five-year-old eyes and his mop of dark, every direction, hair. How could he say no? What was wrong with pancakes? Pancakes every day! Prince would love it, and he himself would be enormous, but did that matter? Prince would love it.

"Sure we can," Brian started, "but why don't we have some nice fruit first, and maybe a little granola?"

Prince immediately pouted, "Why not pancakes first and then fruit?" It was priceless, that pout, something Brian had never thought he would enjoy so much. He'd never tell Prince that, lest Prince use that on him to get whatever he wanted, but it was adorable, and

3

he felt a warm tugging inside him. If it was the weekend, he would have said yes.

"I don't know," Brian said, trying to lead the conversation elsewhere. "I think fruit has to come first, then granola. And then, if you are that hungry, we can have pancakes." Brian had learned that an outright "no" never got him that far.

The two dark eyes brightened, and the pout disappeared into a big grin. How long this trick was going to work didn't matter, it had worked today. "Okay little buddy." Brian picked up his son with both hands, raised him high into the air and carried him over to the table. "You just pull up a chair here, and I will get breakfast on the way."

Prince struggled into his seat as his father put him down on the chair. The table was just a few inches below his chin. "And then, pancakes?"

"Sure," Brian said, smiling. He turned away toward the fridge to see what it was he had available for slicing. "Then pancakes."

Brian took Prince to school. Well, he took Prince downstairs to the carport and put him into a car. The car itself was little more than a chair on wheels with a good stereo system, and a smooth front with a screen where whatever video or movie Prince wanted to watch would appear.

Prince climbed into the car and—obediently or compulsively— snapped the seat belt around his little waist, his dark little fingers seemed to fly as he cinched it around himself. The seat sighed and snuggled around him, keeping him firmly in place. Prince smiled up. "Okay Daddy, off to school."

Brian spoke directly into the car in a louder voice, "Emerald Valley Elementary."

Lights flashed within the car. "Calculating route to Emerald Valley Elementary School."

"Confirmed," Brian interrupted before the car could ask, "Please confirm destination." The door started to close. "Have a good day at school, love you," Brian called to Prince who was busy telling the car what he wanted to view as the door closed.

Brian heard the car lock itself, as a small white bubble encased his child. Very safe. It would whisk him off to school, and before his little Prince knew it, he would be stepping out at the school's carport. This was going to be a decent day after all. Brian felt good as he headed back to his apartment. He too would have to go to work soon, but it was a good day. Everything felt right.

Milky-eyed rescue technicians pried open what was left of the car to see what was inside. It wasn't going to be good, but it still had to be opened. The problem was that the car had just failed, some exception had occurred. The car had stopped reporting its place on the road. It never took long before, *Wham!* But that's what happened to anything out of control. So, pry it open they must.

Most people didn't do so well when seeing an accident: the blood, flesh, and bone mangled by machinery and steel. But rescue technicians were programmed for this, and they never see any of it, just go about their work expertly, quickly and without the nasty reactions that might have happened in the olden days, when eyes that couldn't unsee would have to disentangle the entanglement. Unfortunately, it wasn't a zombie car, it was carrying a passenger. How it got this far was amazing, but exceptions happen.

The rescue technicians set to work trying to extract the body, reaching into the car, getting their hands bloody as they gripped the bones that they could find and tried to pull the body from the restraint foam. The techs spotted the adapter on the right side of the head and brought forth a reader to hold near the temple.

The screen flashed, "686381KAA418," and at that moment a message was sent from one computer to another and to Brian Agarwal's telephone, which he would ignore.

Brian went to work, which was to say he got into his car—his private car. He did not like to take the public cars. They could be dirty. Even though he had just sent Prince to school in a public car, he always checked to ensure there were no unpleasant surprises waiting before he let Prince get in.

Now that almost all cars were self-driving, cars could last for years. Accidents were so rare there were now stories of people having the same car for up to fifteen years, some rumored even more. As long as you relax, sit back, put on a show—if you would like—and let the car do the driving, you were going to be safe and comfortable. Brian usually drew the curtains, so he did not have to see where the car was going or how close he got to other cars. Even with today's precise engineering, it was hard to watch your car bob and weave through heavy traffic, even with private cars getting priority. It was nerve-wracking to see a car popup inches in front of you, with both cars applying the breaks at the same time. Imelda, however, found it reassuring that the technology worked so well.

The Agarwal's car was built for four. Well, okay, maybe two and two really small half-people. Brian had managed to talk Imelda into it by saying they would take trips out to the country, and when Prince was a small baby, they had, once, maybe twice. No, actually once. But it was comfortable, and that's what Brian wanted: a nice comfortable ride to the office and back.

It didn't take long for the car to get him to the office. He got out and directed it to "Make busy, and park," which meant that, based on his patterns of usage, it would drive around, or find someplace to park, or both, depending on which actions were least expensive, always returning when it was summoned or needed. Obediently, the car locked itself up and drove away.

Brian took the lift to the third floor. He had a nice view of an old parking lot that almost no one ever used. *Who drove?* But there were still dumpsters that needed taking out, all the coffee packets, cups, and napkins had to go somewhere, and at 10:36, three days a week, a garbage truck arrived to do just that. For some reason, Brian had never worked out, the building paid for trash removal three times a week; but chose Monday, Thursday and Friday.

From his office he could watch the truck come and dump the trash. If any extra trash fell out, which was the usual case, the garbage collection staff would get out of the truck and pick up the loose papers, broken bits of wood, rotting food and innumerable plastic bags that were sure to be littered around the disposal area.

The office was small room with little more than space for a desk, a largely empty file cabinet, a computer, and a bit of carpet. But the door had a lock and he could pull the blinds. The building was nice but rundown. They had coffee, and maybe that was why Brian stayed there, because he liked coffee. A nice cup of coffee while wedged behind his desk, where it was silent, where he could read the news on the computer and ignore the email and messages until he finally decided it might be a good time to see if there was anything interesting; which there never was. Bills were clockwork each month, but he did his best to ignore them and keep his mind clutter-free.

It was an indulgence of eccentricity that Brian kept an actual office. He could have made himself a cubby-hole in their apartment, and he could have worked there. But Brian explained, rationalized to himself, he liked to keep home and work separate.

The office is where he went to plan how to grow his business. A place to resolve how it was he going to get to that next level. Surely, as he sat at his desk, the how of it all would become clear to him.

Or, perhaps he just didn't like what he did to be discussed with Imelda. It wasn't glamorous, but it paid the bills, and there was tangible value in that. He tried to give it little thought.

He had inherited the staffing business from his father, William, and William had never told Brian how it was he had come into the business. Brian rented out programmable staff to whomever needed them, but one staff was like another staff. Labor was a commodity. With the perfectly competitive market for staff, the money that came in was less and less each month. Brian didn't know how to fix that.

The staffing business had paid the bills for William, and Brian, being a good son, took it over when William passed. He figured he would have to run it and look after his two sisters, Minerva and Chantilly, who he never dreamed would ever get married. To his utter astonishment, though, they did get married, and moved away. He rarely heard from either of them these days.

10:36, always made him smile. He liked that the garbage collection staff always had to get off the truck and chase bits of trash around the lot. He imagined he could see their milky eyes. They didn't even know what they were doing, they just did what they were programmed to do. Don't misunderstand, Brian liked the staff, he even felt fond of them; because these were *his* staff. That's how he had discovered this office: this was a trash route his father's staff had worked for many years. Three times a week his staff came, he watched them from his office. They did their work, they headed on their way, and that's how Brian got paid. He supplied labor to those who needed it.

Garbage was one of the things Brian had always known. He didn't own the truck, but he did provide the staff, and the people who owned the trucks (who didn't want to get into the staffing business) knew that he owned the staff. It was a good relationship.

Not to say Brian didn't have others. There was factory work. Not as much as there used to be, but still quite a bit. Factory owners found that staffing solutions were cheaper and more flexible, considering the relative expense and inconvenience of having a machine break down. Automation came with high overhead and setup/tear down costs. Alternatively, staffing solutions did not.

Brian sipped on a coffee. It was a cappuccino, which he liked, but he didn't remember going to make it. His head was in the clouds today, but it was a good day. He had been right.

He logged into his computer and started reading news articles. Nothing new, the world is coming to an end, the planet is dying, and the banks don't know how to lend money without getting ripped off. There were forty-seven emails waiting for him, and he decided that reading yet another article on something pressing and urgent affecting the world that he couldn't do anything about was preferable to sifting through (now forty-eight) emails about things in which he wasn't interested.

In general, this is what Brian did all day. He sat at his desk, waited for emails, and made sure he had enough staff to pay for all the things that Imelda and Prince needed to live. It was called making a living.

The garbage truck came. There was a lot of paper and plastic swirling around the old parking lot, this would be a two staff job. Brian expected one staff to get out of either side of the cab. But only the staff from the cab appeared. That was odd, where was his other garbage collection staff? Brian stared incredulously. Had one of them decided that they didn't want to help? Was that even possible? Brian looked at the clock on his computer. It wasn't 10:36, but 11:42. His team was over an hour late. That was when Brian checked his messages.

Brian was at the car port when he realized he should have called for his car from the office. He had told it to make busy and park, which meant it had likely gone somewhere to park. Speaking to his mobile, "I need the car, ASAP."

It responded, "It's on its way."

The car took twelve minutes to get to the office. Where had it decided to park itself? Was parking that bad downtown that the car had to drive itself twelve minutes away in order to shut itself off? Oh well, this was not a usual thing. In fact, it was almost exciting, an exception! That was fun.

The car arrived and pulled up, the door slid open, and Brian slipped inside. "Clinic 14," he told the car.

The car's dashboard flickered with a pattern of a map; his route plotted. "Pleased confirm the destination of Clinic 14," the car responded gently.

Brian looked at the map briefly. "Confirmed," he replied, and with that, the car gently yet forcefully pulled away from the curb.

After a short drive of efficiently planned right turns, the car slowed, pulled off the road into a circular driveway in front of the clinic. A voice interrupted Brian, who was still trying to get information out of the Popular's website. In all, he did a lot of searching and got nothing. No worry, but odd—*everything is online*—and when he was at the clinic, it would soon be sorted.

Brian got out of his car, ordered it to, "make busy," and stepped away. He heard the door close, snap shut, the sound of rubber on pavement. The car slid gently away from the curb to go circle until Brian was done.

Brian stepped into the clinic. The waiting room was empty, but there were rows of chairs lined up neatly against the walls. There were tables with magazines on them, all looked crisp and new (though Brian knew they could be years old) and neatly arranged in a carefully measured fan pattern. There was not a speck of dust, and Brian winced slightly at the brightness of everything.

The clinic was quiet except for some gentle instrumental music, not noticeable at first, but effective. Brian felt good, like he wouldn't mind having a seat, relaxing, maybe a cup of coffee. He headed toward the desk where a milky-eyed reception staff sat upright, smiling. Its face started to follow him—though its eyes did not focus—as he approached.

"How can I help you?" it said in a pleasant, slightly mechanical tone.

Brian looked down at the little computer he held in his hand, "I have a staff here," he said, looking for the number.

"Oh," the reception staff said. "Do you know the number?"

"Yes." Brian was stalling for time. "Let me see. I had it." He flipped through pages on his device. "Oh, okay let me see. I think I found it." He turned the display toward the gaze of the staff, it read: 686381KAA418.

The staff looked at the mobile. "Yes," they started, "your staff is here. I have called for a medical technician to escort you." It smiled, straightened, redirecting its gaze toward the door again as if Brian had disappeared.

"Thank you," Brian said.

"You are welcome," it replied, not shifting its gaze, Brian always found it amusing when he could get staff to talk to him without looking in his general direction.

A few seconds later, a large white-clad med-tech with milky brown eyes appeared through swinging double doors. "Mr. Brian Agarwal?"

Brian nodded. "King, please."

"Please come with me." The staff gazed in his general direction.

Brian and the med-tech walked through the double doors, and the brightness, cleanliness, and crispness ended abruptly. The walls went from white to gray, the lights were farther apart and did not cover everything in bright white cool fluorescent. There were areas with shadows. The ceiling did not have any sound tile, disappearing into the darkness above. It felt more like a warehouse than a clinic, an unfinished cement ceiling, power lines and pipes clung to a lattice work of rebar and angle iron; big blue bolts and straps of steel.

The med-tech was walking faster than Brian could, and he found he had to hurry to keep up. A maze of curtains hung from where the ceiling would have been and ended about three feet from the floor. Brian could see there were beds and stands of equipment behind each curtain. The curtains positioned in such a way to create little cubicles of meager privacy.

The staff turned left, and Brian had to almost run to keep up with him. Right, and over two more cubicles. He stopped and turned to face Brian.

"I have to warn you," it said, looking through Brian. "This may be unpleasant. You may find what you are about to see is disturbing." The med-tech paused briefly, as if it were giving Brian a half-second to think about some question, "Would you like to proceed?"

How bad could it be? Brian thought. *And if I didn't look,* he quickly thought to himself, *how would I be able to take this up with the insurance company? I'd have to take their word for it. No way.*

"Yes," Brian replied.

The med-tech turned and pulled back the curtain.

It wasn't all that bad. There was a staff, evidently a male (not that gender mattered) lying on the bed and encased in restraint foam. Much of the staff could not be seen—the foam made them look as if it were floating in a pool of milk, but milk with an iron-clad grip. Brian could see a lot of bruising on the staff's face, two black eyes and the left cheek didn't look like the other one. There were dried brown crumbly bits leftover from some clean-up. The staff was clad, not in work clothes but a thin blue gown that was tucked into the restraint foam.

"This is, 686381KAA418, who I will now refer to as 418, for your convenience," the med-tech began. "Would you like me to begin giving you the medical review now, or would you like a few more moments?"

Brian had seen what there was to see, "Please start," he commanded.

"418 was involved in an exception involving a vehicle in which it was a passenger. The vehicle fell out of the traffic network and contacted, and was contacted by, other vehicles as it was no longer under control." The med-tech took a breath but didn't wait and continued, looking straight ahead, reading a chart only it could see. "The injuries that you see were caused by impacts as the vehicle, and surrounding vehicles came to rest."

"There are fractures to the left side clavicle. A small, fracture on the left cheekbone. There is trauma to the cranium, manifested by contusions in the eye sockets." The med-tech reached over and opened the left eye. "Please notice the eye is bloodshot." The med-tech held the lid open long enough for Brian to see it was bloodshot, then let it snap shut. "The right eye is not, indicating the concussive force may be limited to a smaller section of the cranium. This can only be determined at a future point." Another pause. "418 is expected to survive and will be re-evaluated over the next few days for insurance and rehabilitation purposes."

Brian nodded. He needed to think what that meant. Evidently, 418 wasn't going to die, but would it be functional?

The orderly suddenly continued to speak, causing Brian to jump. "A full report will be made to your insurance carrier, and you can work with them to find an acceptable outcome for this unfortunate situation."

"Oh good," Brian replied, more to himself. Well, there wasn't much to see here. "I think I'm finished," Brian told the med-tech. The staff and Brian stepped out of the cubicle, as the curtain fell closed behind Brian. "Car please."

Somewhere, Brian's car, circling the clinic, got the message he was done—woke itself from zombie mode—and headed toward the clinic.

2

INSURANCE

How could anything look so dead, but not actually be dead? Brian thought about it all the way back to the office. He'd had staff injured before, he'd had one crushed, and he'd even had one—he'd wanted to get rid of—he'd sent off to work at the nuclear plant. But he hadn't had one damaged to the point of unconscious and alive. Surely, 418 wasn't going to make it?

The car pulled up at the office. "Make busy." He did not tell it to park in case he needed it again. Brian hadn't noticed getting out or walking through the carport. The next thing he knew he was back in his office. Opening his computer, he went to the Popular's website and checked his case; useless. It still said pending.

Brian scrolled to the bottom of the page. He clicked the help link, and a video window popped up, "We would like to help you, would you chat with us?" There were two options, a green "Yes" button and a red "No" button. Brian picked the green "Yes" button.

The page loaded in a flash. An attendant, stylized after Brian's own features—brown skin, big brown eyes, a tuft of thick black straight hair, much like his own when he was younger—appeared in the pop-up. "Good afternoon. My name is Rahul. How can I assist you today, Mr. Agarwal?"

Brian answered, centering himself in the display of his camera— as if it mattered, the attendant was only animation and likely didn't care if Brian was there at all as long as it got the audio feedback it was listening for. "I would like to get an update on a case I have pending." Brian started searching for the serial number. "The number ends in 418," he continued.

418

The assistant cut him off. "The case of 686381KAA418, now referred to as 418: The staff was involved in an exception involving transportation this morning. They were transported to clinic 14. The prognosis is indeterminate, timeline, indeterminate."

Brian shook his head slightly, rolled his eyes.

The animated assistant, after it had decided Brian was not going to speak, continued, as if Brian had agreed to something. "Yes, after examination, a prognosis and diagnosis will be made."

Brian had known he should not have gone with the lowest cost insurance company. Something his father used to say echoed in his ear, *"You pay for what you get, but you don't always get what you pay for."* Brian liked to parry back, "Sometimes you paid and didn't get," which his father would concede was true. *"If you don't pay, you certainly won't get."* It was the third part of this, the not getting it, that Brian now feared.

"Look," Brian replied, "can I speak to someone?"

The animation stopped its explanation, didn't look hurt, and didn't argue with him. "I can set up a call back at a time that is convenient for you, or perhaps I can be of assistance?" it replied with programmatic optimism.

"Call me back."

"When shall you be free?"

"Anytime during business hours, anytime ten to five."

"Okay, I will have your account representative call you back at her or his earliest opportunity. Is there anything else I can do for you?" the animation asked.

"No. Thanks." Brian clicked the chat panel closed. It would probably be a good time to go for a coffee.

I felt like I was floating up from the bottom of a deep dark lake, my limbs waterlogged, so heavy I could not move them. It felt like I was moving through thick cold water, as slowly the light from the surface brightened. I couldn't see where I was or how I got there, but at least the light was getting brighter and not darker. I tried to figure out how I got there. Everything was a mess. I must have been buried in

15

the bottom of a lake, water placed on top of me, pinning me in the muck. I was beginning to float back to the top. It felt like the water was flowing through me, I was coming out of dissolution.

When Brian got back from getting his coffee, his computer was ringing. Why hadn't they just called his mobile? He rushed around his desk and touched the screen, where a friendly green box was flashing the friendly word "Answer."

A two-paned window popped open. The smiling face of a young man, a short brown haircut, acne and hazel-colored eyes, appeared in one side. "Hello, Mr. Agarwal."

Brian settled in front of the camera, smoothed down his shirt and made sure he was sitting straight. He reached up and removed the cover from his webcam. His own smiling face appeared in the darkened window beside the smiling young man who appeared on the screen. "Hello," Brian answered, "please call me King."

The smile on the young man faded as he looked away from his camera. "Um, yes," he was reading something, searching, not finding. "King it is." Brian could see him type. He hadn't been doing this job long enough to type and not look like he was doing it. "Well, good afternoon, King, my name is Bolt Greene, and I am your senior personal claims adjuster. I understand you wanted to speak with us directly," he continued, feeling better to be back on script. "What can I help you with?"

"Sure, Bolt," Brian started a little awkwardly. He watched for a reaction that he might have gotten it wrong, but there wasn't. This guy's name was Bolt. "As you know, I have staff in the clinic, at Clinic 14." Brian paused. The young man had been waiting for Brian to say something more definite, but Brian liked saying things that were open-ended to see where it would go.

Bolt got tired of waiting. "Yes, thank you, King. I can see your staff 686381KAA418, to be now referred to as 418, was involved in an exception this morning while 418 was en route to its assignment."

"Yes," Brian tried to prompt him along.

"As a result of the exception, 418 was damaged and was taken to Clinic 14 for assessment."

Smiling, Brian replied, "Thank you, I was there."

The young man smiled, probably because he could see that in the notes he was reading. "Yes, you were." His cheer level went up just a bit. "And you saw we have taken all appropriate precautions with your staff. It is stabilized and immobilized pending review."

"Yes, that is what I wanted to talk to you about?"

"Yes, Mr…" pause, "…King. What would you like to know?"

Brian sat back a bit, feeling more comfortable, "I know you have taken all the precautions and preventative measures and whatnot, but what I saw didn't look good." Brian paused.

Finally, "How so?"

"Well," he continued, wondering how to put it carefully, "it looks pretty dead." He didn't at all put it carefully.

"Oh, I see," Bolt had evidently not seen 418. "Well, we are assured that your staff, 418, will be fine, but we have had to freeze, or immobilize, the body for a few days to let the physical trauma subside, in order to conduct a proper evaluation."

Brian scratched his nose, then remembered he was on camera. "Seems like a lot of work for staff?"

The young man looked flustered, like he hadn't expected Brian to head off in that direction. "Um, I'm not certain what you mean?"

"I mean…" Brian was amazed how calm he was. Perhaps it was his belief in how useless it was to argue with an insurance company. "It seems like a lot of work to do for staff that is pretty much dead."

"Oh, that," Bolt continued, "let me assure you King, we have placed your staff into that state, a form of catatonia so that its body can heal without it being able to hurt itself further." He repeated the same excuse again, as if this wording would stick better.

Brian was nodding at the screen; still not sure this was required for staff.

"Our techs have assessed that, aside from some superficial damage to the left cheek, there is not likely any lasting physical damage that would prevent your staff from returning to work."

"Really?" Brian replied skeptically. *No way! That one is busted for sure,* he thought.

Bolt's voice lowered a bit as if this part was a bit trickier, "We have to do an assessment if there has been any brain damage."

"Right." This was the news that Brian had been waiting for, "I saw…" He had to pause. '418' it sounded odd to say. "And 418 looks pretty brain damaged."

Bolt smiled, back on track. "Correct, and if we find that your staff has been damaged and cannot return to work, this will be reflected in the compensation portion of your claim."

"But why can't we do that now?" Brian asked.

Bolt replied, "Because we don't know if there has been brain damage."

"I'm pretty sure there has been."

"But we don't know."

This wasn't going to work out. Sensing the impasse, he tried a different tactic. "How long will this evaluation take?"

Bolt searched his screen, "I would say," he paused as he read, "about a week."

"A week!" Brian almost shouted. "What do you mean a week?"

Bolt smiled, feeling in control again. His white teeth shone through as he smiled. "First, the swelling and hemorrhaging has to abate." Brian was impressed by the word *abate*. He'd have to look that up. "Then, we will have to do a full check on his education systems."

"Uh, huh." Brian mentally did the math. "Who is going to pay for that?"

"We will," Bolt say cheerfully.

"And who is going to compensate me for not having a staff member while you do all this testing?" Brian asked.

"King," Bolt continued, seeing an end to this conversation. "We here at the Popular Insurance Company are here for you during times like this, and we will compensate you through the claim system for the lost productivity of your staff."

"Oh," Brian answered, not liking the answer, but not sure what else to say. "I guess that's fair."

"We are glad you think that," the young insurance adjuster replied. "Please continue to check our webapp for status on your claim, or you could sign up for push updates on your claim to be sent to your mobile devices."

Brian smiled thinly. "Thank you."

"Is there anything else I can help you with today? King."

Brian searched through his own brain. "No, I guess not."

"Thank you," Bolt replied. "It has been a pleasure serving you today. If you need us again, please reach out to us at your convenience."

I guess I'm getting what I paid for, he thought as he closed the teleconference app. It was silly that he had to wait for the Popular to waste their own money and his time before paying out. Why they just didn't send 418 to retirement, close the case! It was beyond him. What if they did fix 418? Was it really going to go back to work after a wallop like that? It would just break again, and Brian would end up with sixty percent wages from the Popular while they fixed it again. It was preposterous, a terrible way to do business.

3

THE WEDDING

"Hello," Bolt typed into the messenger beside the smiling face of Andrea Dover. "Are you there?"

Bolt sat staring at his screen. It was good to have an assistant, but not good if the assistant didn't respond. If she didn't respond soon, he might have to start to think about doing something about the assistant that didn't respond. Bolt even had an opportunity to take in a deep breath—he was holding it—if she didn't respond by the time he exhaled; she must not be there.

"Hi," the messenger scrolled up with Andrea's reply, "what's up?"

"I need you to do something, I need you to go to Clinic 14 and check on a claim that is in progress."

"Okay! :D :D" came the response. "Send me the details."

"I'll make you a ticket."

Andrea Dover secretly despised her boss. He treated her like an errand girl, and—in her opinion—he was exactly the thing that was blocking her advancement at the Popular Insurance Company. But the thing about bosses is they have absolute power over you. The best way of dealing with them is to say, "yes," to everything you are asked to do, but volunteer for nothing unless it is dead easy to do. She hated going to the clinic—they were dark, kind of scary and, if she were lucky, she wouldn't see something she wouldn't be able to unsee. More often than not, something unexpected and horrible, some mess of mangled flesh, was waiting for her. Being the junior claims adjuster, if it was awful, she was going to get to see it. She had hoped this job was going to lead her to an office where she could reach out to people on messenger and send them places where they were going to lose their appetite. Or their sleep, as sometimes happened to her.

She sat at her desk, looking at her screen. Well, the ticket hadn't come in yet, and she wasn't going anywhere without documentation. Perhaps he would forget. That would be nice. Maybe he'd send the ticket to the wrong Andrea. That had happened loads of times before. She sighed. *He must not have much to do today,* she thought, because in her ticket inbox popped up a "new ticket," red flag.

I seemed to be waking up again. I was still underwater, but now floating just a few inches below the surface. I could feel cold light on my face. I could see light, but my eyes were stuck shut, and my arms and legs were still not responding—as if encased in cement— but now I seemed to be floating. I needed to get to the surface but still couldn't move. I held my breath, if I could hold my breath long enough, I might just be able to break the surface with my mouth and I'd be able to breathe. I was fairly certain I couldn't breathe underwater. Within seconds my heart was pounding, but my head was pounding even worse, the left side of my head was twice the size as the right side, and every pump from my chest caused it to grow bigger. I had to break the surface. I couldn't do this for long. I would have to take in a big chest full of water. I had tried. I opened my mouth, gasped expecting to feel fluid coursing down my throat, turning my lungs into soft coral. But it was air. I must have broken the surface though I still felt like I was soaking in water.

I tried flexing my face in order to pry my eyes open. I couldn't lift my hand. All I could do was wiggle. The pain in my left cheek was exquisite, sharp and grinding. My tongue checked my teeth—those that I remembered being there were still there. My eyes felt like they were going to burst as they watered with the pain. I know I moaned and called out, but I couldn't hear anything as my ears were still below water. Finally, I managed to work my right eye open. There were flecks of crusty, sticky, yellow goo that obscured the light. I could see a ceiling, and if I strained my eyes downward, I could see a flickering fluorescence. The ceiling was gray concrete, and there were pipes and tubes fastened to it. I wasn't in a lake; I was in a warehouse.

I tried calling out but my cheek bit me back hard, and something hoarse came out. I wasn't going to be able to do that again. It didn't matter, no one was coming.

Andrea Dover headed down to the carport. Hopefully this wasn't going to be one of the memorable visits. She tried to put that out of her mind as she stepped into a car. What really mattered was how could she get her boss's job…without it looking like she was trying to get her boss's job. She tried to get comfortable in the car. The door shut behind her, she slid away, turning the problem over and over in her mind.

Some time ago it had dawned on Andrea that, bright as she may be, as keen as she may have been, and as good as she may be at her job, she still had a cap on top of her, and there was a filter through which all her work was presented to management two levels up. That cap and that filter was the same thing: Bolt Greene, firmly fastened in place and blocking her way. The realization of what Bolt Greene was doing to her career sickened and disheartened her.

She had to find some way to get out from under the smothering bushel and let her light shine. As the car drove along and she watched a map view on the screen. At the impressive average speed of sixty-seven mph, her pod wove through traffic. But, how was she going to break through this ceiling? What could she do without arousing Bolt's suspicions?

Bolt, as she had come to discover, had some family connection to the Popular Insurance Company. She had started in sales; it was amazing she had managed to get out of sales. This job, claims adjuster, junior or not, was a desirable position. It seemed to lend to the idea that the next stop would be something policy related. It appeared to be a bottom level management position. She remembered how happy she was when she got the job. This was the first step of many steps she was going to take in a long and prosperous career. Only it wasn't. There was lots of work like this a seemingly unending flow of Joe jobs, fetch-its and "look this up for me, would you?" type of things. Trivial stuff that would have been faster if he'd done it himself.

It took about nine months before Bolt arrived on the scene. She had got there first, since she had been working in claims longer. His connection—an uncle or something—had dropped him in fresh out of college, right on top of her. It might have been okay, but she knew more about the job, wanted the job. But yet, somehow, he was entitled to the job. At first that made her angry, but then she realized his boss's probably felt his sense of entitlement was good. This made her feel even worse: they were rewarding his marginal competence and indolence! How could this be fair? Fair or not, she must not blow it, because she could always find herself starting in sales in some other company.

She had to be smart, she had to be alert for the opportunity, ready to make a shift if there was to be a chance to vault past Bolt Greene. Acting in desperation was not a good idea. That kind of thing could follow you for years, once it was attached to your employment record. But waiting was the hardest part. The car pulled up at the clinic, a soft chiming voice alerting her, "You have arrived at Clinic 14. Please prepare for departure. The door will open when it is safe to disembark."

Andrea stepped from the car, sighed, looked up at the building and muttered under her breath, "I hope this isn't going to be messy," and strode toward the entrance.

Of course, it was whiter than white as she entered the clinic. There wasn't anyone sitting there. The rows of seats were all neatly arranged, and there were magazines that had been arranged on the tables, spread out in a fan, an equal amount of each magazine showing. Andrea moved briskly toward the staff.

As she approached, the staff, who had been sitting ramrod straight, broke into a smile. "Hello, how can I help you?" The reception staff behind the desk asked, its eyes directed but not focused on Andrea.

"I'm Andrea Dover from the Popular, and I'm here to see," she paused as she looked down at her mobile in her hand, "um, 686381KAA418."

As Andrea spoke the last number of the ID, the attendant's fingers—following some ancient artifact of programming—tapped it into an imaginary console that wasn't on the empty desk, and replied, "Yes, of course, I will send for a medical technician to escort you. One moment, please."

The staff went back to sitting or doing whatever it was that staff did when they were waiting for some real-world interaction. Andrea turned to face the two double doors that lead to the back of the clinic. Almost immediately the door burst open, and another staff member gazed in her direction, "Andrea Dover?" it asked.

"Yes," she replied.

"Please follow me," it added, programmed to sound cheerful, but Andrea didn't care. This was Bolt's job. Whatever she did, he was going to take credit for it, and that was annoying her. He should be here, about to see whatever mess she was about to see. She followed the med-tech into the gray, dimly lit back rooms of the clinic.

They walked for quite a while, from pool of light, to pool of light, through the corridors of hanging curtains. Andrea, though she dreaded what she might see, was happy to be out of the gleaming white area of the clinic; so much easier on the eyes. Maybe the relative darkness of this part of the clinic might help her not see something she might not have been able to forget. Abruptly, the med-tech stopped, turned to her and said, "I have to warn you, this may be unpleasant. You may find what you are about to see may disturb you. Would you like to proceed?"

Andrea smiled dryly. It didn't matter if it disturbed her, it was her job. But explaining this wasn't going to get her job done. "Yes," she replied impassively, "please proceed."

Obediently the med-tech turned and pulled back the curtain.

She was braced for the worst and felt a wave of cool relief was over her as the med-tech stepped away, allowing her to see the staff that was laying in the medibed.

There wasn't all that much to see. The body was secured in restraint foam and had been cleaned up efficiently. There was no blood, other than dried crumbs that had become wedged between the foam and the flesh. There were no open cuts, no puss, no broken bones sticking through the skin, and no plastic patches applied to places where skin was missing, allowing anyone to see what might lay below.

What there was, was an awful lot of bruising. Andrea stepped up to the bed to see the extent of damage to the face. The left cheek was stitched shut and almost black with bruising.

"Oh!" Andrea gave a little shout. The right eye was moving around and, shrouded in its deep purple flesh, a tiny slit, caked in yellow goo, had split open and a blue eye was straining to look at her.

Well, 418 was alive.

I was immobilized. I felt like I was alive; certainly, my face hurt, and the left side of my head had been mashed and throbbed at even the thought of moving. Is this what being dead is like? It couldn't be, I was in too much pain, and I'd always imagined death to be rather painless once the dying part was over. And as I was contemplating whether I was dead or not, the light got brighter, like a veil was being lifted away.

Much to my surprise, I didn't see little angels coming to take me away, but dark hair, a rich dark face, clean skin, radiant cheeks and sharp brown eyes appeared over my face. She didn't smile, she looked concerned, puzzled, and somehow relieved. I tried to say something. "Help," I tried to say, "I am stuck here, what has happened?"

Angels must speak some other language, because she didn't reply but simply recoiled at the sound of my voice, a look of horrified disgust on her face.

"No," I tried to continue, "please help me!" I wanted to reach out to her and grab her arm. She would know I was alive, and that I was a person too.

Her eyes widened as I struggled, and she pulled back completely out of my sight.

Andrea wasn't prepared for that. Why had they not sedated the staff? It was always weird to see them when they were offline, they always looked frantic. And the howling sound that it was making… it sounded like it had brain damage. Those sounds did not sound like speech. Andrea was pretty sure she would hear those bestial, horrible, ignorant sounds in her sleep. It made her heart race, good thing it couldn't get up—though she could see it trying—as there was no telling how dangerous it could be. She may not have been a medical tech, but there was no doubt this was a damaged unit.

The med-tech started to read off the prognosis. "There has been a fracture to the cheek. However, it is superficial, and aside from cosmetic damage there is likely not any structural damage to the skull." Andrea felt a wave of something wash over her, the idea of structural damage to the skull made her feel unwell. The med-tech continued, "We have sutured the cheek to prevent further damage and to staunch blood loss." Again, Andrea felt a little unwell. "There does not appear to be any damage to the cerebral interface. However, the cerebral interface will have to be checked for full functionality. Cursory examination does not reveal any issues. There is swelling around the cerebral interface, which must subside before an in-depth examination can be executed."

Andrea let the med-tech finish, its gaze following her as she moved away from the body lying on the table though it never focused on her. It didn't matter what the examination said. Something was wrong with that bit of programming because whatever was laying on the bed was clearly malfunctioning; no examination was going to fix that.

She was certain her report would include the acronym *RFR*: Recommended For Retirement. They would pay the policyholder, and everyone would move on. Everyone, that is, except her. She was pretty sure she was going to remember that frantic look, the straining eye that seemed to be knocked silly and the tormented, muted animal-like screams. This should have been Bolt's job.

She nodded to the med-tech. "Thank you," and the staff stopped talking and listened for instruction. "I think I've seen enough."

It didn't take long for Andrea to write her report. She basically just chose all the negative tick boxes, put in comments like, "subject is N/S," or, "FUBAR," as the prospective outlook of medical treatment. Her recommendation was, "retirement with pro-rated reimbursement of lost labor for the policyholder, based on remaining projected operational lifespan." And that was about it. It would be done. Usually, managers didn't mind getting the lump sum payout. All she had to do was affix her signature to the bottom of the form and press submit—Bolt's job would be done—and he would probably get a five-star rating. Even though he hadn't even left his office, he was probably playing games on his mobile while she was out there doing his work.

How was this fair? "Hrumph!" she flopped herself back into her chair, arms crossed and put on her best pout. "Rrrr," she growled to herself. Even though the shouts were not what they could have been—they could have been worse—it was his job; he'd take the credit and not have to share any of the risk. He was going to get the promotion and likely someone, maybe one of his college buddies, would slide into his place once he was promoted up.

A half an hour later, Bolt's messenger alerted him that Andrea must be back from the clinic. "Hey Bolt, do you have a moment? I wanted to run my report past you?"

Bolt smiled. He liked it when Andrea "ran things past him." Even though he had only been her boss for a year, it made him feel comfortable that she relied on him. This was why he had sent her, because it allowed him to do more things with less time. That always looked good on the yearly review. "Of course, what's up?"

Bolt watched the animated ellipses as Andrea typed her message. "I wanted you to review my report before I file it."

Smiling, Bolt replied, "Sure, send it over."

An attachment appeared in the messenger window. Bolt clicked to download and replied, "Thanks, I'll give it a once over when I have a chance, I'm busy today, it could take a while."

"Perfect." She smiled and rocked back in her chair.

It wasn't like she had said anything wrong. In fact, if you looked at the reports that were created by the med-techs, nothing in her report looked out of order. While it was her job, or really, it was Bolt's job, to personally review the damage for insurance purposes, the initial reviews were created by the programming and observations from the med-tech's. Andrea managed to rationalize, *Given, a large enough expenditure of money and other resources, it would be possible that this staff might recover.* It was good enough logic for her.

The fact that she believed 418 would never recover would not occur to anyone unless they actually went to the clinic and saw for themselves. She had carefully rewritten her report, removing any reference to brain damage, making it look as if it were generated by a med-tech. Likely, it wasn't going to be a problem. Likely, it wouldn't make a bit of difference. But maybe, since she knew Bolt was going to sign off on it and submit it as his own, it may just come back to be something that maybe, just maybe, might help her crack the glass ceiling.

How long have I laid there? I have no idea. I couldn't get online, I couldn't move, but I could think. Thinking and not being able to move is a most exquisite hell. I lay there. Aside from the woman who had come to peek at me, I got infrequent visits from med-techs, but the med-techs, like the woman, didn't speak to me. I didn't know what was wrong with me, but I had, given time—with the pain in my head settling down—been able to untangle events and figure it out.

I had been in an exception involving a car. I didn't think that kind of thing was possible. I had always just got into cars and let them take me where I was going. Hop in and arrive. I never had to think about what was going on outside the car. I had always just moved; safe in my personal bubble. Why should I ever think about it? But now it occurred to me that if I was safe in my bubble, surely, there would be dozens, if not hundreds of other such bubbles. However, the car ride was always smooth. I seemed to float down the street and I could enjoy my own life while I went to or from work. It didn't seem possible I could break my cheek. Such a hard blow to the head; nope, still couldn't figure out how the car had managed to punch me.

By far, the worst thing was I couldn't go online. I'm sure you can understand, *what is life without internet?* You might as well just be laying somewhere dying. Huh, I made a joke. I tried to laugh, but now my chest hurt, a lot, one great big bruise. It wasn't a good joke. I couldn't go online because I couldn't move. My head was immobilized, my hands were stuck in place by my sides and I couldn't tap my activation button.

All I could do was stare up at the ceiling and try to count how many times the light that I could see somewhere over my feet flickered. I had managed to get both my eyes open. My left eye had a purple haze around it. I didn't try to use it. The only thing I could see was cement, pipes and one flickering light. The light was starting to make the top of my head feel numb and I tried not to look at it.

The face had been good; now as I lay there, I realized it had been beautiful. She was radiant. I wanted her to come back. Not so I could ask what had happened, but because she was lovely, and if there was something that lovely out there, I couldn't possibly be dead. This couldn't be where you go after retirement. You didn't just lay there looking up, unable to move. I wanted her to come back.

I think I could remember clearly: she had brown eyes, dark brown framed in porcelain set off by her flawless skin of rich ebony, smooth and firm. Her hair was dark, almost black, thick and styled in waves and curls, not a strand out of place. She must have had perfect dark cherry lips, but my glimpse of her had been so brief, so ethereal and fleeting. I tried to remember everything. There was warmth to her, something real. Then I tried not to think of the face she made when I attempted to speak to her. I must have had something in my throat, and if I'd have known she would react like that, I would have stayed silent. I could have gazed upon her for just a moment more.

Frequently, I tried to re-summon her in my mind. If she would only come back.

The funny thing about laying there, not being able to get online, was that my wife couldn't tell I was thinking of this other woman this way. I mean, if I had been online, I would have been able to interact with her, and she might have discovered I was into someone else. But then again, I could just ask my wife if she would change her hair. Belinda usually liked to portray herself as a tall Asian woman. It was the way she looked when we met, I'll not forget that. She was sitting at a cafe along the Seine, a long leg dangling out from under the table. My eye caught her shoe dangling off her toe, the sheer black nylon running all the way up to where her hair—just as shiny and more silky—hung down to touch her lap.

It's a funny thing: I'd never been particularly drawn to Paris. I'd always felt it was an overhyped city. A lot of old stuff I wasn't particularly interested in. But there I found myself, wandering down a pathway, below street level along the banks of a river. It was a lovely spring afternoon; the sun was starting to begin its descent. I could smell flowers in bloom, perfume, my heart started to beat, hard, like I'd just taken a snort. It felt like I was being drawn to her. There she was, sitting in a cafe that seemed to be tucked under a bridge and cut into the wall below the street. I don't remember walking over, I just seemed to be pulled, I was sitting at her table, which didn't seem like me at all. But there I was, talking with her and she was talking back to me. It was as if it was meant to be.

I blinked up at the ceiling, absolutely nothing going on. I tried to turn my head, raise my arm, anything to activate myself, get back online. Nothing. My teeth were starting to hurt. Did they always do that? It's not like I used them.

The romance was quick. I had to have Belinda, she was too much, and every time I was around her, I felt a dizzy buzz, and I didn't have to pay anything to get it! Oh sure, we went out for dinner, and I did get to pay for that, but I was going to eat anyway, and spending is what money is for. But she was free and seemed to like me, not like the girls at Madam She's. Those girls were friendly, but when it was over, it was over.

We traveled a lot. For a woman who loved her Asian avatar, she certainly did like to tour Europe. Belinda loved the snow—I had never been much of a fan of snow—but she thought it was interesting. The sound of it crunching beneath your feet—if you went to the expensive places—you could even *feel* the snow crunching. I've never been one for cold, but Belinda found the cold fascinating. It made your skin feel like it was burning, but it was cold, odd, and if not for Belinda, I'd never have bothered to experience cold.

Normally we would end up at a cafe and then a hotel where we would sleep the night and do what men and women do. In the morning I would wake and head off to work, keeping her in my messenger. We would chat throughout the day, and I would count the minutes until I was home again, and we could go to some new exotic place.

I knew this was the one. Belinda had a randomness the girls at Madam She's didn't. The girls at She's always acted the same way. They always said yes. They always suggested what I had liked before, and they did it with a smile and without question; but Belinda was more. Maybe it was the unknown, something I hadn't had before. Maybe it was I didn't care that I was spending all my money on travel. I had always tried to keep my balances high in case I ever needed the money, but after being with Belinda, it didn't take me long to pop the question.

I have no idea how long we were dating. It all seemed to flow naturally. We met, fell in love, the next thing I knew I was standing in a great marble and stone cathedral, the sound of an organ shaking me to the core, as if I was melting with the vibration, floating off the floor as everything shook with sound.

Belinda appeared as a blotch of white at the end of a long corridor of pews that converged at the door. She stepped into the cathedral, which was when the music started. Everyone stood and the bride glided down the aisle. I never dreamed I would care so much, but I was excited to get married! I always thought it was much ado about nothing, but I could feel my heart beating as the sound of the cathedral shook me. I was totally immersed in everything; this was awesome.

The next thing I knew, I was holding Belinda's hands, looking at the almond shape of her eyes, soft brown freckles on her face. She had changed her hair; her normally long black silky hair was an almost white blonde. It sort of went with her white vale.

There was a minister, all dressed in elaborate black robes that sparkled and glinted in the colored light streaming through the stained-glass windows. He cleared his throat and began his speech. I looked back into Belinda's eyes, and could see the excitement of the child she had once been and still was. She was grinning; this was the best thing ever.

A face with milky eyes appeared over me. He poked and prodded at me, turned away to make some notes. There was no use trying to talk to the med-tech, it was at work, and it wasn't going to answer me. I wanted to cry out, for pity sake, "Let me back online!" But it wouldn't have made any difference. I lay there as the shape above me finished its examination, and then it was gone.

The first thing Brian Agarwal did when he woke up was to open his computer and check the status of his claim for 418. Every day he checked it, first thing. *Surely it was a matter of time before they wrote off that staff.* He could sure use that money. But every day it was the same, no change. They had set the cheek, the swelling was going down, and they were going to start checking the cerebral terminal.

Hmm, there wasn't much he could say. It looked like they were going to return the staff to him, and they were going to cover sixty percent of the lost wages. Though he'd rather one hundred percent, he hadn't paid for that level of coverage.

My teeth hurt. I was so bored, so restrained, and the numbness I had been once enjoying had been subsiding slowly. I hadn't noticed at the time, but it was true, every day I started to feel more. The waterlogged feeling was giving way to a buttery feeling of wasting.

I wasn't sure I'd ever be able to lift my arms or work my legs again. But one thing I could move were my eyes and my mouth. You work with what you have when you only have a few things. Gritting my teeth was something I could do; it gave me a feeling that wasn't either buttery or soggy, it gave me sharp pain, caused my blood to flow. The harder I bit, the more it hurt, but pain was better than feeling numb and staring at the ceiling. I bit down on my teeth again as hard as I could, letting the pain wash over me. At least it was something.

Bolt reviewed the notes that had been filed by the med-techs. Everything was going well with 418, though it was taking an awfully long time. They would be able to start testing the cerebral interface in three more days. Bolt smiled. He had managed to save the Pop quite a bit of money, he thought. If he had just agreed to write off 418, it would be over, and the Pop would have had to pay. Maybe this would help him move up? A feather for his cap. A popup on his computer notified him that in another week he'd have to sign an extension waiver to keep it in the clinic. *Never-mind*, he thought, he was saving money and making the customer happy.

Sleeping is overrated. It's overrated when you can't go online first, check into a nice hotel and fall asleep in crisp, clean sheets. When you are laying there, and your body is slowly melting, and you can't see anything but the ceiling, sleep is a relief. But there are only so many hours you can sleep, so you stare, stare and you imagine things. Try to remember, try to determine if it's a memory or is it something you made up. Maybe sleep will come and gently take you away from the chore of having to be awake. Had I just been forgotten? Were they just feeding me, keeping me here? And, was I just supposed to lay here until I wasn't anything anymore?

4

REFACTORING

Two med-techs appeared—now this was different—and both looked down at me, without expression, without focus. One stepped to the head of the medibed, the other drew back the curtain, and off we went. The feeling of moving air was good, even though it was sticky with the scent of cement and dankness. It was good to feel the air move against the skin of my face.

Naturally, I had no idea where we were going, but it was good to be going somewhere. Perhaps I would be able to get back online soon? Perhaps I would be able to get out of here? How I missed my home. Belinda must be wondering where I am. We have children, Serenity and little Lucas. I bet they wondered where their daddy was.

We left the larger area and headed through a pair of doors down a short hallway and into a waiting elevator. We went down a few floors and back out, we rolled along into another room. That's when fear gripped me. This was an operating room, and I wasn't under any sort of anesthetic. "No! No! No!" I tried to shout, "Nooooo!" I was rolled into the center of the room where lights and other machines were clustered around where my bed came to rest. But the med-techs didn't pay any attention to my yelling.

They started to adjust things. I could feel straps tighten around my buttery muscles and spongy soft bones. Both the techs stood back, looked in the direction of their work. One of them turned away. As he turned back, I felt cold air rushing all over my body. I hadn't felt cold in a long time. I wasn't wearing my clothes, and as the restraining foam receded, I felt the icy sting of metal as my back came to rest on the table. I tried to move; this was not good.

One of the techs grabbed my head, and I felt a snap on the side of my right temple, for an instant I thought, *Hey, they are going to hook me back up again,* but I knew it couldn't be that. A med-tech checked to ensure the wire wasn't going to come free. I heard them both walking away. Then I felt a warm buzzing near my right ear. There was a current coming out of the wire on the side of my head. I started to scream again; if this wasn't hurting, it was certainly going to. The med-techs didn't notice. I know they pressed another button, and I felt my legs shoot straight. There was a burning feeling in my head, and I felt the bottom of my feet start to contract, tearing against the bone, legs straining against the straps. I let out another scream, this one was real.

I came around. The techs had taken me to the shower room. I was still tied to the table, but I writhed as two bursts of icy cold water blasted up and down my naked, exposed sides. I thought my heart was going to stop! I gasped for breath. No longer did the metal sheet I was laying on feel cold.

After every part of me that could be washed was washed, the techs turned on some fans to blow the water off me. I was shivering— the cold, painful and numb—my chest felt like someone had been beating it with the rubber hoses and not the water. I tried to roll off the table, but I couldn't. The wind continued until I stopped shivering. The med-techs appeared again, roughly and vigorously drying the parts of me that wouldn't air dry. They reset the bed, and this time the restraining foam was comforting and soft. I relaxed into it, not feeling the straps, all the muscles of my legs felt sore, torn and shredded. I was wheeled back toward the cubicle where I had spent so many days staring at the ceiling, and I dare say I was placed in exactly the same spot. The flickering light still flickered.

An email landed in Bolt Greene's inbox. Impassively, he clicked it. It was a report, generated by the med-techs, a button at the bottom for when he had finished reading it. Bolt glanced at the report. 418 had begun undertaking cerebral interface and musculature stress-testing. "Oh good," Bolt thought. He scanned the email for any capitalized words. It was the capitalized words that always meant trouble but there were no capitalized words. Things were good. Bolt pressed the big green button at the bottom of the email. "Append to File."

I woke up sometime later. I felt terrible. My head was full of sand, my lungs were sore, and my legs felt like spikes of pain. Lying there, throbbing, sore in places I didn't know I could be, I wondered what I had done to deserve this. My eyes stared up at the ceiling and I wanted to melt into the table and dribble away so that there would be nothing more left of me, not even a memory.

When you are restrained to a bed, time is a long and gritty steel blade that cuts deeply and jaggedly as it is slowly drawn from one side of your mind to the other. Little bursts of pain, tearing the flesh; moving slowly, granting no rest. Boredom yields no mercy, memories dissolve, bleed into madness; mayhem that may never have been.

A med-tech appeared. I was happy to see them. It made me think I was neither dead nor completely forgotten. It looked at me, then went about checking everything, my catheter, the feedbag, hanging just out of view. It stepped away to make some notes, came back, no expression on its face. It was done, and it was gone. I wished it would come back. It was better to look as its face, even its milky eyes. It could move, it didn't flicker, it wasn't concrete and pipes. I tried to bring them back in my mind, so I could see something different; I wanted to scream and may have.

Sometime later, the ever-constant feeble light was disturbed by a shadow passing over my face. I woke again. My eyes flicked as I struggled to see what was going on. I saw two techs working on me. I was being disconnected from the tube in my right arm. They worked quickly, without mistake, and off I was, oh no! This wasn't going to be good.

Our first stop was not where I thought it would be. We were in a room with a machine with a big circular opening. I was wheeled into the room and right into the middle of the circle. I could feel the wheels of my table lock as I was centered inside the tube. The med-techs stepped away, leaving me there. Whatever this was, it was going to hurt. I heard switches being clicked, heard a humming noise start. I started to scream at the top of my lungs, for the sake of my life.

I began moving, or the ring did. I don't know, I was bracing for searing pain to pour into my body as the ring moved. I was screaming, imagining where some invisible heatwave was searing my flesh off the bone, but there was none. No pain. Maybe I couldn't feel it because I was screaming. I stopped. No pain. Who would have thought? Perhaps this wasn't going to be so bad.

After a couple of passes, I heard the machine powering down, and the techs appeared again. This was too bad; I didn't want to go back and stare at the ceiling again. They unfastened my bed from the floor, and we were rolling again.

But we didn't go back to my cubicle. We went to that other room with the monitors and lights. I tried to protest, but it didn't matter, the med-techs couldn't hear me. They slapped a wire to the side of my head, and the screaming started in earnest as my feet exploded in flames.

When I came around again, I didn't feel like I'd been chewed, but rather I felt like I had been set on fire and allowed to burn, then had cold water poured on me, leaving charred bones for legs. I laid there crying gently, not sure why; it wasn't going to do any good. I only wanted to go home, I only wanted to go back online, see Belinda, hear about the kids. Nothing could be worse than being here.

My thoughtless sleep was broken by the feeling of movement. This time I hadn't been woken by the shadows of the med-techs but rather the steady motion of the bed rolling. Secretly, I hoped my heart would stop; it would save me a lot of trouble. We ended up at the room with the ring where I was locked to the floor. I knew this wasn't going to hurt. Perhaps this time, I'd just die. I'd like that.

The ring did its thing, and we were off again, back to the room with the monitors and the wire for my head. I felt the wire snap into place, the world seemed to go black, I hoped I wasn't going to survive this. The pain began. This time it started at my knees and went up to the bottom of my stomach, waving back and forth, searing, cooking my stomach, hips, twitching. I felt something warm running down the inside of my left leg as my bowels let go. I didn't fight to stay conscious. Hopefully, I wouldn't fight to stay alive.

Every day I wished was my last. Each day was the same: off to the ring room, then back to the torture wire. Every time, I came back to life during my icy hose bath. Each time a slightly higher part of my body felt like it had been chewed and burnt, the flesh torn off. They were working their way up, and I figured when they got to my chest I'd be done, but no such luck. It kept going on and on. And when we got to the top, we started again at the bottom.

I prayed for death.

Brian Agarwal sat staring at his computer. The latest entry in the claim was that 418 was due to be released from the clinic in three business days, so would he like to visit the staff member? It had been almost three weeks. No staff got that much attention at a clinic. *Isn't the rule of thumb two weeks and you are done?* He'd have to see this. Brian sat staring dumbly at his screen. *Would I like to visit the staff member? Did anyone visit staff?* Brian clicked that he would like to visit the staff. Another dialog box popped up, telling him he would be able to come in two business days. *Okay,* Brian thought, *this will be weird.*

I started to think this couldn't last. Someone was playing some cruel trick on me and seeing how much of this I could take before I would just die, but I just wouldn't. No matter how hard I tried to make my heart stop, it kept on going. I couldn't see, I couldn't ask the concierge, but there could not be much more of me left than a shriveled torso with a beating heart and a head that was fixed in place, eyes blinking, a tube running into my arm keeping me alive. Now that I tried, I could almost see myself lying there, waiting to decay into dust and ash.

418

The next morning Brian Agarwal logged into his computer and checked the status of the 418 file. His condition had been upgraded to: "fully functional, pending release." Brian raised his eyes at this. If it was fully functional, why not just release him? He would never have guessed that an insurance company would stay with a claim so long. It would have been much easier just to write it off and let everyone go on with their lives. Brian scratched his head. It didn't seem like a good business move to him, but it was their money.

Brian turned away from his computer—which promptly went to sleep—because it was time to make Prince his breakfast. Tomorrow he would go visit 418.

As the days went on, I started to numb to the pain. I was able to put up with more and more of it. Which was awful. Now they no longer focused on muscles, arms and legs, but on my head. I felt horrible waves of sickness, bursts of pain. Images came flooding up from nowhere, bodies mangled and morphed: I could see myself tied to the table with no skin. As the wire into my head started to buzz, I could feel all the veins in my body start to swell, pushing outward with every pump. Rupturing. The back of my skull filling with blood till it started pouring out of my mouth. I didn't seem to be in control of my own thoughts. My heart would race and I could feel myself trying to run against the restraints. Then fire again and I melted into a red blaze, and some other nightmare was dredged from the armpit of hell once again. All I could do was scream and hope I would pass out.

Brian got into his car. "Clinic 14," he told it. The door was still closing, and he was making himself comfortable while it calculated his route. "Confirmed," Brian interrupted it as it tried to ask him if he would like to follow this route. Now that he thought about it, why did it ask? Did it matter? Did it think for just a moment, that despite the car knowing everything about traffic conditions, that he might somehow know of some other route that was somehow better?

The car snapped him into place, and Brian sat back to enjoy the ride, this time with the curtains pulled aside and his screens down. The car pulled out of the carport with confidence, asserted itself into the stream of traffic. He could feel the car accelerate. It seemed so close to the metal bubble in front of it that he thought he might be able to reach out and tap it, perhaps, pop it as if it were a soap bubble. The car moved into the driving lane and sped up.

This was the less exciting part, where the car followed along as if on a string in a long chain of cars, until it decided it needed to get out of that lane and it gracefully slid into an accommodating gap in the other lane that had appeared moments before. Brian felt the car move sideways, to the right, and he was off on a curve headed in the other direction. Shift to the right, and he was gliding down another street. It was amazing how quickly traffic flowed. He tried to imagine driving himself. It didn't seem possible to make so many decisions so quickly, but once, everyone had to do that. The rich still did that, but they didn't come down here, not to the city. Driving could only be done in the faraway places where there could be fifty feet between cars, not two or three. My, how life had changed.

5

MEETING THE KING

His car pulled up at Clinic 14, and he stepped out. Brian told the car to "make busy," and it zombied off into traffic, circling, waiting for his call. This should be quick.

What a refreshing surprise. I was sinking into agony, hoping to submerge in it, when I popped right back to the surface. A brief moment of shadow, a face appeared, not the pretty girl, not the milky eyes of a med-tech. But an older, brown-skinned face of a man, with a few lines and a few wisps of white in his hair. The man looked at me, his dark brown eyes focused on me. He seemed to be evaluating me as he examined my cheek.

"Hello," I said, and the man jumped back a bit before cracking a wide smile.

"Hello," he replied, grinning as if something was funny. "How are you today?"

I stammered, "I, I don't know."

The man grimaced, paused. "Apparently, you are fine."

"Fine?"

"Yes," he added, "fine."

I had to think about this. I was laying in this bed I don't know how long, "How can I be fine? I'm here."

The man smirked, almost chuckled, but I knew it was not at me, it was agreement. "I see." There was a touch of laughter to his voice without laughing. I liked this man. He seemed friendly, and not because he said he was my friend. "Well, the med-techs tell me you are fine," he continued, "but I had to see for myself."

"Oh." There was a bunch of stuff to think about, so why had the med-tech told him anything? And, who is this man anyway? Why was he here now, and why had he not been here before? "So," I said, "who are you?"

The man smiled. "Of course," he said, "please call me King."

"King?"

"Yes, King," King continued, "it's what I call myself."

"Oh," I replied. I had nothing else I could think of to say.

King seemed to be examining me. There was a look of surprise and bemusement as he looked at the rest of my body. Perhaps he could see my legs were little more than seared pegs of wood. There was little left of me other than a head and a heart that wouldn't stop beating. "Do you think you can walk?"

"I don't know, I don't think so."

"They say you are fine," he continued. "If you are fine, you should be able to get up and walk." It seemed more like thought than speech. "I would think," he added.

I smiled, started to try to laugh but I couldn't quite move enough. It sounded like wheezing. "That's good."

"Why?"

"I can't get off this bed."

King rolled his eyes and smiled. "Of course." He motioned to the med-tech. "Please deactivate the bed."

The med-tech answered, "Certainly, one moment please." It approached my bed, reached under it and I felt the restraining foam recede, cold air rushing in. King watched with interest as the tech's hands worked at the straps restraining me. The med-tech stepped back. "I have unfastened the patient."

"Well then," King started, "you are free, let's see if you can walk."

I tried to move, but I didn't know how to get up. It wasn't like my chair, where I was at an angle. I was totally flat, and I don't know how long I had been on this table. My left-hand slipped as I tried to get it underneath me. I landed on my elbow and discovered it was not a charred piece of wood, but rather bone that hurt when it landed on a metal table with my weight on top of it.

"Here," King said as he stepped forward, "let me help you."

He was holding out his hand, his right-hand, to my left-hand, he grabbed me by the wrist and didn't lift me but swung me around, so my legs fell off the table. I found myself sitting. King let go of my hand after straightening me up into a sitting position.

"There you go. Now let's see if you can walk?"

I sat staring at my feet. They seemed big and floppy and a long way away. I had never given it much thought, walking. Most of it I did automatically. Now that I had to think about it, I wasn't certain I could even stand.

"Is there a problem?" King asked.

I thought about it for a moment. "I don't know when the last time was I stood on my feet."

"Oh," King replied, "well, do you think you can stand?"

I didn't see that I had any choice, if I couldn't stand, then what? "I guess," I answered, not at all certain.

"Well, give it a try," King encouraged. There was humor in his voice again, and that made me feel better, like I was talking to a friend.

I started to slide myself toward the edge of the bed. It was still a long way down. "Um," I said.

"Sure," King seemed to understand. He looked toward the med-tech. "Could you help?"

King was not the strongest man, but his hands were firm, and he helped me move slowly. The med-tech stepped forward, and its grip was like iron. Between the two of them, I was lifted from the bed, my floppy feet planted on the floor. The med-tech stepped away, but King held on, carefully removing his hands as if he would have to catch me. As King stepped away, I was surprised to find myself standing; swaying, but standing.

King smiled and looked at me suspiciously, "are you good?"

I wasn't at all sure. "I think so."

His smile faded, and he became serious. "Okay, let's see you walk."

"Walk?" I didn't think I could.

"Yes, walk."

I stalled. "I just mastered standing."

King smiled again, "Okay," he said, "in your own time, when you can." There was a firmness about the way he said it, which made me feel it might be a bad thing if I didn't. His smile all that friendly.

I put my hand on the bed to steady myself, and I lifted my left foot. I felt a bit of a swoon come over me. My left foot landed on the floor. And that was it, I had done it, taken my first step. Looking up at King and smiling, I lost my balance, and my right foot moved forward and caught me, then my left.

"Hey, hey." King was grinning broadly. "You're doing it."

I had to catch my breath. "Yes," I said between steps, "I am doing it." Each step was getting a little easier, smoother.

King and I walked for a while. Within a few minutes, I was walking smoothly again. I felt very tired very quickly.

"Who are you?" I asked King. "You are not a tech?"

King laughed to himself and smiled. "You know, I didn't think you would ask that."

"Why not?" I asked.

King shrugged as we shuffled and he stayed beside me, watching me to see if I would fall. "I didn't think it would occur to you to ask me." He seemed to measure the words. "Yes, that's about right. Didn't think you would ask."

"Oh," I filled the gap in the conversation. "So, who are you?" I asked again.

King smiled, "Let's just say I'm someone who is interested in you."

"Huh," I said, "like the concierge?"

King was familiar with the idea of the concierge, an online interface that staff could interact with to bring forward issues or ask for things they may want. If there was feedback from staff like "I'm hurt" or "I'm sick," it would come to him through the concierge, and he would get an email about it. "Sort of, but more like I'm in charge of the concierge."

"In charge of the concierge?" I had never thought about that. Someone had to be, but I'd never guessed it would be someone like this, an older, somewhat heavy man, starting to gray, with lines on his face. I had always pictured someone tall with a cape and a helmet and dramatic lighting all around. Perhaps some ominous music should play when he spoke. That would have made more sense for someone in charge of something so important. "So, like you're their boss?"

King didn't know how to answer, "Sure, I suppose."

"Great," I said, "can I go back online?"

King looked surprised, he smiled, "I suppose you can."

I smiled at him. I reached up with my right-hand and tapped the side of my head. Nothing happened. I tapped it harder. Nothing happened. Now I gave it a good swat, just in case there was something stuck. Still nothing happened.

"Stop, stop!" King rushed forward and grabbed my hand before I could bring it up again. "Let me ask the med-techs what the problem is." He started to lead me back to the table where I had been restrained.

As he held my hand, I noticed my wrists were cut up with deep gouges all around. They had healed but looked nasty, like they may have hurt. "I don't remember having these," I commented to King as he led me back, motioning toward my wrists.

King was careful not to let go of my right arm. "No?" he said, lifting my arm and peering into the crevice in my wrist. "They look fresh," he commented softly to himself.

We approached where I must have come from. There was the bed, and a med-tech standing patiently, milky-eyed, gazing at us. King addressed the med-tech as we approached, "Could you tell me why this staff is not able to go online?"

"Certainly," the med-tech replied, then paused for a moment. "It appears this staff has been placed in offline mode, pending the resolution of examination and potential refactoring."

King didn't seem phased by this answer, but I didn't understand it. King replied, "Oh, when he's released?"

The med-tech paused to process, statement or question, "This is correct."

"Okay, thank you," King replied.

"What does that mean?" I asked King, not wanting to know.

"It means you can't go online until you are released from here."

"What do you think?" I asked.

"About?"

"Can I walk?" It had been a while. I was starting to get the hang of it again, though my legs did feel like they were two different lengths.

King looked at me, stood away and watched me walk about thirty feet, turn around and come back. I tried not to teeter, and I think I managed it because King smiled. He even turned a little red for some reason. "I guess you can. Walk, that is."

"Great," I replied. I stopped and looked at him. "So, when do I get to leave?"

King looked at me, almost sorry for a moment. "They haven't told you? Of course not."

"No."

Brian Agarwal felt like a man who had been sold something shiny and gold, only to find the gold was a thin plate that covered something plastic and cheap. It would have been much easier for everyone if 418 had been written off. They could have, should have, gone ahead with retirement. Why had they bothered to work so hard on this? Just to get that kind of result? It was beyond him.

Yes, 418 could walk. Yes, there was nothing wrong with its mental capacities. In fact, it was even pleasing to talk to, though this might have been the first time he had a reasonable conversation with a staff. He was surprised at how communicative it was, for something that lives its life in a make-believe, three-dimensional world of picture, data and neural stimulation. There would be no point in trying to argue with the Popular. They were going to win, and they had spent all that money to get 418 to this state. They were not going to simply retire 418. Brian was going to have to live with it, and either break it, or see what it could do and get what he could out of it.

6

GOING HOME

One day, that's what he had said, it didn't sound so bad, just one day. I watched King pleasantly say good-bye and the med-techs put me back into my bed of restraining foam. It occurred to me that it wasn't much good to know I only had a day to wait if I had no idea how fast time was going. And let me tell you, when they sealed me back into the foam, I was well-restrained. It quickly became maddening to watch that light flicker out of the corner of my eye. I kept thinking: *How soon is tomorrow? Isn't tomorrow now? Why isn't tomorrow now?*

"Honey, I'm home!" Brian called as he entered the apartment he shared with his wife and his five-year-old son.

Hearing his father, Prince dropped whatever it was that he was doing and came running. "Daddy! Daddy!" he called, his little arms up. If he didn't go crashing into Brian's legs, he would have gone crashing into the potted plant they kept by the door.

"Hello, my little cookie of good fortune," Brian said to his son, lifting him up and holding him high in the air. "How was your day today?"

Prince made a face, "Okay, Jenkins beat me at Blitz Commander, but I'll get him next time."

Brian only knew that Blitz Commander was one of those immersive first-person shooter games. It was advertised as super fun and a game that would help build strategic thinking. It was the strategic thinking part Brian hoped would rub off on Prince, not the immersive part. Part of Brian worried it was simply a training tool to make the gullible and naïve actually want to become staff. But what was he to say? Prince loved the game, even if Jenkins Peet, a kid from Prince's school, was able to beat him. But if it made him happy, it made daddy happy. Brian replied, "That's the spirit. Did you play well?"

"Yeah," Prince replied, "I did."

"Well then." Brian hoisted him onto his hip so that he could tap him on the nose with his index finger. "That is all you need to do, play well and enjoy the game, and learn something." Brian was always trying to add to any possible message Prince might remember deep down in his sub-conscious. He should always learn something. He would be ecstatic if Prince found learning enjoyable, though he was only five. Perhaps that would come later.

Brian usually did not tell his wife how work was, there was a good reason. There was never anything interesting to talk about. Work was always the same; work is work. He had staff, he rented them out to places that needed something more flexible and cheaper than a machine. He tried to keep his staff, as replacing them was a real investment; unless he could get the insurance company to do it. The bills rolled in, and he rolled them back out again. Not a lot to talk about, it wasn't like he was doing anything interesting. He was renting out labor and receiving payment for it.

"So, the Pop is going to give me back my staff." It was something to talk about.

"Oh?" Imelda answered as she laid out the plates for dinner.

"Yeah, it's kinda weird." Brian was thinking out loud, something he felt free to do with his wife. "The staff was involved in an exception involving a car."

"Oh no, was it hurt?"

Brian reached into the cupboard and pulled out three glasses. "I would say yes, and the Pop said, not enough."

"Not enough?"

"Sure," Brian continued, "not enough for me to make a claim and retire the staff, but certainly enough that I haven't been able to assign it to any duties."

Imelda stirred a pot with something golden brown in it that smelled wonderful. "But they are going to pay for the time the staff was unavailable?"

"Sure, but only sixty percent," Brian answered as he placed water glasses, one in front of each place setting.

Imelda rolled her eyes as she kept stirring. "I can see. Is that a problem?"

Brian reached into a drawer and grabbed some knives, blunted with years of use, some forks, still pointy enough, and spoons. "Sixty percent is less than I'd like but, you didn't see the staff, it was pretty beaten up. I didn't think it was going to live, but somehow they did it."

"Hmm." Imelda tasted her cooking, trying not to burn herself. "Interesting," was all she could think to say.

"I didn't think they would go through that much trouble."

"Huh." Imelda propped up the conversation.

"I saw the staff a month ago, and they had it in a coma or something like that," Brian was arranging the cutlery. "Its face looked crushed." Brian placed all the cutlery identically. "Its eye was swollen shut and there looked to have been a lot of damage to its head."

"Wow, that sounds serious."

"I figured it was. Serious enough to just write off the staff, but nope, they said it was fine and, I don't know what they did to it, but it took them a month, and they say it's fine."

Imelda turned from the stove and looked at Brian, who had sat down at the table as she let dinner simmer for a bit. "So, it's working now?"

Brian smirked and turned his head a bit. Maybe the shift would cause things to fall into place just a little bit. "I'm not sure they got it right. I know they say it is fine, and I know they have all this diagnostic stuff to check that the staff is fine, but I'm not sure it is."

"Oh." This was more interesting that Brian's usual tales of work, which were non-existent.

"I went to see it today, you know, it could hardly walk." Imelda had never given much thought to the workings of her husband's business. "And, if it can't walk, I'd say it can't work, and it if can't work, what is the good of it? I was hoping it wouldn't be able to walk, that it would just give up and it would be telling me it couldn't go back to work, in which case, I could go back and make the Pop pay for a write-off."

"I see." Imelda sat across the table as the pan of sauce simmered and reduced a bit.

"The other thing about it," Brian said, focusing off into the distance, somewhere to the left of Imelda. "I had to talk to it."

Imelda had talked to many staff. You always got precise answers that had been programmed by some software architect to sound polite, but always sounded tinny. She shrugged. "What's the problem with that?"

Brian shuttered a bit. "It was weird. It was like it had a personality. It almost made jokes. It thought. It was self-aware."

Imelda tried to imagine staff that was self-aware. She looked up at the light that hung over the dinner table, pursed her lips, and tried to imagine. *Hmmm, nope.* Couldn't imagine that.

"I didn't think they were self-aware, I mean, get them offline, and they are totally lost. But this one actually had a conversation with me. Without being online."

It clicked for Imelda, talking to staff that wasn't online. That must have been creepy. The thought of it made her shiver, but she didn't want her husband to be afraid. "That must have been interesting?" she added hopefully.

"It was," replied Brian, following her thread. "I was amazed, maybe even astonished, that staff could think and interact like that. You know they spend their entire lives online, or pretty much. Did you know they have families with partners that they meet online? How weird is that?"

Imelda was demure in her reply. "You know we met on a dating site?"

Brian grimaced. "Yes, I know, but we didn't meet, build a whole relationship, get married and have children online, having never met in person."

"I suppose not," Imelda conceded.

"See, it was weird."

Brian went to bed that night still thinking about 418. It seemed weird to have actually spoken to his staff. He'd tried that before, and it had gone quickly. The staff wanted to get back online so badly that they didn't finish their conversation. It had been like trying to hold a fish as it wriggled, writhed, wanting to get free so it could plunge back into the pool of sensory immersion in which it lived. But this one was different, this one understood it had feet, this one knew that standing came before walking. This one understood, at least at a basic level, that walking would improve with practice, and even—indirectly—told him so. Brian didn't think staff was capable of that.

From a young age, pretty much as soon as the body was capable of doing work, staff went to a clinic where the cerebral interface was put into their heads. Staff referred to this as *going to school,* but it was much faster and quicker. Two weeks and the staff would be good to go, you could upload any task into the buffer of their cerebral interface. During the day, the interface would allow them to do work, while the staff played cards, slots or whatever it was staff did all day when they were not hooked up to their chairs. Normally, staff didn't care about the real-world, they thought the online world was the real-world; you were just an annoyance, and perhaps they missed a raise in online poker.

418 was different, certainly damaged. It wasn't normal that staff should be like that. But, like what? Brian couldn't quite get his mind around it. He toiled with it as Imelda turned out the light and he waited for sleep to take this riddle away from him.

Work came with a sense of being different today. Indeed, Brian's first stop was not going to be the office, but the clinic, and that was different. A change is as good as a rest. Brian woke, got out of bed quickly—no effort to drag himself out of bed—and went to his computer. "Waiting for release back to manager," is what it said on 418's claim. Imelda was right, it was probably going to work itself out. And this was better than just going to the office and paying the bills and mulling over the books, waiting for the day when he too wouldn't be able to pay for the necessities of life.

For some reason, today was one of those inexplicable days where children didn't go to school, but parents did have to go to work. Prince was already watching TV, oblivious to whether or not he had had breakfast. *When the screen is flashy enough, does food matter?* Brian thought to himself, as he breezed past the entrance to the entertainment room, into the kitchen. Breakfast today was a matter of shifting bowls, plates, opening, closing the fridge, a glass got used, coffee poured, drank, ate, drank, scraped into the bin, and down the garbage disposal. Within moments Brian was down to the street and off to the clinic.

"Make busy," Brian told his car as he stepped free of it. He headed toward the front door of the clinic as the car zombied away, neither of them to think about each other until united once again by mobile device.

Stepping into the clinic, Brian was blinded by the bright light of the waiting room. There was no one waiting, but the room was immaculate, the chairs lined up in rows against the walls, magazines spread out in a perfect fan on the tables in front of the chairs. Brian strode toward the attendant who was sitting straight up, staring straight ahead until Brian got within the pre-determined distance. As he crossed the imaginary semi-circle, the attendant's head turned toward him, and a smile pulled at the corners of its mouth.

"Hello," it said, "how can I help you?"

Brian looked at his mobile device. "My name is Agarwal; I would like to see 686381KAA418."

"Yes sir, please wait here, and a medical technician will be here shortly to escort you."

Brian stood, staring at the doors. They opened, and a milky eyed med-tech appeared. "Mr. Agarwal, please follow me."

They stepped into the gray room. Brian took a moment to adjust to the darkness. Forcing him to hurry to catch up, once again he found himself panting to keep up with the med-tech. They turned and twisted through the maze of hanging curtains, until the med-tech stopped and threw open a curtain and went about fiddling with machines.

Brian stepped over. He could see 418 grinning as much as the restraining foam would let it. "Hello old friend," Brian addressed the grinning thing stuck to the table. "How are you today? Are you ready to go home?"

I have never been so glad to see anyone as I was to see King. Could it mean that staring up at the ceiling, that flickering light, the pipes, bolted to the ceiling, never moving, nothing ever changing, was now over? I felt the foam receding, I hadn't been strapped down, I moved my legs so I could sit up. I felt something go pop in my left wrist as my legs moved right, but it was good to not be restrained any longer.

King was smiling at me, pleased to see me. "Hello, old friend, how are you? Are you ready to go home?" I heard him ask me.

"Yes," I replied, wanting to jump out of the bed.

"Good," King replied, he turned to look at the med-tech, "What do we have to do?"

The med-tech turned to King and gazed at him. "It needs clothes. It needs to get to the carport, get into a car and go home."

"Will you bring the clothes?"

"No," the med-tech replied, "the clothes will be coming shortly, but I will not be bringing them."

"Okay," King replied. He turned back to me, "I guess we wait for your clothes to arrive."

King turned to look away. He was not a med-tech—he had no need to see me without my clothes—and didn't seem to want to. I kept grinning at King. It was just too good. After all those hours of staring at the ceiling, the flickering light seemed to be contracting, compressing and turning into a few minutes. "It really is true? I can go home?"

"Yes," King tossed over his shoulder.

"I can go online again?"

King turned and looked briefly, "Um, sure. Of course, you can."

I tapped the side of my head. Nothing happened. "I can't go online, it's not working."

"Huh?"

"Look."

King had to turn to look at me, keeping his eyes on my face. I reached up with my right-hand and tapped at my temple. King did not fade into darkness, and I did not see the green welcome screen of my "at work" profile fade into view. "See? Nothing."

"Oh that?" King seemed a little confused. He turned to the med-tech who was carefully arranging my feeding tube into a nice little coil. "Will it be able to go online? It doesn't seem to be able to activate."

The med-tech stopped what it was doing, straightened and spoke toward King. "The patient has been disconnected during testing of his cerebral interface. Upon release from this facility, you will be able to re-activate its access."

"I will?" King asked, "I have to turn the switch?"

The med-tech waited for King to finish and replied pleasantly. "Yes, you will have to re-initialize the account."

"Thank you," King turned back to me. "Well..." he smiled kindly but looked a little sheepish. "It seems I have to do something, so I'll tell you what: we get you dressed, we get you home, and you get to go online, just like normal. Sounds good?"

He said it quickly, so I had to review. "When I get home, I can go back online?" It had been so long I just wanted to make sure it was true.

"Yes." King seemed a little agitated. A med-tech pulled open the curtain, "Ah good." King was relieved. "Your clothes are here." The med-tech placed them on the bed beside me.

The clothes didn't fit me. They were loose and baggy. "What seems to be the matter with these, why are they so big?"

King shrugged. Now I was mostly dressed—save for buttons and zips—King wasn't trying to avoid looking at me. "I guess these used to fit you."

I looked at King, puzzled.

"You have been here a long time; I suppose your size changed." Then he thought about it. "I bet you can get yourself resized when you get back online."

I smiled. It would be good to be back. I finished cinching up my pants. "Okay, ready," I told King.

King smiled, "Good."

We walked through the maze of curtains, following a med-tech. King had asked it where the staff carport was, and after being told he asked the med-tech to lead us there. I loved how King could just order around the med-techs, and they did everything he asked. Without question, all promptly, and usually with an oddly broad smile. They wouldn't even respond to me, and I'm not sure they even heard me. For King they responded exactly, precisely and with a *Yes sir!*

We headed down a walkway that curled around on itself twice. There were several burnt out lights here and a terrible smell as we passed some double doors. It smelled like garbage. The tech turned left, pushed open a different set of double doors and held one side open for King. I managed to squeeze through before the door could hit me as it slammed shut. We were standing in a carport, and a car was heading up the ramp toward the loading curb where we stopped. The car came to a halt. I stood back; King motioned with his hand that this car was for me.

"Aren't you going to get in?" I asked King. "I am sure there will be another car around in a second."

King chuckled. "No, this car is for you, my friend."

"Oh," I was confused, "if you insist."

The car was opened, waiting. I stepped in. I tapped my head, nothing happened.

"You are going to have to wait until you get home," King explained, "Just be patient."

I had just been a patient, and I didn't want to be one again. I didn't know what he meant, but the door was sliding shut, and before I knew it I was sliding down the ramp from the carport, making my way back out to the road. I felt the car lurch—this wasn't going to be good; I didn't feel well—and we made four short right turns. The car started to slow again.

When the car stopped, and the lid opened, there were two med-techs waiting to hoist me out of the car. They stuffed me into a medichair, activated the restraining foam and wheeled me back into the dingy gray area of the clinic, placed me facing a wall.

I wanted to scream, and for a while I did. King did not return.

Finally, after what could have been days of staring at the same bit of concrete, I was grabbed from behind, wheeled back to the carport. Without any explanation, I was released and loaded into a waiting car that, this time, did not loop back into the clinic.

I have never been so sick in my life. I'd taken thousands of car rides, I'd taken a car to work every day of my life, and I'd never had this problem before. As soon as the car pulled into traffic, my stomach started lurching around, shaking like a maraca. I felt myself swallowing hard as my throat went sour and my head started to swim. A few bumps and turns later, I felt my chest convulse. I thought my head was going to explode with the pressure. My mouth opened and nothing came out. I tasted blood in my throat, and as the car lurched from one side to the other, I felt my chest compress again, trying to toss my stomach out my mouth. This was awful.

When the car pulled up at my condo's carport, my clothes were all covered in blood, and little brown flecks of stuff that looked like it should have come out of the other side. I almost fell out of the car. It was good to be home. As I staggered away, the car sealed itself up, pulled away. and was replaced by another car. I clutched a handrail to get out of the way. There was a line of cars all waiting to drop off their passengers. I had to pull myself up to get out of the way of the next staff, and the next and the next; they just kept coming. There I was, alone in the carport, staff streaming by, no one around, but at least I was back in my own building.

I couldn't get to the elevator. The tromp of incoming staff was too quick, too steady, they didn't seem to see me, and I didn't want to get trampled. But as steady as the flow was, with seemingly all the residents of my burrow arriving at the same time, it stopped just as fast. I was literally alone.

The carport empty, I headed to the elevator, pressed the button and a door opened to my left. I stepped into the car. I had to think and remember, there seemed so many numbers, fifty to choose from. I knew the general area, but which one? I closed my eyes and let my arm reach out to where it always does, and it pressed "19." I looked at it, it seemed right, I was usually online. I felt my midsection drop again as the elevator began to move and we descended to the nineteenth floor. For a moment I felt like I was free-falling, then the elevator started to slow.

The door opened, and I stepped out into the hallway. A bare place with doors every eight feet and a single fluorescent light bar every sixteen feet, except where burnt out. I turned to the left automatically, though the corridor stretched equally in each direction, and started to walk. I got to the spot where my legs felt like they wanted to turn and looked up at the door. But it was a wall. I hadn't taken the right number of steps.

I looked at the doors on either side of the wall I was standing in front of. They looked identical, except they had a string of numbers and letters on them, in the same large block print. The one to my left was, 9644452479E2 and to my right was 43166AD170F5. I approached the door on my right—it didn't open. I moved past it to 1204F976WC90. No luck. This was the general area I thought I lived, and the nineteenth floor seemed more and more correct when I thought about it. Why weren't the doors opening? This wasn't good. What if I couldn't get into the condo? I could get lost down here. I started to run. Just as I did—almost to prove a point, as if it were making fun of me—a door slid open as I ran past. I stopped.

The light flickered on. The two fluorescent tubes struggled, caught, and came to life. I didn't remember it this way. Had staring at the ceiling changed the way I see things? It was bleak. The walls where white, the chair cream-colored vinyl badly worn, and a thin metal tower stood where I hooked up my feeding bags so I could relax and eat at the same time.

I stepped into the little room, it was about as wide as it was long and about as long as it would have been if I had laid down. There was a toilet on the far-left wall, a sink. To the right, there were drawers where I could get clothes from, and on the far wall was the cupboard where I would find food packs I could hook up to my catheter. I supposed this was all I needed, but I couldn't help feeling, is this it?

I looked at my chair, shuffling around the narrow condo. I worked my way into the chair. The chair seemed to remember the way I was shaped, and I sank deeply into it. It was comfortable. I reached over and found the hard wire. Hard wire connections were always so much better than wireless. I paused for a moment, looking at the connector. It must be the same as they had at the clinic, but they had caused such horrible pain with their hard wire. I hesitated to connect it to my head. Would it even work? Would it hurt me? Would I be able to disconnect it? One way to find out.

I felt the wire lock to the side of my head with a great satisfying snap. I waited for the world to fade and a screen of green to rise up in my field of vision, half-expecting it not to happen. "Whoo hoo," I said aloud. The world was dissolving and up came a field of blue, not green. Why was it blue and not green? It had always been green.

A kindly face appeared, an older man with salt and pepper hair, pale skin, almost delicate in contrast to his iron-colored hair. "Hello," the man said as he materialized in front of me on the field of blue. "Let me introduce myself, I am Samuel, consider me your concierge. What would you like to do today?"

"Samuel?" I asked the man. He was wearing the right uniform, something that looked like a fitted tuxedo. He spoke with the right air, but my concierge is Ernest, and he was shorter with dark hair and a little more olive complexion. "What happened to Ernest?"

Samuel smiled. "I'm sorry. I have no information about Ernest. Is there some other assistance that I can provide?"

How do you argue with the concierge? Concierges are the one-stop for anything and everything. They know everything. "Ernest used to be my concierge," I explained. "I'd like to talk to him."

Smiling, Samuel replied, "I'm sorry, I do not know who Ernest is."

"Is there any way you could?"

Samuel continued to smile. "I'm sorry, I don't understand the question."

"Why not?"

"I can't know a concierge. It doesn't work that way."

I didn't know what to say. It didn't occur to me to ask how it does work.

"What would you like to do today?"

"I don't know," I replied. "I'd like to go see my wife."

Samuel smiled again. "I'm sorry, you do not appear to be married."

When someone tells you something you know isn't true, but that someone is supposed to be someone who is not supposed to be able to lie to you, what do you do? I felt like I'd been smacked backward by some invisible hand; staggered, astonished. "What do you mean?"

Now the concierge was annoying in his pleasantness. "I have no record that you have ever been married."

This concierge wasn't helpful, but he was supposed to be. I didn't know what to do. "How could I not have been married? My wife is Belinda Boyle. Look that up."

The concierge hardly paused for a moment. "There are fifty-three persons who call themselves Belinda Boyle. Forty-two are married, two are male. Shall I send them a message and ask them if any of them are married to you?"

"Sure," I answered.

There was a brief pause. "Done," the concierge said.

"Okay," I replied.

We stood there for a moment.

"Any response?" I asked.

"Not as yet."

"Oh." I waited some more. Finally, I asked, "how about now?"

The concierge answered cheerfully, "You have a like but no other responses."

Can I see who?

"Sure." The concierge motioned to his right, where a face formed into view. It was a young man with a finely trimmed hairdo. "Here is your like, but I think it's unlikely this is your wife as..."

I cut him off, "Thank you, that's not my wife." She would never have presented herself as a nerdy white teenager. It occurred to me that this was hopeless.

"What else would you like to do?" the happy-faced man asked me.

"I need to eat."

"You do not seem to be connected to your external feeding apparatus. Would you like me to connect it?"

"Sure." The background went a little fuzzy as the concierge took over.

Somewhere in a condo, deep underground, a milky-eyed staff got out of its chair. It stood up, turned, and reached into the cupboard at the far end of the little square that was its condo. Expertly, it grabbed a bag, hung it on a rack, obtained a sanitary tube, plugged one end into the bag. It sat down, its eyes looking forward, focusing on nothing. Its left-hand moved down to the end of the sanitary tube where a wipe back had been fixed to the end. It tore it open, wiped its arm where the tube was to connect and snapped the tube into place with a gentle, but firm, click.

Samuel, the concierge, came back into focus. "Your feeding apparatus has been connected. Where would you like to eat?"

"McDonald's," was the first thing out of my mouth. I didn't think about it. "I'd like to go to McDonald's," I said again. It sounded better this time.

"Okay, let's go," Samuel said. The blue screen faded and a street-front with cobblestones and people on bicycles bouncing down the road. Samuel stepped toward the door. As it slid open, he held out his hand. "McDonald's."

I stood there for a moment. It didn't seem real. It had been a long time since I'd even had something as simple as McDonald's. I stepped past Samuel into the store and was hit by all the smells and sounds, the beeping, the rich scent of salt and fat cooking somewhere behind the counter. I could feel my mouth water. It had been so long since I'd had any sort of formal dining. They had just kept me alive at the clinic, but now I would be allowed to enjoy it. Too good to be true.

"Hello sir," said that smiling teenager behind the counter. "How can I brighten your day?"

I felt myself smiling. "I would like two big macs, extra-large fries, a chocolate shake, iced brownies, oh, and two extra double cheeseburgers." It all slid out at once. My whole order left my mouth at one time, and the teenager started to punch in the order.

"Could I interest you in an apple pie?"

"Sure," I replied, "why not?"

"Okay," she said with enthusiasm. "Uh-oh..." The countertop where she was entering my information had turned red. "It appears you do not have enough to cover the payment," she mused as she stabbed at the countertop. "Let me see. If I remove, the apple pie?" The countertop went white again and then flashed red. "Nope," she continued to stab at the counter. "Let's see," the counter went white again, and then red. "How about if we just do the two cheeseburgers? Hmm, nope," the countertop was flashing red again. "I'm sorry sir, can I offer you a complimentary glass for water?" She held out a small plastic glass.

"No." I turned away. The smell was delicious, I just wanted it, I really wanted it. This stunk! I stepped out the door. "Samuel," I said, and the concierge appeared in front of me. "I can't order anything."

Samuel smiled. "Let me see," he said, his pause almost imperceptible. "Yes, it appears you have no money in your account. Would you like to visit the bank?"

"Sure," I answered, "why not?"

The street around the McDonald's dissolved and reformed itself into a different street where the American Bank stood. The concierge smiled. "Here we are." He held out his hand and motioned to the door. "American Bank."

"Thank you," I said, and turned to head into the bank.

The bank was a large room with some desks in it, so I could stop and write a note or something. There were a few colorful chairs no one was ever meant to sit in. Three tellers stood smiling and standing straight behind their bulletproof glass cubicles. I approached the nearest one, and she smiled. "Welcome to American Bank, how can I help you today?"

"Hi there. It seems I don't have any money in my account."

The teller looked at a computer screen that was set in the table. "Yes, that seems to be the case."

I tried to lean over the counter to get a look at the screen, but I couldn't read anything on it because it was dark, as if it was not on, or perhaps just supposed to represent a screen so it would appear the teller was looking something up. "How is that the case?"

Still smiling, the teller replied, "Our account displays a balance of V$0. I'm sorry."

Somehow, I wasn't surprised, but my head felt like it was spinning, "How can that be? I used to have a couple of hundred thousand."

The teller didn't blink. "I'm sorry sir, when I look at your balance, the highest it has ever been was V$0."

"What?"

"Yes, the account was opened today and has never had any money put into it."

"What?"

"Yes, this account is new."

"Oh." My head was hurting. "How can my account be new?"

"It was only opened today."

"Right." Perhaps that wasn't the best question. I thought of a better one. "How do I get money into my account?"

The teller blinked, then, blinked again. "Normally, funds are deposited in your account by your employer in exchange for services rendered."

I stood there silently. The teller looked at me, smiling. "Okay, I see." I turned and left the bank.

7

HOLIDAY

"There are many places you can go when you don't have any money," Samuel tried to say cheerfully. "Being in the street usually does not cost anything. You could tour various different cities or destinations without incurring any costs."

I felt myself scrunching my face at the idea. Just wandering around, and I couldn't go into any of the stores, amusements, and restaurants? What was the point? I couldn't gamble, I couldn't enjoy food, drink or other ingestibles. I couldn't attend a show, I couldn't go to the club. But I could wander around outside, thinking about all the things I couldn't do. Yeah, that sounded like fun. I disconnected myself online, Samuel started to fade into a billion dots, and the lights flickered on in my condo. The outline of the cupboards assembled into straight lines cut into the otherwise white wall.

I sat. The sound of online had dissolved, and I could feel my heart beating—for some reason. It was slowing back to normal. There was a rushing noise in my ears that also seemed to be dying down. Sitting in my chair I looked around. The feeding tube had emptied, which I thought was funny because I hadn't been able to order any food. How was it that I had eaten? I thought you had to eat in order to engage the feeding system. I disconnected the bag and sighed. I disconnected the hardwire and threw my head back.

Tapping my right temple, online mobile came into view. Good to know this worked. I asked what time it was, and Samuel told me it was 3:39 and I could see the numbers projected into my mind. I tapped my right temple again, going completely offline. I still felt hungry, even though the feeding bag had emptied. It just wasn't right if you didn't get to sit down and go through the process of eating. I lay there, staring dumbly at the ceiling. How was it I had nothing? How was it my wife hadn't responded to me? Wasn't she waiting?

I was still breathing harder than I thought I should. Taking deep breaths, I tried to slow everything down. That's when I noticed, the room I was in, was small. Nothing online was this small. You never went to a restaurant and sat in a room this small. Even the opium dens didn't have rooms this small. As I looked at the walls, the cupboards, the shower, everything seemed to be moving toward me, shrinking, getting smaller, and instead of getting easier to breathe, it was getting much more difficult. I could feel my chest pounding harder as my eyes tried to gauge if the walls were moving in on me, and how fast.

I wasn't going to let myself get crushed. Whatever was going on in my condo, I wasn't going to sit around waiting for the walls to cave in on me. I got up, I stepped toward the door. For a brief moment, I panicked. The door didn't open. I remembered that I was usually in mobile mode. I had to reach out and touch the door with my hand. I did, and it slid open. I stepped out the door.

The hallway seemed long. I couldn't remember walking to the elevator. I just knew it was to the right. As I passed each door, a tiny red light on top of the door blinked on, then off, noting my passing; registering that this door did not belong to me. If you walked far enough, you either got to a wall or an elevator. I found the elevator, pressed the button and waited for a car to descend to my level.

The door opened. Stepping into the empty box, I turned and looked at the control panel. There was a big button, heavily worn. Beside it was the word, "Carport." Above the carport button, was another small shiny button that looked like no one had ever pressed. "Ground," it said. I reached out and pressed the "ground" button. The door slid shut, and I began to rise from the nineteenth floor toward...what I guessed was the ground floor.

As the elevator opened, I found myself looking out into a dusty, dirty room with cinder-block walls. There was a banging sound somewhere off to the right. I stepped from the elevator, displacing some dust from the floor. At the end of the building, some fifty feet away there was a metal door that was being pushed open or pulled closed by the force of the wind in the elevator tube. When my lift door opened, it then slammed shut. My elevator moved away, and I felt suction as the car dropped into the earth. I moved away from the lift, stepped over some old boxes of tile, bags of sand and cement, and picked my way to the door. The door wasn't locked, in fact, there wasn't a lock at all. It was just a door, easily opened.

I had never seen anything like this before. I had expected to see buildings or streets, perhaps stores and restaurants like I had seen online. What I found was nothing; there was no place like this online. Just a large flat surface, heading out in every direction. Every so often there was a light, and under that light there was a little building. I walked toward one of the other little buildings. It was a long walk—despite it being dark—and it was still hot, hotter than I liked. I found myself sweating. I didn't like sweating; my clothes were sticking to me. No wonder no one ever went outdoors, it was disgusting.

Having made it to another building, I looked in through the meshed glass of the door. I reached out and pulled a long thin metal handle, and the door opened easily. It was the same, as my building: discarded construction supplies, a mop in this one, and dust and dirt everywhere. I could hear the whistling of the elevator cars going up and down their shafts.

Leaving this building, I wandered to another and another. They were all the same. Not even the color of the paint was different, just the rubble that had been left behind changed, but was one pile of rubble any different than any other pile?

I don't know how long I did this. I tried walking in one direction, seeing if this plateau would ever come to an end. But I grew tired, I'd just spent untold days in the clinic, and I wasn't used to walking. My feet were starting to hurt. The pavement was uneven, these buildings had been here for a long time, the asphalt had cracked and been clumsily patched, if at all. Because I was looking up and not paying attention, I felt my left ankle turn underneath my weight. It didn't take long before my heel was swelling and I was stepping on pulpy mush, a skin wrapped bag of hurt squeezing around under my foot.

It was surprising how fast my body broke down once I'd managed to hurt myself. I couldn't say I had ever hurt myself before. I had come home with cuts, I had been notified by Ernest—my previous concierge—that I would have to report to the clinic, or that I had been taken to the clinic. I had even asked to go to the clinic. That's when I realized I no longer knew where I was. Sure, I was still on the same plateau, but where was my building?

I turned around and tried to figure out where and when I had made turns. I walked a few yards, backtracking, but realized I didn't know if that was backtracking or not. I turned around and around looking for a landmark. There were none, and that was a bad idea. I was now just lost: plateau, small buildings, orange lights, and dark brown sky. I tapped my temple, nothing. My foot really hurt. I walked to one of the buildings. Maybe I would get lucky and find my condo building. I was hobbling and hopping on my right foot to try to save a few steps on my left foot.

Pulling open the door, it was more of the same, rubble, dust, but not the same rubble and dust. It didn't look like anyone had walked through here in a while. I found an old box that sagged under my weight as I sat on it. Dust plumed up from either side of it, and I felt myself cough as the air became gritty. Tapping my head, I was relieved I was able to go mobile. Samuel appeared on his blue screen. He was standing behind a counter, and only his face was animated.

"Hello," Samuel greeted me. "How can I help you today?"

"Hi Samuel, am I glad to see you. I'm lost; I've hurt my foot."

"Uh-oh?" Samuel answered. "Which is it, are you lost, or are you lost and hurt?"

I was glad to see Samuel. "Both, but I really am hurt. My foot, I can barely walk."

"No problem," Samuel replied cheerfully. "I see where you are. Did you know there is a carport just one floor below you? You could use that to go to the clinic. I will summon a car for you."

I got up from my box and walked toward the elevator and pressed the only button to call the lift. "Thanks Samuel, you are a life-saver." While I was talking to Samuel, the door opened, I got in and descended the single floor to the carport. *Wow! Does my foot ever hurt.*

Before I knew it, I was on my way to the clinic in a car Samuel had summoned. Keeping Samuel online, being in mobile mode, made the drive more bearable, but I still felt every move. I'd never had problems with cars, at least, not before the exception. I'd never even noticed being in them. Unfortunately, I didn't have much to say to Samuel. "Has Belinda responded to my message?"

Samuel smiled. "No, I have not had any responses that are serious."

"Oh." At least wondering what had happened to my wife gave me something to do other than think about how I was being tossed around in this tin can.

Finally, the ride slowed down and appeared to be coming to a stop. Samuel interrupted our staring and smiling contest. "Well, George, you seem to be at the clinic. Please let the car come to a complete stop before disembarking."

I couldn't wait to disembark. If I could have, I would have jumped from the car to stop this torment. But the car slowed, and it wouldn't release the restraining foam—or open the door—until the car was at a complete stop. As the car opened, I could feel myself being lifted out of the metal pod by two med-techs who flipped me around and fastened me to a medichair.

"Congratulations George," Samuel started speaking to me, "you have arrived at the clinic and will be helped shortly."

"Oh good," I replied, being somewhat relieved.

Smiling as always, Samuel answered, "It was my pleasure." A few moments later, I felt hands on me, and I was being wheeled off somewhere. I only felt a little fear, which would have exploded if I'd lost contact with Samuel. "George, you are being taken to an examination room where they will examine your foot. Would you like to play solitaire in the meantime?"

"Sure." What else did I have to do?

8

WHOOPS HEHE

"I don't believe it," Brian muttered to himself as he sat in front of his screen looking at the message from the Popular Insurance Company. 418 had checked itself back into the clinic, this time with a foot injury. The claim was being processed, but in the meantime, he could come and view his staff, if he wished—or subscribe for push updates—at Clinic 14.

Brian sighed. Normally he wouldn't have cared, but he hadn't even got a day's work out of 418, and it was back at the clinic. He would have to go and see if he was going to convince the Popular that 418 should be written off. He would ask them again why we all just couldn't get on with things. It would have much more fun to go to the office and take care of paperwork. With minor annoyance, he set about getting Prince ready for school and himself ready for a trip to the clinic.

Stepping out of his car, he told it to make busy, this wouldn't take long. He strode into the spotless white area of the clinic, where nobody was waiting.

"How may I help you today?" the reception staff asked, looking to where Brian had walked. He was standing in the place where the med-tech would come out to meet him, not in front of the desk. It was just faster this way. "My name is Agarwal, and I am here to see my staff." Brian didn't really have to look at his mobile. "686381KAA418." Brian tossed the character string over his shoulder toward the reception staff.

The staff smiled and said, "Yes, one moment, a medical technician will be here shortly to escort you."

"Thank you," Brian added, still looking at the doors that would be bursting open at any moment.

And sure enough, the doors burst open and a milky eyed med-tech came forward. "Mr. Agarwal, please come this way."

This time, instead of turning right, they turned left and headed off to a different wing of the gray area. Brian arrived at the cubicle, and this time, 418 was sitting up in a restraint chair with its foot set into a plastic boot.

Normally, when Brian had gone to the clinic to see staff, he would find them sitting there all milky-eyed and dazed playing games, chatting or doing whatever it was they do all day when they were mobile. He would turn to the med-tech and ask what had happened, and the med-tech, who was also milky-eyed, dazed, playing games or somehow occupying the other part of its brain, would read back whatever was in the file. But, this time, 418 was sitting there grinning at him. "Hey King. Nice to see you."

Brian was taken aback, "Yes, it's, um, nice to see you too."

Samuel told me I was going to have to wait until a VIP came to check in on me at the clinic. I didn't need Samuel to explain what VIP meant. King was coming, and I think that was who I needed to talk to. He seemed to be someone who could get things done. Since I was going to be sitting anyway, staring at Samuel, not able to do anything, I figured I'd go off mobile and just wait. The nice thing about where they had put me was there was no flickering light.

I heard the footsteps coming, I saw a shadow rise on the curtain that defined my room, when it opened, I was ready.

"Hi King, what do you think?" I motioned to my leg.

King blinked at me, his jaw hanging open, "Yes, um, it's nice to see you," was all he could manage. It took him a moment, like he had to re-adjust something in his mind. "Um, so, what happened?"

The med-tech stood by obediently. King had not spoken to it, he wanted me to tell him. I tried to shrug. "I went for a walk, and I hurt my foot, but I don't know what's wrong."

King straightened, as if I had said the most amazing thing ever. "You went for a walk?"

I smiled. "Yes," I answered cautiously, as if this was something weird or something.

"Why?"

I hadn't thought about that. "Um, I didn't have anything else to do?"

Now King looked confused. "You didn't have anything else to do?" He repeated what I had said, as if there was something wrong with the order of the words. "How could you not have something else to do?"

"I don't know," I answered honestly, "it was better than sitting in my condo all night."

King seemed to be rejoining the conversation. "But what about online. You got back in, right?"

"Oh yes," I answered cheerfully, glad he didn't seem baffled. "I was able to get online, but there's a problem."

"A problem?"

"Yes, a problem."

"And what is that problem?"

"I can't find my wife, and I don't have any money," I answered as directly as possible, just to keep it simple.

King seemed confused again. "You can't find your wife, and you don't have any money? Are they connected?"

I hadn't thought of that. "I don't know, maybe."

King looked around for some place to sit, but there was none. He turned to the med-tech. "Could you get me a chair?"

The med-tech smiled, gazed at him and answered, "Certainly, sir."

We heard the footsteps as the med-tech walked away, and then heard them coming back. It reappeared holding a small, sturdy and simple looking chair, which it placed down at the edge of the cubicle. "Your chair," it said in a friendly voice.

King moved the chair so we could have a nice conversation. "Okay, you can't find your wife?"

"Yes," I answered. "I was married and now I can't reach out to her."

King looked like he was thinking. "I see," he said after a long pause. "When you say you can't reach out to her, what does that mean?"

I tried to explain. "I used to be able to send her messages and reach out to her online and she would answer immediately, but now the concierge says that I've never been married." I didn't think that made sense.

King looked lost in thought. "Oh, right. Huh."

I waited for King to finish, but he stopped talking and went off into thought again. "What do you mean, huh?" I tried to bring him back.

"I know you are married. You know you are married. Why would the concierge say that you are not?" He was thinking out loud. His eyes didn't focus on me when he was thinking. "I'll have to look into it," he added, quickly coming back.

"Thanks," I said. I guess this is why he is King.

"And you have no money either?"

"No, I went to the bank, and they say that not only do I not have any money, but I've never had any money and my account was opened today."

King rolled his eyes, "Ooohh," he said, "that makes sense." King sat up and looked at me earnestly, "You disconnected yourself and went for a walk?"

"No, not exactly," I corrected him. I needed to tell him that I tried to have dinner, and if you haven't got any money, they don't let you eat anything. I told him that if you haven't got any money, they don't let you into places. And what good is it going to interesting places if you can't get in and you can't enjoy anything or do anything? I had to explain to him that all I could do was wander around and look at things from the street, the street was free, but it wasn't that interesting.

King agreed. There wasn't much point in wandering around on the street with nothing to do. "And instead of wandering around online, you decided to unhook yourself and go wander around your condo burrow."

"Sure, I guess." I thought I needed to add something else to explain myself. "It was different, I've seen all the online places before, but I'd never been to the ground floor of my condo."

King was thinking again. "Gee, why would you?" I don't think he was aware that he had said anything. "And you went for a walk, and you hurt yourself?"

"Yes." It was interesting how King seemed to be thinking of something else and then leap to some other thing.

"Okay."

I smiled. "Good."

King turned to the med-tech. "What exactly is wrong with it..." he paused awkwardly, as if he'd said something that didn't sound right. Then he tried again, "What is the diagnosis?"

The med-tech told King I had damaged some coating of a muscle on the bottom of my foot. I knew I'd damaged my foot, but I didn't know my muscles had coating on them. King asked for the prognosis and was told I would have to stay off the foot for quite a while. That I should be returned for a regular checkup to see if I can be re-instated for duties and that I had received cortisone. King seemed satisfied with this. He was also told he could check the status of the claim using the website or mobile app and push notifications were available.

King turned back to me. "I will fix this."

"Great!" I had not expected to hear anything like that. "But if you don't, how will you know?"

King smiled. "Leave a message for King with your concierge, and I'll get it." With that, King wished me a good day and told me to get well soon. He also said that he would be in touch, though I wasn't sure about that. The med-tech told him that I could leave any time after he released me. King told the med-tech to release me, and the med-tech paused for a moment, didn't move, and told him it was done.

King helped me to my feet.

9

FAMILY IS IMPORTANT

Brian got out of the carport at the office. "It is staff," Brian kept thinking to himself, "and because it is staff, it isn't supposed to matter." But the whole idea that someone had managed to lose their wife, staff or not, didn't sit well with Brian; after all, he had matched them. Yes, he would have to look into this.

Arriving back at the office, he logged into his management screen. With annoyance, he noted the bank had wiped out the payment history to 418. It annoyed him that re-initializing meant recreating 418's account. It annoyed him he hadn't thought of that.

Brian opened the Popular's website and clicked on his claim. The website said 418 was due to be discharged at 20:00. Brian raised his eyes as he read. *Well, that has to be a mistake,* he thought. He knew better, he'd escorted 418 to a car and even put him in it. He'd have to sort this error out; it couldn't be right. He selected the previous button in the claim history window. And the screen changed again.

"Advanced Details," Brian choose.

Brian clicked the button. "Speak with your adjuster." The dialog box went away, and nothing happened. They would call him when they were ready.

Brian clicked around on his screen. It didn't ring. He moved some papers on his desk. Silence. He looked at his mobile, it didn't ring either. He clicked on his screen again. Nothing. *This is useless,* he thought, *a watched kettle never boils.* Annoyed, he decided he knew just the trick to get this call happening. He'd go make himself one of those fancy coffees they had in the galley area.

Sure enough, as he re-approached his office, steaming coffee in hand, he could hear the chiming of his computer. There was an incoming call. He jumped around his desk, jamming a corner of it into his thigh, scalding himself and spilling hot coffee all over his desk.

Accepting the call, he tried to slide into his seat and make himself look presentable all at once. "Hello," he said to the computer. The face of Bolt Greene smiled into one side of the chat window.

"Hello," Bolt answered back. Looking down briefly, he added, "Mr. Agarwal, can you see me?"

Brian reached out and uncovered his camera, "I can see you, and please, call me King." Brian could see Bolt looking a little perturbed. He would have to make another note, and *why didn't the nickname field pop-up properly?*

"Sorry about that, King, what can I do for you today?" Bolt added, resuming cheeriness.

They talked about 418, and Bolt told Brian since 418 had been in the clinic for over twenty-one days, it was automatic that his accounts had been terminated and archived. Whether it was terminated or archived, Bolt—when pressed by Brian—had to admit he didn't know, Brian assumed it was termination, not archival. Bolt told Brian it was his understanding that he would simply have to go into his favorite banking app and set up an automatic payment scheme for 418 and that would take care of the problem.

Brian asked Bolt about 418's wife. This is where the conversation slowed down. Bolt didn't know anything about a wife, how would he? He is an insurance adjuster, and wives are not the type of thing that ever came up, certainly not online wives. Bolt wanted to say it was too remote for him, or anyone, to have thought of and tried to maneuver the conversation so Brian might agree.

No, Bolt didn't know how to re-associate 418's wife with 418. To the best of Bolt's understanding: a) this sort of thing wasn't supposed to happen, as while promiscuity was acceptable online, actual mating was a one-time thing, and b) 418's wife, who, interestingly enough happened to be 814, had a mind of its own that it could choose to make up for itself.

Though Bolt couldn't tell for sure, he and Brian speculated that what had happened was, after twenty-one days, when 418's accounts were disabled, 814 must have decided its partner was dead. It had probably had a funeral and changed their status to single and moved on. It only seemed logical knowing that 814's concierge would have told it that its partner had been involved in an exception and it had been taken to a clinic for treatment. And likely that would have been about all it would have done. 418's mate would have waited online for 418 to return, asking the concierge daily, and getting the same answer, until one day, the concierge told 814 that 418 no longer existed. Perhaps *index undefined* meant something had died in its sleep. 814 must have been told, and it had gone about its life.

While Bolt and Brian were talking, he had looked up 814. E098FH836814, was its exact name. Of course, it was still working for Brian, as were their two children: a female, 1154472DE6D6 and a male—pending schooling—7R5E2A12H279. But Brian didn't know how to connect them back together, and Bolt wasn't really of any help. He had started saying things like, "the Popular's responsibility was to return your staff to working order." Brian didn't like this and contended that, while the staff might be able to work, it was not in working order because it had gone out and hurt itself because it didn't find everything as it had been before the exception. Bolt disagreed that the scope of working order should be narrower and that 418 was in working order because the Popular couldn't be held responsible for any of the consequence of any relationship it had formed online.

What was missed—while Brian and Bolt were talking about what working order and why had the accounts of 418 had been terminated—was that 418 had actually made a choice to not be online. *Anti-social behavior is always a sign of much larger problems.* But Bolt was worried about some potential blowback. It was true that any clinic visit longer than twenty-one days resulted in statutory retirement, and that would have meant a different payout to the manager. Bolt had been proud of not making the payout. Andrea had given such a glowing review that Bolt had been surprised when twenty-one days had expired, and he had to sign a waiver to keep 418 in the clinic, but in for a penny…

And so the claim had moved downstream. Despite his best attempts to smile and be friendly, Bolt got the distinct impression that Brian was annoyed with him. He dared not ask.

As usual, talking with the insurance company was not a gainful thing; you always get what they want. Things were tight, Brian didn't have any extra money—too many people running employment agencies. The price that labor fetched these days was getting lower and lower, and he had no way of making his labor look any better or different than anyone else's. He had to take whatever the market would pay him. He needed that insurance payment in order to feel a bit more comfortable in his own life.

The question of *how* to jumpstart his business, *how* to make his staff look different so he could charge more and *how* to make more money preoccupied and paralyzed him. It was all he could do to keep his staff working. Sometimes he rented his staff out for a loss, given all the things he had to pay for: insurance and feeding, clothing, living spaces. Those things added up.

Thinking of this reminded him, he had to keep 418 happy. He logged into the bank and pulled up the staff management section of the site. It seemed that he had not scheduled a payday for 418. The box for recurring weekly pay was V$0. The box for current balance was also V$0. That wasn't right.

He normally paid his staff V$150,000 a week. Truthfully, he had no idea how much he should pay them. It was advised to make sure that staff had everything they wanted to buy online. A happy staff is a complacent staff, and when it came time to retirement, if they have had a happy life, they would go easily and quickly. Brian was about to fill in the usual V$150,000 when he gave it some more thought. Why not make 418's day? Let's start with V$300,000 per week. What did it matter? Brian put in 300,000 in the box for weekly pay, then thought about it…nah, how about 200,000?

It was closer to 150,000. Brian pressed submit, and a dialog box popped up warning him that, "This staff would have no money until their first pay period is complete. Would you like to add a starting bonus?" Sure, of course Brian would like to do that. He added a V$200,000 starting bonus. He felt better about that, giving the poor sot a bonus for his distress. He thought again, Why should he even care? At the summary screen, it was displayed:

Weekly Obligation	V$200,000
Conversion rate V$ to $US	1:0.0000
Weekly Obligation in $US	$0.00
Starting Bonus	V$200,000
Conversion rate V$ to $US	1:0.0000
One-time Bonus in $US	$0.00

Confirm | Decline

Brian pressed confirm. He smiled. He had been generous to add an extra V$50K per week. It was wise that he hadn't gone nuts with it, given the whole 300,000 that might have caused 418's head to swell. Brian felt warm. *It is good to treat people well, but important to keep them in their places.* He'd done the right thing.

It was not an exciting day. King had dropped me off at the carport and even watched me get into the car. King had told it to drive me home. The car door closed, and I braced myself for a sickening drive, but the car simply headed out of the carport, looped around and headed right back in. The door opened, and King had been replaced by two med-techs who reached into the car, pulled me out of the car, placed me back onto a restraining bed, and wheeled me back into the clinic, facing a wall.

Frantically I reached for my right temple. As the world dissolved, I breathed a sigh of relief. I hadn't been taken off mobile. "Samuel," I called out, as Samuel completed initialization, "what is going on?"

Samuel smiled. "You are at the clinic."

"I know," I answered feeling exasperated, "but why are they taking me back inside. I've been released."

Samuel paused for a moment as if that answer was further away. "You haven't been discharged."

"What? What's the difference?"

"Released means that you can go, discharged means that you can leave."

I felt sick trying to figure that out. "But," I tried to object to Samuel, "when can I go?"

"Ah, you mean leave." Samuel smiled. He seemed to like knowing answers. "You are scheduled for discharge at the end of the workday, twenty hundred hours."

"Oh no! The end of the workday!"

I didn't have much to do. I talked with Samuel, "Has anyone else responded to my message to my wife?"

Samuel took a moment, responded cleanly, "No, no one else has responded."

"I have a daughter."

"I have no knowledge of that."

"Could you send a message?"

"To whom?"

I was about to reply to my daughter, but I would have had to scream if I'd heard, one more time, Samuel reply happily about what he did not know. "To Serenity Sanelli."

"Okay," Samuel answered, "what would you like the message to say?" Samuel added, "There are seven Serenity Sanellis, please keep in mind that many of them are not your daughter even if one of them is, phrase your message appropriately."

"Yeah, sure," I muttered back to him. "Hello Serenity, this is your father George Wojciech, how are you?" I stopped. "How does that sound?" I asked Samuel.

Samuel read back the message and concluded that it sounded no more or less unusual than any other message, though likely most recipients would believe there to be no context to respond.

"Well, send it," I told Samuel.

A moment later, "Sent."

We watched each other for a few moments. Well, this was fun. I wondered why they had chosen this concierge for me and not Ernest. I liked Ernest much better.

Suddenly Samuel broke the silence. "I have a response from one of the Serenity Sanellis."

"Great," I replied, "please read it."

Samuel cleared his throat. "Hello Weirdo," he began, "you are sick. My father is dead, and you pretend to be him. I will block you as soon as you read this message. If you try to contact me again, I will report you." Samuel stopped reading. "That is the entirety of the message. Would you like me to re-read it?"

"No, forget it," I said glumly.

Brian had nothing else to do but play cards on the computer. But cards weren't exciting, so he started looking into how he could re-connect 418 with its wife. Searching the internet, he found all sorts of instructions on how to make a staff member find a mate within your pool, but not one on how to re-unite one. It seemed like this was not a common problem, and the knowledge of it fell off the edge of the internet into the dark abyss of space beyond.

He toyed with the idea of just trying to re-initialize the relationship. 814 was still, after all, his staff, but her last child had come with complications, and he had been told that it would not be safe for her to reproduce again. The point of initializing a couple is so that they would create new staff that could be grown, schooled and managed. But if he did re-initialize, he wasn't going to get any more new staff, and there was a problem. 418, and likely 814, still remembered how things were, and if he re-initialized them, Brian was worried that somehow, they might break. 814 would not likely be able to cope with this many new unexplainable things thrown at it. It might just go into meltdown, he would lose another staff, and if he did it, the Popular might not want to cover the retirement payout. Better not do that, he decided, but it still wasn't right.

The problem was that he couldn't get 418 to forget it, and he didn't want to explain to 814 what had gone on. He imagined himself in that situation, if someone took Imelda and Prince away from him, made it so that they didn't remember him. He didn't think he would have been able to keep it all together after something like that. And then, to take all his money away. Even if 418 is only staff, it felt it, and it knew it was happening.

He had never given much thought to his staff, what they did after hours. Whether they went to the club or this fantasy restaurant or that one, it didn't matter to him, it just wasn't important. He had spent the first years of Prince's life carefully building the walls needed to keep Prince from doing the unforgivable: diving into the pool of sensory immersion and joining the staff. Brian shuddered at the thought: having an implant put in his head because school was too hard, or because the sensory immersion of the internet was too appealing and just couldn't be fully understood without a cerebral interface. Brian had nightmares about going to wake his son for school and having Prince tell him it was no problem, he didn't have to go, it was done, and having him point at the purple wound on the side of its head.

Brian frequently said things like, "Staff have basically had their brains scooped out and pixels poured in through their ears." In the presence of his son he compared them to zombies. Prince was a sharp boy, and when he had asked Brian why this was, that staff were always "it," Brian had responded with what he felt was amazing honesty: "They are 'its' because they have lost their humanity and are now only things." This strategy of not overdoing it, but, whenever possible, re-enforcing that staff were inferior species, had worked well with Prince. Prince reacted negatively whenever the idea of social immersion came up. Brian didn't mess with it, didn't want to oversell. And yet, here he was, dealing with 418, who was showing real signs of being a human.

I sat. I couldn't stand staring at Samuel. I'd run out of things to say, and Samuel was intended to be a servant. He's not a real person. When you ask him for opinions, he simply repeats what he thinks you want to hear. He smiles at you and tells you that everything is wonderful. But it's not wonderful, it's just that I can't do anything else, and I can't go into full immersion when I'm mobile. I turned him off. I'd rather sit and listen to the sound of the med-techs moving around, guessing what it is that they are doing and trying to see with my ears.

I knew time would pass; it always did. Time is a force, nothing stops time. I just had to sit and feel time move me, slowly. It would take me out of this room. If I wanted, I could always ask Samuel what time it was, and it was always sometime later than it was before and not nearly as late as I would like. Slowly, I was being carried down some hallway, toward the carport. Eventually, I would be on my way home again.

Brian headed home. It was five o'clock and about time to go enjoy dinner with his wife and son. As he packed up his things, he thought again, if he wasn't heading home to his wife and son, what would he be doing? What would be the point? How could he bear it? If someone took the smiling face of his little Prince away, what would he do? Brian decided he was going to enjoy this dinner, eat his food more slowly and try to stretch every moment as long as he could. He locked the office door and headed down to the carport. He looked at his mobile. The car was already waiting outside to take him home.

Like clockwork, at 19:52 a med-tech came to release me from my chair. It didn't say anything, just started pushing my chair. There was a car waiting for me. Adeptly, they released me and loaded me into a car. The door slid shut behind me as the car seat began to swell to hold me in place. I went online briefly. "Good news," Samuel chimed as soon as he ceased to be a swarm of dots and turned into himself. "You have been discharged."

"Great," I answered.

"Certainly, we are on our way home," he chimed happily. "Would you like to play a game?"

"No." I turned him off. As soon as I did, my carsickness hit me hard. I started to throw up. It would all come to an end, and it wasn't my car. Who would care? It's not like I was throwing up on purpose; someone else could clean that up. I was on my way home.

At the carport, I put Samuel back on and let him do the walking. He was better at coordinating my legs and the big plastic boot.

"Would you like to play a game? Or watch a show?"

"No. I know this sounds weird, can I just watch?"

"Watch?"

"Yes, watch me walking."

"Sure," Samuel replied, "but it isn't interesting." Samuel minimized to the right corner of my vision. For the first time, I watched myself walking.

Whoa!

10

I'M BACK

I was amazed at how close I stood to all the other people waiting for the elevator. I had never noticed it. I could hardly breathe. Occasionally, I'd get bumped from in front or behind as everyone swayed gently waiting for the elevator. The doors opened and we shuffled and packed in. I felt people pushing into me as they tried to squeeze into the elevator. The doors slid shut, brushing against arms, legs, and midriffs, the doors not catching anyone and not bouncing open again. The mass of flesh packed into the square metal box started to plummet toward the floors below. If the cable snapped, would they be able to tell one of us from another, or would we just be a mass of death splattered on the bottom of an elevator shaft?

I felt like I was being mashed into the floor. We were stopping, coming to a halt and my knees pressing into my ankles. Having nothing to hold on to didn't make me feel at all good. But we were all being crushed down, and as we all tried to spread out at the same time, we all stayed in place as we all squeezed to a halt.

The door opened and everyone got out. We unfolded, expanded and spilled into the hallway. I headed to the right, but I had to move quickly because there was someone behind me, stepping on my heels. How weird was it that everyone got out on the same floor. As we moved along the hallway, doors opened, and people shifted left and right into their condos, the door sliding shut behind them, no one ever going into the wrong room. It was orchestrated, silent, except for the sound of shoes on the hard-concrete floor, the swishing of doors opening, the sliding of doors closing. Quickly, the crowd was absorbed into the building, and I found myself alone in the corridor, listening to the gentle whistle that came from underneath the elevator door.

A few more feet and my door slid open. There was a chair, facing the cupboards on the far wall, and not much more. Slowly I entered the room, taking in how small the room was. The door slid shut behind me. It was a really small room. But, does it matter how small your space is, when you can travel to any place in the world? I hooked myself up and climbed into my chair. There wasn't anything else to do.

Samuel reappeared out of his haze of black and blue dots, with the hardwire to my head. He was in three dimensions. I could actually reach out and touch him, and it would feel like I *was*. Just for fun, I walked up to Samuel and slapped his face. I don't know why, I just felt like it. What was he going to do? It wasn't like I was actually slapping a real person; everyone knew that concierges were just interfaces. It felt good to feel my hand slice through the air, my palm contacting his face, the weight of his jaw being thrown back and the sting that followed.

Samuel staggered a bit. He turned, adjusted himself and smiled. "Thank you," he replied, "that was refreshing."

"You are welcome," I answered. "It was good for me."

"That's all that matters," he added quickly, "What can I help you with today?"

"Messages?"

"I have one from American Bank, a deposit has been made to your account."

"Whoo Hoo!" I think I actually did manage to leave the ground with my jump. "Details?"

"A deposit of two hundred thousand virtual dollars has been made to your account. It is available today," Samuel announced, reading the contents of the message only he could see.

"Two hundred?"

Samuel answered the question, "Yes, two hundred thousand is what it says."

"Fantastic." I only ever got one fifty. Well, don't ask good fortune too many questions.

"There are no other messages," Samuel added, closing his file on my first request. "What can I help you with today?"

"Dinner!"

I felt like I had been cheated the last time I went to McDonald's. I had to right that wrong. This was our first stop. I went in and I ordered the same thing, plus an extra double half pounder. The smell of grease and salt was so good, it got into to you, lifted you off the ground and carried you around the restaurant. I found myself in my seat, up to my elbows in polystyrene. It all tasted so good. It had been so long, I'd missed it, something so good, pure, wholesome and wonderful tasting. My teeth tore through the soft bun, ripped through the hundred percent pure beef. My tongue hummed with the tang of the sauce, and I munched my fries like logs into a pulp mill. It was so good, my head spun with savory, flavory deliciousness.

With a great burp, I rose from my table, leaving wreckage behind, where it would fizz back into pixels and bits. I strode out of the restaurant. I needed something to drink, something strong. I decided I would go to that Big Wheel thingy in Vegas. I mean, what is better than Vegas, or, better than Vegas at night?

"Samuel, let's go to Vegas," I called out, as I stepped into the street.

Samuel shimmered into existence, as the cobblestoned street in front of McDonald's shimmered and became the rubberized surface in front of the *Welcome To Las Vegas* sign. "Okay," Samuel said, "Vegas sounds great, and we are here. What would you like to do in Vegas?"

"I want to go on the Big Wheel!"

The world shimmered again, and we were standing in the concourse in front of the ticket booth.

"Thanks," I said to Samuel, stepping past him. Of course, there was no line, even though there were dozens of people walking this way and that way. I liked this ride because you could see the city, all the casinos, the scrubby little houses that used to hold people who used to work here. I liked that they still kept those buildings around. It looked more how I thought a city should look. Tall buildings that attracted all those thousands of tiny little workers from far and wide to feed off the mighty, towering businesses. Sort of like how thousands of tiny bugs appear to feed off a chance piece of bread or cheese, dropped by a child on the way to the beach.

Stepping up to the attendant, I said, "I want an all-you-can-drink ticket."

"Okay," the attendant said chirpily. She stabbed at the countertop, and a piece of paper came out of the counter and landed in my hand. "Yes," I said to myself as I stepped around the ticket booth. "Vegas here I come!"

Whenever I did Vegas, I always went the big Ferris Wheel first. There are three reasons: first, it gives me time to think. It's peaceful up there. Second, you get to see the city, and if there is anything new you might not have known about. Finally, thirty minutes of uninterrupted drinking!

I ordered a Manhattan, two Cosmos, one for each hand and three shots of Tequila. I had to stop and wash it all down with a beer and two Gin and Tonics with lime, because I can drink them fast, and a double rum neat, to go. When the ride was over, I wandered out of the carriage. I stumbled and somehow caught myself on the escalator. The night was young. I'd eaten, I'd quenched my thirst. A show would be a good thing.

The next thing I knew, I was sitting front row at a show that involved tigers and motorcycles. It wasn't clear if the tigers were driving the motorcycles or simply sinking their claws into leather-clad figures driving the motorcycles. I had a good stiff joint in my hand, and I was busy watching the tent ceiling shift and gently twirl a kaleidoscopic pattern on the edge of my perception. I was feeling pretty fine.

The next thing I knew, I was at the ultimate fights. I had put ten down on the Mascarpone Kid, who didn't look like a kid. He was about seven feet of taught brown muscles threaded with pumping veins all wrapped around a heavily-set skeleton. I figured even though the odds weren't that good, betting on the favorite was my better option. Given my recent brush with being destitute, I'd get twelve back, which I thought was a good deal. Some suckers had taken the other guy. The other guy was just going to be used to test out the blood drainage system in the ring. Betting on the favorite gave me the feeling it was all right to scream and cheer when the blood did start to flow. You know, *"If it isn't someone's finale, it isn't an ultimate fight!"* I'd never been disappointed before.

Sure enough, there was blood aplenty, and the floor of the ring was sloppy with guts and grime. I was shouting and did a couple of lines of coke from the coke girl who came by to sell some individual nose bags. It was awesome, nothing like ultimate fighting and cocaine! Just feel your heart hit the top shelf, blast off, drilling through the sky. It was awesome to be back online.

I found myself at the skydiving site. It was probably the cocaine, because I still felt like my engine was firing in overdrive. What do you do when you are in overdrive? Simple, you Go! Go! Go! Why wouldn't you? I was about to go skydiving at night.

The airplane was something from an old movie. It might have been used in a war where soldiers were dropped from the sky on tiny little peasants who scattered as the drone of the propeller wailed high over their heads. Except it was night, and the cool air of the desert seemed to be sucked into space, making it even colder as the plane, with its door halfway open, continued to climb. The air got colder and colder.

I've never understood cold. Why does anyone think it is good to be cold? Why do they make you feel cold on rides like this? Are they trying to create drama? I don't like visiting the places that are cold, if they don't have an option to turn off the feeling of cold. Who wants to get all bundled up in layers of clothing when you can go to a ski resort and enjoy the slopes in the comfort of your usual clothes, or no clothes? It would be my suggestion for this attraction: allow people to turn the cold off, and you would get more takers.

The airplane must have turned again. We could see the city displayed in lights below us. We would get a lovely view as we jumped and plummeted toward the desert below.

Black air whistled past my head. It was cold and sharp, and this cold I liked. I felt my stomach lift and the giddiness of being weightless. Looking down, I could see the lights starting to move, expand and spread out. At that moment, I thought I could ride this feeling all the way down. I could just let the force of gravity continue to pull me until the earth stopped me. There would be a loud thump, but I would simply wake up in my chair in the morning, well-rested, ready for the work. It had happened to me before. Samuel would give me the cautionary speech about death, that death is no joke, and, if not for online safeguards, I might have experienced real death, for which there would be no recovery. I'm not certain if it was the lecture, the fact that Samuel, who was not Ernest and would never be, was giving me the death lecture (for which there was no *TLDR* option) or if I wasn't ready for this night to end.

But this was skydiving. And the whole fun of sky diving was to dive as fast as you can, to watch the world rush up at you, pull the cord at just the last second, cheating death. I could feel my heart pounding, this was awesome, I was tearing through the cold desert night. I felt like a meteor cutting a bright streak through the sky, about to hammer into the earth, to destroy whatever was below. I looked at the altimeter on my wrist: its circular dial had moved way out of the green part of the dial and was over halfway through the yellow. You have to pull the cord when you hit the red. The further you go into the red, the harder the landing. If you go too far, you might as well go all the way. It's far worse to survive the drop and experience bouncing off a tree than it is to just pancake and get a lecture from your concierge. I was at the edge of the red. I counted, one, two, three, and I pulled the cord.

A tremendous yank forced all the air out of my chest. My shoulders shot up, my spine dropped down and my legs dangled as the chute caught the air and slowed me down. I had let the lights get as close as I could. Looking back, I wouldn't have bet on me: the next instant my boots were coming up through my knees. I sort of bounced as I tried to roll to one side. Good thing I hadn't hit a tree. Nothing but dirt and a tremendous wallop! However, I was otherwise unhurt, except I couldn't get my breath back for a moment or three. Isn't that why we skydive? Awesome!

Casino or opium den? Well, the casino was always open, though, when mobile, the games were less exciting, basically just the games themselves. You didn't get to look at the shine of the pretty girl's dress who just wafted by with a glass of champagne in her hand, trailing one long red fingernail at you as she headed off to wherever it was. No, I needed to calm down. Opium den it was.

Now, don't get me wrong, the opium den has its attractions too. Just like a casino, you can always rent someone for an hour. But it's different, it's calmer and slower, and instead of the thrill of excitement of the casino, it's about melting and forming and savoring, a totally different experience.

I felt peaceful as I walked into Dr. Pong's. It was like going home. I'd been away for too long. You come here, all your troubles melt away. I'd had a good party, but there were still things that bothered me; like, what happened to my wife? How could I get my old life back? Ernest, not Samuel?

Dr. Pong himself was a kindly soft-spoken man with a wispy goatee and red and black mandarin hat that covered up a spreading bald spot. When you entered Dr. Pong's shop, The Golden Poppy, he was always there to greet you. It was like visiting your exotic Asian uncle. Only this one got you stoned, took your money, and wasn't going to tell anyone.

I found myself sitting in a darkened room with large cushions and lamps that hung from the ceiling that let out a soft glow, not bright enough to recognize anyone who was not standing right in front of me. I took a pull on the pipe that seemed to be in my hand. Instantly I felt better. Instantly, things that had been bugging me started to melt. That whole time in the clinic didn't matter. Talking with King—who was King anyway? Some sort of keeper?—seemed to shrink in size until it amounted to nothing, something trivial I shouldn't worry about. Each breath I took made me feel much better. I could feel myself cool, my heart rate dropping, everything getting better, everything just fine. I drifted off. Everything was good. Good to be home. Good to be back online.

11

BACK TO WORK

"Good Morning George," Samuel said.

I opened my eyes and saw the chandelier and the vaulted ceiling of, well, not my favorite hotel, but a hotel, and a nice one. I guess Dr. Pong had forgot me, too, but at least the good doctor had found a nice place for me to wake up. I expected nothing less. "Good morning Samuel, what's up?"

"It is time for you to go to work," he said with the usual cheer. "How do you feel today?"

I've never understood why Ernest—now Samuel—used to ask that. I figure it's some nag subroutine programmed to go off if you have too good a time the night before. "I feel fine," and I did. If you kept it going, partied till it was time to go to work, they would just turn off your feeling. It's not smart to waste your money buying drinks, smokes, coke, opium, crack or weed just before wake-up time. They turned it off, and you were sober as a judge, so you didn't get bang for your buck.

With a sigh, I told Samuel, "Alright, alright, just let me get up."

"I can do this for you." Samuel added.

"Sure, thank you," I said, and I felt myself get up. I took my clothes off and stepped into the shower. I pulled the door, and the jets activated as soon as the door snapped shut. The first blast was cold, I'd never noticed that. Even though I was letting Samuel do the driving, I still wanted to jump, though I didn't. "Hey!" I called out to Samuel, "what is wrong with the water, why so cold?"

Samuel seemed confused. "The water is set to the settings last used. I did not change it. Do you want to adjust the temperature?" I could feel the water warming up.

"Um, yeah." It probably wasn't a good idea to argue with the concierge. "It's fine," but I could still feel the initial burst of cold.

"Glad to hear it."

It's not possible to clean yourself faster than the concierge can do it for you. I wasn't in a hurry, but the shower is narrow, just a few inches of space to maneuver in. If I were to try to do it, I might break the stall or bust my elbows. I could feel the air jets come on, and I turned around and around, letting the air squeegee the water off me. I spun out of the shower and in one smooth movement pulled the clothes out of my work drawer. I was dressed in an instant.

"You are dressed," Samuel notified me. "We are going to head to work now." I felt a desire to let out a little fake cheer. I probably did.

The stuffiness of my condo was replaced by cold damp air from the hallway as I stepped through the obediently opening door. I was down the hallway, joining the crowd to wait for the elevator. Together we would enter the lift as one mass of people. We would rise up and all step out and shuffle into the carport where cars would take us away to our jobs. All of it automated, leaving us to chat, play cards, slots, watch movies, videos, or whatever it was they wanted to do during the day.

Work had always been a painless thing. You did it and didn't pay any attention to it, and by the end of the day, you would find yourself being reminded by the concierge that you were home: Would you like immersion? I can't think of any reason why anyone would say anything other than "yes," and you got to sit back and enjoy the fruits of your labor. If you wanted to, you never had to take control back from the concierge. The concierge could—and would—wake you up, get you washed and dressed, put your clothes, take you to work, have you do all your work duties, bring you home from work and set up feeding, put you back in your chair, and orchestrate your entertainment for the evening. Whence, everything would start all over again the next day. It was pretty sweet.

Except today wasn't sweet. My foot hurt. That was odd. I normally didn't feel anything. In fact, handing over control to the concierge was the best way to not feel anything that might have happened to you. I'd gotten some pretty bad cuts that I had found out about when I got home. Things the concierge didn't notice, but still hurt enough for me to feel. You could report those to the concierge, and you would get a trip to the clinic, get things all fixed up. You didn't notice any of it ever again and went on with your life. But that wasn't happening today.

My foot hurt, and it hurt enough I couldn't concentrate on my slots and blackjack. Every step I took jabbed at me, and I started to make mistakes in the games I was playing. Good thing I had an extra fifty thousand in my bank because I wasn't playing well.

Brian got himself to work. There had been no messages from the Popular or from his staff management software. As far as he knew, everything was as it should be, and when the garbage collection staff came to dump the garbage from his building, and they had to get out of their truck to pick up the swirling papers, he would see two staff and one of them would be 418. He would sit there, coffee in hand, watching them go about their job with automatic aplomb. Systematically picking up and tidying. They would get into the truck and head off to the next building to pick up whatever had escaped or failed to make it into the dumpster. As Brian headed into work, he felt good about this, reassured that everything would be as it should be.

Nothing was amiss as he stepped out of his car. "Make busy," he told the car, holding on to the "and park," as if there was some relief in being able to tell his car to go park itself. The car obediently closed its door and slid away from the carport, in search of the lowest cost combination of fuel and parking.

He walked into the building. The entrance was dirty and dusty and there as a foot and a half wide pathway worn in the ancient linoleum leading to the elevator. The elevator squealed a thin hard blade of pain that dug into your ears as it descended or ascended. It also smelled like hot pee when you got in. No matter how he complained—and even if it was scrubbed—it always squealed and smelled. Today, Brian did something bizarre that not even he understood: he stepped off the blackened path worn into the linoleum and walked right past the elevator and pushed open the metal door—glass, glazed with a million fingerprints—and stepped into the stairwell.

He looked at the stairs. He hated stairs. They were practical, but whoever had invented them must have hated humanity. Why use the stairs if you have an elevator or escalator? They didn't move, they were pointy, hard, and unforgiving. He started up the stairs, and it didn't take long until his head was spinning. One after the other, he could feel cracking in his knees. The air was harder to breathe. But he also knew they were just stairs. He remembered he used to be able to sprint up them when he was younger. He seemed to fly up the stairs. Somehow, he imagined his father waiting for him at the top, hands out to greet him as a miniature version of himself pelted up and around the landings.

That was a long time ago, and he was much older now. As he climbed, he tried to think of how long he had been working in this building. This might be the first time he had seen these steps, that splotch of paint, the missing screw under the railing, the crack in the wall and the plaster job that seemed to miss. This was work! He was breathing hard as he rounded the last landing and looked up at the last flight. Relieved that his father wasn't standing there waiting for him, he put his head down. It was something he should do, should have been doing, and he was going to do. One after another, his feet climbed the stairs and his hand ratcheted up the handrail until the handrail went suddenly flat. He shuffled forward on the landing. He'd done it. It was a good thing, he knew it was. *May it never be that hard again!* But why had he done that? The elevator was still perfectly good. It even had a gentle scent of urine, for authenticity.

Brian rewarded himself with an extra-large mocha based coffee drink. He loaded it up with some sort of whipped topping he squeezed out of a can. *I've done exercise today. I've earned it!* The computer in his office still said he had no outstanding messages. He needed to celebrate the fact that everything was back to normal.

The building was quiet. Most of the offices were either dark or had obstructions, boxes, posters, or paper to make sure you couldn't see what was or wasn't going on inside. Brian didn't care, he liked that he could walk around the building and not see anyone, whatever they were up to. He didn't have to worry or be aware. He had his business, and that was good enough. He looked at his mobile. It would be soon time for the garbage, if everything was all right, it would be on time. He would get a full day's pay for a full day's wages, as it should be.

Opening his office door, he saw the truck just entering the parking lot. There were lots of papers and plastic bits of rubbish blowing around the old parking lot today. The truck pulled up in front of the dumpster, a staff got out and headed to the gate in front of the dumpster. It was 418, it was hobbling and moving as if its foot wasn't fastened on correctly. It was wearing some sort of big plastic boot and looked like it had been shot or something.

The truck lifted the garbage high into the air and the wind sprayed a stream of papers all over the parking lot. The dumpster dumped and was reset with a clang that must have been deafening, as it was loud through the glass window.

Brian could see the truck lurch as the driver took it out of gear and parked it. The driver got out and helped 418 try to pick up the papers and trash that had sprayed around the parking lot. It was sad to watch 418 hobble around. If it hadn't been his staff, Brian would have wondered why it had been sent to do that job at all. As it was, it just looked pathetic, a small child chasing after paper birds, not able to catch any of them and not understanding why. This was not as it was supposed to be.

The truck had gone some time ago, but Brian sat thinking. Brian knew that injuries happen. Given time, 418 would return to normal. Picking up garbage would be something it would do without question. But in the meantime, this wasn't right. Perhaps he would have to find them some better work. No, that was nonsense. That's the thing about staff, they don't care what they do as long as they get paid; they have internet, something to eat and whatever recreational materials they are told they want. 418 had all those things, it was nonsense. Brian told himself he would see that, in a few days, maybe weeks, 418 would be back to normal and would not care. It was totally immersed.

12

WHY DO I SMELL?

None of my poker friends remembered me. What good is it to play poker with complete strangers? It's like playing against a machine. You can't make jokes, you can't tell when they are bluffing, and you can't trick them into thinking you are bluffing when you are not.

My foot hurt. No matter what I did to try to distract myself, I was always aware I was walking around on it. Every step sent out pulses of pain. I was grateful when we had some place to ride to and I could sit in the cab, but the pain was constant, not pulsing. It never went away. I could take care of that tonight, I could, after dinner, go straight over to Dr. Pong's, partake, and be off on a cloud of bliss. The day seemed long, dragging, painful. But like all days, it eventually came to an end, and we returned to the depot to drop off the truck and head home.

The car came and picked me up. All the while I played solitaire, but it was boring; however, being online kept the nausea down. I made it home, instead of just going from mobile to online, I stopped and turned my access off. I was tired, I never imagined I could be so tired. My leg ached and the pain seemed to stretch up the thick part at the back of my leg, through my knee, through my hip, and up into my back which ached for the pain in my foot.

Sitting back in my chair, I tried to get my breathing to slow. Why was I breathing so hard? I seemed to have lost so much ability to not breathe hard. I don't ever remember breathing that hard, ever. Why did I notice it now? It must be my foot that was distracting me.

I felt like I had been running, doing something at full speed, or faster than I should. Turning off was just a way for me to try to catch my breath and not feel tired; I tried to slow the thumping in my chest. But the more I rested, the more tired I felt. The weight of everything that I didn't understand, couldn't quantify, was heavier now that I sat in silence. But what? What was it? I took a deep breath, funny how that seemed to calm me—I knew not why, but it did—and that's when it hit me. I smelled! It was a thick smell, like ranch salad dressing gone bad. Had I always smelled like that? Was this something new? Did I only notice because I'd been in the clinic so long? Is this what work smelled like?

I got up from my chair and had a look in the mirror of my tiny washroom area. The mirror wasn't flat, my face bulged as I bent down to peer at myself. Nothing looked wrong, but I looked at my arms and I was covered in a fine gray silt. I smelled dirty. I rubbed my arms. The gray silt was smudgy. There was another smell, not of spoiled food and rotting. It actually seemed to be coming from me. I lifted my arm and hit my elbow against something. I didn't notice, as I was busy following my nose to my armpit. It smelled horrible. Something animal, something sick, oily and nasty. The combination of body odor and bad salad dressing seemed to get stronger and stronger.

I undressed. I was clumsy as I smacked into walls and fell against my chair, my elbows taking much of the brunt. I put my clothes in the used uniform cupboard. Careful not to touch any of the cold metal bits, I stepped into the shower, activated the wash cycle myself. I didn't want to tell the concierge I was having an extra wash—something I didn't trust about that guy. The water jets came on cold, causing me to jump, and writhe a second or two until some warmth introduced itself into the jets. The jets started to move, up and down, soap bubbles coming out with the water, the gray shine starting to be scrubbed off, the pressure of the jets digging it out of my skin. The water turned to air, blades pushing the water down, off me and into the grate on the floor. In moments I was done, standing there, naked, mostly dry. Most of the smell was gone. My pits still smelled, they would take more work, but the only thing I had was the shower, and it didn't seem to do that good a job on pits. It was true. I had always smelled like this.

Stepping from the shower I opened the new uniform drawer. There was nothing there. I sighed. I'd have to get into the old uniform. it was sticky. I fought against the friction and the grab of the damp and soiled patches as I struggled to get back into it. Once inside, I could feel the damp bits soaking my skin in rotten perfume. I hooked up a feed bag, sighed and went back online.

I went straight to Dr. Pong's. I didn't even bother eating. My foot hurt much more than my desire for food. Opium was the solution—always the solution—after a long day. Within moments I was traveling the silk road toward blissful paradise of mountain passes and fields of poppies. I breathed deeply, letting the fresh air fill my lungs. I didn't have a care in the world.

Samuel woke me up, and I was off for another day of work. He walked me into the shower, and I was washed once again. I didn't tell him I had a shower the night before, and he didn't seem to know or was too engrossed in routine to notice.

I was dressed; a new uniform had arrived during the night. I was off, down the hallway, jammed into the elevator, into a queue, into a car, jolting and rocking my way to wherever work was.

The day was largely the same, I tried baccarat, but I wasn't playing well because my foot hurt. We went from stop to stop, and my foot would hurt on and off like someone was flipping a switch. It was getting to the point where I wanted to hurt something else so my foot would just stop being the most painful thing. Other parts of my body were hurting in sympathy: the top of my back, my shoulders, my left-hand.

I tried to make it through the day, but it wasn't getting any better, it never numbed. It wasn't going to make any difference, I had to go to Samuel. I left the baccarat room. Samuel appeared.

"Hello George," Samuel greeted me, "what would you like to do today?"

I felt some relief as I drew my breath in to speak, "I would like to see King?"

"King?" Of course, Samuel wouldn't know who King was. Why would he? He wasn't Ernest.

"Yes." I felt some frustration. "The man who I met at the clinic."

Samuel didn't answer, but his face lost its pleasantness and he squinted at me as if he was deciding what I was really saying and how much I might know.

It leapt from my mouth: "I want to talk to the boss."

Samuel seemed to be taken by surprise. "Okay," he replied, "I will send a message."

"Good."

"Is there anything you would like to say?" Samuel asked, "in the message that I will send?"

"Yes, tell him I want to see him," I answered. "And ask him, 'Why do I smell?'"

13

BRIAN AND IMELDA

Brian's margins were thin, very thin, but his work was steady. Unfortunately, new customers only wanted to buy from him if he could offer lower prices. Brian's business was in paralysis; he just didn't know how, to break out of it. Finding something new seemed like an impossible task, and he tried not to think about it: How could he find new customers? How could he find something new? How could he make more money? How? How could he get out of this spiral? The more he thought about it, the more "how" questions he had, the harder it seemed. Hopefully things would work out— 418 would heal—and everything would resolve itself.

Brian went and made himself a coffee. He'd sit down and watch, see how things are, see how 418 was walking. Did he really want coffee, or did he really need tea? No, coffee was a good distraction— taking a sip—and Brian sat back in his chair and waited.

And waited.

And waited, until he realized that, indeed, this was not garbage day. Brian laughed. *Good.* He was smiling and chuckling, turned back to his computer and started pecking at the keyboard. *Very good.*

The day went on without incident, everyone showed up at work, Brian was going to be able to collect for everything he had been contracted for. It had been a good day, an uneventful day. It was four forty-five and Brian was thinking about calling for his car and going home, but the office was comfortable, and he wasn't awake enough to bother walking down the stairs. He shut off his screen, stretched his arms and made himself get out of his chair. He needed to get his heart beating first; his legs felt tight from the stairs and the long day of sitting. He took a stroll around the floor, taking long steps to stretch himself out and deep breaths to try to wake himself up. Imelda would be cooking dinner, Prince would be playing some game, but Brian was determined to have some father-son time. He smiled, he always felt so good with his son—a little bit sad he couldn't be a small boy again—but was glad he could share the gift of innocence.

He passed his office one last time, then checked that the door was locked. Headed for the stairs, oh yes, the walking had been a good idea. It was a little shocking what years of elevators, desk job, apartment and cars that drop you off at the elevator doors will do to your body. He felt a deep pinch as he stepped down the first stair. Going down seemed easier than going up, but he had to catch himself, and he felt his knees straining to support him. This: doing the stairs, was a good idea.

At the bottom, Brian was shocked that he was breathing hard. Blood was pumping through his head, making little dark sparks fly, and the walls seemed to beat with his heart. He tried to put out of his mind how bad a thing that might be. He'd take the stairs tomorrow.

Striding out the door, he found his car was waiting. He sat down in the car and decided to check his messages once again. Every day he did this, as a point of responsibility, but today there actually was a message. Brian opened it: it was a message from his staff management software. Apparently, one of his staff wanted to meet him, and had the specific message of what the conversation should be about: "Why do I smell?"

Why do I smell? Brian laughed and continued reading. The staff was 418. Of course, it was 418. He'd been doing this job for thirty years and never, not once, had a staff ever requested to see him. There was a link at the bottom of the message—would he like to accept or decline the meeting request? Brian thought about it. Properly, this was such an odd thing that he might be able to use it to complain to the Popular that 418 had brain damage. This never happened. Staff didn't ask to see their managers. They hardly even knew about their managers. But, then again, it had happened, and should he decline it? Brian pressed Accept and a dialog box popped up asking him where he would like this meeting to occur, and when. Where do you meet someone who spends their entire life online, submerged in bits and pixels?

Brian left the location open. He would meet 418 before work. That way, he wouldn't lose the day's wages. But where should he meet him? At the clinic? It might be faster if he wanted to have him evaluated. But there was no rush and doing that would likely mean losing another day's wages. There was time enough to have him retired, if that was what needed to be, but for now, 418 would report to work, and Brian would get paid.

As the car worked its way through traffic, it occurred to Brian that perhaps he should be frightened. It was unusual for staff to request a meeting with management. Perhaps 418 was dangerous. For a moment, fear passed through Brian, but it went out the other side. Brian found himself laughing again. 418 didn't even know what it really was. It couldn't do anything, and any sort of outbursts could be easily handled by having it sent to the clinic for mental examination, which would not go well for 418. They would literally slice them up.

Brian gave himself a deadline of bedtime to decide where to meet 418. Certainly, it wasn't going to be his home, and Brian didn't think it would be safe for him to go to 418's home. He shuddered when he thought of going far underground. The whole thing was claustrophobic to him. What if the power went out? What if the elevator didn't work? What if he couldn't get out? He'd be buried under the ground, with all those staff who would not be looking for him—he shouldn't be there—and he could get trampled by their blind obedience.

The car had left the city and he was zooming through the crumple zone. Brian didn't live in the best neighborhood. He certainly was not affluent enough to afford to live in a big house, with grass and room for cars that didn't drive themselves. He lived in a small apartment, but it was beyond the crumple zone.

Brian had never believed the rumor that the crumple zone had been created by some toxic event that had happened in the city, and if you lived there, you got sick and died. For Prince, it was a convenient enough lie. The crumple zone had supplied the first waves of staff when the Economic Prosperity laws were passed that allowed for personal foreclosure. When those laws were put into place, it was like a chain reaction, as individuals and families were foreclosed on, which only caused more foreclosures. Businesses and neighborhoods folded as their customers and employees were converted to staff and moved to underground condos. Bankruptcy spread like a virus, ripped through neighborhoods, crushing everything. Eventually, the crumple zone became little more than a mix of commercial buildings, apartments, houses, roads, old storefronts, small factories and other odd bits of city that no-one used anymore. All of them slowly dissolved, crumbling with passage of time. Great highways, like the one Brian's self-driving car was on, had been built over the crumple zone with high walls on either side of the road. No one ever had to see the unpleasantness.

The zone was dangerous. There were lots of wild dogs, cats, rodents, snakes, and Brian had heard tales of spiders as big as a dinner plate. It wasn't something he wanted to check out. If it was true, it would be dangerous, and if it wasn't true, what would he have gained by all of this? The crumple zone was best avoided.

The majority of the crumple zone was impassable. Many of the streets had not been set up for self-driving cars, the danger of falling buildings, light poles, cracks in the road made it too dangerous. On the inner side of the zone, the city, it was self-driving cars only. Outside the crumple zone, it was still a hybrid. Only the truly rich could afford the insurance of driving their own car. Exceptions were rare, except in the case where a mad man tried to drive a car into the self-driving car lanes. That usually ended quickly. But still, rich young people, bored with their lot in life, would try it and find out why it wasn't such a good idea. The machine was an unforgiving thing. If something happened that it didn't expect, or hadn't been programmed for, you can expect something messy to be the result.

This was the whole reason Brian and his father before him had been able to make a living. Machines, compared to a pair of human hands, are inflexible, and when things went wrong, the results were never good.

Brian's apartment was on the good side of the crumple zone. If he went up onto the roof, which he had done as a much younger man, he could look into it. If you stood long enough, you could imagine that you were seeing parts of buildings falling down, right before your eyes.

They, the last remnants of some long-ago municipal government, had even blocked off the streets into the crumple zone. They said it was a way to stop the spread. Someone had drawn a line. It would be easier to know where to stop providing fire services, ambulance, animal control. And by and large, the animals observed it. They stayed in the zone, because if they didn't, they were aggressively trapped and disposed of.

Brian was the first exit out of the crumple zone. He lived on Station Close, which was a street just five blocks from the edge. Often, he thought of how lucky he had been, even though his apartment was humble, he was still outside the zone and still not staff.

What Brian wanted more than anything was for his son to do better than he. And so, there were times when Brian wanted to rip off his son's headset and destroy all the screens in his house because he didn't want Prince to stay where he was, or, heaven forbid, descend into staff. The only problem was, aside from damaging equipment, he had no real idea how Prince should go about trying to learn or do whatever he had to do to make it to the next level.

The screens, headsets, and partial immersion devices were tools used to teach children. You can't take them off it, there are laws about not educating your children. What is a man to do? And it wasn't like Brian could stop what he was doing himself. He had to keep working to keep his family from slowly melting into staff. Their apartment may be small and rented, but it was still his. He didn't get paid in Virtual Dollars, and the things he saw in his apartment were real and not just polished representations of other places and events that may or may not have ever been.

The car dropped Brian off in front of his building. "Go park," he told the car, and obediently it packed itself up, shut the door, and drove away. Brian looked up at the building. It was old red brick, and now that he looked at it, it was starting to age pretty bad. The brick was dirty and the great steel numbers that hung over the door, "515," were starting to bleed rust, even though they should have been stainless steel. The "i" had fallen out of the Station Close, making his address rather messy looking, almost like a bleeding tattoo on the brick above the entrance, "515 Stat on Close." Brian tried to ignore that. He'd like someone to fix the sign, but he didn't want to give management another excuse to raise his rent; annually was enough.

He buzzed himself in and stepped into the lobby where there were two elevators, one on each side of the hallway. You had to press the button for each elevator. If you pressed the button for only one side, that would be the only elevator that knew you were waiting. Brian pressed both buttons and felt slightly out of breath. This was awful. He straightened himself, caught his breath and spied the door to the stairs. Lowering his head, he strode toward them. He was going to start taking the stairs, even if it killed him, because it probably wasn't.

At the top, Brian stopped, clutching the handrail he felt himself swoon. Good thing he had a good grip, or he might have found himself bouncing down the stairs, pinballing off the walls all the way down the four flights to the lobby. Four floors, that was one more than the office. If he kept this up, he'd be in excellent shape in no time. He felt good about himself. *Small things are things that matter.* He seemed to remember his father saying something like this, and if he hadn't, it sounded wise, and he'd give Papa credit.

There was a bead of sweat running down Brian's back as he opened the door. "Hello," he called, "I'm home."

He heard the footsteps of his wife Imelda approaching the door. "Hello honey," she smiled. She was cooking and had been splattered by something that was likely very tasty. "How was your day?"

It sounded weird as it came out of Brian's mouth, "Interesting," he said, and he didn't think he had ever said that before.

They walked together past the family room. Prince was busy playing an immersive game. From the way Prince was jumping and making "shoo-shoo-shooting" type noises with his mouth, Brian guessed it was Blitz Commander.

"Hello?" Brian called, but he didn't use his son's name. Prince was wrapped up in his game—he likely didn't hear him at all. With the eye mask on, he certainly didn't see Brian, just continued to jerk and move, reacting to the game. Brian felt part of his heart sink. It would be nice if Prince would come to greet him, but this wasn't the way that little boys were these days. Prince didn't mean anything by it. He'd probably been playing for two hours, and he'd be annoyed if Brian broke his concentration, which is precisely what Brian wanted to do though he couldn't bring himself to do it.

Imelda had already set the table. She was busy stirring something, and a steaming basket of Garlic Naan was sitting on the table, all wrapped up in a tea towel. Brian reached for the cloth. Imelda shot him a look and Brian pulled his hand back.

"So, tell me what was so interesting," she asked, returning to her cooking. She was a master at reductions, bringing out all the flavor in a dish.

"I got a message," Brian started, trying to make it sound dramatic, "from a staff."

Imelda stopped stirring, turned to face Brian to see if he was joking. "From staff? A message? Are you sure it wasn't *about* staff?"

"No." That's what was interesting. "It was from the staff, to me."

Imelda thought of all that she knew about staff. They weren't supposed to have any consciousness about the world that wasn't online. They just played and did whatever it was they did all day, without question and without desire. "How did that happen?" She stepped toward the table and pulled back a corner of the tea towel to expose the steaming naan.

Brian plucked out a piece, tossing it from one hand to the other as the steam escaped, trying not to burn his fingers. "I got a message from the staff management software." Imelda looked at him, letting him continue, "418 asked its concierge."

"418? Concierge?" Imelda made a scrunched up, confused face, trying to imagine.

Brian tried to help her out, "Yes, online, they, it, 418, has a concierge, think of it as one central place to ask to do anything. Like if they want to feel like they traveled to see the Taj Mahal, they tell the concierge, and poof, they think they are in India."

Imelda looked at him. She got that they were the travel agents.

"But they can also use the concierge to send messages," he added. "Normally we don't hear anything, because staff send hundreds of meaningless messages to each other every day, but today, this staff sent me a message. Not just the usual message to everyone, that no one will pay any attention to; but to me, and only me."

Imelda leaned against the stove, almost feeling how dinner was progressing with her elbow. "Huh?" she thought out loud. "Should we be concerned?"

Brian took a big tear out of the naan. It was hot, full of garlic, butter, and salt, and the taste was wonderful. "Yes and no," he answered, paused to chew and swallow. "Yes, it's weird, and it almost certainly means something is wrong with this staff. And no, because I don't think it's out of control. What can it really do to us? It's talking, that's all." It sounded like Brian was trying to reassure himself.

Imelda turned to move dinner off the stove. "I don't know, staff don't really talk, better safe than sorry." The more she thought about it, the more it sounded like a stupid idea to be talking directly with staff. Only violence could happen, or that's what she had heard. Otherwise, no one ever talked with staff.

"I know," Brian agreed, "but the staff asked, and I've talked to him before."

"Him?"

"Well, yes. It's the staff that I was telling you about. The one that had the exception in the car. I had to go see it at the clinic." Brian used the more conventional *it* pronoun this time. "Three times. The first time was for insurance purposes, and it was pretty banged up.

And the second was also for insurance purposes, I guess." Brian took a breath. "That was pretty weird. It was conscious, and I wanted to make sure it could work. But instead of it being online and just responding to my voice, it was like really there and it even tried to make a joke about, 'Walking, I've just mastered standing.' You see, it is sort of like a person."

Imelda started ladling out rice, sauce, and goat meat. She kept her eyes from her husband. Everything she'd ever been told about staff was that if they went offline, they could be dangerous because they were uneducated and basically had the IQ of small children. You could never tell with staff where they came from, if they had been born into being staff or it was its punishment for committing a crime. That was where the first staff came from, corrections, and volunteers. The ones from corrections could be dangerous, because if they went rogue, they did know how to do things. They were not big children, and they could hurt you. It occurred to her to ask, "Where did this staff come from, is it one of ours?"

"Yes," Brian answered, "actually it's one of the last from my father. We have had it for its entire working life."

"Not a criminal?"

Brian felt better as he was answering these questions. starting to feel better about the request. "No, not a criminal. It's a natural."

"That's the word I was looking for," Imelda also felt better. It was good to have a lot of naturals. If anything went wrong, they were docile as they had never known anything other in their lives; they were converted to staff as soon as they became economically viable. "A natural. So, if it's a natural, I guess I don't see any problem."

"Me neither," Brian conceded, "but it does feel weird."

Imelda didn't bother to ask how Brian planned on talking to this staff—she had probably decided there was an app for that—and Brian decided that it was best not to tell Imelda that he was actually going to meet the staff. There was silence as dinner was served, until Brian remembered that he had to go unhook Prince so that they could eat together. Brian decided to try not to say anymore, until this staff situation settled itself out.

14

JAZMIN'S

Brian did decide he didn't want to meet at the clinic. He'd had enough of that place, and he wanted to meet someplace neutral, but not anywhere near Brian's apartment. He remembered there was a coffee shop, some old chain that was teetering on the edge of bankruptcy, but he thought that they still cooked things, and if he was going to have a meeting with staff, he was going to enjoy the meal. Perhaps it would be a good distraction.

When Brian went to sleep, he only felt a little uneasy about the meeting. It was odd, but somehow it gave him a little thrill. Something different. Something new. Something that he hadn't ever imagined happening. It made him feel good, as if life wasn't bleak and hopeless. He slept well but had odd dreams of weird things that didn't make sense. Everything, all those whispered suggestions and inciteful thoughts from his sub-conscious mind, shriveled and died in the pale light of daybreak.

Like some sort of kid, Brian got out of bed fifteen minutes before his alarm was supposed to go off. He went about the morning routine, making a bit more noise, hoping that everyone would get up. Prince appeared wiping his eyes. He looked like he hadn't slept at all, or maybe he was saving his most restful sleep for the last fifteen minutes of sleep, which he now had been cheated of by clanking pots and clattering cupboards. Brian looked at Prince. His son was always a symbol of hope for him, that things would be better for Prince, and even better for his children's children. Prince looked like he had been dumped there, a stuffed giraffe hanging from his right-hand and his left-hand wiping the sleep from his eyes. Brian smiled. Things were going to be better. They had to be.

The self-driving car was supposed to be the solution to all traffic problems, and for a short while it was. Brian had set the meeting so there would not be traffic. He did not want 418 to be late to work, though whatever time Brian got to work didn't matter. What happened now was there just wasn't enough road for all the cars. Nobody wanted to park. Brian himself wasn't even certain that his car ever went to park when he told it to go park. It likely just trolled around, making busy until he needed it. Since cars were fueled by staff, it was hard to tell. The car always had gas, the car was always ready to go, air-conditioned or heated and always waiting.

He could feel the car slow in traffic. Had someone not kept up the maintenance on their car? A bad sensor or two and everything slowed down to a crawl. Either that or the city was bigger than Brian had remembered it. Maybe it was growing, the crumple zone getting bigger and bigger as it spread like a bruise eating up the neighborhoods, where people could not stay because they could no longer afford to pay.

Thinking about that didn't make him feel much better. He must avoid becoming staff—he could feel the pull. But how? He knew what would happen if he couldn't keep his company in the black. He could work at a loss and hope things worked out. He might already be doing this. But sooner or later, working at a loss will catch up with you. Not paying your debts is a crime. If you commit crimes, you can be rehabilitated by being forced to join the staff. Or you could just join the staff—lose your freedom to commit crimes—and be absolved of your debts. Which wasn't quite true, but you would never have to repay them. Dereliction was a form of absolution.

Typically, if you did that, you went to work for whoever owned your debt. It was important that as an employment agency, you were always lending money to whoever would take it. Brian's father, William, could never get the hang of it. He never understood why it was you wanted to loan someone money back in the days of negative interest. The idea of paying someone to take money from him baffled William, and so he didn't do it. Nowadays, things had flipped, you couldn't find a loan for under 16%.

Ideally, you lent someone money, and if you were lucky, they wouldn't pay you back for three months. When you set up the loan, you had to do an amortization schedule, and that schedule had to be adhered to. If a debtor fell a total of two entire months of payments in arrears, you could apply to a debtor's tribunal to foreclose on the debtor. If the debtor fell three months behind after giving the court proper notice, a sheriff's deputy, which nowadays was also staff, would come and arrest the debtor. If the debtor did not have enough assets to liquidate to pay the loan, that debtor could be considered eligible for a repayment program which included the necessary medical treatment that would allow the lender to recoup their losses through the labor of their new staff. Negative interest rates were just incentive to get people to borrow money and overextend themselves.

William never figured this out. He didn't lend, and while there were many other families who made their fortune off foreclosures and re-assignments, William thought this was wrong. *"Usury,"* he called it. William tried to staff his firm through naturals, and participating in lottery assignments of recidivist offenders, a good old "three strikes and you are out!" William Agarwal always thought it was too risky to lend out money. What if, by you lending out money, you overextended yourself, and what if someone foreclosed on you? He had heard horror stories about this, too. Entire families being foreclosed on, disappearing overnight because of overextension.

His father had imparted a sensible and prudent fear of being dragged into staff. Despite his father's best intention, Brian, who had filled his shoes, could see that month by month the Agarwals were slowly sliding down the slope. Brian tried to keep panic from his thoughts. He knew he had to do something about it, but *how?* Likely he would not survive long enough—or he would die soon enough—and so avoid being sucked into the crumple zone. Though each day that passed he had a little less than the day before, and less to hand off to Prince when that day came. Thank goodness they had only had one child.

The car veered right, and a voice told Brian to prepare to disembark, that they had arrived at Jazmin's cafe. Brian looked at his in-car screen. 418 was almost at the café, as well. That wouldn't do. He told the management software to delay 418 by twenty minutes. He needed time to get seated, feel comfortable, order something and have it arrive. The car let him off in front of the cafe. "Make busy," he told it. Off it went to join the swarm of other little metal cells pumping around the veins of the city.

The cafe looked less like a cafe and more like a discount shop. All the tables were of different sizes, heights, some wood, some plastic. Odd chairs littered the room. Inside there was a kitchen with high opaque plastic panels that prevented you from seeing the kitchen staff. Those panels had been added later. They looked newer and cleaner; a decade newer than everything else in the cafe.

Brian sat down at a table. A wait staff immediately approached him and asked him if he knew what he would like to order. He did not, though it wouldn't take long. By the time he had managed to get the menu the right way around and focus his eyes on the choices offered, the staff was gone, off on its rounds. Not to worry, it would be back in about three minutes.

Checking his mobile, the tracking app showed 418 heading away from his location. He was sure glad he'd put in the delay. Imagine the awkwardness, sitting there, with staff, waiting to be served breakfast.

The wait staff reappeared, "What would be my pleasure for me to get for you today? Or would you like to hear today's specials?"

Brian was not a fan of specials. He felt it was like settling for what someone else wanted you to eat.

"I'll have two eggs over hard, the bacon, half potatoes, and half grits and coffee." Brian smiled. The eggs never came over hard. They were always soft and runny, barely cooked, sunny side up.

The wait staff moved its hand across its notepad but made no real marks on the paper. It was all recorded and would automatically generate the order and keep track of the bill at the same time. With programmed efficiency, the wait staff was gone, off to look for more orders.

A few minutes later, food arrived, just as he had ordered, with a side of white toast. He hadn't ordered that, but it must have been included with the eggs. Every order of eggs got a side of white toast. He could almost see that as a subroutine written in green letters on some engineer's screen. He'd probably eat it anyway, he always did, but he knew he shouldn't have so many empty calories, and if you didn't draw the line somewhere, where did you draw it?

Brian took a deep breath. Well, the food looked good. Even if this place was a dump. He had been so wrapped up in his own business that he hadn't noticed the restaurant had filled with the oldest and most decrepit people he could imagine. They looked broken, old men and women with arched humped backs trying to corral and suck up eggs sunny side up and chasing the yellow liquid around their plates with the complementary white toast soaked in margarine. It was disgusting to watch. Not everyone had teeth, and food was slopping out as much as it was being sucked in. There wasn't much chatter, only complaints about backs and hips. Now that Brian looked down at his food, it didn't seem as appetizing. He looked at his mobile. 418 was almost here. He took a bite of his white toast; glad he had ordered his sunny side up eggs over hard.

Samuel had woken me early. I was crashing out after a night of relief at Dr. Pong's, and Samuel came early to tell me I had to get going because I was going to meet King. Wow, was it as easy as that? You ask, you get! He got me out of my chair and got me washed. We put on my work clothes and off we went.

We were early. I was not joining the queue to shuffle down the hallway, pack together, and wait for the elevator. I was able to walk freely and there was no one waiting at the elevator. I was the only one in the lift, and I was the only one in the carport. There was a line of cars that were marshaling up to take people off to work. I got in the first one, and Samuel told me he would handle the directions. He omitted the part about how he always handled the directions.

Almost instantly, before the foam could hold me into place, we were off. I chatted with Samuel. It was better than thinking about if I was going to be able to handle the next curve. "Where exactly am I going?"

Samuel answered matter of factly, "You are going to a cafe called Jazmin's."

"Oh, where is that?"

"It is here." And Samuel showed me a map. The map was interesting, but it didn't mean anything to me, and it wasn't all that colorful like the maps online. It was wordy, and without pictures.

I tried something else, "It's a café, like a cafe that we have online?"

Samuel, who was smiling gently, said, "Yes, it is."

"Oh." That was interesting. I didn't think I'd ever been to a real café. "Can I order something?"

Samuel had to think about this. I'd noticed that the amount of time it takes for him to find an answer is related to the obscurity of the question. "Almost certainly not," he answered firmly.

"Why not?" I felt a little hurt.

"The staff there are not looking to answer to you. King may order, and if you would like, you may ask me to order, but they do not take Virtual Dollars for payment. Likely it will be unsuccessful if I try to place an order for you." Samuel gave me a surprisingly factual answer. I felt a little cheated.

The ride wasn't as awful as I thought it would be. There didn't seem to be as many turns as I would have thought. As we headed out of the city, it was a straight line and then a right. Another right, and we were pulling up at the carport.

"We are here, sort of," Samuel told me, "there has been some sort of blockage..." I turned him off, I didn't want to be mobile while I was talking to King. What would be the point of that? I don't think I'd remember anything. The door opened, and imagine my surprise when, instead of a dingy old carport with grime and dirt all over the crumbling concrete walls, I stepped out and felt the early morning sun on my face.

Wow! What a feeling. I'd experienced sun online, I'd been to see the pyramids, and I'd been to the Caribbean, at least some of the tourist places Ernest had taken me to, but this was real actual sun. There was something about it that was different. The way it felt on my skin, it felt like I was reacting to it, and not as if my brain was being told about it. I took a deep breath, the air was different, it wasn't damp, but it was moist.

There were smells too, not of concrete, but of fat, salt and something gritty that I didn't like. I liked the smell of fat and salt, instinctively, I started to move toward it. There was a door to a shop, the worst looking shop I had ever seen. There were papers stuck all over the door, the door was metal with glass, and it didn't hang straight, slightly ajar, because it was scraping on the ground where it had dug grooves in the concrete. Samuel had dropped me off here. This must be the place.

I pulled open the door. It ground against the cement, sending a shrill charge up my spine, rattling my teeth. Doors were different here. You had to step around them. Online, you could almost step through them as if they were symbolic or unimportant. My foot ached as I pivoted around the door and stepped into the cafe.

I expected to find something like McDonald's, all nice and clean plastic, with *shove you in the back* padding on the benches and chairs. I expected King and I might be the only two in the cafe. I was always the only one in the restaurant, but that wasn't the case. It was cram-packed full of people, all sitting, most of them with real plates of food in front of them. A number of wait staff were bringing plates of food, or otherwise circulating around the room with notepads they didn't need.

King waved to me. He was sitting at a tiny little table over by the wall. He wasn't sitting in the middle of the room, and he didn't have a great view of a waterfall or some other spectacle. He looked small, crushed over there. There was a lamp that hung over the table. The table itself looked like it wasn't level, and it matched the other tables in the restaurant by not matching any other table in the restaurant.

Instead of just floating through the restaurant, I had to navigate my way past chairs that stuck out too far, and arms and elbows. I picked my way through the maze. It would have been easier to let Samuel do it, but then I would have been just like all the other wait staff. I noticed one of the diners reach up and grab a wait staff as they tried to pass by on its rounds. Even though it looked like it might have hurt, the staff smiled sweetly and asked if there was anything it could get for him. He barked orders, and it pretended to write.

I pulled the chair out. There wasn't a lot of room for my chair. There was an old woman who was talking loudly to her friend across the table. I wanted to stop and listen. She stopped talking and looked up at me, first with her mouth open and then with a look I could only describe as horror. "I think we had better go," she said to her friend, and they picked themselves up as fast as their aged and bent bodies could move and started to shuffle to the door.

King was smiling. He motioned that I should sit. He had a small breakfast in front of him, only two eggs. I always had at least six, if I felt in the mood to do the breakfast thing. I sat down, I had lots of room now. King smiled at me. "How are you?"

"I guess I am fine," was all I managed to say, but that wasn't true. "No," I corrected myself, "my foot hurts."

King took a bite of his toast, the toast looked good, it was simple, small compared to the feast sized items you got online. He crunched it and I watched him chew. He was eating it, not just putting it in his mouth. There was a procedure, not just an intention and a taste. He swallowed. "But you did that? You hurt your foot."

"I guess, does it matter?"

King thought about it. "No, it doesn't matter." He took a sip of what I guessed was coffee. I could smell it. I'd never smelled coffee before. I'd tasted it—online—and it tasted bitter, and gave you a kick, but not as much as cocaine or adrenaline. I didn't bother with it, but it was interesting to watch King drink. I was waiting for him to speed up, but he appeared much the same. He continued asking questions. "What do you mean by hurt? How does it hurt?"

"I'm not sure what you mean. It hurts all the time."

King raised his eyebrows. "All the time? Like when you are at work?"

"Yes," I straightened up. He did understand. "It hurts when I am at work, and it never used to. I never used to feel anything."

A wait staff came by and asked King if there was anything else he wanted. They totally ignored me, as if I were not there.

"No," King replied firmly to the staff, and it immediately turned to continue its round through the cafe. "I see," he said to me. "When you are at work, and you are online, you can feel it?"

"Sure," I answered.

"Did that happen before?"

"Before I hurt myself?"

"No," King corrected, "before the, um, the exception?"

"The exception?" I asked.

"You know, the thing that landed you in the clinic, the first time."

"Oh, that. No, not that I remember."

"Interesting," King said wistfully, his eyes had a different type of glaze over them, without going gray. It was as if he'd gone someplace else to think. Finally, he asked, "What do you want me to do about it?"

I sat for a while, watching everyone eat. Everyone was eating something similar but something different. If I told King I couldn't work, I didn't think that would be good. It occurred to me, it wasn't work that I couldn't do, it was this specific work. "Well," I said, and I looked around, wondering if what I was about to say was nuts. I didn't want it overheard. "I'd like to do something else."

"Something else?" It must have been a crazy suggestion, because King needed some time to think. "Something else," he repeated, trying to make it sound right to himself. After a long pause: "Okay," he agreed, "we have a deal. I will find you something else to do."

"Great!" I said with great surprise. I didn't know what to say.

King kept looking at me. He looked amazed.

I looked back at King. He had eaten all his toast and was starting on the eggs. I had nothing in front of me. "Now what?"

"I suppose you have to go to work. I can't change that," he started, still thinking of something. "But I promise to try to do something to change things around."

"Great!" I was starting to sound mechanical, but I didn't know what else to say. I sat there grinning at him.

"I guess you go to work now?" King said rhetorically, taking a sip of his coffee.

"Yes." I didn't want to go to work. This place was nothing like anything online, I wanted to stay, and I wanted to try the eggs, real eggs. "I suppose."

King placed his cup down. "I will have to go to work myself and try to find you a solution."

"Oh?"

King smiled, seemingly amused at me. "That means I can't do anything for you here."

"Oh," I nodded.

"Go to work and I will sort something. Leave it to me."

I didn't know how to leave. Online, when you leave, you just go. But here, when you leave you have to turn around, you have to walk somewhere, and you have to go somewhere. It's strange. Awkward, I got up and I walked out the door. I think that's how it's done.

Outside I tapped my forehead and went online. In a few instants, the pixels stopped swirling, and Samuel came into focus. "Hello Samuel," I said, before he could greet me and ask me what he could do for me today. "Take me to work."

15

YES, YOU HAVE BRAIN DAMAGE

Brian watched 418 stand up abruptly and clumsily, then march itself stiffly out of the cafe. Everyone looked. It looked as if it was walking out on his tab, but staff don't get served. There was no reason to stop it. It hadn't had any real food, and the wait staff didn't even notice. It was all very odd to watch 418 cut its way out through the maze of tables. A few seconds later, the door opened again, 418 appeared again, milky-eyed, and headed directly and expertly through the maze of tables toward the back of the café. The wait staff moved out of the way as it approached and, as quickly as it had appeared, it was gone.

The coffee was lousy, but it gave him time to think. There was no doubt in Brian's mind now that 418 is indeed, one hundred percent certain, brain damaged. But what to do? To simply retire 418 was a loss. He'd have to take 418 back to the clinic and open a new claim, and they would do the re-examination, and maybe they would find what he already knew. But they didn't find it the first time, why would they find it this time? Especially since it was going to cost them money. They would say it was fine. Brian knew his best course was to stick with 418 and see what he could get out of them.

Brian took his time. He might as well enjoy his breakfast. He tried not to look at anyone else eating. It was disgusting, slurping undercooked eggs. If he thought about it, he wouldn't be able to eat. The chewing, open mouths, bits of food popping out, and a snack for later sticking to a wrinkly, stubbly, chin. He needed some time to think about this. He sighed and finished his coffee. It tasted like dirty water boiled in an aluminum pot.

Back at the office, the first thing Brian did, after he made himself take the stairs, was go get a real coffee. There is no substitute for good coffee. At his desk, he gave it some thought. Well, it would be simple, but he could have 418 work at a factory. He'd provided staff to factories before, but the problem with factory work was that it wasn't always stable. There was always garbage, but there wasn't always work at the factory, and to work in the factory, Brian would have to commit 418 for the day, and if it got there but wasn't used, he wouldn't get paid.

The alternative was to continue to hurt 418, which would ultimately get worse and worse and result in trips to the hospital, the best that Brian would be able to get was sixty percent of 418's wages. It wasn't likely that a factory would allow 418 to hang around and not be used. 418 was in pretty good shape.

Brian would have to make some phone calls.

I stepped outside the cafe and went online. Pixels swirled, and Samuel came into view. "How can I help you today?" he asked. He always asked.

"Take me to work."

Samuel smiled. "Good news, the blockage in the carport of this building has cleared. I will lead you to the carport where I will arrange transport." Samuel seemed pleased, as if he'd had some hand in fixing something. And with little more fanfare, Samuel took control of my arms and legs. We marched back into the cafe, expertly through the maze of tables, and out the back door to wait for a car.

Work was the same as it always was. I was taken to a depot, and I marched myself over to a truck where another staff was already sitting behind the wheel waiting to go. As soon as I got in, the truck switched into gear and away we drove, without a word. Oh sure, if I wanted to, I could have Samuel open a chat, but since the other staff hadn't done that, why bother? It probably didn't even know it had been waiting while I had been late, so why disturb it?

The truck bumped. Samuel asked me if I would like to go to the casino or participate in a show. I didn't want to do either. I sat there with Samuel, feeling the ride, smelling the smells.

Our first stops were in downtown. In most places, all that was required was for me to step out of the cab and unlock the gate. The other staff would drive the truck and do the dumping. If everything went well, the dump would be clean, I would shut the gate, get back in the cab and we would be off. Inching around the town, crawling from dumpster to dumpster.

If things didn't go well, we would be wandering around the parking lot. I could feel myself doing a lot of walking and bending. It was funny, I was staring at Samuel, who continued to smile and occasionally suggest some distraction or another, but I could feel everything I was doing. Had it always been like that? And I had just chosen to not feel what I was doing?

Some of these stops had to be a lot of work, and occasionally, I would feel my hand touch something mushy or slimy, and seconds later the smell would hit me. Now that I was paying some attention, it dawned on me why I smelled: I was picking up garbage with my bare hands, and that was the smell that was staying with me. Okay, that seemed to make sense. At least it wasn't me.

"Samuel," I said, "why am I staring at you?"

Samuel smiled back. "I am the concierge and you have not chosen an activity."

"Oh." I had to think about this. Samuel continued smiling. "As long as I don't choose an activity, you stay here?"

Samuel shrugged, "That does seem to be what happens."

"I have a question?"

"What would that be?"

"Why is it I can hear and smell things, but I can't see things?"

Samuel smiled. "Default setting. But there is no reason you couldn't, but why would you want to?"

"You are not that interesting to stare at." I answered a little too quickly.

"That's why we have activities and entertainment. To relieve you of the tedium of work."

"I can see what I'm doing?"

"Yes, you can," Samuel replied, "but you won't like it."

"Why?"

"It's boring."

It turned out, even though I was at work, all I had to do was ask Samuel to allow me to see what was going on and he would have faded away into the distance and become a little icon on the edge of my vision. Well, now, wasn't that better? I will concede that the offline world is much drabber, and is often not exciting, but it was totally new and completely unpredictable. Perhaps it was because it was something different, but different was fantastic.

The inside of the truck was dirty and grungy. The first thing I saw was the cracked dash of the truck, covered in baked-on dirt and grime. The other staff was totally unaware of me. We drove along in silence. It was fascinating to watch someone actually drive. When we got into places that were tight, they automatically started pushing the pedals and turning the wheel as if it knew what it was doing, as if they had been doing it for years. We were in and out of tight spaces, with inches to spare on each side. I saw no new paint scrapes on that beaten up old truck.

The flies were the next thing I noticed. And why not? It seemed that at some time the garbage had been dumped inside the cab, not over the cab, and into the bin on the back. The cab itself smelled horrible, and now that I was not playing slots or staring at Samuel, the stench was undeniable. Things were rotting in here. I moved my feet and there was a squelching sound. I was stuck to a mass of paper and minced plastic. We had pulled into another tight parking lot. I got out and the smell stayed with me. It was the smell from the rotting garbage inside the cab. This is why I smelled!

Brian smiled as he saw the garbage truck pull up and 418 got out, hobbled around the truck—tried to wipe something off its feet—and unhitched the gate that housed the dumpster. A sinking feeling rose in Brian as his smiled dropped. It wasn't right to watch 418 walking, dragging its foot around. He'd have to do something. The dumpster sprayed papers all over the parking lot, as it always did, and 418 and the other staff tried to pick them up. 418 looked like a fish with a broken fin as it tried to chase after paper and plastic that moved about just faster than they could.

It was sad and pathetic to watch. What Brian should have done was send 418 back to the clinic and make a claim. If 418 couldn't be made to work, Brian could certainly use the retirement benefit the insurance company would pay. As Brian watched, he knew what would happen. There would be a lot of talking. This would drag on for a long time, but 418 wasn't young anymore, and the foot may not heal, or it might take months, maybe even years. During that time, Brian would receive a portion of his wages in between times that 418 could be made serviceable. Eventually, 418 would get retired, and that would be the end of that, but it would be a long, money-losing process.

Brian watched the staff and 418 get back into the truck. Most of the papers and plastic had been corralled, stuffed back into the dumpster until the next time they would fly out and litter the parking lot. Yes, he would have to do something about this.

Not all jobs paid the same. Brian had found garbage collection was a good job. Perhaps people just didn't think about it, but there was always demand, and it normally got his staff home okay. Certainly, there had been injuries, and there had even been deaths, but those were covered by insurance.

A less profitable job was working in a factory because it was a little more irregular. Brian didn't like committing staff for the day and not getting paid. Most factories didn't like to overstaff, but certainly liked to have staff for all the things it was too difficult to get the machines to do. Doing things machines couldn't do also indicated a level of danger, so it was best to send older, less resilient staff to work in factories. The potential for loss was lower when the eventual exception occurred.

Brian sighed and stabbed at his mobile. "Hello, Suresh, this is Brian, Brian Agarwal."

There was a lot of noise on the line. It was obvious that Suresh was busy out on the factory floor. "Hey Brian, how is it going dog? You still the King?"

Brian bristled. He liked being called King, not being reminded that his name wasn't King, which went back to when they were kids. "Of course, of course, I'm still the King," Brian almost shouted into his mobile. "How is everything, my old friend?"

Suresh was walking off the factory floor. He kept an office behind a thick glass window with mini-blinds he usually had open—so he could see what was going on—but could still be drawn in case he needed to have a snooze. "Things are good for me," Suresh yelled into his mobile, "but you, my old friend, must have some sort of problem."

"No, how do you figure that?"

Suresh stepped through the heavy steel door that secured his office against the noise of the factory floor. "You wouldn't have called me *old friend* if you didn't need me to remember that we are old friends," Suresh continued to yell. He was pretty deaf after years of tending to the factory. "What do you need?"

Brian sighed. He knew he had not done a good enough job staying in touch with his friends, "Okay, you are the best," he replied. "I need you to help me out. I have a staff..."

16

THERE MUST BE SOMETHING BETTER THAN THIS

Brian had to work it out with Suresh. "You know I am a businessman," Suresh chided him. "What makes your staff better than anyone else's?"

Brian didn't have an answer for this. *How his was any different?* was a question he avoided, even if it meant it would be months or years between talking to his business friends. He knew his staff was the exactly same as anyone else's staff, and he didn't want to get beaten up on price. "Oh, you know me Suresh," he stalled.

"Yes, I do," Suresh cut him off. He was enjoying this. "I know you need something, and you don't want to tell me."

"No," Brian lied. "I just have an extra staff, and I don't have a garbage route for them. I was hoping to keep it busy."

"Good." Suresh seized on the opportunity. "I want ten points off."

"No, how can you do that to me?" Brian complained. "We have been friends since I don't remember, and you want ten points?"

"Okay," Suresh enjoyed the parry. "Five points."

"You are killing me."

"No," said Suresh, "That's not me. Okay, send it over."

"You will find it work?" Brian added, hopefully.

"Sure, we are old friends, or did you forget?"

"Oh, thank you! Thank you, thank you."

Downtown is not very interesting. Samuel was right, it was pretty boring, I never dreamed there were so many dark places and dirty back lanes, and all of them had a dumpster buried somewhere. Most of the dumpsters were beaten and old, with doors that didn't fit, and the trash came spewing out when it was lifted. But that didn't matter. We were there to pick it up and put it back into the bin so whatever wasn't dumped this time might make it next time by virtue of being on the bottom of the bin.

The day seemed long, and there was no stopping. I could feel my foot, my arms and legs aching every time I got out of the cab to open another set of doors and wait while the truck picked up the trash. Silently we went about our work. I couldn't do much more of this, I was going to need Dr. Pong's again tonight. This wasn't funny. I went back online briefly. Samuel was as cheerful as always: *'Would I like to play a game, or see a show?'*

"No Samuel," I explained. "I'd like to send a message."

"Oh, that sounds like fun. Who would you like to send it to?"

"Please send this message to King, 'My foot hurts, have you found anything different for me to do?'"

"Okay, I can send that to King."

"Good. Please do."

"Sent."

I stared at Samuel for a few moments. "Did he answer?"

Samuel smiled again. "The message has been delivered but not read."

"What?" How could that be?

"That's all the information I have," Samuel apologized. "The message has been delivered but not read is all the information that I have."

"Yeah." I had to think about it. "I guess."

The idea that I could send a message to King and that it might be delivered but not read ate at me. It made me feel uncomfortable. It didn't seem right or even possible. I went back into seeing mode because I didn't want to stare at or talk to Samuel any more than

127

I had to. It amazed me that he couldn't tell me something that he didn't know.

Samuel minimized, turned into a smiling head, moved up and to the right, and the world reappeared. We were out on the highway. The other staff was just sitting there, the truck was driving itself again, and we were heading out of the city. We seemed to be on some sort of long bridge with high walls. Every now and then, there was a light post atop a building, or some sort of antenna stuck out over the wall, but generally there was nothing to see but cars, road, wall, and sky.

We were whizzing along. I didn't think anything went that fast, but there we were. I looked down at the little bubble of a car in front of us. We were so big and solid. If that bubble stopped, I couldn't imagine how we could possibly stop this heavy mass of metal in time to not crush that little metal egg. The little egg seemed to know this and stayed just ahead of us.

After a long while, the road started to look less like an open tunnel and more like a road. We were still zipping along, but the sides of the tunnel had gone, and I could see trees and walls further off to the side of the road often obscured by greenery. I'd never seen so much green in my entire life. Everything I knew was gray concrete. Green was fascinating, it came in many different shapes, shades, and sizes. There were great bushes, towering trees, vines that clung to things and grass. I never knew grass could grow to such a height.

We slowed, headed to the right. The staff with me was still sitting there, no expression on its face. Did we do this every day? Just sit here, not seeing any of this because we had chosen to distract ourselves?

We headed off on a long road and the truck slowed down dramatically, less than half the speed we were driving in the city which had been tight and congested. Now the truck left large spaces, drove slow and even came to stops from time to time where it waited for other cars. This was weird. It actually pulled up at a stop sign, and another vehicle drove up, never stopped and continued plowing through, and we just sat there like dummies the whole time.

The other driver was actually driving their shiny red car. It looked like something from online. It was clean, pristine as if nothing had ever touched it, ever!

After a stop or two of these, we headed off on a long road. On one side there was a lake, calm, perfectly smooth, reflecting the trees in a perfect green mirror against the dark, glassy surface. We slowed and turned right and headed down a long drive. There were great stone houses. I saw horses, and we went behind what appeared to be the largest house.

The truck pulled up, and I felt myself get up. It had been a while, and my legs creaked as Samuel hoisted me out of my seat. While I could see, I still wasn't in control of my body unless I went offline, and I was supposed to be at work. I couldn't go fully offline.

I watched as I got out of the truck, wobbled a little and headed toward a gated enclosure. I opened the gate and pulled the great green painted doors open. These did not scrape against the ground. They were well designed, and, while heavy, rolled easily once I got them moving. I had to rush around to get on the other side to stop them.

As the truck lifted the trash, nothing came out the sides of the bin. The truck dumped the trash, backed away, and I found myself closing the gates. I was back in the truck. We went through a turning loop and back out the way that we came, off to the next lane.

This one featured tennis courts. I'd been to Wimbledon online to see who was going to be the online champion, but this was different. I was struck by how big and empty the tennis courts looked. The grass on these had real texture and was mowed, with fresh chalk for the lines. As we moved along, I noticed this house had been made differently: it was made of brick and had large windows and massive rooms. I could even see people walking around. They looked tiny compared to the massive windows. I'd seen enough online to know that these people lived here. But how massive the house was! It was staggering. Didn't they get frightened living in such wide-open spaces?

Another stop there were two women sunbathing and a man out playing with a small girl. She had a bicycle with pink tassels on the handlebars, and she was going around and around him. Even though we were speeding past in search of garbage, I could see the smile on his face and almost hear the laughter of the little girl.

How could these people have so much? Some of the places we went to, it wasn't clear which was the main house because there were many large buildings. And the cars, none of them looked like they were self-driving. The drive between some of the houses was minutes. There were houses with golf courses in front of them, duck ponds, horses, elaborate play toys for their children. They took little notice of us as we drove in, only if we got in the way of their cars, in which case our truck stopped, and we waited from them to pass safely by.

The most amazing thing was that these people didn't seem to actually do anything. They were all looking relaxed and happy. Smiling, playing, having a good time, if we saw them at all. And each place we went to only had a few people, never more than five or six, people living there. How could they do that? Didn't they live underground? They seemed to spend a lot of time wanting to be above it and having large windows so they could see green all around them.

The other thing that amazed me was how it went on and on. I didn't think there could be so many large houses. How did they do it? Where did it come from? How could I have it?

As the sun set in the west, we headed back to the city. The same route, I guess. The same roadway that had walls up on either side of it. The same cars danced, jockeyed and tried to pack themselves as tightly against each other as possible. We hurtled along as tight as we could to the car in front of us. All the time, the other staff with me just grinned to himself, he must have been winning whatever it was.

Finally, we made it to the city, the walls dropped away, but we were still on streets lined with buildings, no open spaces, circling around until we found the depot. It was dark outside now. I got out of the truck after it parked itself. The other staff sat there for a moment, just long enough for me to wonder if it was going to stay there all night. It got out and headed for the changing area full of broken benches and bashed-up lockers no one had used in decades. Silently, we changed out of our shoes, staying in our filthy work uniforms. Calmly, we walked toward the carport.

It was time to go home. I felt tired. Even though I hadn't done anything, it was seeing all those new things that made me feel tired. Too many things for me to process. I called for Samuel as he walked me to the carport. "I'd like to play solitaire," I told him.

"Oh, good," he answered, "that sounds like fun."

"Hmm," I mumbled. I wasn't feeling cheerful.

As if Samuel had heard me—of course he had, he was in my head—he announced, "I got a message back from King. Shall I read it?"

"Yes, what is it?" I was tired.

"I have found you a job working in a factory. You should not have to do as much walking."

"Oh, good."

"Would you like me to send that back."

"Sure, why not?" I didn't mean it.

"Done and sent."

17

WORKING
AT THE FACTORY

Some mornings were rougher than others. Despite the fact that Samuel woke me and made all the goodness Dr. Pong dispensed go away, I was still groggy and tired. I let Samuel drive because I was just asleep on my feet. I didn't want to wake up, I didn't feel alert. Thankfully, I didn't have to be.

I had spent my night thinking about all the stuff that I had seen the day before. I wondered how they ever managed to get lives like that, and I wondered how it was I had managed to get so little. I remembered the horses, the family. I don't remember ever experiencing my family all at once. It was always one-on-one and through chat. Watching the man play with the little girl while the woman was sleeping. Young boys playing basketball or driving small cars around. They lived their lives differently; they lived in a spatial plane. It wasn't like they were in a room where they chose to see what they wanted and who they wanted to see. It was like they were in a place and had to move around in order to make the scenery change. It was fascinating, but, at the same time, disturbing.

How did anyone live like that, having to move? I didn't have to move. I could travel all over the world. I wondered about the places that I had been. They must exist. I remember meeting Belinda in a cafe on the Seine. Why I'd chosen to go to Paris, I don't know, but I had. I had wanted to go back, but Belinda was always busy.

I wondered where she was. I mean, I knew she was out there. "Samuel," I asked.

Samuel smiled before me. "What can I do for you?"

"You still haven't got any message back from my wife?"

Samuel frowned. "I'm sorry, no further responses have been received. Would you like to send another message?"

"No," I told him, then, "Yes." I changed my mind.

"Very good, to all of the Belinda Boyle's?"

"No," I replied wistfully, "I don't think that will make any difference. Could I send one to King?"

Samuel shrugged. "Why not? What would you like it to say?"

I had to think for a moment. I remember talking to King about it, but the idea of a message was fresh, and the words were still swirling around. "Hmm, how about this: 'Hello King, do you remember that I once had a wife? I was wondering if I could meet her again. It would be great. Let me know what you think.'"

"Okay I've got it. Would you like me to read it back?"

I didn't want him to read it back. It was going to sound odd no matter what I said. "Nah, send it."

"Sent." There was a long pause. "What would you like to do today?" Samuel asked, filling in the silence.

"Nothing."

"As you wish, you know where I will be." Samuel minimized and drifted up to where I could ignore him in the top right corner of my vision. The blue background fizzled, and shapes of gray, black, white and other colors sizzled into shape.

I found myself standing at the front of a queue. Within moments, a man came and took me by the elbow. I felt my feet obey the tug he gave me, and I started following him. The factory was a large warehouse with towering steel shelves that held heaps of materials and half-finished stuff. There were large machines for doing various things, some had red lights, some had yellow, and some had both on top.

There were lots of staff standing around, the same lifeless look in their milky white eyes. Some had tools ready to go, tongs, clamps, long metal bars and some just stood with gloves on, waiting for things to start. We moved through the factory and entered a place where everyone had a grinder. There were lots of metal boxes that looked almost finished with rough edges.

I was led further down to where a long conveyor belt unified a sea of much lighter equipment. The belt ran into some machines and out of some others. There were already staff here, and I felt some relief. It didn't look like I would have to move much. I was placed beside the conveyor and a number of other staff quickly followed me until there were six of us, three on each side of the conveyor.

This conveyor was part of a simple set up of adding stoppers to bottles. I could see by peering through the maze of poles, belts, shelves, and machinery that not all the bottles were the same size. I looked beside myself. There was a bin full of twisted metal wire with caps that had been fitted into the loops. I could see this was going to be a good job. I even had a stool to sit on. However, for now, Samuel was in charge, and I was standing like all the other staff.

The small team of men who had placed us started the machines, and slowly, items started to move. As the conveyor brought the first item to the first staff along production road, one of the men grabbed the staff's hands, told them to pay attention and walked them through what it must do. Then he stood back while he watched the staff do the same, without his help. Once the man was happy with the work of the staff, he moved on to the next unoccupied staff and showed that staff what to do.

Soon it was my turn.

"Pay attention," I heard the man say to me, and I felt my head pull down to look at the work. My hands were held, and I reached into the bin and took a chunk of metal wire. I was shown how to wrap my hands around the bottle without lifting it and wrapped the wire into place. My thumb stung as the wire made a loud snap into place. "Good," the man said. "Keep doing this, adjusting for the size of the bottle. You are to handle every 6th bottle. Let five go by, grab the sixth one."

I felt myself nod and heard myself say, "Yes sir, I would be happy to do this to every sixth bottle." The man stood back and watched as the conveyor moved slowly. I counted the bottles, even though I didn't need to, just to make sure I was doing it right. The man moved on to the next staff and repeated the same procedure.

It did take a while, but soon enough, the men had worked their way through the line. One of the men mounted a scaffolding where a chair had been fixed to oversee the entire production line. There was a big metal box mounted beside his chair, the man got into the chair and looked about the production line. Everything was going as it should. Satisfied, he pressed the button, and everything started to speed up. Soon my hands were flying around, and I couldn't keep track of them. Good thing I wasn't controlling them. My arms moved left and right, my right-hand dipping into the bin, grabbing a chunk of wire. My left-hand steadied the bottle as it moved past, as my right-hand expertly snapped the capping mechanism onto the top of the bottle. I was a spectator; not even aware I was doing it. Only my point of view made it undeniable that it was I who was capping bottles.

After a while, I noticed the belt was moving even faster. My arms automatically adjusted and moved faster along with it. A few moments later, we were going faster still. My hands moved about, blurring in front of my eyes, moving too fast for me to follow.

This continued, and I noticed I was starting to breathe hard. I looked at the other staff. I could see sweat starting to bead on their faces. They didn't seem too concerned about what was going on, the same blank looks. I was breathing harder than I normally did. The line sped up again.

After a while, it was clear that the line would go as fast as the slowest of us would go. This was awful, my heart was pounding, my hands were flying around, and I felt sweat pooling uncomfortably at the small of my back.

The flow of bottles never stopped. We just went on and on and on. The man in the chair swapped out after a long while, and another man sat and watched carefully, keeping an eye on the whole production to see if we could go faster.

All of a sudden, glass flew everywhere, alarms sounded and the conveyor ground to a halt. My hands slowed with the bottles as they went past, still grabbing every sixth bottle.

Another man in a long blue coat came running. I could see out of the corner of my eye that one of the staff behind me, also stopping bottles, had had something happen. There was blood all over the conveyor. One of the men got on his mobile and said something into it that I couldn't catch over the noise of the factory. Now that I wasn't moving around at warp speed, I could hear how noisy the factory was.

A third man was walking over with another staff by the arm. The staff beside me was replaced and taken back to the front of the factory. The other staff was put in place, and the production line was started again. Slowly, as they had to show the new staff how to cap bottles. My hand started to move automatically as the first, seventh, thirteenth and nineteenth bottles appeared from the opening of the last machine. It all began again.

Sometime during the day, I got a message from Samuel, "King says, 'I will meet you tomorrow to discuss it.'"

I went into full-screen mode, "Oh good," I told Samuel.

Samuel added, just before I asked, "I will guide you to the meeting place."

"Oh, good," I repeated.

I noticed something. My arms were still zipping around, and my heart was still pounding. I had been hoping that there would be another breakdown in the production line again, but if I went online, it didn't feel so bad. I could feel myself breathe, my hands hurt, my fingers were raw, and I felt cramps in my wrists that I worked through anyway. But it didn't feel quite so bad. I guess if I had gone off and played poker with my friends—too bad they didn't remember me—I might not have noticed anything, or I might have just felt a little discomfort that I would have scrunched up in a little ball and tossed away with the thought, "What do I expect? I'm at work."

But it was boring, staring at Samuel. I turned him off and went back to watching my hands fly around. It was impressive what I could do when I wasn't thinking about it.

The day was long. Very long. There was another time where something got stuck, and a shower of glass came spitting out of one of the machines. This caused the men to come running again. Lights were flashing, and buzzers started to wail. With gratitude, I watched my hands slow until the belt stopped. I wanted to use my hands to shift myself. My backside was hurting, the stool was little more than metal with a layer of wood bolted to it, and I think I had found where all the bolts were. But Samuel was still driving, and I did not have discretionary use of my hands. No one had been hurt. It was just a matter of putting the machine right, and starting up the conveyor again, no training of new staff required.

Other than this, there was nothing eventful going on. A never-ending stream of bottles. It was with heavy hands and heavy heart that staff came by to swap out my almost-empty bin of wire chunks with a fresh one, full to the brim with twisted pieces of metal. Clearly there was no end to supply of material. The production line would stop when someone broke, or the day came to its end.

The man in the chair changed seven times throughout the day. I asked Samuel what twelve into eight was—there had been eight men in the chair. He told me it was one and a half and asked me why I wanted to know. "No reason," I told him, "just something I saw." Samuel was happy with this, but it did mean their shifts were one and a half hours on this production line, and mine was twelve hours. Good thing someone else was doing all the driving.

At the end of the day, I was exhausted, my hand cramped and blistered underneath the thick gray sheen that had built up in the spots where I grabbed the wire and twisted it. There was a great dent in my thumb where I always, precisely, grabbed the wire. As the whistle blew and the conveyor slowed, Samuel got me up off my chair. I don't think I could have done it. I could feel my knees creak. My feet felt like blocks of fuzz burning away on the bottom of my legs. Still, though, Samuel managed to keep me upright. We strode out of the factory, past the line of staff waiting to take our place. It was good to be going home.

18

MORE OF THE SAME

Samuel was smiling over me as my eyes fluttered open. I looked up and saw the smooth clean ceiling painted an immaculate white, with a small-but-elegant crystal and gold chandelier hanging delicately from the ceiling. "It's time for you to get up." And the next thing I knew I was on my feet, stepping around my tiny cubicle of a condo and into the shower.

"Samuel, why don't I shower when I get home?" I asked him.

"We shower for hygiene purposes, so we don't smell."

"Sure, I know that."

"When you get home, you actually are not around anyone. All you have to do is get undressed and get into the chair."

"Oh, but if I am showering now, why wouldn't I shower then?"

Samuel smiled. "That's simple. When you get home you want to eat, you want to be entertained."

"Yes."

"Why wait?"

I had to think about this, "I guess."

"Sure, you like it better that way, everyone does."

"Why do I shower at all?"

"Because you stink," my concierge answered cheerfully. "It's for hygiene purposes. Okay, all done with the shower, I will be getting you dressed. We have a busy day."

Imagine my surprise when the car pulled up, and Samuel announced, "Here we are, Jazmin's cafe, would you like me to guide you inside?" I had totally forgotten about the meeting with King, I was preoccupied with wondering if my hands were going to fall apart.

"Right," I exclaimed. "I will take it from here. Thank you, Samuel." And with that, he gave me control. I was standing in an alleyway, and as Samuel turned off, I noticed it was spitting rain. Not enough to be cool, but just enough that it would make my clothes sticky and soggy if I didn't get moving.

A small white metal sign—*Caution, Staff*—on the door indicated that this was Jazmin's cafe staff entrance. Even though I wasn't online, I guess I was still staff. Besides that, I didn't know how to get around to the front door. I pushed the door open; the place was a buzzing beehive of automation. Staff moving quickly everywhere, took no notice of me. Carefully, I made my way through the kitchen.

Entering the dining area, I found it looked the same as it did before, but everyone had moved around. This time King was over by a window with his back to a wall. There was an empty seat in front of him and lots of room this time. The only problem was navigating the room. The staff did it quickly, but I didn't have that much practice with obstacle courses and had to move slowly and carefully, avoiding the staff who did not see me at all.

King had a slightly bigger breakfast than the last time, but still had only three eggs, not the normal six. He also had a large sausage that had been split lengthwise and looked like it had been grilled that way. The smell in this place was wonderful, fat and grease and salt. All the things that are good for you. Today King had a pile of white toast and was busy spreading some chunky orange-colored jam on it. I'd never seen jam that was chunky like that. It was always smooth every time I had seen it before.

"Good morning," King said as I got close enough, smiling at me. He enjoyed watching me pick my way through the mess of arms, legs, elbows and the backs of chairs that seemed to be juxtaposed in the walkways from every possible angle. "Have a seat," King said.

"Thank you." I pulled the chair out so I could sit down.

"What can I do for you? How do you like factory work?"

I didn't know which question to answer first. Do I answer them both, in which order, and did he mean to just discard the first one? "I don't like factory work," I explained. My hands hurt, I held up my hand, and he could see the blistering which made King recoil. "All my fingers hurt, and I lose feeling in my legs because I am sitting for so long."

King smiled. "That's funny, it's either feast or famine, with you. First your foot hurt, and now your fingers hurt. By the way, how is your foot?"

"My foot is fine," I blurted out, and then I thought about it. "No, it's not, it still hurts a lot when I walk on it, I just don't notice it right now."

"Okay, well I can try to find something else for you."

"Oh, that would be great!"

"Fine," King said as he cut off a piece of his sausage and popped it into his mouth. "That's settled, tomorrow I will find something different for you to do."

"Great!"

We sat there for a few moments, then I said, "Do you think I could try some of that? It smells great in here."

King stopped chewing. He looked at his plate, then he looked at me. "Are you sure?"

I didn't know what to say, but I felt weird being the only one here with no plate in front of them. I unwrapped a napkin that had been wound around a set of cutlery. The fork felt weird in my hand, I'd used them online, but there it was again, the feeling of actually holding something. I was sure I didn't know how to work it. I kind of stabbed toward King's plate.

"What would you like to try?" King asked. He was carefully arranging what remained of his toast.

"An egg," I said. I'd meant to say, whatever you want to spare, but somehow the truth blurted out.

"Okay." King pulled the plate back, turned it, placed the empty side plate that had been covered in soggy bread. Carefully, he cut off and slid one of his eggs onto the plate, then slid the plate over to me with the tip of his index finger.

I looked at the egg. There was more detail to it than I remembered, and the yolk wasn't as yellow as I was used to seeing. It looked limp, glossy in a different way, not as sparkly under these lights. I stabbed at it with my fork, and it slid just a bit before being pierced by the prongs. It bled yellow. I looked at King, who studied me intently. Perhaps this wasn't such a good idea. King nodded at me.

There went nothing: I put the egg in my mouth. It seemed to burn the top of my mouth. Little flecks of pepper scraped and bit at the top of my surprisingly slack and flabby mouth. But the egg was warm, and I didn't have to chew it. It slid down my throat as one lump and landed with a crash in my stomach.

My head started to spin, and my stomach tossed as the egg tried to find someplace to settle, this one warm glowing dot inside me, trying to work its way into my stomach. I thought I was going to be sick. My face felt hot, and I thought the egg was going to be coming right back up at twice the speed.

I felt myself gag. I swallowed again, and this time the little egg, with the help of some fluids that I didn't know I could produce, found a way to slide a little further down to where it wouldn't compel an upheaval. I took a breath, smiled. "Wow, delicious," I managed to say, wiping sweat from my brow.

King was laughing as much as he could without attracting attention. "Are you sure? You look like you swallowed it twice."

I was starting to feel better now, though there was a sour taste in my mouth and beads of sweat running down my back. "I think I did, but I did it anyway."

King nodded. "I didn't think you would."

Aside from the waxy, acidic taste of stomach fluid, the egg left a wonderful taste in my mouth. The gentle burn of black pepper, the sting of salt, and that glorious warmth of the fat. Mmmm, good! "That was good," I managed to add. I could still feel my chest beating as it struggled with the first food that I could remember eating since before I went to school.

King took a sip of his coffee. He held the cup up for me.

"No." I shook my head. "I'm not sure I could handle that. But thank you."

"So," King started, "I know you didn't come here to eat an egg."

I straightened. "Right, thanks for reminding me. I wanted to talk to you about my wife."

"Yes," King added, keeping something back.

"I'd like to meet her," I blurted.

King wrinkled his brow and held the cup up as if he was going to take another sip. "Why do you think I can arrange that?"

"You are in charge of the concierge," I stated flatly. "Maybe you could make her meet me somewhere."

King put down his coffee and rubbed his head. "Are you talking online?"

"Online, offline, I don't care."

King grimaced. "Yeah, that's part of the problem. If I introduce her to you, she might—" He stopped altogether, looked at his plate, and poked some pepper flakes with the tip of his knife. "It might not go well for her."

I sat for a while. It didn't seem right. I asked, "Why not? I mean, we were, are, married."

King sat back and took in a breath. "I'm not sure how to put this, but your wife, she almost certainly thinks you are dead, and for me to reach into her life and interrupt it and tell her you are here, um, it's not recommended."

I crinkled my brow.

"It could break her." King pointed to his head and made a circular motion with his finger.

"Hmm." I felt awful. I had no idea how much I wanted to meet and talk with her, but what King was saying meant that I'd never be able to talk to her again. "Can I at least see her?"

King sighed. "I don't see how?"

"I mean just see. The privacy settings won't let me see her online unless it's just random or she lets me."

"I feel for you," King said, "I just don't see how."

I left King in a reflective mood. He was clearly thinking about what I asked, but the rest of the conversation resulted in short answers. He was clearly someplace else. It is a little frustrating talking to someone who wasn't there. I thanked him for the egg and headed off to work. He nodded at me and told me he would give it some thought, which made me smile. I wasn't sure he even knew I had left. Slowly he pushed at his food as I walked away, gave Samuel control, went to work.

What can I tell you about the workday? It's called work for a reason, it's stuff you would never do otherwise. Samuel took me back to the factory where I found a man was waiting to place me in the front of the line. I was led through the factory to a stool beside a big machine with a round turret. The way this worked: a belt would feed me little squares of steel. I would grab one, push it into the machine using another metal jig until it settled against two edges. I would push a button on the machine with my other hand, and bang! A tremendous crash, like the sky falling down, vibrated through me, causing my teeth to rattle and my ears to ring. The concussion from the machinery shook me on my seat down to the base of my spine. The whole machine rocked and shuttered as each plate was smashed.

Rollers were supposed to take the trashy bits away and carry the smashed part off the machine to where another staff packed it on a pallet so it could roll over to some other part of the factory. But the rollers didn't always work, and the machine didn't always tear the metal the right way, and from time to time, I would have to reach in and grab whatever was stuck with a long metal rod that had a magnet welded to the end. The magnet stuck to many parts of the machine, but I had to get the mangled metal out, quickly, before the next piece of metal was propelled my way.

In all, a boring job. Easy, too. Normally, the machine worked without a problem, but the machine got jammed often enough that I always seemed to be sticking my hands into it. Wham! Wham! Wham! The machine beat out a steady rhythm as I continued to feed it all day long. A very boring job punctuated by the opportunity to get yourself maimed. If I should be lucky enough to make it out of here with both arms, I'd sure feel better about not having sore fingers.

When the buzzer went, I watched all the machines slow and stop. The staff slowed down in time with their machines and men dispersed themselves through the plant to grab the staff and lead them back to the front of the factory. A minute later, Samuel alerted me, "George, it's time for you to go home, congratulations on another excellent day at work." Funny, either Samuel was late, or the factory was early. I didn't think clocks could get out of sync.

19

MEETING BELINDA

"Good morning," came Samuel's cheerful voice.

"How are you Samuel?" I asked as I opened my eyes and looked up at the perfectly smooth ceiling, chandelier: shiny gold, sparkly crystal, where a reflection of some morning light splashed across the ceiling.

"I am fine and ready to help you with your day," he responded, far more cheerfully than I would have liked. Something about the enthusiasm in his voice made me not care.

"Let me guess, it's time to go to work?"

"Right you are."

"You can drive," I told him. I don't think he waited; I think I was moving before I told him I was going to let him move me.

This morning was no different than any other morning. I had the option to send messages, go play games, slots, maybe watch a movie. I think I had seen all the movies, and I think I had seen every possible poker hand. What is the point? I just sat, feeling glum, watching as Samuel made me have a shower and dressed me in the uniform that was appropriate for the work I was going to do.

Uniforms are normally big and bulky. If they didn't get your size right, it didn't matter. You were dressed, and you would be able to work. Who cared, anyway? Mine was bulky today, and I watched as my thin little legs disappeared down the pant legs and Samuel dressed me. He stood me up, put my arm into the bulky sleeves and zipped up the front. I was ready to go; it was too much effort to let out a cheer.

I was marched down the hall, jammed into a lift, marched back out to join the queue for the cars. I got into a car and felt my stomach lurch. I went back to staring at Samuel. "Can I see a current event show?" I asked.

"Current events?" Samuel asked, "Don't you mean the news?"

"Okay, the news." The news was always boring, but I was hoping it would make the ride a little less nauseating.

In a moment, Samuel dissolved, and I was sitting front row in the news set. There was a super-hot model and an older man with just a touch of white on the side of his head sitting behind a round desk. They smiled and spoke to me, "Hi there, welcome to the real news show. The only news you need." I smiled back and they seemed to like that, though I wasn't sure they had seen me.

There was an article on fire safety and a dog that had been credited with putting out a forest fire by stopping it before it started. That was interesting, and the dog was cute. Another story was about lemonade sales in Kansas and about two young children who had built an old-time lemonade stand off interstate 70, with the help of three of their parents' staff. I felt myself transported there and I could feel the immediate desire to have a lemonade. The staff were standing in the background and the little kids were talking about how hard they worked to get this idea up and running. I didn't believe them. The staff did it! But I did want some lemonade, really badly.

I was glad when that story was over, and we went back to a story about trees and woodpeckers. Apparently, the American woodpecker—who pollinated the great redwoods of the golden west—was making a big comeback, and in the future, we might see a return of the great towering redwood trees of California and Oregon. "Wow," the female anchor said, "that would be neat."

Samuel interrupted. "I'm sorry to interrupt, we have arrived at Jazmin's cafe."

I was relieved. "Jazmin's cafe?"

"Yes, King would like to see you. He asked that I not tell you. It is to be a surprise."

"Really? That's so cool."

"Let me guide you in, then you can take control."

146

Today King was sitting in a booth, but he wasn't alo c   ne. There was staff with him. King had ordered and was eating breakfast, the staff sitting beside him and fully engaged as if neither of them knew anything about each other. King smiled as I disengaged. "How are you?" he asked.

I didn't know what to do. Sit down, stand up, go get coffee.

"Sit down." King motioned to the other side of his booth. "Make yourself comfortable," he ordered, but in a kind way. "How did the egg go, yesterday? Any aftereffects?"

I shuffled into the booth. My uniform seemed to stick to the seat and spin around me, so it was clutching at me in an uncomfortable manner. "I'd forgot about it," I said, which was true, "I guess that means it went down well."

King was smiling. "If you say so. Are you ready to try something else?" There was a big side plate of bacon, almost as much as I would eat if I was online. "Bacon?"

Cautiously, I reached forward, not sure why I didn't feel like I should move too quickly. "Thank you." I took a piece, held it up, examined it and looked for a place to put it.

"Here." King held out a small metal box with paper napkins sticking out of it. "Use these."

I took a napkin, smoothed it out and put the bacon on top of it. "It's not hot?"

King smiled. "And that is one of life's little disappointments. Bacon never seems to be hot, but this is the cost of eating out, cold bacon. But," he continued, "try it, I think you will like it anyway. It must be good if people eat it, even when it's cold."

I love salt and fat. They taste so good. Everything should taste like salt and fat, and online it does. I wondered how close to bacon they had actually got the offline version of bacon to taste. I examined the striping. Online, it seemed simpler, as if drawn to look like bacon. Offline, I could see through some of the white parts. I tried to snap it, and unlike bacon online that snapped and crunched immediately, this had a bit of give to it before it cracked and tore apart. "It's not as crispy as I'd imagined."

King raised his eyebrows and lifted his coffee cup to his mouth. The staff beside him sat still, not looking at me, milky eyes glazed over, focused on nothing. "Taste it, tell me what you think?" King added.

I sniffed it. The scent of goodness was strong. I immediately felt my stomach rumble and my mouth wet. Cautiously, I took a bite and nibbled it. There was a crunch, but not the exaggerated like crunch you get online. It was a gentle crunch, my mouth was filled with aroma, smoky, salty and fatty. The bacon seemed to hover in my mouth like something blessed that I had, perchance, been allowed to taste.

I swallowed. It took two swallows to get all the gorgeous little bits to go down. I immediately felt better, my head felt warm and all was good in the world. "That is tremendous."

King smiled nodded and carefully placed his coffee cup back on the saucer. "I'm glad you like it."

"Thank you," I said, "but why?"

"Why what?" King wrinkled his brow at me.

"Why did you do that? I mean, we have bacon online."

King shrugged. "I'm not sure, I just wanted to see how you would react." Then he volunteered, "Strictly speaking, you are not supposed to be able to eat, or at least that's what everyone says."

"Oh." I wasn't feeling good about this, like I'd done something wrong. "Why is that?"

King looked a little surprised at this question. "Because you don't eat. How can you eat if you don't eat?"

"I don't know."

"Maybe that's why I did it. Just to see if you could?"

I didn't like the idea of being a test thing for King. "Well, I did." I felt a little put out. "Now what?"

King smiled and shrugged. "I don't know." He took another bite of his eggs and I had another bite of my bacon. I probably couldn't eat much, but it was still heavenly.

Finally, I had to ask, "Who is this?" I pointed at the staff sitting idly beside him.

King's smile dropped off his face and he became super serious. "I want you to take this calmly," he said. "Promise me whatever I say, you are not going to make a big thing out of it or raise your voice, storm off or do something silly."

I blinked at King.

"You have to take this in stride, like the bacon. You did that well. Everything was quiet and good. Nothing weird?"

"Nothing weird?"

"Yes, nothing weird."

"Okay, nothing weird. Who is it?"

King sighed. "I wanted to make sure you understood that I couldn't fix it. You know—you wanting to talk to your wife, and all that. It just isn't possible."

"Yeah, I know, you told me. No, are you telling me?"

"Yes." King nodded. "This is your wife."

"Belinda?"

King shrugged. "I don't know what it calls itself, but this is." King had to look down at his mobile, poke the screen, scroll through. "This is, E098FH836814, and that is your wife."

I sat there like a boulder had been dropped on me. I looked at the staff sitting there, so engaged that it was almost lifeless. It was short, pudgy, folds had been forming around her chin, her eyes were blue gray under the thick milky haze of engagement. Her wispy hair was brown not black, and there was a good bit of gray in it. Not straight, not shiny like silk. Her skin was white, but not healthy, just pasty. "That, is my wife?"

King was making shushing sounds and motioning with his hands that I should keep the volume down.

"This doesn't look anything like her?" I managed a much quieter tone.

King rolled his eyes. "I think you can make yourself look like whatever you want, that's what I'm told, online."

I nodded. "Yeah, I guess that's true, but I always thought you had to start with something that looked sort of like you."

King shrugged again. "I'm sorry. I didn't want you to think that your wife had been taken away from you, though I guess it was. I went home last night and thought about how it would be if I lost my wife, and I thought you deserved to know."

I couldn't take my eyes off of her. There was no way in a million years that I would have picked her. She had moles on her face; I didn't like moles. Of course, online she was tall, porcelain skin, Japanese. This was totally different—she was short, pallid white skin with pink blotches, dull blue eyes tired and old, certainly not Asian. How could it be so different online? Her eyebrows needed a trim, her hair, thin and brittle—like every staff—and her nails looked like someone had trimmed them with a hacksaw, not the beautiful candy red talons she showed me online. "This is way different to what she looked like online," I said, shaking my head. "Are you sure she's my wife?"

"There is no doubt," King replied. "You know I don't know what anything looks like online?"

"You don't?"

"No, how would I?"

"I don't know, you know everything."

King smiled and didn't say anything.

"Can I talk to her?"

King cocked his head to one side, "Talk?"

"Yes," I explained, "can I talk to her?"

"But it won't know who you are?"

"So?"

"If you talk to it, it's just going to, well, I don't know, but even if it knows who you are, it's just going to think you are crazy or mean, it could get ugly."

I thought about it for a moment. Even the online version of her didn't react well to surprises. "Okay, I won't say anything about that."

Now it was King's turn to think. "I don't know, this might be a bad idea."

"Aw, come on, please,"

"You promise to keep things cool?"

"Cool and quiet," I promised.

"Okay," King reached for his mobile. King opened an application and selected a line from a long list. A dialog box opened, and he started to type something. It took a long time. A button popped up, and it was all red: "Force Offline." King stopped before he pressed the button. "It's not often I have to do this. Usually it's done in a clinic where they can be restrained. It may react strangely, don't let it hurt its or start running somewhere."

I nodded. "But I'm offline and I don't feel like running."

"Yeah, but you've been different since you had your melon cracked," King said as he looked at her again, sizing her up in case he had to grab her. "You, we, have to keep it from scratching, punching or swatting itself; scratching is more common for some reason." King completed his evaluation. "Okay, this could take a second. I think it must feel like how a blender feels when the plug is pulled." He pressed the button.

Almost instantly, there was a change in her face. It went from being slack to one of tightness, almost pain. The milkiness of her eyes started to clear. King and I watched; the look of pain went as quickly as it had come. Her eyes started to flutter as they turned an actual shade of gray blue. Those eyes came into focus, and she looked right at me, I smiled, she blinked. She looked at King, who was studying her intently. She reached up and tapped the side of her head. "Hey," she said, her voice was groggy as if she had been asleep for a long time. "Hey," she tried again, her throat was clearing. "I can't get online, what's going on?" She was starting to look panicked and starting to swat at the side of her head. I found myself reaching out to grab her hand so that she couldn't hurt herself. "Stop!" she tried to shout, but it didn't come out right. The glare she gave me was unmistakable: fear mixed with anger.

"Shhh, shh, shh." King motioned with his hands and continued to talk in a soft quiet and calm tone. "I'm sorry, we needed to speak with you. Hello, how are you?" He asked before she could argue or protest.

"I want to go back online," she said. It was almost a bleat. "I want to go back online."

King had turned to face her as well as he could. "Shh, shh, shh, it's okay, just a moment."

She tried to get up, but she didn't know how to get out of the booth, and she slipped and fell on the floor.

"Ow, ow, ow," she complained and went back to tapping her right temple.

"Shh, shh, shh." King continued to try to be soothing as he tried to shuffle out of the booth, some people had turned to look, and when I looked, they looked back to their tables but continued to shake their heads. "Let us help you up."

"Ooh, my bum, I think I broke it," she complained. This was sad. She was like a child in a grownup body, "owie."

King had made it out, and he motioned to me to get up myself, I had been too busy hanging my mouth open to do anything else but stare. I got up and grabbed the other side of her, preventing her from smacking the side of her head again. Together we managed to get her up and slide her back onto the bench. I sat down and King motioned for me to shove over.

"Okay, I'm sorry for having shocked you," King said, once he had managed to get seated. She was no longer compulsively tapping her right temple. "We wanted to speak to you. Is that okay?"

"I don't know." I think she was going to pout. "I'm supposed to be at work."

"Don't worry about that now," King said. "Let's just have a little conversation."

She looked suspicious. "Why?"

"Well," King started, and I could see he was just making it up. "You see, you have friends here." He paused for a moment, thought of something better to say. "I've heard that you are really good at work."

"I am," she seemed to beam.

"Yes, I wanted to meet you because you've been so good at work and I wanted to give you this award," he said.

"An award! That's awesome!"

"Yes." King looked around, unwrapped a napkin took out the cutlery and handed her a fork. "I wanted to present you with this pure silver fork, which is symbolic of all the good work you have done. A fork is a tool, we use it to get things done."

Her mouth opened and she almost bounced on her seat. "Pure silver!"

"Yes," King smiled. "Pure silver and it's all yours." He extended the fork to her and she grabbed it from his hand. She studied it intently. Under his breath, while Belinda was occupied with the fork. "You see what I mean?"

I nodded.

"Isn't that pretty silver?"

"Yes! Yes, it is." She turned it over and over and tried to see herself reflected in it. It was an old fork, beaten up and looked like it been bitten by a thousand sets of dentures.

Again, King whispered to me. "Have you seen enough?"

I nodded. He opened his mobile again and pressed another button.

"This is wonderful!"

"Yes, and it's all yours," he told her.

"Wait till I tell everyone." She reached up and tapped her right temple and her face went slack and her eyes clouded. Her hands went limp, but she managed to cling to the fork.

King heaved a sigh of relief. "Take that fork away. I should have used the spoon; it might have hurt itself with the fork."

I took the "*silver*" fork away. "What was that?"

King smiled. He had made his point.

I ate some more bacon, and King dismissed Belinda. He had to do it by typing into his mobile, and, without a word, it got up and marched its way back through the kitchen. It was weird to watch someone walk around like that. It was completely oblivious to everything, being run by a computer-generated assistant. I felt a little unwell. I didn't want to talk to that thing, and now I wondered why King wanted to talk to me. I chewed on some more bacon.

"What do I do now?" I asked.

King looked a little confused, "You mean now? Or now that you have seen that whatever happened, it can't be undone."

"I don't know, I wasn't ready for that."

"Would you have ever been?"

I shrugged, "No."

"I guess," King said thoughtfully, "you go to work, and we try to get on with our lives."

"About that," I stopped him, "working in the factory is boring, and scary at the same time."

King shrugged. He seemed to be thinking of something. "Yes, I suppose it is. But work is work."

"I'd like to do something different."

"Something different?" King seemed really surprised. He said it like 'something' and 'different' were two words that should not be together.

"Yes," I continued. "The factory is boring, scary and I ache when I get home."

King straightened. "Okay." He rolled his eyes up and to my left. "I'll see what I can do, just be patient."

"Patient?"

King smiled. "Seriously?"

"Seriously what?"

"You don't know what patient means?"

I shrugged.

"No problem," he added. Now he looked pleasant and kind. "Just give me some time, sometimes things take a while to arrange."

20

THE CHOPPER

Today I found myself working in something they called a shear gang. It was four staff who work a big uninteresting machine that slices steel. You might have thought that all this stuff we use comes made to order. However, I was beginning to understand that little of what was made to order actually comes that way; someone, or something has to make it that way. Today our job was to take flat sheets of steel and cut them into thin strips so they could be loaded up onto a pallet and driven someplace else in the factory and turned into something else.

Two of us were to stand behind the machine and pick up the parts as they fell. One of those two would feed large sheets of steel onto the shear, and I was one of the two staff who would center it and start chopping it into little thin shards of steel.

The machine itself is large and wide with a flat portion where the steel can be laid and pushed up against the backstop. When you step on the pedal the whole machine shutters, the steel bulges and pulls up against you and there is a crash like thunder as the sky falls from heaven above. The steel slams back onto the metal table and a thin slice tinkles to the floor behind the shear. In itself, the shear is a fairly simple machine. You have to set the backstop, hold the metal square before you activate it. A giant blade smashes through the steel and rips a strip off the sheet of metal by tearing it against the bottom blade.

It's all quick. My job was to square the steel and one of us would hit the foot pedal when the steel was square, causing the shear to drop and the steel to slice. In all, it sounded like a machine gun going off as we pushed the steel in toward, first to the handguard, and then right up to the edge of the slicing blade.

This was the worst of the jobs for me to watch myself doing. I wished I had not looked. I wished that I'd let Samuel distract me with some card game or slots or maybe a memory game for some virtual dollar prizes. But I didn't. I watched as they showed me what to do. As the machine went bang, bang, bang, I was to push the steel ever further into it. Always closer and closer to the slicing blade. And I was to stop just before my fingers were crushed by the guard or sliced off by the blade.

Going online didn't work. I could still feel the cold metal, my gloves damp with slippery grease, grit on my fingers, as I pushed against the thin edge of the steel. I was pushing hard, the sheet had to be square, and the it was very thin. There wasn't a lot to hold onto. I felt myself lean forward. I was sure that I was going to be disturbed from my game by the sharp tang of having a finger removed. I had to watch—couldn't concentrate on anything else—and with each sheet finished I heaved a sigh of relief. With each new sheet, I felt fresh waves of fear as I watched my hands approach the slicing blade. The last couple of slices, when the blade and the guard getting close to my hands and there was no way I could pull them away. I was at work, and all I could do was watch.

Sickening. Each time I would lean into the machine, I could imagine the next strike would be on me. Bang, bang, bang, bang... crunch? Nope not this time, reload. Another sheet: bang, bang, bang.

And so it went, on and on, through a whole stack of sheet metal. One other staff and I squaring the metal. Someone, I think it was me, tapping out the foot pedal to bring down the blade, and two other staff picking up the pieces and feeding more metal to the loading plate of the shear. Just before we ran out of steel, a forklift appeared with another pallet of steel for us. This never stopped. I kept watching my hands, and every time I would get them back, with all the fingers, I was relieved.

I imagined it would be a sickening crunch, but it wasn't. The shear slid through the steel just as easily as it always did. The loud crash was as loud as any other crash. I didn't feel a thing. But the other staff straightened up, held up both hands, the ends of three fingers were missing on both hands. Something had gone wrong, the steel hadn't sat right, had missed the backstop, and the blade had come down. The staff seemed to look at me, gazing in my direction, holding up both hands, stubs of fingers extended as if I was supposed to count them. For a moment there was nothing, just a clean-cut.

Then blood started pumping out. Lights and sirens started going off, and the men who ran the factory came over with dirty towels and oily rags to staunch the blood that oozed out through the stubby finger holes.

Through luck or providence, I managed to not to have any accidents. The staff was taken away and quickly replaced, and we continued to do things just the same way we had been doing them all morning. At the end of the day, I reached out to King. "I need to get out of here. I just watched someone cut off their fingers," was all I said in my message.

21

EXCITING RETAIL OPPORTUNITY

"Good morning George, rise and shine, time to get up."

In the moment before I opened my eyes, I thought to myself that this was going to be a good day. I had sent King a message, and I knew he wouldn't let me down. I was looking forward to seeing him. My eye snapped opened and I smiled at Samuel. "Good morning Samuel, yes, let's go." And before I knew it, the hotel had dissolved away, and Samuel was getting me out of my chair and into the shower. It was going to be a good day.

Cheerfully, I let Samuel dress me, walk me down the hallway, pack me into an elevator, and shoot me up to the carport. I happily let him put me in the queue, and stuff me into one of those little vomit capsules and off we went, right turn, right turn and turn to the right until we got to where we were going. Everything was going to be all right because I knew precisely where I was going: to see King. Maybe I could try something new, perhaps orange juice or maybe some potatoes.

Imagine my surprise when I arrived not at the restaurant but at a strange carport that I'd not seen before. It was the largest I had ever seen, with two entrances, cars streaming in. The motion of the people gave the feeling of waves and water flowing everywhere. At first I couldn't tell where I was going. Everywhere I turned, I seemed to be face-first into staff headed in the other direction.

As it turns out, we took a backway in. I had to let Samuel lead, and boy, did we ever walk up the stairs, flight after flight. I was either going to work somewhere high in the sky, or the carport was buried far below the ground.

Finally, we pushed open a door. I found myself in a room full, from floor to ceiling, with boxes. There were shoes everywhere! I was disappointed, it wasn't the cafe, and I didn't see how this would be where King would meet me? But at least it wasn't the factory. I'd managed to escape with all my fingers.

A man walked into the back room. He looked at me and sighed. He approached me and looked at my overalls. I watched him inspect them, sigh again and head off to a little desk behind which was a number of red and white vests. He took one off a hanger, looked at the tag inside, held it up as if measuring me with it and proceeded to approach me and fit me with the vest.

Once he had put the vest on and made sure it was sitting the right way, he addressed me, "Do you know how to sell shoes?"

Much to my surprise, I answered, "Yes I have been uploaded with retail sales 10042 and the shoe sales module seven has been added as a compliment," he seemed to know what that meant.

The man nodded, held up a shoe. It was a reddish-brown; looked like it might even be leather or something like that. He held out the shoe to me. "Get me a size ten in black."

"Yes sir," I heard myself say, "may I have the shoe for a moment?" I saw myself reach out and take the shoe from him. I turned it over and looked at the bottom of the shoe. There was a little white tag, I glanced at it, but I didn't have time to read it myself. "You may have the shoe back, and I will check the stockroom. Please make yourself comfortable and wait here, I will return shortly." Again, I was amazed to hear myself say this stuff.

Handing back the shoe, I turned and headed to the shelves, my eyes breezing over the tags and labels. I found what I was looking for, reached over for a step ladder, which was attached to a runner around the storeroom, then slid it my way. I climbed, took down a box, opened it, saw there were two black shoes of the same style that I'd briefly seen before, and headed back to the man.

"Would you please be seated so we may try on your shoes?"

"No, just hand me the box," the man said.

"Certainly sir, it would be my pleasure." I handed him the box. He opened it and looked at the shoes. "Size 11," he said, peering inside of one of the shoes. He looked at the box. "But the box says size 10, so you're good. The box is wrong, but you were right." The man put the shoes back on the corner of the desk. "Follow me," and he led me out of the backroom into the store.

About twenty feet from the front of the store, he stopped. "You stand here when you are not serving customers." He straightened me up, so that I was facing the door. "Smile, and if anyone enters the store, please serve them." I felt myself smile. It wasn't comfortable, but it wasn't cutting steel.

I stood there, thinking how lucky I was. This was a much better job, putting shoes on people's feet. No problem, is there anything that could be easier? An idea occurred to me; I probably didn't need Samuel to guide me. I maximized Samuel.

"What can I do for you? Would you like to play a game or go see a show?" he asked as he came to full life, and the world faded away into blue pixels.

"Hey Samuel," I started, not sure how to go about this, "about this work..."

"Yes," Samuel answered, "what would you like to know?"

"It's easy, right?"

Samuel shrugged. "I don't know what *easy* is supposed to mean in the context of work. Work is work."

"Okay, but the things you are having me do, they are simple, right?"

"If you are asking if they are physically demanding, they are certainly less demanding than the factory."

"Oh, no, not what I mean, I mean I could do them without you?"

Samuel blinked and paused. I got back one of those detailed answers I liked. "While it is within the realm of possibility for anyone to do anything that is considered work, no, it is not possible for you to do this yourself. You are at work, and I must ensure that the duties thus assigned are executed within the parameters of the programming."

Now I had to think. I started slowly trying to untangle the logic. "Because you know what I have to do. I am not allowed to try to do the job without you?"

Samuel smiled agreeably. "That is a correct statement."

"That doesn't seem right," I countered. "How come I can turn you off sometimes, but I wouldn't be able to now?"

Again, Samuel smiled agreeably. "Because we are at work. You can't deactivate me at work. Sorry, I have to ensure the tasks are completed within design parameters."

"Oh." I felt ripped off. This looked like a job I could do myself. "Well that sucks."

"I'm sorry you feel that way. Is there something else I can do for you? Perhaps a show or some gambling?"

"No, just minimize."

When the world came back into view and Samuel slid up and to the right corner of my vision. I noticed that the man was busy setting another staff into position. I was looking ahead at the doors, which were still shut; but there were people walking around outside, strolling and peering into the store. The man finished with the other staff, shook his head, looked at me and let out an audible, "tsk." Then he turned on his heel and headed to the back of the store.

The thing about being immersed: even in mobile mode, you don't notice time. As I was standing there, I could feel the blood pooling in my feet. My bad foot was starting the throb numbly. But what was I to do? I suppose I could ask Samuel to shift my weight, but I don't think I'd ever asked Ernest to do that. I stood watching the people walk by. It was like watching fish swim behind glass. Sometimes they kept right on going, as if they didn't see you, and sometimes their eyes got stuck on something and they stopped to make faces and peer in at something. Usually they were alone, sometimes in pairs. They would drift by, or get stuck. But as time passed, a collection of them, seemingly attracted by something shiny or colorful, seemed to converge around the closed glass doors of our store. You know,

I could never remember a store being closed online. What a drag it must be to wait for a store to open. It's so nice to walk right in, be the only customer, and be served right away.

The man who had placed me marched between us and up to the door, where he turned a lock. The doors slid open and in came the small crowd that had been waiting outside. I heard my voice greeting people and felt myself start to move in reaction to the incoming throng.

I found myself doing rounds of the store, asking if I could help with something. I was getting tired of saying it and I wasn't even saying it. But I thought back to the wait staff at the café. That's what they did, after all. If you didn't want anything, they circled around until you did. I was in circle mode.

Finally, an old woman held up a pair of shoes. "Get me these," she ordered me.

"Yes ma'am," I said with nauseating obedience, "what size do you take?"

"I don't know," she snapped. She actually snapped back at me. "Just get me the shoes." She fired the shoe at me, and I quickly flipped it over to examine the bottom.

"Yes ma'am," I replied, though I really didn't want to. "Please make yourself comfortable and I will return shortly with your selection." I put the shoe down and I felt myself turn and march off to the stock room. It was sickening. I wanted to stop myself, but I couldn't.

I grabbed six boxes of shoes, carefully balanced them, and headed back onto the floor. Even though I didn't see where she sat, I found her immediately.

I put the stack of shoes down and bent down. The woman had not taken off her shoes. "May I remove your shoes, ma'am?" I asked.

"Duh," she replied.

Expertly, I unlaced the shoes and slid them off her foot. Despite the fact she was wearing shoes, she had no socks or coverings on. I could see all the corns on the sides of her feet, the plantar wart under her big toe, blue veins, saggy skin and bones that seemed to stick out at the most impossible angles.

"Ma'am, I am going to have to place a sanitary covering on your foot," I told her, "may I do that?"

"No, can't you clean them?" It sounded like a complaint, and definitely an order.

I wanted to say no, but I rose to my feet. "One moment." Much to my surprise, I returned from the back with a bottle of sanitizer and a bottle of foot cream. I knelt down and began to work at her feet with the sanitizing gel. The smell was strong and went up my nose. I felt dizzy, though my hands didn't stop their work: first her left foot, then I reached for her right.

"Ow!" she yelled, pulling her foot away and kicking me in the forehead with her cleaned foot. "Be careful, you truck driver," she bawled, "my foot hurts."

"I see ma'am," I replied. I saw myself reach for her other foot again, this time moving more slowly.

Once I had her feet cleaned, I reached for that funny looking device to measure her feet. How I knew how to use it? Not sure, but I did.

"What are you doing?"

"I am going to measure your foot, ma'am," I replied with complete calmness.

"Don't do that, just try on a shoe," she ordered.

I must have had her foot on the device long enough to have caught the measurement, as my hands expertly reached for the third from the bottom of the six boxes. Before I knew it, the shoe was out of the box, laced, and on her foot. "There ma'am, how does that feel?"

The truth was, it fit well, and so did the other one. But the amount of complaining was impressive. She found other things to complain about, and she made me try them on in a different color in case they fit differently. All of this I did cheerfully and with a smile—at least when I caught glimpses of myself in various mirrors throughout the store. I was always smiling.

In the end, the first pair of shoes we tried on was the one that fit. When I went to the cash register to ring them in, she asked to see a real person.

"The manager, I will summon the manager immediately, one moment please." And I turned and headed into the back room.

The manager didn't say anything to me when I announced that a patron wished to see him. He simply sighed, and his shoulders sank a little bit more. We headed back out to the floor.

"Hello," he addressed the lady, "I'm the manager, what can I do for you?"

I stood there staring at the two of them.

"It's about these shoes," she started, "can you give me a discount? I think they should be only half price. I thought I saw an advertisement that said I could order them for half this price."

The manager disagreed, though the lady kept raising her voice and he kept lowering his. In the end, she picked up the box and slammed it back down on the counter and stormed out of the store, exclaiming, "This will be the last time I come to this store."

The manager sighed, I heard him say under his breath, "I should only be so lucky," as he turned to the backroom. He stopped, looked at me and I felt myself smiling even wider. "You. Go back to your station," he said, and I felt myself march back to the spot where he had placed me at the beginning of the day. And that is the story of my first day as a shoe sales staff.

This line of work is not physically demanding, and, compared to factory work, there is far less chance of an injury which would also be far less severe. For a while I didn't say anything to King about it. What this line of work does is make you feel humiliated. No wonder no one wanted to do it, and it got assigned off to staff. And, if I thought about it, just like the wait staff at the cafe, where they got grabbed in inappropriate places, this happened to me, too: people seated would reach out and grab anything that happens to pass by. Just because someone else is driving doesn't mean it doesn't hurt when you grab the soft, fleshy bits. But the footwear business, now that's work I could handle—except for the nauseatingly mangled feet and the occasional smell of pee or other interesting odors.

However, one day, I had a particularly bad day. It started with a particularly particular customer. She was a younger woman, below the age that usually came into this store, and no matter what shoes I fitted her, for they were either too small or too big, even though I saw myself measure and heard myself tell her the shoe, as it was placed on their foot was the correct size. *The customer is always right!* I tried on the size larger and the size smaller and when I didn't have anything to try on, I tried on the size larger and the size smaller. Even though I was saying all the nice things I was programmed to say, this was wearing pretty thin. And after one particular set of shoes, I was told to take them off, and as I took the first shoe off— perhaps because she was frustrated with the whole procedure—she stood up and put her full weight on the back of my left-hand. I felt a bright burst of pain in the back of my hand, some of the bones seemed to slide and pop.

"Look," I heard the customer say to her friend, who was yawning and falling asleep in a chair on the other side of the store. "I stood on its hand."

"Oh, I am sorry," I heard myself say, and I wanted to be sick. My hand was cracked up, I wasn't sorry, and if I had been able to take control, I might have said something different.

This was not enough for me to want to get out of this job. Nor was the little boy who decided he wanted to smear his chewing gum onto my scalp. I was fitting his mother for shoes and she was holding him on her lap. I had suggested, as I was programmed to do, that it would be best if the little boy sat in his own chair. But mother knew best, and despite the fact he was flailing his feet around and he was rather big, she put him on her lap, and I had to manage to fit her shoes.

There was a moment, when she switched sides to present her other foot, that the boy lost his balance, fell forward and all I felt was sticky hands and something glop into my head.

"Oh no!" I heard the mother cry. A second later, I felt hands tugging at me. Whatever was in the boy's mouth had escaped and landed on me. But the hands were frantic, these two little hands trying to grab his sticky treat and shove it back into his mouth. The problem was it was already stuck to me. He gripped and he pulled and pulled, and I felt a layer of my mushy soft skin rip from my scalp.

Another explosion of crying, as the boy realized that whatever he was eating was full of bits of me. "Oh no!" I heard the mother cry again. "Look at what your staff has done."

The man who ran the store rushed over. Even though I was still on my hands and knees, I heard myself apologizing to the woman and asking if there was a*nything I could do to put the situation right?* The man reached down and grabbed me by my right arm, causing my full weight to fall on my busted-up hand. The pain was exquisite, red, sharp and cutting all the way down to my stomach where it made me sick, still I issued platitudes and offers of *how can I make it better?* We got me to my feet and the store manager pushed me into the back, where I stood, my hand throbbing and chewy goo slowly tracking its way down my head.

Finally, the noise out front died down and the man who ran the store came back to see me. He looked at me and sighed, led me over to a chair and pushed me into it. He disappeared into the store's tiny closet of a washroom and reappeared with a roll of paper towel. Actually, it was more like paper—it didn't absorb anything as he tried to clean the messy goo off my head. He muttered to himself. "This is disgusting. What do they feed these kids?", but never did he say anything to me.

When he decided he had done as much cleaning as he could, he disappeared again. I could hear him rummaging around, and he came back with a small baseball style hat. He plopped it on my head and tried to make it look like it fit. "Okay," he asked me, "Are you all right?"

No, I was not, my hand hurt just sitting here doing nothing and I still felt like I'd been gooped. I was definitely not all right. I felt my mouth open and I said, "Yes sir, I am fine. It would be my pleasure if I could go back to work now." *Nooo!* I thought.

This, in itself, was bad. Normally this would not have been a problem, but it was the combination of all three that made me send off my message to King. I was sent out onto the floor, and a pair of older women were ready to have footwear tried on. I graciously greeted them. "Oh my," I heard myself saying, "you both want the same style of shoes. Tell me what your sizes are, and I'll be back in a jiffy with something I know you will love."

The women told me, and I asked them if they could get comfortable while I got their sizes from the back. I did the best I could with only one hand. My left hand wasn't working correctly. I was having problems squeezing anything with it. I had to take the shoes down one box at a time, manage to pick them up and carry all the boxes at once with only one hand.

I knelt before one of the women and she didn't put her foot out. I had to crawl with one bad hand toward her. I lifted her foot to take her shoe off, and as I did, she let out a loud sharp fart into the chair that snapped off the vinyl. I dare say, I almost felt a draft. The smell was almost immediate, the scent of rotten eggs. I heard the two women laughing and talking. Oh lovely, that had been on purpose. What horrified me was that I said, "Excuse me, I'm sorry, looks like I've unsettled you. I apologize." I *apologized*. If it hadn't been for the horrible smell of burnt eggs, I'd have been sick for my own toadying.

I moved onto the next woman, not getting up off the floor. She was also sitting with her feet back under the chair. I reached for her foot, and as I lifted it, she let out a long soft fart that smelled creamy, whipped, as if someone dropped a loaf into a pot of boiling water. At the sound of the second fart, the two women burst into laughter and high fived each other.

"Samuel, please send a message to King, 'I'd like to get out of here.'"

22

REALLY? THAT'S ODD

My message was successful. I found myself at the café, waiting. I turned off Samuel, though I could still turn him off since I wasn't at work. I made my way in through the kitchen into the dining area.

"Good morning," King said. There was an egg and two pieces of bacon set across from King's breakfast. "How are you today?" King was smiling like he was pleased about something.

I sat down and I held up my hand. "I got stepped on."

King reached out and I gave him my hand. He gave it a squeeze, and I almost jumped through the roof. "You aren't going to work today," he told me. "I can feel something that isn't right."

I smiled, "What's this? My own breakfast?" I asked, motioning to the egg and bacon.

"I wanted to see if you could eat and keep it all down."

Still smiling, I said, "I'll try."

"I get the hand, but what's so bad about the shoe store?"

"Oh, that." I felt almost ashamed now that he'd acknowledged my hand. "It's humiliating."

"Humiliating?" King squinted at me, as if he wanted to know if that's what I meant to say.

"Yeah, the way that I get treated. I don't like it."

"Really?" King asked, "*you don't like it?*"

"No."

"That's odd," King continued thinking aloud, "you aren't supposed to care."

"Well I do."

"Okay."

I looked at the egg, cut it with my knife, stabbed it with the fork, and took a bite. It wasn't so hard to swallow.

"Okay," he said again. "Let's enjoy breakfast. Then you should go to the clinic to get that hand fixed."

"Okay," I replied, and broke out into a big smile.

"Welcome back, George," Samuel greeted me, after I left King sitting at his table. "I have something unfortunate to tell you."

"Oh, what is it?"

"It has been reported that you have been injured, and I am obliged to guide you to the nearest medical clinic, where you will receive an examination and treatment where required."

"Wow, that's great."

Samuel looked a little puzzled. "Actually, being injured is not great, and can be dangerous."

"No, I know," I tried to explain. "I think it is great that it is going to get looked after." I could feel myself getting into a car, the door sliding shut to seal me in for my trip to the clinic.

"Yes, this is true," Samuel seemed to muse. "Would you like to know the specifics?"

"Sure."

"You have an unspecified injury to your left-hand."

"Really?"

"Yes, it occurred at an unspecified time in an unspecified manner."

"That is helpful," I commented.

"Thank you." We were pulling into traffic.

Soon enough, the car was sliding back into the clinic. I was getting used to being there. When the door opened, it almost felt like home again. Two med-techs were waiting for me. Before I could get up, they grabbed me, flipped me around and landed me into a medichair. I had to squelch a moment of fear. Right, I thought to myself, they are just going to fix my hand. I was pushed up the ramp through the doors and into the dimly lit clinic, where I was parked in shadow between the sparse lighting. Facing a wall, I heard the med-techs walk away.

"Hey Samuel," I asked, summoning him from his minimized state. "What time is it?"

"Really?"

"Yes."

"9:05."

I thought about it for a moment. "You know, I don't know what that's supposed to mean. "I mean what time means in general."

Samuel shrugged. "Why do you think I asked, if you wanted to know? It's just a fact, nothing you can do with it."

"True, but now I know what time it is."

There was silence between us for a while. Was it better to stare at Samuel, or the wall? I suppose I could play cards.

"Hey," I interrupted the smiling contest. "Why are there twenty-four hours in the day?"

Samuel paused. "This is not a popular question," he added finally, "all I can see is that it is because it has always been."

"That doesn't seem like a good reason."

"No, but it's reason enough," Samuel drew the conclusion.

We sat there for a while, smiling.

"I suppose if I asked about the sixty-minute thing?"

"Same," he answered. "It is because it always has been. The word they use is arbitrary."

"Arbitrary?"

"Yes, something that just is because it is."

I thought about it for a while. "I'm not sure I like this arbitrary thing."

"You don't have to, it's arbitrary."

"Hmmm."

We sat in silence some more.

I was about to say something when the chair moved. "Whoa, hey Samuel, what time is it?"

"Again?"

"Yes."

"9:16."

"I found something to do with it." I was pleased with myself. "I can tell how long something took, eleven minutes."

"Ten minutes, fifty-six seconds," Samuel tried to correct, but he simply sounded pouty.

We went off to a big room where they put my hand on a table that had a big cross on it. There was a light that they focused from above, and the med-techs stepped out of the room. There was a buzz and a clunk, and the med-techs came back. I was wheeled out of the room and made to sit in the hallway, again, facing the wall. I sighed—something I had picked up from the manager of the shoe store.

There are times and places where you feel like you have been abandoned by everyone. I suppose that's why, unless you just turn off altogether, the concierge is always there somewhere, to keep you from getting lonely. But staring at this wall, a second time, I felt like I was buried under the earth in some great bunker with the weight of the world above me, and no one was coming to find me, and no one was looking for me. Well, I had the concierge, but I didn't like him, he wasn't Ernest, and he smiled too much—even though I knew it was the same amount of smiling that Ernest must have done. It didn't irk me when it was Ernest doing the smiling. This concierge seemed, somehow, less trustworthy. Sitting there was better than staring at Samuel, but I felt small, tiny, insignificant.

"Hello," I heard from my right. I turned my head as far as I could. It was King. He was being led by a med-tech. "How are you doing?"

I smiled. "You know, I don't know."

"Yeah, just messing with you," King replied. "Guess what? You broke your hand." He pulled me around and crouched a bit, so that we could look at each other on the same level.

I looked at it. It didn't look obviously broken, but it sure hurt.

"It's a hairline fracture," King added. "I mean, it's not dislocated. You don't have to have it set, just, it's going to hurt for a while and you should try to not move it because it'll only get worse."

"When did you become a med-tech?" I asked him.

King didn't like that. He stood up and took a step back, looked around. He realized I hadn't meant whatever it meant to him. He smiled again. "No, that's not for me. But I did ask about you and they told me."

"They told you, and not me?"

King grimaced. "Yes, they do tend to do that?"

"Why?"

King rolled his eyes. "I don't know what to tell you."

I tried to shrug.

"You are staff, they don't tell staff about staff." His face brightened. "It's some sort of privacy law."

"Not to tell me about myself?"

"Yes, it's an insurance issue."

"Insurance?"

"Someone has to pay for your medical treatment."

"Who does that?" I asked quickly.

"The insurance company."

"Oh." My eyes dropped down and I looked at my left-hand. It was purple on top, but otherwise looked the same as I always remembered it. "Why do they pay for me?"

King stood back, measuring his response. It occurred to me that he would have made a terrible poker player. He didn't always say all that he knew, but whatever he did say was never a lie. "You and I are friends." It sounded so awkward. "I pay them to look after you." The second bit sounded like it was right.

"Oh, well then, thank you."

I didn't make it to work. I got sent home from the clinic at the end of the day with all the other staff. I had my hand wrapped and something put in my palm, so I didn't bend it in any sort of strange manner. But King left shortly after our conversation. Whatever it was, I was his responsibility and that was something I wasn't going to be able to get out of Samuel. I dared not ask. There were probably questions you could ask that would get you into all sorts of trouble, and the nature of King was likely one of them. I remember how long it took when I asked to send him a message the first time. It was like Samuel was checking to see what he should do, what he could and could not say. He'd said little, but I knew there was little that he was allowed to tell me. It was a long and boring day, staring at the cement wall.

Brian didn't go to work that day. It was weird: 418 was becoming more than staff. The conversations, the answers, the questions got better with each meeting. Each time, he was more surprised about what 418 might say or do.

He went home. He needed to think. He knew what the law said, that if 418 was brain-damaged, he should petition his insurance company to have him retired. The insurance company would relieve him of the liability of a malfunctioning staff and would provide payment for the remaining serviceable lifetime. He would be free from accountability.

But if something were to happen, what would that mean? He knew 418 wasn't just playing cards and watching videos. 418 was actually *thinking,* and that wasn't supposed to happen. There were the horror stories of criminals who had been assigned to staff, snapping and going nuts. But why would that happen? 418 was a natural, not at all threatening. But, if it did become threatening, Brian would just call the medics and get a psychological retirement and he would blame the insurance company for returning him a defective unit. Yes, that's what he would do, blame the insurance company. Hadn't they done their checks? What about due diligence? And didn't they say it could be rehabilitated, that it could go back to work?

That was precisely what they said, but Brian didn't feel good about it. Instead of sitting around his office and playing games on his computer, moving papers around his desk, he decided he would go home and see his wife. Maybe that would make him feel better. She would have wanted him to do the right thing. She was always big on that kind of nonsense, but the question was: what was the right thing?

The car dropped him off in front of his building. He sighed, climbed the stairs. At the top of the stairs he sighed again. Again, at the door to their apartment. He opened the door, Imelda came out from the living room, "What's wrong?" she asked. Something must be wrong, he was home.

"Oh, nothing."

"No, it's not nothing, you are a terrible liar."

"Okay, I just wanted to come home," Brian tried again.

Imelda looked at him, squinting through one eye. "You don't want to tell me. That's fine, sit down. But if something is wrong, you let me know."

"Okay, sweetie, I'm just glad to be home." It was good to stop thinking about how he was going to handle any of this. It was simply good to be home.

23

BACK AT THE CLINIC

The next morning, I was surprised when Samuel came to get me from my restful dreams. "George, wake up George, it's time for us to go to work."

"Mmm," I said. I had managed to flip myself over and bury my face in my pillow. "What do you mean? I have a bad hand."

"Nonsense," Samuel countered, "you are able enough to go to work, so off to work you are going to go. Do not worry, I will get you up, washed and dressed."

I felt myself getting up. It still felt like I was in a hotel room. There was a snap on the side of my head and the hotel evaporated, blue dots swirling in my vision, pushing out the blackness as Samuel came into view in mobile mode. He'd gotten me up without waiting for me to ask him. Not that it mattered. He'd have done it sooner or later. I was off to work.

I got dressed in light gear, the softest and lightest I'd ever had. "Hey Samuel, are you sure I have the right clothes on?" My hands kept moving, pulling the V-neck orange pullover over my head and fitting it to my body. These clothes did not fit two sizes too large. They were what I can only describe as comfortable. I even had matching orange pants that were not baggy. There was also a plastic badge or something that I put on my pocket, and I got to wear soft-soled shoes. They felt good, they didn't bite back at my feet. I felt them squeeze from side to side as I walked, but they supported my feet. "Samuel, I'm pretty sure something is wrong. I've got the wrong clothes."

"Impossible," Samuel answered, "those were the clothes that I found."

"For selling shoes?"

"Ah, you are not selling shoes today."

"I'm not."

"Nope."

The stupid matter-of-factness was getting a little tiring, "What am I doing today?"

"You are working at the clinic."

"Working?"

"Yes."

"Whew, I guess working at the clinic is better than being worked on at the clinic."

"Work is work," Samuel chimed, "all work is the same as all other work."

"No, it isn't. Do you believe that?"

Samuel sighed. "It's not what I believe, it's a fact. I can look it up."

I was puzzled. "Just because you can look it up makes it a fact?"

Samuel paused. "Yes, all facts can be verified. Because I can look it up, it must therefore be a fact."

"Good to know." And off we went. This was the lightest and most comfortable work gear that I had ever worn. Clearly not all work was the same. This was already much better.

The trip to the clinic was exactly like all the other trips I had made to the clinic, only I wasn't in emergent pain or complete discomfort. The car turned right and right again and with each turn I felt my stomach lurch. I was getting better at that, though nothing had changed. It didn't make me feel quite as sick, but by the time I got out my head was swimming and I needed a handrail to steady myself. However, Samuel was driving and, despite the feeling that I was going to go pitching over the handrail or I might go striding face-first into a wall, I kept moving until the world started to settle and my stomach decided to play nice once again.

I was marched out of the gray area into the white area. I did a quick circle around the waiting area, reached down and arranged the magazines just so they had the same space between each corner, and were arranged in a fan shape on the table in front of the chairs. There were some plastic flowers that I felt myself touch and arrange right back to exactly the way they had been before. I tried the door of the lavatory and found that it was all clean inside, like no one had ever been in there. I must have been satisfied with the state of everything. I looked around for marks, dust or grime, and found none. I made my way back to the desk behind which I would sit and stare out peacefully out with a smile on my face, waiting for someone to approach me.

I don't know how long I sat there. I forgot to ask Samuel, but it was boring, I didn't even move. While it was good for my foot and good for my hand not to be doing anything, it was rather tedious and tiring.

The boredom was broken when the door opened. Despite the pure white of everything inside, the opening of the door let in such sunlight that the pristine white walls of the clinic flashed quickly into gray. The blinding light was cut by a silhouette outline that I couldn't look at for the brightness of the sun behind it. As the figure walked out of the sun the doors slid shut behind it, returning the walls from gray to pristine white. The figure was King. He was grinning. I tried to say something, but nothing came out. I tried again. "Good morning, how may I be of assistance today?" which was not at all what I had thought I was about to say.

King smirked and laughed. "One moment," he said, reaching into his pocket for his mobile. He held it up and started poking at it.

"Please take your time. We are here to be of assistance to you. If you would be so kind as to tell me what is wrong I may better triage, or direct you to treatment." I couldn't believe I was saying any of this.

King poked at his mobile once again, looked up at me and smiled. "There. You can take a break."

I felt my face droop. It was sore from smiling so much. "Oh, thank you," I said, raising my hands to my cheeks. "That was weird. I wanted to say hello, and I said all that other nonsense."

King was vibrating with the laughter he was trying to hide. "No problem. You were at work. I just wanted to see how you were doing."

"Good, I guess, I mean this is great, it's easy and I don't have to either stand or use my hand."

"Yes, I have to apologize I didn't think of this." He was looking down just a bit. "I mean, I didn't think of this until last night."

"Oh, why last night?"

"I don't know. I got home, I saw my wife, and bang, it hit me. I could have you work here."

I felt a little annoyed with him. "Why didn't you do that before?"

King nodded as if it was a good question. "You are a big strong guy and this is normally a job for staff who happen to be female. Though does anyone see the difference between male and female when it comes to staff?"

I felt a little more annoyed. "I suppose not," I said, though I certainly knew if I was male or female. I remembered meeting Belinda. I suppose I could understand. Staff was staff. No one gave it much more thought than that.

"Well, anyway, it hit me. I have one staff here. I could swap out for you, and so I did."

"You sent them to the shoe store?"

"Nah, I sent them to do garbage. It pays better."

"Huh, I thought work was work and all work is the same."

"True, but some work pays better than others and some work is easier than others." King smiled. "I know you know that."

I did, though I felt dismayed at what Samuel had said. "Thank you for getting me this job, but it is boring."

"Well, heal up," King said. I felt like he wanted to rub the top of my head like I was a little child. "And I will see what I can do."

24

FINDING MEANING

This was the best job I had ever had. Despite the boredom, it was a rest.

I realized, because King had said as much, that King was in control of whatever job I had, or would have. Nothing wrong with that, but I wondered why it was no one had ever told me this. I suppose that since it didn't matter, I wasn't told. It was like that with Samuel. He couldn't tell you things he didn't know, because they didn't matter.

The job was good, but there were days where at the end of the day, I got up and my face hurt from twelve hours of non-stop smiling. The door to the street was never locked, but it was hardly ever opened. Days would go by when no one would come in, and it was tempting to just play cards. I have to confess I did; it was boring. Really, really boring, but it was a rest. My hand was getting better and my foot no longer hurt when I made normal walking motions.

One morning, I got up and Samuel dressed me and guided me to work. I found I was on the gray side of the building, being checked in. "Samuel, what is going on?"

Samuel only answered, "Your hand needs another checkup."

"Did I hurt it again?"

"I don't think so, this was scheduled as part of the original injury. It means someone wants to see if you are getting better."

"Oh, that's nice." And it was. I felt good about it.

After the examination, I was held for the rest of the day in the gray area. This was getting old, why they face me into the wall? Was it too much effort to turn my chair to face anything more interesting than the wall? It was all I could do to not go a little funny.

"Samuel, tell me, is there anything wrong with me?"

Samuel came into focus again. "It appears you have a fracture in your hand. However, it is the same fracture that was recorded three weeks ago."

"Why do I have to face the wall?"

Samuel paused. "It seems that this is the most efficient place to put you."

"Can I be moved somewhere else, or at least turned around?"

"I will enquire," Samuel said with the same stale sounding enthusiasm he always had. His answer was short, and followed shortly, "No. You have been placed in the optimal overall position, and there is no method for reconsidering your replacement unless the clinic requires this location for other patients."

"Oh." This did suck. We sat for a while. "Can I send a message to King?"

"Sure, what would you like to say?"

"Help this is boring, they have me staring at a wall."

"Is that the entire message?"

"Yes,"

"Would you like me to play it back?"

"No, just send it."

"Sent."

I was hoping that King would come and find me, and at least turn me so I could see something different than the uninteresting, unpainted concrete wall I'd been pointed at. I could hear stuff, guess what it was, but I could never confirm it. All I could see was gray. Unfortunately, even though my message was sent, and Samuel was even able to confirm it had been read, King did not arrive. I felt miserable. The only thing that was going to rescue me was time.

That night, when I got home, I was in a sour mood. I didn't want to eat, but I had to, so McDonald's it was. But the food did not have the same zing and savor it normally had. It was food, pure, simple, basic food. I was eating staples; the flavor somehow removed. I tried some travel. Every city I went to held no excitement. None of the lights, sounds and smells were interesting at all. Everything was just so intense and so real that I didn't think it was real anymore. It was as if I was still sitting in the clinic—staring at the wall—only I didn't see the wall. I saw something else that wasn't there.

It had never bothered me before: the fact that it wasn't real. Perhaps I had always known. None of it was anything other than what I perceived it to be. And now that I perceived it was a wall in front of my face, it wasn't any more than just a light show put on for my benefit, or lack thereof.

I went to the opium den, hoping to have a little peace from this rather dour realization, but the opium, while making me feel no pain, simply made me feel that there was nothing real. Perhaps I wasn't real. Perhaps I was just someone's imagination, something someone thought up, a thought come into being, which was the extent and the depth of my menial existence. It could be easily and quickly removed so no trace of me remained. I drew in more opium, hoping this thought would go away, but it was like I was drawing in myself and consuming my own being with each breath I took.

I knew that tomorrow would be another day. I would get woken up and Samuel, or whatever it was, would march me through the shower, put me into clothes and take me off to work where I would do whatever it was I was supposed to do. I inhaled deeply. If you did enough, darkness would come from all sides, inking out the light, muffling the sounds of traffic, Chinatown, and soft music they played in the background, slowly fading until you were a little island surrounded by inky black silence. If you reached out, the silence would envelop your hand, until you pulled it back, its smoky wisps holding onto your fingers for just a moment before receding back into the wall. If I drew in more breath, the wall would tighten, my island cell becoming smaller. The wall, the darkness, an old friend. If I drew in enough, it would close altogether. I could put my head down and just bathe in the dark smoky ink, safe, free from pain and sadness. I drew again, dipped my head and let the dark take me.

"Good morning, George." I was woken by the smiling face and voice of Samuel. "How are you today?"

"I'm fine, and what is good about it?"

"What's good about it is that you are fine, and we are off to work. Isn't that great?"

"Yes, that is amazing." Did I have any choice?

"Would you like to see a show, play a game or visit a casino? While I guide you to work?"

"Hmm, tempting." I tried not to sound sarcastic. Best not to be sour with the concierge. "But no thank you."

"Alright, off we go."

At least today I would be staring at the doors. They were opaque white glass doors that let the light flood in, but didn't let you see what was on the other side. Occasionally a shadow would cross the glass, leaving a dark impression in my vision, and then be gone. Other than that, not much moved in the reception area, and I sat there smiling, waiting for someone to arrive and see the nice smile I had been wearing all day and the day before.

As I contemplated a day of staring straight ahead, I wondered why it was I couldn't make the effects of opium last any longer than the night. I would have thought it would have taken some time to wear off, but Samuel was able to turn it off. And if that was true, and I had to sit there all day, smiling, waiting for people who may never come—hopefully there would be a real patient today—why couldn't I enjoy the effects of opium while I sat there?

Samuel interrupted my mope. "We are here. You likely want me to let you do the guiding now."

"I do, um, okay."

The world started to spin and re-assemble itself into Jazmin's cafe. "King," I said. With true surprise, he smiled broadly. "What am I doing here?"

"You called, I answered," he motioned, "have a seat." Today there were two eggs, bacon and toast; almost a regular breakfast! "I don't suggest you try to eat everything, just what you can."

"Wow, thanks." I slid into the booth in front of King.

"What is it? I didn't understand your message. I thought it would be better if I met you and just asked you."

"Oh." I studied the food in front of me. I could feel my mouth water and my stomach protest that it might have to do some work. "The message?"

"Yes, the message."

I felt myself get warm. "I, I don't remember exactly what I said."

King smiled. He looked at his mobile. "It says, 'Help, this is boring. They have me staring at a wall.'"

"Oh." I smiled, looking up from an egg I had been poking at. "Right." I felt a little odd. "Um, it's okay now."

"Oh, that's good."

"It's just that..." I was talking without measuring what I was saying. "It's just that, when I go to the clinic..."

King nodded. "Uh, huh," he tried to prompt me.

"After I'm done, they don't let me go."

"Huh?"

"Well they do, but only at shift change."

King sat back, his eyes rolled up and to my left. I could see him thinking about what I had said. "They keep you there till eight?"

"No, that's usually when I get there, they let me go at twenty hundred hours."

"Oh," King's face looked like he now understood. "That's a long time, I wonder why they do that?"

I shrugged. "I don't know, but that's not what I care about, it's how I have to wait."

King crinkled his brow.

"Once they are finished with me, they wheel me out into some hallway and point me at the wall."

"Really?"

"Yes, and what's worse, they leave me restrained. I can't move, can't get out of the chair, or even turn my head."

"Oh."

"Do you know how boring that is?"

"I can guess," confirmed King.

"I was hoping you would come. My concierge wouldn't help me."

"Why not?"

"He said I was in the optimal position already, with my face facing a wall."

King crinkled his nose. "I see." He took a sip of his coffee. "I'm sorry, I didn't understand." He stopped talking, just looked at me.

After a long pause I smiled. "What can I do about work? It's boring."

King smiled. "Your hand is getting better. I'm working on something so I can move you out."

"Oh, can I ask what?"

"You know, I think this is the first time a staff has ever asked what their work was going to be. That was never the intention."

"So?"

"Don't ask. I think you will be surprised."

"Hrumph." I tried to snap a piece of bacon to show that I was angry. It didn't work. King was having a chuckle. "No, I want to know now."

The breakfast was wonderful. This was even better than eating online. When you eat online, you feel like you ate. You taste everything, and you never feel full. It's just that the more you eat, the less it tastes. You always want to eat the best-tasting thing first, because after you have eaten for long enough, everything loses its flavor.

The food at the cafe was different. I felt it as I ate it, in my stomach. Not all the food tasted the same and not all of it made me feel the same. I started to feel heaviness as I ate, but the taste didn't go away. It's just that I didn't want it as much. But after I had finished eating, I could still feel it. It wasn't like someone had just turned off a light. It lasted. As I walked, I could feel it. It made me feel good, the salt, the fat, wonderful.

I found myself back at the clinic, sitting there like some fence post, waiting, but I was feeling good. And it was nice that King had not forgotten about me. He had heard my message, just didn't understand it. He'd done what he thought he should do. Somehow, I was okay with that.

25

A CAREER

I would love to say that something happened that day, or maybe even the next day. But it didn't, and that's why I'd love to say it had. As the days went on, the pain left my foot entirely and my hand became like it always was. I knew I had one more final trip to the clinic, so the day that I woke, and I made it to the wrong part of work, I was not disappointed at all.

Again, I was put in a restraining chair. Again, I was pushed around, my hand placed under the light. The med-techs left the room, returning after a series of clicks and a buzz. I was wheeled out and placed in a hallway with my face into the wall.

This particular wall was even worse than the wall I had stared at before, because I was in a dark area—one of the sparse lights had burnt out—and I couldn't see a thing! This did give my imagination a chance to come up with interesting things that could be happening to that wall, but really, how much interesting stuff could be happening on a wall in a dark cavernous building?

"Samuel." I summoned the concierge. "I'd like to send a message to King: 'Help, they have done it again. I'm at the clinic, staring at a wall. Could you please come and find me?'"

"Yes, George, would you like me to read back the message?"

"No, just send it." It was good to tell Samuel what to do without asking or getting his suggestions first. I quite liked this feeling.

"Okay, it's sent." I went back to staring at the wall.

A few minutes later, Samuel resized himself. "George you have a message from King, would you like me to read it?"

"Yes." Of course.

"Understood, I am on my way, sit tight."

I started to chuckle.

"What's so funny?"

"Nothing."

King appeared sometime later. I heard someone walking, not like how the med-techs walked. Their gate was always the same, measured. They were either walking, or they were not. This one was three-quarters of the step, so it didn't match the rhythm of the med-techs. I knew it must be King, or someone with a limp.

"Hello 418, my old friend."

By his voice I could hear it was King. I tried to turn but I could not—the footsteps were getting closer to me. "Who's 418?" I asked.

There was some hesitation in his voice. "You are."

"I am?"

"You are. Um, 418 is how your messages come through. It just says message from...418." He seemed to be trying to explain something bad as not being his fault.

"Don't worry King." I didn't want to make him feel uncomfortable. "I knew you were coming. Who else could it be?"

"Right." I heard King laugh as his hand appeared in my vision and he spun the chair so we could talk.

As he spun me around, I realized I probably looked a little ridiculous—or maybe just sad—because King spoke to me with great sympathy. "I know I said I would be finding something new for you. I had to wait until you were declared healed."

"Oh." I replied trying to figure out what doing something different and being healed had to do with each other.

"Guess what?"

"What?"

"You are healed!"

"Fantastic," I replied, genuinely happy. "Can I get out of here?"

The answer was sadly not, but at least King put me in a place where I could see things and not have to stare at a wall. He wheeled me around so I could look directly at the med-tech's station. That was interesting. It was like watching fish. They went in, they did stuff, they came out, all with a calm but deliberate sense of urgency. Sometimes they wheeled staff this way and sometimes they wheeled them the other way. It was far more interesting than just staring at the wall. In spite of my not facing the prescribed direction, the med-techs did not touch me again, and I sat there until the end of their shift. It was interesting to watch.

At the end of the day, I sent another message to King: "Thank you for moving me. It wasn't fun sitting there all day, but the view you gave me was far more interesting than the optimal view I had been given before."

"No problem, sleep well," was the answer I got back.

I did sleep well, though habit is a horrible thing to have to break. I didn't go to Dr. Pong's, I just spent my time seeing the sites and I went to a restaurant in Paris. I still missed my wife. I went back to the Seine and I watched the day go from daytime to nighttime, the lights come out and watched as the dark blue water that flowed through the city turned to coal-black as nighttime fell. I wondered if any of it was real. I knew it wasn't, but did it exist somewhere? I wanted it to.

There was a pleasant smell in the air, not like most cities which don't seem to have any smell whatsoever. Trees and flowers were in bloom. I strolled along the Seine side pathway toward the cathedral. A barge would slip past in the night, and from time to time there were men and children fishing from the bank, trying not to catch anything but enjoying the gentle rush of the water, the cool air and the darkness the trees provide.

I kept walking, trying to feel good. King was going to arrange something. But as I took this walk along the Seine once again, I couldn't help but feel I had been naïve. I wondered how I had ever chosen this place. I liked sports and action. A bullfighter's ring would have been more my style. But that day I met Belinda, I had chosen this, a total mystery. Though now I think I could understand why she chose it. It had magic. I found the bridge where, once upon a time, I walked under, and there had appeared, so long ago, an improbable cafe.

Expecting to see tables with carefree diners all talking to each other. Lovers whispering romantic plans over café noir, cappuccino or maybe something a little more bubbly. I wanted to see people sitting at cast iron tables on chairs with embroidered cushions. There should be sharply dressed waiters, with white aprons and clean black uniforms shuttling trays and bottles amongst the clot of tables. This is where an eddy of foot traffic could spin-off and spend some time enjoying the sound of water, the coolness, a break from all the traffic above. Tall trees creating an oasis of moonlight shade, reaching right up to the roadway. That is what I expected to see, but what I found was just...wall.

There was no cut-out, no place for foot traffic to eddy. There was no café. Had I dreamed it? Had it been there? Had it been real? I sighed, of course it wasn't real. The place where I had met my wife wasn't real. With a great pang in my heart, I knew I had to move on.

I traveled for a while and found myself walking up a hill. I needed a place to go to sleep. Sleep would be good. It would take me faster on to the morning and whatever King had lined up. I tried not to let the fact I couldn't find the café bother me anymore. It wasn't that I didn't remember. It was simple: you start at one end of the Seine and you walk toward the cathedral. You cross under a bridge and there it is. But I had made it all the way to the cathedral, the wall did not open for me this time, so I climbed the stairs from the riverbank, onto the streets, full of old style cars that needed a driver. I wandered into the old city.

Somewhere, uphill, where the street seemed sideways, I found a sign that I could get a room. That's all I wanted. I pressed the buzzer and a woman in a light blue terry cloth robe wandered downstairs and opened the door.

"Hello, what can I do for you?" She yawned and wiped her eyes sleepily, as if she was letting the cat in or out.

"Do you have a room for the night?" I asked hopefully.

"Ah, yes." She rolled her shoulders, as if she had just got up from a not-so-comfortable bed. "Yes, it's seventy-five a night. Would you like it?"

"Yes please," I said. She stood aside and let me enter the doorway, which led immediately to stairs.

We walked up the stairs and, with each turn, there was another door. After about four floors, she stopped tried her key. "This is your room. The washroom is down two flights of stairs."

The room was a little bigger than my own condo. I stepped in. There was a washbasin, a twin-sized bed and a little desk with a chair. But the most intriguing thing was the window. There was a hand crank. I opened it and could hear the sounds of the street below, the city and the nighttime flowed in and I felt immediately better.

"I'll take it."

The woman smiled. "Thank you, it's nice to have you here."

She closed the door, and I pulled the chair out from under the desk and sat beside the window. This was nice, very nice.

I wanted to go to Paris. The real Paris, not this one. This one was what someone remembered. How much of it was real? Probably not much—it was based on something long ago. But there must be someplace like this, someplace where you would want to breathe the air, like the places I had been during my garbage run. Wherever that other place could be, I think I wanted to go. I breathed deeply from the Parisian air and soon I found that the single bed was too attractive for me not to want to go lie down on. I slept well that night, dreaming of other places and other things I'd never seen before.

Samuel found me (as always) and when I heard his voice, "George, it's time to get up," I felt myself mumble and sigh.

"Come on George, rise and shine."

"Okay," I answered. I could already feel myself moving, disconnecting myself from the hard net and unplugging my feeding line. "You don't have to bug me." True, I could have slept all day long and he would have picked me up, washed me off and marched me off to work.

"Today is another exciting day," Samuel said with his annoying cheer.

"Yes." And I remembered that King said he was going to do something. I'd learned that things took time in King's world, not like online, where changes were applied instantly.

We dressed, and we were off. The trip to work felt the same as it always did, the same number of right turns and the same spaces of time between turns. I was a little disappointed to be heading back to the clinic. When they came to a stop, I got out and I asked Samuel to let me watch. We strode up the walkway. It was the clinic, again.

I expected to see myself walk through the gray area, quickly heading through the maze of curtains that served as rooms in the clinic and into the white area where I would take my seat. I tried not to feel disappointed. I'm sure I'd be out of there sometime soon, and I should probably just enjoy the easy work.

I did walk through the doors the same way, and I turned right instead of going on through the maze. I stepped right into the med-tech's service area. Well, how about that. I was going to be a med-tech!

I was amazed. As soon as I arrived, I picked up a chart device and headed out into the gray area, going from cubicle to cubicle— or as I discovered: personal treatment center to personal treatment center—and checking on the patients.

The first thing I was supposed to do, at the beginning of the shift, was to check whether each patient was still alive. If they were, I was to take simple readings. Even though they were still connected to machines, I still had to manually take temperatures and check for a heartbeat. I even counted them. I had no idea there were so many things to check in a body. If the patient was no longer alive, I would have to summon another med-tech to confirm the pronouncement. Ultimately, we would wheel the body to the respective disposal area. In the white zone, we would move the body to the pickup area, where someone would come and get it. If in the gray zone, we would take it to the incinerator, take pictures to complete the insurance forms and wait for permission to load them onto the conveyor and press the big red button.

Despite the fact that it was a big deal when someone dies, we still batched the bodies during our rounds. If you found someone had died, you did call for assistance, but you had to move on, complete the round in a timely and efficient manner, go back, collect, marshal, move and deal with the bodies.

Once you start a task, you never stop it. It made things make a lot more sense. I could never have gotten the attention of a med-tech. Not only because I was staff, but once they started rounds, they did rounds. When they started doing x-rays, they did x-rays. It didn't take me long to understand this was because everything was automated, and the cost of stopping and doing something different was not justified. There were no gains, only losses when the task that was started was not completed.

Because everything was new, the day seemed to fly by quicker than any other day I could remember. It was like watching a show. None of it seemed to be real. After my first day, I could see that a clinic was a complicated thing. So many things had to be done. All of them at once, and concurrently. It was a mastery of programming: the setting of bones and the cutting of flesh, and the sewing of it back together again, all of it, had been automated and perfected.

26

THE DOWNSIDE

Let me be clear: this is a great job! I don't have to wear heavy workwear. I don't get exposed to as many nasty people. I don't go out in the rain, and I don't have garbage poured on me or come back with mysterious pokes and gashes in my skin. It is all civilized, and, for the most part, like all work, it is pretty boring.

What I didn't know about a clinic is, because they are heavily automated (everything runs on a schedule) there is no moving the schedule up or down. It didn't take me long to understand why it was I hadn't been allowed to go home until the end of the day. From a purely administrative point of view, it's easier to marshal all the discharges for the same time and do them all as a batch. It provides a more effective, higher quality service with fewer missed issues. Of course, in the white area it doesn't work like that, but there is a technical reason for that.

Imagine, if there was no plan, and no schedule, things would go haywire quickly. Without automation, it would be chaos. There would be staff running this way and that way, and nothing would ever get done. Order is the only thing that works in medicine. But it's not the type of thing you can understand when you don't work in a clinic.

Take the job I had before being a med-tech. I was sitting out front. If someone had come through, and there were people who did come in the front door, I would have to record all their information, see if they were in our system, and ensure that we have billing and insurance information. I would have to triage their complaints, and based on that, I would open a file and the clinic would assign med-techs as required in the order in which they were required. Because everything in the gray area was planned, checked in via concierge, anything in the white area was always much more emergent.

I remember one day we had a man come through the white area. He was having pains in the chest and numbness in his hand. After I ensured we had billing information—I scanned his ID card and it returned as valid and current—I quickly took note of his symptoms. As soon as I had entered them, two med-techs came running out of the gray area with an old-style bed, not the one with restraining foam. They pretty much pushed the man onto the bed and wheeled him off. I knew where they went. The white area had one of all the same rooms as the gray area, an x-ray, rooms with various machines, but they were kept clean and sterile in case someone came through the front door.

Within seconds of being pushed onto the bed, I heard the peep of machines and the buzz of other machines. I could hear something that sounded like whooshing, and I heard the clattering of metal things against other metal things. Whatever was wrong with the man was fairly serious. I wanted to get up from my station and see if there was anything I could do to help, if there was any way I could be of assistance, and just what was going on. I wanted to know. I even asked Samuel if he knew what was going on, and he told me that work was work, that I need not be concerned because the med-techs were well programmed to take care of whatever it was that was going on.

I did find out what the problem was. Sometime after I admitted the man, a woman and a young girl came by. They did not appear to be in any discomfort when they entered through the front door. They approached me and I felt my smile relax as I spoke, "Hello, how can I be of assistance to you today?"

The woman looked like something horrible was going on. Her face was strained, drawn tight and there were folds cutting into her skin as worry tugged at her. "I am here about my husband."

I smiled some more. I knew exactly who she was talking about, but the smile was programmed, and so was my reply, "And your husband's name is?"

"Oh right," she stammered. I wanted to tell her to relax and not be flustered, that everything was going to be all right, but I couldn't. "His name is Graham, Graham Ainsley, they said he was here."

"And what is your address?" I asked, as if we were full of Graham Ainsleys today.

"Um, 34280 Garrage Court Way," she answered. She looked like she was about to go charging off somewhere.

"Very good," I answered. It was the same billing address we had on file. "Please wait here, and I will have staff come to escort you."

Within an instant, one of the med-techs appeared from where they were working on Graham Ainsley. "Good Afternoon, Ms. Ainsley, and who do we have here?" the med-tech said, looking toward the small girl.

"This is our daughter Abigail, she's seven," Mrs. Ainsley added quickly, trying to get preliminaries over with.

"Good," replied the med-tech. I had seen in the file that they had a daughter, though it made sense that this should be confirmed first. "Ms. Ainsley, if you could leave Abigail here in the reception-triage area, I can take you to see the patient you have come to enquire about."

Ms. Ainsley sent the little girl to go sit upon the seats that no one ever sat in, where the girl started sifting through the magazines no one ever read. I felt my head pivot to keep the child in the center of my general gaze. That was kind of interesting. It must have been part of my programming to look after children that had been left in the waiting area. I wanted to smile, *that's nice,* but I was already smiling.

I don't know what the med-techs said to the woman. I knew the patient was expected to survive, and that he had what she would know as a heart attack. But it was there and then that I knew what I wanted to be. I wanted to help people, anyone. That's what I wanted to do, and it was killing me that I was stuck behind this desk.

The only problem with being a med-tech is when you are working on staff, you don't get to talk to staff. In fact, if it is staff, and there hasn't been a head injury—which would require the forcing offline of the staff member in order to isolate and evaluate damage to the cerebral interface—staff stay pretty much online all the time.

In the rare case where we must force staff offline, it is done with caution. Not all staff are able to manage the strain of being offline. Sometimes they become damaged psychologically. However, that kind of damage usually sorts itself out and manifests itself in self-damage at some future date. In general, to protect managers' investments, it is best to not disturb staff if they are fully engaged.

I could see the risk King had taken by bringing Belinda offline. But I, myself, had been forced offline, and maybe that was what he meant (I didn't think I was brain damaged) but being isolated with nothing to look at for so long does make things go a little funny. I must thank King for taking that risk with Belinda; it was very human of him.

The other problem with being a med-tech, and any other type of staff, is that there is no one to talk to. I could see why you would want to control what sales staff are able to say, but as a med-tech, with real people, it would have been nice to be able to say something other than what was programmed. That said, compared to all the other jobs I had had, this was by far the best. Even though I didn't do anything, and it was all programmed and driven by the cerebral interface, I felt the best about it.

But not all jobs are all roses. In fact, it wouldn't be a job if it was enjoyable all the time. Here are some of the things that we saw all the time, most of which was easy to treat and somewhat commonplace. Within the staff world, very little ever went wrong. This was because the life of staff was all virtual. If you jumped out of an airplane and you go smashing to the ground, you don't actually end up in the clinic. We don't have to fix you. If you are street racing and crash, we don't have to scrape you off the pavement and pour you into a bucket. You just simply go offline, sleep, if you would, to calm you down. Then you wake when it's time to go to work. The incidence of accidents was low with staff, sort of.

What we saw with staff were things like boils, rashes and infections. All of these can be taken care of, but it can take a while for staff to notice these things, if they ever do notice. It could also take the concierge quite a while to notice a rash or infection is impairing work if no one reports the staff as infected. Notwithstanding how these little infections are reported, they are easy to deal with. Just deal with the symptom and find the right antibiotic to deal with the infection over time.

On rare occasions, a staff may develop something that cannot be treated or does not respond well to treatment. But this could be handled humanely through a course of pain killers, more powerful antibiotics, and, if that failed, the option for a staff member to retire from active work. I was pleased to discover that there was nothing we cannot treat in the lines of infections.

The other type of thing that we tended to deal with—for staff—is what I call accidents of misadventure. Things like cuts, broken bones, amputations, burns and electrocutions. These are all the things that happen to the staff while they are at work. Something bad happens when they are doing something. I thought back to my time in the factory. I remembered my shear partner standing there, missing half of six fingers, holding them up for me to see the clean-cut.

It was common for us to have staff patients come in with missing fingers, hands, the bottom of a leg, perhaps most of an arm. We would simply try to make a clean cut above the amputation, so we could close the wound without getting any infection. It's infection, not the loss of a limb, that kills staff. And with the staff being online, I'm not even certain they are aware that anything has happened to them. All one has to do is to make sure they have enough pain killers in their body, make the incisions neat and restrain them so the adjusters can come and have a look.

The adjusters were weird. They are not staff; they are never staff. They are always people, and they always act like there was someplace they would rather be. Most of them didn't have much stomach for what we had to show them. When an adjuster would arrive, we would have to lead them to their patient and recite all the information we had on that staff. The adjuster would sometimes make notes, but usually they would make faces, comments about how little they cared, or make motions that we were speaking too slow. But we were required to read them all the details. They may not have been required to listen.

Whatever it was, the adjuster was required to look at it. Some things didn't always look that good. Someone who had been hit by a forklift and dragged across the factory floor didn't look good, and where the skin was missing it was red or yellow. More than once, I had to fetch a bucket for an adjuster. I can't say I liked the adjusters all that much. They spoke to me sharply and often referred to me as a stupid robot or tin can head. I had not, to the best of my understanding, received a lobotomy, though I had an adjuster say something like this to me. I had received a cerebral interface, which was hardly the same thing.

Finally, there was a third category of catastrophe, and those were exceptions. Exceptions were far more random than accidents and infections. Infections could be planned. You knew that, if you had a hundred staff, over a five-year period seven percent of them were going to have a catheter infection. It was just going to happen. You also knew, depending on the line of work, that a certain percent of workers were just going to get hurt or maimed when at work. But the exceptions were much wilder, unpredictable, and could affect anyone.

The most common one was the traffic exception. This happened more often than you think, but there was a strict warning that divulging any information about a traffic exception is a *Class A Felony,* and punishable by lengthy jail time and a fine. I can't imagine being locked up with no internet. I did a few weeks and I almost lost my mind. So, you can't talk about traffic exceptions, but who would I tell? I mean, no one online would care. I don't know anyone who isn't online other than King, and he might just agree with me and tell me to keep quiet.

The injuries from exceptions tend to be the ones where the victims look battered, as if they put their face in a blender. They tended to have body parts removed and stuffed into the car with them so they could all arrive together. Sometimes the included parts

EDGAR SCOTT

didn't match. Not that we could attach them, not for staff. We simply made it so they didn't bleed to death.

Internal injuries were the worst. This means that we had to wait and see if there was going to be too much bleeding for the patient to survive. It could take days before they die, and there wasn't much we can do to help them.

The other characteristic of exceptions is, there is never just one patient, but almost always multiple. It was rare that one car would crash. It was always a group. It was rare that the machine only took out one staff; usually everyone around the machine got hit with some flying shard of metal when the tooling broke. The safety system that was supposed to protect staff from breathing in paint in a painting plant wouldn't just stop working for one staff. It stopped working for everyone and everyone got a lung full of color of the day.

We saw industrial accidents where staff had become mangled together. Ultimately, we there wasn't much we could do for them. We made sure they didn't feel any pain and kept them online until they went dead.

A funny thing happens when you give someone a real painkiller when they are online and immersed: they can't tell between the real thing and the virtual pain killer they are used to. But their bodies relax, and they have no incentive to come offline. Also, you can't take them offline if you used virtual painkillers. When you have staff that is in real pain, just give them real pain killers and they won't come back for quite a while. It's quite convenient.

I found out about my situation, though I was not allowed to read my own file. It was still "classified." Apparently, staff are not allowed to read their own files. But I could now gather that I was an exception, and I had to be kept in place while they checked my head to ensure I was still capable of working. I don't know if it was a good thing, but someone decided I could be rehabilitated, even though that might not have been the correct diagnosis. Yet it was not me, but the adjusters who made the decision. I could, and we did, provide a prognosis, and I was programmed to answer, factually and clearly, any question posed to me by an adjuster, but they often didn't ask, and I was not programmed to tell them when they needed to ask me something that they haven't. I wonder if, in my case, some questions should have been asked that were not. For this, I am grateful.

27

THE DARKSIDE

This didn't sit well with me. I suppose it doesn't happen often, but it did happen once, and I didn't like it.

We were working on a staff that had been involved in an exception involving a company that shipped frozen meat. I don't know all the details of what happened—because it's not important—but something had happened with a forklift and one of the staff got crushed. Several of the staff's ribs were broken, and there was bleeding. We were going to conduct surgery. The staff had got to the clinic just in time. There was a high probability of saving this staff. So, we set about our job.

We opened up the staff. We had to drain the chest cavity of extra fluid, a couple of stitches here and there. We could stop the bleeding, too, even though I wasn't in control. I was cheering for the good guys on this one. If we could save a life, even if I was just the hands that someone else used to do so, it would somehow make all of this so much more bearable. Helping people is what I wanted to do.

I had blood all over my hands as I was going in with precision and a needle to sew things up. The staff looked more like stew than a person once we cut them open. I was pulled back. I put my tools down, I left the staff open on the operating table. I headed to the sink, and I threw away my gloves, washed up and walked out of the room. The other med-tech accompanied me; we even turned the lights off in the operating theater. We headed to the white area. There was a man, a large fat man, who was complaining of indigestion, chest pains and diarrhea.

It turns out that, after we gave the man an EKG, there was nothing wrong with his heart. He had only said that to get attention. He had taken a car to this clinic because the clinic near his home was full of people waiting and he knew that here he would be the only one in the white zone of this clinic and so he would be seen straight away. He didn't have indigestion, but the diarrhea was real and while I am certain it was unpleasant it wasn't going to be fatal; however, it caused us to shift our staffing.

After we treated the man, he was grateful, though he didn't thank us. He probably didn't think we were listening. He left and we went back to our surgery. When we turned on the lights in the theater, the blood had all gone cold and congealed. There was a heck of a mess there, which the adjuster would have to come and examine in the morning in order to complete their report. Something didn't seem right about this.

28

VIRTUAL OPIUM

The worst thing you can do is to educate someone. Absolutely the worst! It takes the fun out of everything. I used to love going to Dr. Pong's. Opium, that's the thing for me, though you have to understand that just about anything you can think of (cocaine, ecstasy, codeine, morphine, *flakka*, crack, caffeine, taurine, niacin, alcohol, glue, paint solvents, adrenaline, gasoline and even just the effects of concentrated sugar and pure oxygen) can be replicated online. And online, there is no danger of overdosing.

You can get a buzz—you can get several buzzes at the same time—and you can see the stars come down from the heavens and kiss the ground or you can fly a thousand times through the sun and no harm ever comes to you. It's truly awesome. As destroyed as I've ever gotten, I was always able to just snap it right off whenever I woke up, be straight as an arrow and head off to work. And I liked to indulge in something, at least every night. It was awesome to be able to feel something after a long day of feeling nothing and playing boring card games with the talking heads online while being forced to be at work.

It occurred to me, why? Why was all this being provided? What was the point of it all? Just to let people get as smashed as they wanted so they could be turned off, sent back to work, so they would do it again at the end of the day? Maybe. It's possible. It kept people happy, so that might be the reason. Happy people are docile people. There was a reason we always used restraining beds and chairs on staff at the clinic. It was in case they were not happy. Pain can do strange things and it can make you unhappy. When people are unhappy, they can become dangerous.

But did they have to make it so available? It was everywhere. You could get high on sex hormones if you wanted. You could take virtual Viagra if you wanted to feel that way. I admit, I've done it, it's great. Online, it was like you couldn't start doing anything without first taking something, swallowing something, drinking something.

I learned in the clinic that it's simply a matter of stimulating the brain in the right way, that's it. So simple, and you can experience anything. But the question I had was: why?

I didn't think I wanted to take virtual opium anymore. I'd enjoyed it, it was my go-to. But I just didn't feel right. Perhaps I am getting old.

29

RETIREMENT

I had always thought that retirement was the ultimate goal. Something to be strived for, pursued, chased and won. It is your reward for a life of hard work and toil, doing things you didn't like doing, passing your time so you could choose how to pass your time. I've come to understand that it is not.

We had all been told that when you retire, you go to a place where you don't have to work. You go to a place where you can play games all day, talk to whomever you want. Spend as much or as little time on the internet as you want. But best of all, the drugs are real. Sure, you can still take the virtual ones, but the good ones, the ones that would otherwise be illegal, are legal when you retire.

Yes, it is the best of both worlds. You get all your friends and all your online activities, and you get real physical stimulation. However, you don't get to stay in your condo, no, you sell your condo and you move to an assisted living facility. That's how it works. That's where people come and wait on you hand and foot to make sure that anything you want, you have. Sounds wonderful!

A clinic, by contrast, is in the business of the maintenance and upkeep of human and staff bodies. However, we did do a lot of work with retired people. First thing, you could tell when people were going to retire by the frequency with which they came to the clinic. The closer they were to retirement, the more often they came. I noticed—though it does seem obvious now—that the older I got, the older anyone got, the more their body breaks down and the more they needed to come to the clinic. When we are young, we never come to the clinic unless something is urgent. As we age, we come to the clinic more often because things we never noticed before start to trouble us.

If you visit the clinic frequently, there appears a checkbox (that isn't normally there) in the gray *office use only section* near the bottom of the insurance forms, which is, "RFR," or, recommend for retirement.

But wouldn't that be great? Who wants to work when you can just gad about all day doing whatever you want, drinking, eating, taking whatever? Sounds good to me. Perhaps this was why I couldn't see my own file; I couldn't retire myself. I could see a lineup of people wanting to do that.

We actually had a name for it, *geriatric care*, when we had to work on staff that was retired. We didn't get a lot of non-staff coming to our clinic for geriatric care. I'm not sure I ever saw one, but we do get staff.

The problem is, aside from broken legs, sprained ankles and the complications of whatever work-related injury they have suffered, there isn't a lot to do. We bandaged whatever it was, and we prescribe either an antibiotic or an antibiotic with a pain killer. Pain killers are huge in geriatric care. In fact, if all you knew about was painkillers, you might have most of modern geriatric care covered.

The sad thing about retirement, is that once you get there, you are usually too banged up, messed up or otherwise effed-up to be able to enjoy it. For all the perks and benefits retirement holds, no one can enjoy it. We usually see people who are little more than sitting statues, wheeled in, hopefully grinning, but usually with the same sorry blank look on their faces. I check them out. They have bad joints, bad bones. I give them painkillers, and at the end of the shift, they are shipped back to wherever they came from.

That would be it, for a few days. Remember, these people were not well. They were not able to work, so they were usually right back at the clinic, and I'd see them again. What strikes me as odd: we were good at keeping staff going, but the retired staff, they didn't seem to live long. A far shorter time than they spent working. I'm not sure if it was not right or not fair, but whether it was a few hours or a few weeks, we invariably found ourselves looking over their breathless bodies. Since they came to us like this, all we could do was confirm that they were indeed, dead, wheel them off to the incinerator room and take some pictures for insurance.

Perhaps I had too much time on my hands to think about these things, but I decided I didn't want to retire. Something bad happened to everyone who retired. It wasn't right. I didn't want it to happen to me.

30

GETTING CLEAN

I was being given just enough to be able to rest up, recover and head back to work. Day after day after day. Nothing more, nothing to accumulate, nothing to enjoy and nothing tangible that I could say, "Hey, look at this." The sum total of my life was going back to work and when I was gone, there would be no more memory of me. The sad fact was, as I got up each day and as I worked, at the end of the day I took into my hands the means to make sure that, within this workday, I no longer had any more memory of me.

Virtual opium, that was my thing. I don't know if I learned it at the clinic, I don't know if it just dawned on me. There was more to the addictive process than just the feeling one gets. It was about habit and routine. Wake, work, and wash from my mind anything that happened that day. All the tedious hours of card-playing, casinos, endless casinos, more card games, unending petty gambles. When you look at them, they don't pay off. Sometimes I win, usually I lose, but over a long period of time, nothing changes. But that's okay. It's about the game.

It's funny that I didn't have much interest in the casinos after the exception. All my friends didn't know who I was, and I didn't feel like taking the time to try to find new ones. The games became predictable. I didn't know if I would win any particular round, but it was always the same. I was either going to win or lose, and over a long period of time, I was going to lose. But now, I didn't want to play.

As much stimulation as I found online, it was no longer enough. Perhaps I was burnt out. I could go to the ultimate fighting competition and watch someone get completely destroyed. Now that I worked in a clinic, the idea of blood and of being dead meant something more to me. It was no longer funny to watch someone get maimed, cut in half, pummeled to death or die in any other way.

My work was ruining me: online was dull, and on a day to day basis, nothing of consequence happened. Work always had lots to do and many things to attend to. But I didn't like working on staff. Staff didn't respond at all. They were off playing slots or roulette, but real people, they were different.

When I stopped to think about it, we got a surprising number of children in the white area. A child would have an accident, break an arm or a leg falling from something. Not like online, where you might feel the break for a while, but, once the point has been made, you went back to feeling fine because you were fine. But a real injury doesn't just go away. The people in the white area of the clinic didn't have access to virtual morphine or virtual Oxycontin.

In the white area, we had to administer anesthetics and prescriptions for tablets that had to be taken. The children we get were often the type that I would say have had minor exceptions, though exception is not the right word. Invariably, it was not because something unexpected happened to the child; it was because the child had been doing something they should not have been doing, and the consequences were totally expected. Which was a different type of thing, and so it was called an accident. There was no programming that could have avoided this or failed to consider it.

As such, I set a lot of bones, and I got to be there with the parents who were trying to keep their child distracted and to help them understand that this was just what happens when you do whatever it was they shouldn't have been doing. It was a completely different interaction that they had with their children compared to how I interacted with my children. I used to get notes from my children. We would have online meetings, and I thought I could reach out and touch them. At least it felt like I did, and when we did meet, I was given a burst of good feeling in my brain. But I'd never got to hold either of my children when they broke their arm, dislocated a finger, or got a nasty cut that wasn't going to stop bleeding.

I enjoyed taking care of these patients. Even though I couldn't say anything more than I was programmed to say, and my hands did what they were programmed to do, I could tell when things were going well. The tears would dry up, the color would return to their faces. I could see the levels of tension reduce in the parents too. I could even record it if we had a heart and blood pressure monitor hooked up. I felt like I was making a difference, even if it was only my hands. I tried to watch what I was doing, in case I ever had to do it offline. It might be good to know.

But who was I kidding? My life was online, and my family was online. Neither Lucus or Serenity had ever broken their arms or any other bone I knew of, and I never had to comfort them through the setting and the healing of the bones not broken. I felt a strange sense of missing something, like I'd been ripped off.

Perhaps the video conferences I had with Lucus and Serenity had meant nothing at all. I remembered the great flood of emotion the first time I saw baby Serenity. It was a torrent of emotion, burned into me so I remember it today. But now, I see it was just an online representation, a surge of neural stimulation. I had never known my children.

I noticed on days that I saw real people, when I worked in the white clinic, that I didn't feel like I wanted to go to Dr. Pong's. It was only habit that took me there. On those days I'd rather go for a walk, and sometimes I would. I would find a place, maybe a forest, or a lake, maybe a city, where I could walk and walk and think about the good I might have done. I felt warm. I didn't need Dr. Pong's or any other distraction. On those nights, I didn't need my reward, but I still felt empty. What else was I to do during my off hours? However, I was sure I did not need Dr. Pong anymore.

31

BOREDOM

Another thing happened when I decided to give up Dr. Pong's, that is, aside from my nights becoming incredibly long; I started to feel sad.

The more real patients I saw in the white area of the clinic, the worse I felt. Okay, not the man who came in complaining of diarrhea, but children and couples, people who were scared, they needed to see someone now and they couldn't wait around at the clinic where they lived. The pain, the distress, the fear would make them come downtown and I could treat them. I started to dread going home. Those twelve hours I was away from the clinic were the longest twelve hours. I saw no one. I simply went to my condo, sat in my chair, fed myself, tried to not think about things. The day was long, the nights longer.

Through my time at the clinic, I started to realize the concept of a week. I had heard myself say it a few times to people in the white area of the clinic: "Take two of these, two times a day for two weeks." They knew immediately what a week was. I didn't. But I could count, and I did see that some pills, when I had to go to the dispensary and package up a bottle, were only one per day.

"Samuel, how many is fourteen divided by two?" I asked Samuel one day.

Samuel smiled. I was beginning to think he was feeling a bit neglected. His smiles seemed larger and perhaps even less genuine, if that was possible. "I am glad you asked," he said, as if he needed a moment. "Fourteen goes into two seven times," he pronounced proudly. "Is there anything else I can help you with today?"

"No thanks," I replied cheerfully, "that's it for now."

"Okay." And he would give me back control. There were seven days in a week. Something no one had ever bothered to teach me, but something everyone else knew. I finally knew what a week was. The funny thing was, I got paid every week. The only thing I was told was that I was paid every seven days—why not ten?—but there it was. I was paid every week. Must have been an offline thing.

In order to make myself feel less alone, I sent frequent messages to King. I didn't have anyone else to send them to, but the answers I got back were always short. They didn't always make sense either; things like, "Enjoy, it's good?" or "I tried to find you something like," and "That was not this." I'm sure they made sense in King's world, but not mine. So, I discovered that I could ask King if I could meet him once a week. I looked forward to those meetings, talking to a real person in a real place.

We had a case come into the white clinic where a man had overdosed on drugs, the real type. It was a big deal. He was dropped off on our doorstep by friends of his, of course. They used a self-driving car, so the car was turned around by legal override. Law enforcement staff were summoned as soon as we made the diagnosis that this was, at best, a misadventure with a *controlled* substance. Funny—if they were controlled, how did they get misused?

I and the other med-tech immediately ran out and placed the patient on a bed. We wheeled him into the back and hooked him up to monitors. We stuck a tube down his throat and started pumping everything we could out of his stomach. We watched the man's vitals. We watched the blood pressure go up and up and then down and down. When the heart stopped, we injected him with more drugs, and brought him back with a gasp. He bucked against the restraints.

A few minutes later, the law enforcement staff showed up. We had to get a hand free, even though he was restrained. He was to be handcuffed to the table. The friends who had dropped him off were returned by the self-driving car and the law enforcement staff extracted them from the car. One of them must have put up a bit of a fight, because we had to examine the hands of the law enforcement staff and had to treat the resisting man for numerous contusions, lacerations and a broken eye socket. He was also handcuffed to a restraining bed in the next treatment bay, until more law enforcement staff arrived to securely remove him.

The man who had overdosed was able to recover. Though we kept him there for a full day, a law enforcement staff stayed there and ensured that no one mistakenly discharged the patient. He wasn't looking so good when he was finally released into custody. Apparently, it was some sort of crime to try to kill yourself. And the taking of controlled substances was illegal, which was funny: I could take all the virtual drugs I want, but I couldn't have any of the real ones. Why would they let me do that? Why had they let him do that? If there were going to punish him, what did that mean for me?

This was the first time the idea of taking my own life occurred to me. I was lonely, tired, and, on many days, felt totally unfulfilled. Why wouldn't I want to take my own life? When was it going to get better? When I retired? I'd seen the retired, and they didn't seem to live long after they went to retirement homes. But taking my own life didn't make much sense, either. I was bored, not in pain. It was possible that things could get better. I waited. Roughly every seven days, King and I would have breakfast together. It was all that made it bearable. Otherwise, I would have gone back online, never to re-appear again.

With each meal, King would give me something different to eat. I was up to eating small breakfasts, a bit of everything, but not very much. There was a downside to all this eating. After I ate, for the next day or so I wanted to eat again. I wanted the feeling of having food in my stomach, and I had nothing to eat.

"King, why is it that my money doesn't work here like it does online?" I asked one day. It wasn't that I wanted to pay for breakfast, but I figured if I could find a restaurant, I could eat on my own without King. Except, just like that time at McDonald's, if I didn't have any money, it wasn't going to happen.

King finished chewing as he thought about it. "I guess," he started. "Well," I could tell he couldn't come up with anything better, "it's because online money isn't the same as physical money."

"Why not?"

"Because you can't take it physically to a bank," he smiled, pleased with his answer.

"Hrmph," I answered, "Can I be paid in real money?"

King snorted into his coffee, making a little mess on himself. "No, I don't think that's possible."

"Why not?"

"It's just the way it is."

I didn't like this answer, but I could see that King wasn't going to tell me anything else. I smiled, nodded and went back to the eggs that I was chasing around my plate.

The days I didn't get to see King were unbelievably boring. Nothing online had any interest, and I couldn't do anything else. I started to go for walks in the real world. I'd done that before, the first day when I'd found I didn't have any money to spend online, but there wasn't much to see. I lived in a silo in the middle of a large field of silos that were otherwise identical. It was all I could do not to get lost in this desert of sameness. I didn't want to alert Samuel that I was heading out, but there were so many identical condo buildings buried in the ground I couldn't get anywhere. So, I tried taking a car. But I couldn't summon one.

"Samuel," I called.

Obediently he appeared. "What can I do for you today?" he asked in the same cheerful voice.

"Can I have a car?"

"Sure, where would you like to go?"

"I don't know, how about Jazmin's café?"

"One moment." An instant later, Samuel replied, "I'm sorry, I can't get a car for you, you do not have any business at Jazmin's cafe."

"Sure," I answered, "I know that, but I just thought I wanted to go."

"I'm sorry," Samuel answered earnestly, "transportation is only provided for authorized purposes. If you would like to go online, I see there is an online representation of a cafe that is similar, if you would like me to find it for you."

"Hmm." I was feeling hurt, almost trapped. "I can't go?"

"If you can obtain authorization, yes."

I didn't like days like these. They seemed to go on and on and I was trapped, waiting for that one day a week I got to talk to a real person.

32

MEETING BELINDA

Thank goodness for work. If I didn't have work, I think I would have gone totally off my head. I guess this was why so few who suffer exceptions survive long. Work, while boring and the same, offered me exciting random events. Truth is, when I went to work, I never quite knew what was coming through the doors. Emergencies came in through the white area of the clinic and casualties came in through the gray area of the clinic. Although, on any given day, there was little that went on that wasn't planned, pre-scheduled, sorted and classified. There was always a chance that something random could happen. Random—a word I had heard myself say to families of patients and adjusters—was what I lived for.

The day started like every other day. Exactly like every other day. I hoped and wished for something random to happen—as if hoping and wishing ever had any effect on random events—but as I went to work, everything was exactly the same.

We had someone come back from the retirement home. They looked a little dried out. They had died. It had been two days since their retirement. Not everyone lasted that long, though sometimes people lasted a week, even two. This one was like all the others: the heart had stopped, nothing left to do. She, it, looked like it was relieved to be gone. I checked for vital signs. There weren't any, and its face had already yellowed. We photographed it and took it to the incinerator room, where it would wait. If the insurance adjuster was here today, we could press the red button. Other than that, everyone at the clinic was alive and everything was going as it should.

Then, something random happened. We were notified that there had been an exception, and we should expect a staff casualty. We headed to the carport and waited with a restraining bed. The information was that this was not going to be a lot of work for us. We were not told to prepare any machines or any operating theater. I knew this meant that likely it was a fatality, but that was what we were here for, to pronounce the diagnosis and wait for the adjuster to confirm the diagnosis.

Quietly, a car entered the carport. Slowly, it pulled up and the door opened. We could extract the patient. Expertly, we removed the lifeless body and sent the car away for cleaning.

It was obvious that there was little for us to do medically. The staff had suffered head injuries, the right side of their head, and the back—upon examination—was crushed. The face was pretty much intact, but the right shoulder was badly broken. Professionally, I could see the staff had been hit by a heavy object falling from a significant height, and death would have been quick if not instant. I checked for vital signs and found none. The body was already starting to drop in temperature. There was nothing to do. In all of this, there was nothing special to note, and I probably wouldn't have noted anything other than the fact that I'd seen this staff before. And even though someone else was driving my body, it made my blood freeze and my head feel dizzy.

It was Belinda.

With expert precision, I prepared the body for final examination by the insurance adjuster. It was a good thing Samuel was driving. I couldn't have done it by myself. Even though I hardly knew this Belinda, I still felt waves of anger, fear, dismay. All of which I couldn't express. It was like I was locked in a closet, left to scream all to myself with no one to hear. *What was the use?*

We wheeled the body to the incinerator room, placed it beside the woman from the retirement home, and I went about my business.

33

DISSATISFIED

I tried to find out as much as I could about how Belinda had died. Samuel didn't know anything about it, and still insisted that I had not been married. So anything about Belinda Boyle was strictly secret. I even tried reading her number from her file, E098FH836814, but he pretended he didn't know what that was, and said there was no way for him to look up anyone by this means. I felt crushed.

A messenger window popped up on Andrea Dover's messenger application. "Hey, it's me," it said. It was beside Bolt Greene's avatar.

Oh, how she hated him. She'd tried several times to put him in positions that would expose him for what he was: incompetent and lazy. But it hadn't worked. He was still the cap on her career. She smiled as she typed, "Hi Bolt, what's up?"

"I need you to go to Clinic 14 and do a confirmation."

Oh joy, Andrea thought. Bolt left pretty much all the confirmations for her, *another dead body.* "Sure," she answered, typing as pluckily as she could. "When do you want me to go?"

"Anytime, but before EOD," he answered. EOD was an acronym he had learned a couple of months ago, one he would not stop using. The word today would have been fine. She sneered at the messenger window and typed her response.

"Ok, sounds good to me."

"Ty."

"Np." A ticket instantly appeared in her inbox.

Andrea still didn't like going to the clinic. The bodies usually weren't too bad. If they were messy, they got cleaned up, and you didn't have to do much more than check that the catheter matched the serial number on file and well, dead is dead. Usually one look was enough. She slogged off to the basement carport, and off she went to Clinic 14.

The place was as dingy as it was on every other day she went there. It was a wonder how anyone in the gray area of the clinic ever got better, and, in her opinion, quite often they didn't. The number of infections that took staff out of service was, in her imagination, on the rise. She'd watched some old movie with her boyfriend—which was a mistake, because he didn't have a job like this—that was all about a contagious disease spreading throughout California. Once it went airborne, it was impossible to stop, and everyone died. Or that's how she remembered it. This gave her a new reason to dread going to the clinic. She didn't want to be exposed to patient zero or catch some superbug. Looking at the darkness, the dirt, the dank walls and the smell of leaking water and what must have been some low-grade mold, she figured if there was going to be a place where a new disease would be born, it would be Clinic 14.

She walked into the clinic and right past the receptionist that didn't even pay any attention to her. It must have known she was coming, or maybe it was the way that she marched in, without any intention of slowing or staying longer than she had to. She walked straight back to the med-tech station.

"Hello." She addressed a med-tech that was busy moving papers around, from desk to cabinet and back to desk. "I am here to check out the stiffs for the Popular."

She was just like all the others. They may have looked different, but they all acted the same, as if they didn't want to be here. But even if you weren't staff, work is work. The woman came up and told me that she was "Here to check out the stiffs for the Popular." I didn't know what the Popular was, but I could guess. I was pretty certain that *stiff* meant body, but it didn't matter. I responded automatically. "Yes ma'am, right this way," and I led her off to go see Belinda.

When we got to the incinerator room, the woman took a look at the body, briefly. It was pretty clear Belinda was dead. She was yellow and her eyes were clouding without being online. Her chest did not heave like normal people did when they were asleep.

I saw the woman shiver. I was watching her as best I could. She poked Belinda and nothing happened. She turned to me. "Give me the details," she said, hoping that I could save some time and tell her everything at once.

I started to read the details as they had been recorded in the file. "This is E098FH836814. It was doing garbage duty when a garbage bin broke, the metal bracket that was supposed to house the prongs of an automatic lifting mechanism sheared, and the bin became unsteady, slipped and struck the staff on the right side of the head and right shoulder. Death was quick, and before any medical assistance could be obtained." Well that was interesting. I wanted someone to give some acknowledgment more than this. It was, after all, my wife. Even if I couldn't prove it.

The woman adjuster was looking at me as I was speaking. "Do I know you?" she said finally.

"No, ma'am," I heard myself say. "I don't believe that we have met before," I added. But it was weird how she was looking at me.

"Yeah," she replied. "Silly of me talking to staff. I should get my head checked." She turned and took a photo of Belinda. "There," she added speaking over her shoulder, "I think that just about does it. You can throw the body in the fire now."

"Very good ma'am!" It almost sounded like I was cheering. "Is there anything else that I can do for you today?"

"No, just get me out of here."

I led the woman back to reception. She took another sideways look at me, shook her head and picked up her pace. When she was gone, I met the other med-tech in the incinerator room. Without words we loaded Belinda onto the conveyor. I watched myself press the red button. The oven roared as the door opened, and the body rolled into the flames. I still wanted to cry, but I couldn't.

If things had not sat well with me before, they really didn't sit well now. I used to do garbage. That could have happened to me. It was true that one of the nice things I liked about this job was that I didn't smell. And I didn't smell because I didn't have garbage or garbage water falling on me and I didn't have to sit in the dirty, grimy cab. But I never thought death could happen in or around a garbage truck.

I wonder if she even knew something happened. Was it just that she was sitting at the poker table and all of a sudden, the lights went out? Or did her concierge come to tell her she had been injured, and that she was in route to the clinic and they would do everything they could to save her? Or was it that she was just hit by falling garbage, suffered a system malfunction and the other staff just called it in?

Thinking about these things was all I could do after I had pressed the button and went back to my rounds. Literally, it was all I could do. Nothing else. I couldn't help but think that somehow this could have been me.

Imagine my surprise when King entered the clinic. Which was odd. He couldn't be here to see Belinda. We had already loaded her and pressed the red button. King didn't look like he was happy. He was serious, solemn, and he also didn't look like he wanted to be there. Even though I saw him, I didn't acknowledge him as he approached, I couldn't. He slowed, pulled out his mobile and started poking at the screen.

I felt my arms slouch and my face relax as the world dissolved. Samuel, who had been hovering around in the corner of my vision, disappeared into a tiny swirl of black dots that dissolved as the discretionary use of my eyes was returned to me once again.

"Oh, thank goodness," I blurted out, "you have no idea how horrible that is."

"What is?"

"Being stuck like that. I could see you coming, and I couldn't say anything. It's the worst."

"Yeah, I figured you were having a bad day."

"You did?" I was amazed.

King nodded, "Yes, I saw the exception report."

"You did?" I suppose so, but I was still amazed he was here.

"Yeah, that's pretty sad, crushed by falling garbage."

"No, you mean crushed by a defective garbage can."

King looked to my left and smiled. "Yeah," he said. I could see him thinking. "Falling garbage, garbage can, what does it matter?"

"Well, falling garbage would mean that the job itself isn't safe whereas the garbage can would be an exception." I realized that this wasn't a question. "Oh, I see, it doesn't matter."

"No," King said with genuine sympathy. "I'm sorry for you."

"Sorry for me?"

"Yes, for your loss."

"My loss?"

King shook his head. "It's something that we say, *I'm sorry for your loss,* when we know someone has someone close to them die."

"I've never heard that before." Thinking for a moment, I added, "Thank you."

"Are you okay?" King asked, looking me right in the eye with force, so that I had to look away.

"I, I..." I didn't know what to say. I looked at the floor as if the words I was looking for might somehow be down there, "I think I'll be fine, but I don't think I'm really okay."

King reached out and put his arm on my shoulder. "I get that," he said. "I wish it weren't so."

The rest of the day I thought about that visit from King. He came down to the clinic just to see me. Took me out of work, just to see me. He didn't have to. He could have carried on like everything was okay. Who was Belinda to either of us? But now that she was dead, it didn't matter if she thought I was dead. Whatever I thought of our marriage, it was over, and I couldn't help but feel twisted up about that. However, I felt good that King had come. It made the twist I was feeling seem better, not like something I wasn't supposed to feel.

I went home that night and I took a long slow walk along the Seine. Belinda would never sit there by the side of the river in the café that didn't exist anymore. She would never flash her nails, and she would never smooth her smoother-than-smooth, shiny black hair again.

I thought of her—pale, short, head half-crushed. She looked like she had been in a lot of pain before it happened, and that it was some relief. Could it have been that she had stepped under the garbage? It's not possible for us to control our bodies once we are in work mode, but maybe she'd just stepped into it all the same. Maybe she felt life was pointless.

I didn't even want to get stoned. I kept walking until the night got darker and darker. The lights of Paris dimmed and became farther and farther away. The river stretched on and on, or maybe it just looped around on itself, but it never seemed to end. I'd have jumped in, but it wouldn't have made any difference. I was a prisoner in a world I couldn't get out of, even if I had wanted. That night, I found, if you just kept walking, you can disappear into the night.

My eyes fluttered and I looked up at the pristine ceiling. Samuel leaned over me. "Good morning George, how are you today?"

I rolled my eyes and looked around. I was flop in the middle of a great big bed with puffy white covers, just as I was on almost every other day. Yippee! "Good morning Samuel," I said flatly. "Let's get on with it."

Samuel always seemed to enjoy taking control, "Okay, away we go," he said, and I felt myself get up and out of bed. I was on my way to another glorious day. The pattern of the car was so regular that even if I wasn't paying attention—this was one of the few times I did play solitaire—I knew every turn. With great joy, I noticed I wasn't going to the clinic. We didn't swerve right when we should have. I knew we missed that exit.

King was glad to see me. He was smiling as I stepped into the café. "How are you doing?" he asked me. I was glad that he seemed to care.

"I'm okay, but I have to tell you, that was horrible."

"I bet." Today the breakfast was almost the same size as his. "Here, eat whatever you want."

"Thanks." I grabbed the mushy white toast and began prodding my eggs with it.

King sat there for a while, watching me eat. He would smile and take a sip of coffee. Leisurely, he ate his breakfast. "I think there is something you haven't asked." He paused for a moment, then continued, "No, I think it's that you don't know how to ask it."

I stopped eating. "What do you mean?"

"You know how far you have come? I have to tell you, when I saw you the first time, I thought you were brain dead."

"Brain dead?"

"Nothing happening inside." King sipped his coffee. "And now, look how far you have come: you have feelings, you are bored, unhappy. Isn't it wonderful?"

This annoyed me a bit. I was about to say something, but I had to think. I sipped the orange juice that had appeared on the table, then found my retort, "not brain dead, I think I just wasn't aware." Thinking some more, "of pretty much anything."

"No, you weren't."

We ate for a while. "You know," I said. King raised his eyebrows. "If it weren't for you, I don't think I'd be aware of a lot of things."

King smirked and shook his head. "Don't blame me for that. I didn't curse you."

I kept eating.

"It would have been a lot easier for everyone if you had just stayed the way staff stays," King added.

"How?"

"Stay in your world, just be, exist. Let everyone else move on."

I shook my head, "I don't want to do that."

"I can tell."

"What do I do?"

"I don't know."

34

FURTHER EDUCATION

Brian stepped out of his car. He was having to get up earlier and earlier on these days when he met 418, because the breakfasts were getting longer and longer. It was a puzzle to Brian. He had been assured that staff not only had no requirement for eating, but they had no desire and no capacity. But every time he met 418, the amount of food it ate was more and more. Staff were supposed to lose the concept of self and lose the concept of there being a real-world beyond the world that they saw online. Not only that, staff were supposed to be happy. Staff are supposed to like their lot in life and would choose nothing else if they had a choice in it.

Brian felt a strange kinship to 418. It wasn't like they were friends, but Brian could imagine that if you didn't want to be in that world—if you didn't want to be online all the time—nothing would be worse. And it was kind of the same for Brian. He didn't like what he was doing, but at least he knew the reason why he was doing it. It paid the bills and allowed him, Imelda and Prince a life together.

Until 418, Brian had thought his life was pretty fixed. He was, if he was skillful, going to stay where he was, avoid being declared bankrupt and, with any luck, finish out his days as he was in his apartment with his wife. Hopefully, he would watch his child go on to better things. He didn't want Prince to take over his business, but it was keeping them out of the crumple zone. He would rather have Prince flourish, thrive, shine and enjoy life, but what else was there?

Entering the building, Brian sighed as he opened the screeching door for the stairs. The stairs, still dusty except for the narrow pathway where he walked, were dirty, unforgiving and hot. No air conditioning. He started, ascending one step at a time. There had to be some way to break out of this, he thought, as his knees complained bitterly about the angle and the weight they were forced to support. If 418 can do it, he could do it. Suddenly, it became clear to Brian, that even though it wasn't supposed to work this way, 418 would want out.

418 should be happy. 418 shouldn't care, and anything 418 could possibly want would be provided to him online. That's how Brian remembered the rationalization. There were even people who held this conviction so strongly that they chose to undergo the conversion process and join the staff. The working part was just a natural moral imperative. *It isn't right that a man, woman or staff should not work. Indolence is morally wrong.* Everyone knew this! Staff happily accept the trade of reduced internet exposure while they work in exchange for a life where everything is provided. They have no worries, about anything.

Brian turned the first landing. These stairs were getting easier, but as he gasped and wheezed for air, he knew he had put them off for too many years. It was going to be hard work to shift all this fat, all this plaque, everything that was making him feel old and slow. But he was determined to do it. What was the alternative? He wanted to see Prince grow up, he still loved his wife. He just couldn't give up, no matter what. But what was he trying to do? Just get fitter? Just stay alive? There must be something more. Whatever it was, he knew that by climbing upward, he might discover it. It was at that moment, when he reached the next landing, he realized that he and 418 were in exactly the same predicament.

Brian stopped, his head swimmingly dizzy; he held the handrail and it all came to him. "Yes," he said out loud, "Yes, that's it." Taking in a deep breath he realized, *Things cannot go on this way,* and then he realized that even though he didn't know how, he had to understand that not knowing didn't make it impossible. The *how* was not—was never—important. *If things are to change, then I must change them, and I can change them!*

Education is the process of facilitating learning. The process of giving or receiving systematic instruction or an enlightening experience. The first day of school was always the saddest day, the end of childhood. A literal loss of innocence. The children were typically about six years old, coordinated enough to do tasks, but not yet adults.

The children were always happy. From birth, they had been raised in daycare to believe that the absolute best thing in life was the internet. The internet was all things to them, and they were lucky, because they were going to get to enjoy the true, fully-immersive internet. The only downside was, the internet was for grownups. They were too little to be able to be on the internet, and so they have to stay in boarding school until it was time for their higher education, which took place at the clinic. But after that was over, it was immersive internet all the way. I, like all the other kids in my class, couldn't wait.

There was another group, almost as naïve, maybe more. They are the people who volunteer to join the staff. Some of them believed that life was hard, and why should the staff get all the fun? They want to enjoy the internet, which is better than life. I'm not sure if I feel sorry for this group or disgusted.

There were actually two more groups, though they looked like one. One came from the jails; violent criminals or "three strikers." The other were debtors. If you couldn't pay off your debts law enforcement staff brings them to the clinic. Both of these were easy to deal with, though I felt sorry for them. They came heavily sedated, and we would restrain them and keep them sedated. If we didn't keep them sedated, they started yelling and screaming. The screamers were the worst—they would damage themselves screaming. Staff without the ability to respond to questions is a less useful staff.

The process was fairly painless, at first. No one knew about the painful part, but we anesthetize the patient. The first surgery was the inserting of the catheter into the arm. This was always done first, because once we did the second surgery, we started using feeding tubes to feed the converts.

The second surgery was the implanting of the cerebral interface into the front right side of the head. I don't know the details any more than I can describe them. If I was selected to do the surgery, I'd cut open the temple and, with a tool, hollow out a cavern immediately in front of the frontal lobe. We'd insert a thin black wafer that has a magnetic contact which we slid in between the skull and the brain tissue, then cover with the skin of the right temple.

The final step was to insert a liquid, a kind of thick goo which was supposed to repress infection, and promote the healing of tissue. It actually caused the tissue to adhere to other things. It was like glue, though we only seemed to use it for cerebral implants. It'd work wonders on connecting skin.

We'd keep the patients sedated, heart rates low, for a few days as the incision healed. Then the painful part began. The testing of the interface connection. We had to make sure the interface could control the entire body. If it couldn't, then you couldn't be staff. This portion of the education process was called calibration. The interface had to be able to execute the full range of motion of your muscles and joints. You had to be able to exert maximum strength and the interface needed to know its limits and how to achieve them.

Finally, programs had to be uploaded. The basic instructions, concierge, were already on the wafer, but we had to be able to upload and download without any nasty bits coming off and damaging the brain.

The whole procedure took about two weeks, depending on age. The younger the faster. Those who came from debtors court or the corrections facilities could take a few days longer to heal. In all, about nineteen out of twenty education procedures were successful. For those that weren't, we have retirement. The working world was just not for them.

I hated those days. Thankfully, there weren't many of them. I looked at those poor, the guilty, the innocent and the naïve who had been brought before me, and I wished I could control myself and somehow not do what I knew I was about to do. Sometimes, I screamed inside my own head for them, because I knew that this not only could have been me, it *was* me. I was one of those small children, clamoring for the immersive internet. We were told it was nothing like anything we could understand, and they were right.

35

OVERDRAWN

Vomit welled in Brian's throat. He struggled to keep it down, swallowing hard. The sight of it made him dizzy and sick at the same time. He had to hold onto his desk, and he fell back against the door at the same time.

A registered letter. Did they have such a thing? He had to even sign for it. Signing for it was a formality, an important formality. Someone needed to know he had received it. It was someone else's checkbox obligation. Brian staggered back around his desk. He landed in his seat. He opened the drawer, shuffled around his desk, chasing pens, papers and office supplies that had long since broken but never managed to make it from drawer to garbage can. Finally, he found a long thin pen, which didn't work but he kept just to open letters. Sliding the pen into the envelope, he tore it open, leaving chunky bits as he ripped his way along the edge of the envelope.

It was one thin piece of paper addressed to him, printed on one side.

Brian Agarwal
1720 Marbeth Drive
Suite 303

Re: Petition for Compulsory Foreclosure.

This notice is intended to serve as the first notice of the filing of motion for Compulsory Foreclosure against you, your assets and any related properties for the purposes of paying debt outstanding and delinquent.

This petition has been filed against you, Brian Agarwal (party of the first part) by Sheila Grantner of BCPL LLP (party of the second part) with Fairview County and is witnessed by Olivia Gerrard of Seventh National Bank (party of the third part).

If you have any questions about this petition, you may view it at Fairview County Courthouse.

If you have any questions about the debts outstanding or delinquent, please contact Olivia Gerrard at Seventh National Bank for details on these accounts.

A tribunal date will be set for you to attend in no fewer than 30 days from the date of this letter and no more than 60 days of the date of this letter to assess if you have made good the debts outstanding and delinquent. If, after that hearing, these debts remain delinquent for an additional 30 days, the party of the first part may be declared in bankruptcy by the party of the second part witnessed by the party of the third part. At such time all assets of the party of the first part may be disposed of, in accordance with the discretion of the party of the second part.

Warm Regards
Susan K. Woland
Foreclosure Petitions Clerk
Fairview County

The room spun. Things went black and he could hear his heart pounding in the back of his head. Cold sweat was running down his face. He struggled to keep breathing. Images of being taken in the night, anesthetized by the medical rescue techs, loaded onto a restraining bed and being sent to Clinic 14, all flashed through his head.

The image was clear in his mind, even though he was anesthetized, he could see what was in front of him. Surely someone would help him. The trip was bumpy and lights flashed in the ambulance as he stared up at the ceiling. They arrived at the clinic and he was wheeled in. He tried to scream, he tried to move, but either the restraining bed or the paralytic worked too well and he was stuck.

Brian imagined he was handed off to the med-techs. He saw the face of 418 from below. He tried to say something but 418 was fully engaged and it didn't notice. Hey, this wasn't fair, this was his own staff! But his own staff worked efficiently, as programmed, and rolled him straight off to the operating theater. There were blinding lights and the room smelled like rotten flesh and there were flies everywhere. He was released from the bed and carried to another table. The table was sticky. He could feel the crushing of hundreds of dead insects as he was laid upon the table. Brian's head was clamped into place and he heard the whirring sound of a high-speed drill or cutter. 418's face appeared, eyes still glazed, but with a strange smile on his face.

Brian fell off his chair and landed on his right elbow. Pain shot through his arm—it was relief—now he felt sick for another reason. Should he tell his wife? He had to tell Imelda, she'd be furious with him, but how would he be able to explain if they got foreclosed? She'd be even more furious with him, though he probably wouldn't have to hear it for long. When they came, they didn't wait around. They would break down the door, streaming in, screaming orders, law enforcement staff would hold you in place while medical rescue techs administered sedatives. There was a lot of shouting. It wasn't like he was going to be able to calmly explain to Imelda that he had tried, but, sorry, we were in bankruptcy and now we were going to go work off our debts, it's been a slice. He wouldn't even get to kiss her good-bye.

Getting himself up off the floor, Brian realized he was going to have to get the facts. Sitting back in his chair, he had to calm himself. "Okay," he thought, "if I can pay off whatever Seventh National thinks I owe, this all goes away, right?" He wasn't thinking he was muttering to himself. "I just have to find out what it is. How much is it? That's the first thing." Brian looked up the Seventh National Bank, he'd never done any business with them before. Using his computer, he looked up an O. Gerrard at Seventh National. He pressed the dial button that popped up on his screen.

It took about forty-five minutes for Brian to get through to Olivia Gerrard. She was well guarded and well defended by automated attendants, push-button menus and minor minions that appeared to be offering helpful advice but were there to make you think it was your idea to hang up. Truly the most expensive thing a company could do is answer the phone. It was one of the first jobs that had been automated, once labor costs had dropped with the development of staff. Using staff allowed a company to keep quality high, costs low and still have it sound like a first language person was answering the phone. They were good at keeping people from talking to non-staff, who got paid a whole lot more. The fact that Brian knew this made it harder not to feel panic. Cold fear surrounded him; he didn't even do business with Seventh National. This was crazy.

Finally, he got through. "Hello Olivia Gerrard?" Brian tried not to sound like he was panicked, angry or scared.

"This is Olivia. How can I help you?" The voice on the other end belonged to an older woman who had been sitting in some stuffy office where the air conditioning didn't work.

"Hello, I am Brian Agarwal," Brian started, hoping this would get things going. It didn't work.

"Hello Mr. Agarwal. How can I help you?" Her voice dripped with the thick gummy malaise of, *I don't care.*

Brian tried to stay calm. "I received a letter," he started. "It was from the county clerk's office and it was witnessed by you." He said it quickly, far quicker than he'd meant to.

"Do you have your account number handy?" the woman replied in even, paced monotone.

"No." Brian heard his voice crack a bit. "No. I don't know the account number. I didn't think I had an account with you."

"Oh," was the response and nothing more.

Finally, Brian thought of something to say, "You witnessed a letter from someone called BCPL claiming that I am in arrears."

"Oh, now that I can look up. One moment." Brian could hear something rustling and her breathing on the other end of the line. Music sprang up on the in Brian's ear as she put him on hold; it was all he could do to not lose his mind and start ripping his hair out. Finally, the music stopped, "Oh yes, we have underwritten a line of credit that you have with them. They are calling it in. You haven't made a single payment."

Brian's jaw hit the ground. "A what?"

"You took out a line of credit with BCPL in March and you haven't made a payment on it."

"I did what?"

"Yes," said the voice, still dripping with I don't care, "I can see all the e-signatures here, you received twenty crypto credits and you have to pay 24.49% interest, no principle in the payment, with the balance due in 120 periods so that would have been a monthly payment of 0.4082cc, for a balance of 1.23cc that you currently owe. However, you have missed the first two payments, accelerating the repayment of the principle to due immediately."

Brian's head was reeling. "I don't know who BSPL is?"

"BCPL," she corrected.

"Whatever, I don't know who they are."

The voice on the line paused, as if she was waiting for Brian to say more. "Apparently you do, your e-signature is all over these papers."

"But I don't. How can this be?"

Olivia Gerrard truly didn't care. "I don't think it matters how, it is," she answered flatly, hoping to end this call.

Brian was frustrated. "But, no, I don't have an account. There must be some mistake. I'm trying to explain…"

Olivia Gerrard cut him off. She had lots of files to review and she didn't need to waste her day talking to this guy. He'd be staff soon enough and it wouldn't matter. "Well then," she tried, again, to close out the conversation, "you can explain all of that when the tribunal date comes up."

Wracking his brain, Brian tried to think of how this could happen. There must have been some mistake. He'd be able to take this up at the tribunal. He thought about it: the tribunals were not known for being merciful when it came to debtors. He tried looking up BCPL. There were lots of warnings to not use them, that their lending rates were high. One review said they were a lender of last resort. He tried calling them, but it was fruitless. With the banks, there usually was a way to get to speak to someone, but this company was well hidden behind automated answering staff and frequent misunderstandings, misdirection and strategically placed hang-ups. After three hours of trying to get through, Brian decided he had to think of some other way to address this. There had to be some solution.

It was the fastest ride home Brian had ever had. Imelda wasn't going to handle this well. She would call him a fool and she would sob that all was lost and that they were going to be turned into staff. She would point out that he should have seen this coming, and was this the future he wanted for Prince? And, how could he have done this to her? Perhaps she would go into denial, not knowing how serious this was, and she would simply ignore it and let him try to figure out something. Maybe she would surprise him and have some big stack of money hidden somewhere, or maybe she would know someone who could make this all go away. A fellow could hope, but his car drove him home quickly and surely. Before he knew it, he was standing at the front door of 515 Station Close, looking up at where light from a screen flashed. He knew Prince was home.

Head hung; Brian entered the building. He looked at the elevator. It would be easier, and faster. It probably didn't make any difference that he was taking the stairs these days. Nonetheless, he turned and headed up the stairs. There were not as many of them as he had hoped there would be.

To his surprise, Imelda was not nearly as angry as he thought she would be. In fact, she wasn't angry at all. He, by his own judgment, had always been a careful and considerate husband. He failed in all the ways women always feel men fail them, but, in all, he had given everything that he could to his wife and family, and he had enjoyed them with honest warmth and cherished them every day.

The idea that someone was attempting to foreclose on them was not as surprising to Imelda as Brian had hoped it would. He'd always seen himself as provider, and now there was someone who was willing to try to take him before a judge and accuse him of not being so. It implied that he was a failure, and Imelda didn't rail into him about his shortcomings. He felt like he was going to fall flat on his face.

She was understanding, worried for sure, but understanding. When he told her, he had no idea how it was that such a debt could have been linked to him, she believed him. She told him everything would be all right, even though she didn't know any way that it could be. She agreed with him that falling on the mercy of the tribunal was not such a good idea. You never knew what they would do, and if things didn't go their way, there would be no appeal and no aftermath. It was likely best to avoid the tribunal.

It was good to tell her all of these things, to share his worries even though in sixty days they could all be hooked up to a wire, sitting in a chair waiting to go work for someone else. She was compassionate, and Brian didn't think he had ever loved her more. He would find a solution!

36

FAST FOOD

I used to love to go to the ultimate fights in Las Vegas. What could be a better time than to watch two people beat each other, one to the edge of consciousness and the other, to death? But now, the idea of the roaring crowd, and the beating that would go on until someone was scraped up off the floor, made me feel a little unwell. Blood was actually a bother to clean-up, it got sticky fast. There was a distinct smell to it, too, like meat and salt, that made me recoil just a bit.

I didn't like it when exceptions that came in were messy and not pleasant. I couldn't help thinking that whatever had happened could have happened to me. If I'd have been in the same place at the same time, it would have been me, and I might not have even noticed it happening. Exceptions give no warnings, they just occur. It was like that one day: there was no warning, there was no notification of what was going on. The cars just started to arrive.

The first car arrived in the carport. I was summoned to go get it with the other med-tech. We opened the car and found a staff had been stuffed into the car. There was blood everywhere, and the staff had the gray of death some time ago in its eyes. We pulled the body out of the car and plopped it onto the bed. There was quite a mess in the car. No time to worry about that now. We would tell the car to go out of service, so it could be cleaned up. Thankfully, cleaning cars was not one of my job tasks. As we were busy restraining the body, I noticed another car enter the carport and queue up behind the car we were working on. *Oh dear.*

As we began wheeling the first body away, another car entered the carport. Well, the good thing about cars is that they will wait their turns. Normally, the passengers were blissfully unaware that they were stuck in traffic. However, in this case, I think the passengers were just unaware.

That was when we were summoned to the white area of the clinic. We left the staff where it was, lying in the carport, then headed off toward the white area. We burst through the doors to find two medical rescue techs unloading a stretcher. There was a man on it, and he was moaning, clearly still alive, but he had a big chunk missing from his left arm where something had passed through it, and a wound to his leg that looked like it still contained a bullet. We took the man into a clean theatre and started working on him. He started screaming when I reached into his thigh to dig out the metal. The other med-tech tied off his arm so he would not bleed out. Then, mercifully for all of us, he passed out.

I continued to work on closing up the wounds when another pair of med rescue techs came to drop off another victim. This one was a woman who was shrieking about her hand. It didn't look good—she'd put it up and it had been obliterated. A nice round hole remained where the pass-through had occurred. The other med-tech took her away and sedated her.

I finished up my sewing as two more sets of medical rescue techs arrived. Neither of those victims were alive. We pushed them away into the hallway as a child arrived with a hysterical mother. The child had been shot in the hip and was pretty close to death. The bullet had hit the base of the spine and shattered everything. I wasn't able to save him, but I tried.

Other people, family, were starting to appear in the white reception area of the clinic. There was lots of screaming and wailing and crying. We didn't save many that day. Twelve people were brought to us. Eight of them went straight to the hallway for cataloging and pickup by the removal people. Eventually, two law enforcement staff showed up with a medical rescue tech. There was no attempt to save this one. They had already put a blanket over the body, but the clinic went quiet when that body was wheeled in. It was almost as if all the air had been sucked out of the room.

There was a tremendous crash of screaming and shouting as the air flooded back into the room when the body was wheeled into the removal area.

I wished I could do or say something, there had been a shooting at a *fast food* restaurant. I didn't know what fast food was, but I imagined Jazmin's cafe, and how awful that must have been. Apparently, the *sicko* under the blanket had walked in with automatic weaponry and opened fire on everyone he could. Law enforcement staff had come and taken him down quickly, there weren't a lot of places to hide. He had jumped the counter, was shot and fell into a fry machine.

It was awful dealing with that much blood and flesh and not being able to say I wish I could do more. But there wasn't much that can be done with injuries like that. If something important was hit, it's pretty much the end, and most of the dead had multiple wounds. It all seemed senseless.

The day seemed to move quickly and slowly at the same time. The patients died so quickly, and there didn't seem to be an end. Thankfully, Samuel—or whoever was driving—handled all the questions.

"Is my husband going to make it?"

"We are doing everything we can." And I noticed I kept on working. Thankfully, I kept on working.

Mercifully the day did come to an end. The bodies were put in the removal area, and those that could be helped were. When there was no longer anything for us to do, we went back to the gray area of the clinic... oh, wait, I forgot... We went to the carport and found seven cars lined up, two of them actually dripping blood from around the doors. All the staff from the restaurant were waiting for us to offload them from their cars. They had been patient, sat in their place, and waited for their turn.

Methodically, we opened the cars and pulled the staff out of their blood-soaked seats. We had to use water to free some of them. They were model patients, didn't even complain once. I wondered if they ever even knew they were about to be slaughtered. We loaded them onto beds in the incinerator room. It had been such a busy day. It was a small mercy that the insurance adjusters had gone home. I was tired of all the blood.

37

HOLISM

The next day wasn't so bloody. There were no new dead bodies to be found in the clinic, and nothing new had rolled in during the night shift. We waited for the insurance adjusters to show up, but only one did. All the staff were insured by the same company, NAIKI Insurance Co-operative. I had no idea what NAIKI was supposed to mean or stand for.

A young man with too much acne, the type that was going to leave dents on his face when he got older, walked into the clinic. It looked like he had been given a suit two sizes too big in the hopes that he would grow into it. He looked a little intimidated, uncomfortable, and kept looking behind him as if there might be someone coming or watching him. I wanted to tell him, whatever he was looking for, we didn't have things like that here, but I couldn't.

"Hello sir, how may I be of assistance today?" I said as the man approached me.

"I'm Grady Schmidt from NAIKI." He looked around quickly, giving me the feeling that he might not either be Grady Schmidt or from NAIKI. "I've come to see the casualties that belong to us."

"Right this way," I answered cheerfully, and led him off to the incinerator room.

I liked Grady better than any of the other adjusters that I had met. Perhaps it was because he actually checked that each body was his, and took some sort of look at each body, to just to make sure it was dead. "This is horrible," he said.

I smiled. "I am sorry you feel this way. Is there something I can do to make you more comfortable?" I asked for some reason.

240

He looked at me strangely. "It's horrible that they died like this," he clarified.

I wanted to agree with him. "It is unfortunate, but exceptions happen." I was mad at myself for allowing those words to come out. It was horrible, but I wasn't allowed to say it.

Grady didn't take much time looking at the bodies. With each cover he lifted, each photo that he took, he looked a little greener. I stood by, an impassive but pleasant look plastered on my face, saying nothing unless I was spoken to. When he was done, I escorted him back to reception, then returned to the incinerator room and, with the other med-tech, we pressed the red button seven times.

No one ever thought about it again. The oven shuts off by itself.

The day went back to normal, not random, but nice comfortable boredom. It was good, I needed a rest. You can't have something like that happen every day. It gets to be too much. I welcomed the taking of temperatures, the cleaning of equipment and the mopping of floors—in the white area only. There is a certain solace one can feel in the proper and precise execution of tedious work, like sorting things or filing papers.

I was disturbed by another call to the carport. The other med-tech and I prepared a bed and walked out. When we arrived, the car opened. There was a staff in the car, and from everything I could see, there was no apparent injury. What I did notice was that it was offline. Hmm, perhaps something wrong with his cerebral interface? That wouldn't be good.

"Hey, what are you doing?" it protested as we reached in and pulled it out of the car. I suppose I had been programmed how to do this when someone didn't want help. It didn't matter how it moved, we had too good a grip on it—I could feel the pain in my hands as we gripped it, and wondered how badly my fingers were damaging its arms and shoulders. Expertly, we flipped it over and smacked it onto the bed. I pinned it down with my weight and the other med-tech activated the restraining foam. It was stuck now.

I did a physical on this staff. Technically it was a male. I did the checks that were appropriate to a male. There was no physical problem with this staff. After my examination, I sat them up, still in its restraining chair though it looked a lot less frantic sitting up encased in restraining foam than it did laying down in restraining foam. The staff was offline, and it was in this manner that I began to question them. It was strange for me to talk to staff as staff.

"How do you feel?" I asked.

"Frightened," it answered truthfully.

"Why are you frightened?" I parried right back.

It looked around, "I'm here, this is where the damaged go."

I felt like nodding, but I couldn't. I simply continued, "Are you damaged?"

"No."

I expected myself to ask, *Why are you here?* But I didn't. "How is work?"

"Okay, I guess." It added trying to look away, which meant it wasn't okay. If I could, I would have told them that everything was okay and maybe it should just go home and go for a walk and try not to think about it.

"Are you having problems with work?"

"No," even I didn't believe its answer.

"Are you experiencing headaches?"

"Yes," it answered. It looked at me hopefully, but I continued behind my inscrutable face.

"Could you describe these headaches?" I asked, and for some reason added, "please."

"I get them in the top of my head, my eyes are sore, and my head hurts like I just don't want to look at anything anymore."

I took out a flashlight. "This is a retinoscope," I told it, "please keep your eye open. Tell me if there is any discomfort when I activate the light." I looked into the eye, and something inside me noted that there did not seem to be anything wrong. "Did you feel any discomfort?"

"No." I was about to pick up another instrument when it continued, "It only happens when I am at work."

"It does?" I asked for confirmation.

"Yes." It seemed to be relieved to be able to tell someone about this. "When I get home, I find I have to take off my clothes, soak them in water, place them on my forehead, and that will make me feel much better."

"Do you close your eyes?"

Confused by this question, it stammered a bit, "Why, yes, of course."

"And when you close your eyes, what do you see?"

"Well..." It looked around as if it knew that it shouldn't say anything. "I see all the things that I do at work."

"What do you do?"

"I file taxes, make assessments, send out bills."

"And you remember this?" I remembered much of what I did, but I had my eyes wide open.

"Yes," it added, "I don't want to, but I do."

"So, you are online, and you remember filing taxes, making assessment and sending out bills, do you remember how to do each of these tasks?"

"Every detail." It looked exasperated. "I don't want to. I'd rather play slots or attend a game show, but when I close my eyes at night, all I remember is bills and taxes, what to look for, what has to be there, where do they go, what shelf, where do we send them, how to log in, where to store the documents." It was starting to get worked up. It was a real torment for them. "I don't want to know these things. I just want a normal life. Can you make it stop?"

"Of course, we can," I answered. I even heard certainty in how I said it, but I had no idea how we would do it.

It was late, we kept the staff, that one suffering from working, overnight. We let them be online because it had suffered no physical injury to the area of their cerebral interface, but first thing in the morning, after the usual rounds of heartbeat, temperature taking were done, we wheeled them off to an education theater. This was going to be a test of his ability to upload, download knowledge. For the patient, it was probably going to be painless.

I snapped the patient into place and anchored the table under a great light. It still looked like an operating theater, but there were no machines for drilling or trays of tools for cutting. Just a computer with a cable attached to it. I cleaned and sterilized the cable and snapped it to the side of its head.

I stepped behind a counter. I could still see the patient restrained in their bed, and I started to operate a machine. There wasn't much to it. There was a button marked *Up* and a button marked *Down* and a button marked *Switch* that would stop doing whatever and start doing the other. At least that was all the controls I was using. The rest of the panel was wide and full of dials, sliders, and levers. I had no idea what any of them did. I just turned on the machine and after a while pressed the switch button.

Every time I pressed the switch button, the patient convulsed, as if it was in pain. I was pretty sure that wasn't supposed to happen. About the eighth time I pressed the switch button, I heard the patient emit a soft groan. That groan got louder, until it was a cry each time I pressed the button. The frequency with which I was pressing was getting faster and faster, until I was keeping the patient writhing and groaning, jolting them again and again.

The patient was exhausted, sweaty and I could see it had been straining itself against the restraining foam. When I disconnected the wires the patient fell limp, its chest was heaving. It was going to be physically all right, but I could tell there was something wrong in its head. I unlocked the bed and wheeled them back to a suitable place in the corridor where there wasn't much light. Sleep can be soothing.

The patient dozed, with occasional groaning throughout the remainder of my shift. We had put them on the *to be monitored* list. It wasn't going to die, but I didn't think it was resting very well. I knew I would find out all about it tomorrow when I questioned the patient about its experience.

The next morning, I came to work and did all the usual things. I check on the living, and I found a staff to take off to the incinerator, but it was not the staff who I had treated the day before. The staff we took to the incinerator was a street sweeper that had been hit by a car. It was fairly obvious: broken bones, pulverized hip, lots of blood loss. It had arrived during the night and the night shift med-techs had tried to save them, though I couldn't imagine what they might have done to reverse whole body blunt force trauma. But they tried. Isn't that nice?

Returning from the incinerator room, I was surprised that I was not sent to examine the staff suffering from headaches. I started doing other things. I caught a glimpse of the patient in the hallway. It hadn't moved, and neither of us were examining it. Unfortunately, I was at work, and there was nothing I could do but work. Work is work; I don't get to choose anything.

An adjuster came and I figured we were going to the incinerator room, but we didn't. We walked over to the staff. The adjuster was a wrinkled woman who wore a lot of flowing clothes and bright colors. She was unmissable in this gray and darkened area of the clinic. Loose materials were not advised here as they can snag on things. She wore flat shoes, hair in a bun, big glasses and long flowing silky fabrics that draped around her like fine curtains of red, yellow, white and green all mixed together, as if someone had painted her clothes with a broad paintbrush. She had an airy sound to her voice.

"Tsk, tsk, tsk," she said, as we approached the staff. "This can't be good."

I'd liked to have pointed out to her that if it were good, she wouldn't be here, and neither would the staff.

"Oh dear, oh dear, oh deary me," she said as she looked at the staff. The staff had been taken offline again. I watched and waited to be addressed. "How does your head feel?"

"Horrible," it said. "I feel horrible."

"Mushy?"

"Like I've had a thousand horses stampeding through it."

"Oh dear!" she said, she turned to me. "What is the diagnosis?"

The file appeared in my vision. "The staff has suffered cognitive infection due to the leakage of electronic charge and information from the cerebral interface."

"Oh," she nodded. She did look genuinely concerned. Most adjusters looked at me impassively. Some of them rolled their fingers in small circles hoping I'd speed up. They never interjected because that caused me to pause. "What can be done for it?"

"The fault exists in the conjunction between the interface and the cerebrum, which is causing the staff to suffer when information is moved either way. Additionally, it can be asserted that the firewall between interface and cerebrum has become compromised, resulting in neural data bleeding into the staff host."

She squinted at me. "So, that means?"

"The staff has data bleed. This accounts for the soreness in the eye. It may have been caused by an infection and spread to the optic nerve. The staff is re-seeing things that were recorded by the cerebral interface as if they were things that the staff has seen as themselves. This is causing discomfort which appears to be in the central area, in the corpus callosum. This could be the sign of further brain injuries but will not be treatable without surgery."

"Surgery?" she interrupted me. "We don't want that!"

I wasn't able to stop my speaking and ask why we wouldn't want that. "The prognosis is that this phenomenon is not going to attenuate and will become more pronounced until such time as the staff is unusable for either reasons of loss of co-ordination or unmitigated discomfort."

"Oh, so it will not stop?"

"Correct," I answered and stopped, but I had so much more to say.

"Okay, get me the chart." I handed her an electronic pad. She scrolled her way down it and tapped the button for the checkbox RFR. She pressed her thumb to the bottom of the page and her signature sprung into place. "There," she said cheerfully, the concern she had shown just a few moments ago had evaporated into the ether. "All ready to go. Do you have anything else for me to see today?"

I took a moment, as I knew I was searching the inventory of our patient list. "No, we do not," I replied to her. I could feel myself smiling outwardly.

I watched her leave, some old painted bird, flying out of this cavern. I went to the dispensary, obtained some medicine, administered it to the staff so it wouldn't move when we released the restraints. Together with the other med-tech, we headed to the carport. It was time for that staff to move on. We loaded it into a car that was waiting, closed the lid and went back to our duties. Quietly, the car drove out of the carport.

The next day a car arrived, it was the same staff I had helped place in the car the day before. There were no signs of life, but it had a smile on its face. The pain it had been suffering and the pain I had put them through had been washed away.

38

THE DEAL

This was to be my fate. A long life of working, until something stopped working and then I would be sent to a retirement home. Then, with any luck, I might avoid dying for a while. What kind of horrible deal is that?

I had all day to think about it. That staff, the one we just loaded into the incinerator, was me; a naïve me. If it had just managed to keep its mouth shut, it might not have been retired. I could see how easy it was. *Just don't be able to do work.* All I would have to do was start complaining to Samuel about headaches, and I'd be at the clinic. What amazed me was the honesty with which the staff had answered all my questions. When was the last time that an authority figure questioning you ever did something good for you? I'm not sure if the naïveté made it worse or better. I can't deviate from my programming, perhaps, neither could it.

"Hello Samuel." I summoned Samuel back into the foreground as I went about the duties at the clinic.

"Yes, George, how may I help you today?" Always cheerful, and always there, I could minimize him, but I couldn't make him go away.

"Please send a message to King," I stated. "Hello King, how are you today? I am having one of those days where I just don't know what I am supposed to be doing? Could we meet up and have a little chat about that, whenever you can? Thank you."

"Would you like me to read back your message?"

"No."

"Would you like me to send the message as is?"

"Yes."

"Sent." There was a pause. "You know you are here to work, and I can do that for you."

"Huh?"

"Well, I noticed you stated you don't know what you are supposed to be doing. That's what you said." Samuel was talking an unusual amount. "I just wanted to let you know, I can take care of everything. You don't have to know or do anything."

I was confused and tried to remember exactly what I said. Had I said the wrong thing? "Did I?"

"Yes, you did."

"Oh." I was about to say that that wasn't what I'd meant, but that would have led to what I did mean. "I must have been confused." I thought about it for a moment—that wasn't a good choice. A bolt of fear shot through me: when you think about not saying something, it can be hard not to.

"Well, then, see, that is why I offer to read back your messages, in case you have said something that isn't going to make sense. Would you like me to recall the message?"

"No," I answered a little too quickly, then tried to sound calm. Samuel had read—or listened to my message—and was even capable of not sending them even though I've asked for it to be sent. Another bolt of icy cold went through me. "No, just let it be."

"Okay." I imagined he sounded a little suspicious. "I am here to help, remember that."

"Yes. And, thank you very much." I didn't bother waiting around for King to respond, he didn't respond right away, and I wanted to end this conversation. "May I go back to seeing once again?"

"Your wish is my command."

I think not. I remembered how I tried to take a car ride and wasn't allowed to go anywhere. "Good to know."

I woke up the next morning and everything went as programming dictated. I was showered, I dressed, I headed out, stood in line, jammed into the elevator, waited my turn for a car to whisk me away.

It was utter disappointment that I did, in fact, make the turn that meant I was going to the clinic. I hoped King had got my message. I was sure he did, and he'd always kept his word in the past...sort of. It would be a long day—hopefully uneventful—but long. Twelve hours of being marched around, watching myself do things with speed and precision but no explanation.

And I was right. The day was long. By the time I went home, I was glad to be free. All I could want was to get out of there, go someplace no one ever went. I decided I would go for a walk someplace where it snowed, all the time. I asked Samuel to turn off the temperature sensation. I didn't need to feel cold. I just wanted to walk someplace, down a country lane, to a pathway by a ravine and be the first to put my feet in the newly fallen snow. The land, trees, rocks, road, fence posts and whatever I would walk up to and past were all clean and blanketed in the first sticky snowfall of a year that had never been. I didn't care that it wasn't a real place, just that it was nowhere, and it was something different.

The next day, I was equally disappointed. Again, I didn't get redirected to go see King. There was another exception involving automobiles. Four staff were brought in suffering from various injuries. One had broken ribs from where the restraining foam had held on long past the rib's ability to absorb the sudden stopping motion.

Another had part of the car sticking out of its right arm. After removing the bar, they would be fine, though likely the arm would never be the same. Hope they didn't have a job that required a lot of the use of that arm.

The third car that came in had a staff that had a crushed face, as if the restraining foam had not worked properly. We operated and pushed the cheek back into place. I was amazed at how quickly I could sew and how easily we pushed the bones together. They were lucky-ish. It didn't look like the cerebral interface had been affected, but you never can tell with head injuries. The cerebral interface is a delicate and complex piece of technology. It's best not to take chances with a concussion.

The final car contained a staff who had suffered a left temple impact, like myself. But by the time we had taken care of all the other staff, as we dealt with them in the order in which they arrived; there was nothing to do but put them in the incinerator room. A one car exception, I thought, that's pretty rare. I suppose I was near the front of the line when I got here. I'd have smiled wryly at that. Instead, we hoisted the body out of the car, not a word was said, and we wheeled it away.

I was pleased with myself. If I learned anything it was that King is a good man who would help me whenever he could. I was lucky to have such a good friend. I'm glad I didn't just pepper King with requests. I figured he was busy working on something, and that's why I hadn't heard anything, but it had been bothering me. Today I was comforted by the facts: I had got up early, was ahead of traffic, and the car didn't swerve to the right. It made me know I was on my way to Jazmin's cafe.

King looked troubled. I approached him with a smile on my face. I was glad to see him, but he only returned half of the smile and motioned that I should sit down across from him.

"What is on your mind?" I think that was the first time that I ever led the conversation.

"Nothing," he replied, waving his hand but looking at the food he had ordered for me to eat. "I got your message," he said, though he still looked distracted and slightly annoyed, "What do you mean, you don't know what you are supposed to be doing?"

I had to think, "Yeah, about that," I started. I wish I remembered exactly what I had said. "About that, I guess I had a hard day."

He raised his eyebrows.

"There was a shooting or something, and I got to work on some of the bodies, and, well, you know, that kind of thing doesn't make you feel good," I tried to explain.

"Do you want me to find other work for you?"

"No!" I exclaimed, briefly thinking of how mind-numbing every other type of work is. "No, this is just fine. In fact, I like it a lot."

"Okay." He looked like he was lost somewhere else like something bigger was on his mind.

"It's just that, well, you know, I get up in the morning, and I go to work, and I work and sometimes good things happen, and I feel like I did something good, but most of the time it's just boredom. I go home, and I eat, and I rest, and I entertain myself, and I probably sleep, but the next day it starts all over again."

King nodded. "Sounds like life to me."

I straightened. "Yes, it does, but is it?"

King sighed. "I don't know. I guess."

That response didn't give me much to go on, "That can't be all that there is."

"I don't know," King answered. He wasn't eating much, and he wasn't strategically sipping his coffee. He looked a little limp.

"What happened to you?" I asked. Finally, I might have been overstepping my bounds, but it was getting obvious that he was elsewhere.

King sighed again, took a long breath, and sighed again. "You know, I guess it doesn't matter if I tell you, because who are you going to tell, but things have been pretty tight for me."

"Tight?"

"Yes." King picked up the sugar and poured it into his coffee. I'd never seen him put anything in his coffee, but he poured it and poured it long past what I would have thought could go into a cup of coffee. Taking his spoon, he languidly stirred circles in the coffee sugar mixture. "Do you remember when you got to go home and get online once again? After the exception."

I smirked and stifled a laugh, thinking about how eager I was. "Yes. That seems like so long ago."

"You told me that you couldn't do anything."

I nodded. "Yes, I had no money."

King nodded slowly back at me. "Yes, so you do understand. Except imagine you have some money, but not enough."

"So, like I could get some things, but not everything?"

"Yes," he continued, "but imagine that the things you could get were just not enough. So while you had some money, it felt like you had no money. That's feeling tight."

I tried to imagine what would have happened if I could have ordered just a sandwich or a drink and nothing more. I wasn't sure if that would be frustrating, infuriating or just devastating. "Oh," I finally answered. "What do you do? When you feel tight."

King sighed again. "I don't know."

I brightened. "You can have some of my money."

King laughed. "No, it doesn't work that way."

"What do you mean?"

King looked me in the eye. "Your money only works online. It doesn't work here."

I looked at him confused, "So?"

"Your money has no value."

I wished he had not put it so bluntly. Isn't that why I went to work? So I could get money, so I could spend money, so I could enjoy life? I felt a wave of sickening misery wash over me. *My life wasn't real, and my money wasn't real. What the*...I reeled with that for a moment. I caught a glimpse of King. He looked dejected, and I felt dejected. Maybe he was kidding. "Is there anything I can do?"

King sighed again. "I don't know."

It was the worst breakfast I'd had with King. The charm he had, the confidence and common sense he normally exuded, was missing. He looked like a man carrying a lot of weight. The only time that a glimpse of the King I knew flashed in his eyes was when I asked if we could meet up tomorrow. Briefly he smiled, and said yes, and that it would be a pleasure. Perhaps tomorrow would be a better day.

The next day, good to his word, I found myself up early and redirected to Jazmin's cafe. We got a booth this time, not a table. I think everyone prefers a booth, except the people who can't fit into them. They prefer tables. But I liked the booth: the seats were more comfortable, and you didn't have wait staff and customers bumping into you, or making you duck so that they didn't crash into you.

I slid into the booth. "Good morning King, how are you today? Any better?"

"Yes," he said. "I feel better today."

I felt genuine relief, other than King, I didn't know anybody, quite literally, I didn't know anyone. "I'm glad. Did you sort out the tightness problem?"

King smiled, took his cup in his hand again. "No, I'm stuck." Then he corrected himself. "That's not what I mean to say. I don't see a solution."

"Oh." I felt my shoulders slump.

King put his cup down. "Just because I don't see a solution doesn't mean that there isn't one." He nodded at me, but over my shoulder.

I turned to see who was behind me, but there was no one. Or, anyone who was there was turned around, not looking and clearly not the recipient of the nod. I turned back. "That's good right?"

"Yes." King smiled. The old King was back. "That's good. Let's talk about you."

"Me?" I said.

King nodded again. "You said that you didn't know what you were doing, or something like that."

Ruefully, and feeling red in my face, I said, "I guess."

King looked away to let me get the color back out of my face. "I think I know what you were asking, and you are right not to put it too exactly, you can't trust your concierge."

"Huh?"

"I think that you just realized that there is more to life than being entertained, gambling, doing virtual drugs, having virtual parties, visiting virtual places, doing virtual things and going to work the next day."

I'd never heard it put that plainly. "Um, yes, I suppose."

"Right." King sliced a sausage and popped it into his mouth. "Real food tastes better," he stated after a good chew.

"It does!" I almost shouted. "I mean, it does," I managed to say it quieter.

"Why do you think that is?"

I shrugged.

"See, and you didn't answer me with anything more than just a shrug." He sat back and smiled. "It's because real food actually engages your whole body. It's not just the stimulation of some neural cluster in your brain."

I blinked at King, who continued to eat. He ate everything, and I sat there and so did he. We finished our breakfasts. He was right, it was delicious.

I think you know you have a friend when they annoy you, but you still manage to like each other. That was what King had done to me. He politely excused himself after breakfast was over, told me he'd ask me what I wanted tomorrow. Then we both went off to work. It's annoying, but food does taste better when you eat it than when you imagine it.

The next day, I was woken early again, and off I went to Jazmin's cafe.

I was smiling as I made my way through the maze of chairs. "Three days in a row? I could get used to this," I said. King was smiling. He was starting to look better.

"Good morning, how are you today?"

"Do you want to know?"

"Sure," King was back to hiding behind his cup after talking. "Of course." He took a sip.

"Well." I took my time answering. "I'm glad to be here, because I didn't want to go to work. I mean, if I have to do work, that's it, but I mean, what's the point?"

King smiled. "I'm glad. Have you figured out what it is that you really want?"

I stopped what I was doing and put down my knife and fork. "I, I," I hadn't given it much thought.

"I can tell you what you don't want, you've already said it."

"I don't want to go to work?"

"That's true, and that's what you did say." He held his coffee cup in front of his mouth again. "But we all have to work. Work is work. It's not so bad?"

I smiled, not sure how that was a question. "I don't want to work but I have to go to work."

"Yes, that's true."

"So?"

"What is it that you want, if it's not the work?"

I smiled. I took a big link of sausage and cut it in half. I put it in my mouth and chewed while I looked at King, who was smiling at me. "I get it, I want out."

"The spoken word! Once said..." King replied playfully with drama.

"I want out?" It sounded so strange to me, but upon hearing it, I knew that it was true. I did want out. I wanted to help people, not just be something that might be used to help people or, in greater measure, be used to harm them. "I want out." It still sounded weird.

King nodded. "I needed to hear you say that."

"Why?"

King shrugged. "No man should impose his will on another as to how they live."

I blinked. "Okay, nice, now you're showing off."

"I mean, I can't tell you what you want. Only you can."

I drank some orange juice; it was my turn to use a drink as a prop to buy myself time to think. "I suppose that makes sense."

King smiled. "The food is good today."

I didn't see King the next day, and I was crushed about it. That was a long day and I was alone in my thoughts. I did want out, but to what? Perhaps I could travel, try to find some of those online places offline? I would need to find a job, but I didn't know how to do that. How would I get rid of the concierge? That pesky Samuel was always lurking somewhere just out of my sight.

I set a child's arm. That was a nice distraction, but I had a conversion come in from the prison. I got a glance at the file: this inmate had been too violent or too disruptive while serving their term, so the order was given by the warden and signed off by some judge that the inmate and their sentence was to be commuted into staff, and to work at the discretion of Fairview County Prison LLP. I did my work in both cases the same. Effectively and efficiently. I just enjoyed fixing the little boy more than I did fixing the problem for the prison.

As I let Samuel take me home—I figured it was best to let Samuel do as much as Samuel could—I felt that things might be about to change. There was a weird, almost optimistic feeling, though I had no good reason to feel it. Like there might actually be some reason for going on. It was warm, and I wanted to wrap my arms around it and never let it go.

When I fixed the boy's arm, and he stopped crying, he looked up at me and said, "Thank you."

I wanted to say something back, but Samuel spoke for me, "You are welcome, how can I help you today?" I would have just said that he was welcome and left it at that.

The boy looked up at me. "How come your eyes aren't gray?" he asked.

Again, Samuel answered, "The graying of the eyes has to do with the absorption of light. In this case, this staff is not absorbing the light." Indeed, how could he say that? Hadn't he got that backward? The light was only absorbed when it didn't reflect back.

The next day I met with King. "King," I said, as I walked toward the booth where he had set himself up. "I want out." It felt great to say, and I wanted to say it louder.

King smiled. "Now that's what I thought. You even say it like you mean it."

"I do mean it." The good feeling started to dissolve. "I just don't know what *out* means. And, I don't know how."

King could see the smile sliding off my face. "Stop right there, don't think about it too much. I have a plan."

39

A BAD PLAN

The first thing King told me was that he couldn't tell me anything. Strictly speaking, I wasn't supposed to know anything. What he did tell me was this—and I love this part—that there was no doubt I had brain damage! Perhaps it was for that reason I was beginning to understand. I had worked in the clinic for a while now, and I knew what brain damage was. It was an impairment of cognitive function caused by some injury. Okay, simplistic, but that's what it was. King explained that once a person has been commuted into staff, you were not supposed to remember anything that was uploaded to your head.

I nodded.

"You are supposed to walk around," he explained, "and you are supposed to do things because you were programmed to do them. And at the end of the day, when you go home, we could take that knowledge out of your head, and you would not know how to do any of what you have done during the day."

"That seems simple enough," I offered, "but I remember things." I didn't want to say the words out loud; but I had to agree, *I did have brain damage.*

King nodded, sipped his coffee. "I've given that a lot of thought. You aren't supposed to remember what is uploaded, but you remember what you see. It's the difference between learning and stealing."

"Stealing?"

"Yes, stealing. It's actually a crime for you to steal the knowledge that is uploaded into your head."

I remembered the staff that I reviewed. "I ran into a staff who was having data bleed."

"And what happened to it?"

"It was recommended for retirement."

King smiled, waved his hand as if something was to follow. "And then, what happened?"

I frowned. "The next day, it came back to us dead."

"Exactly," King replied, "if I knew you were stealing data, I'd have to turn you in, but you aren't."

"I'm not?"

"Nope. Just be careful what you say."

I blinked at King. He was serious. "Who am I going to tell? I only know you."

"You have a concierge?"

I nodded. "Right."

"Why didn't you turn me in?"

King smiled and shook his head. "They said you were fine. I had some deniability."

I nodded, but that didn't sound like a good thing.

"Besides, someone like you doesn't come around every day. I'd never heard of it. I don't think my father had, either. You were online but didn't want to be online. Everyone wants to be online. You didn't shout and shriek when you were not online. Well, you did at first. But you know what I mean?"

I thought of Belinda. It was unnerving thinking about that.

"Here's what I want you to do," he said, leaning over so no one would hear him. "I want you to learn everything you can."

I had leaned in to hear him. "Okay," I said, then sat back. "Why?"

"Learning stuff, may help you; and I may need your help."

"My help?" I replied. This was exciting. "How could I help you?"

"I don't want to get into it yet. It's a just-in-case thing. Just learn everything you can. And for God's sake, finish your breakfast." He pointed at my plate and shook his head. Eagerly, I started eating.

40

CLASSIFIED

As the days passed, Brian didn't feel any better about the impending tribunal date. True to expectations, the county clerk's office sent him a tribunal date in the mail. It also arrived registered, just to make sure he got it, though he didn't think it mattered. They would have held the friendly review without him.

He had to come up with some ideas. He spent most of his workday brainstorming what he could do, what he could sell. He needed to come up with twenty crypto coins, plus, at worst, three months' interest which would be 0.41 coins per month, or 1.23 more coins, it total, he calculated 21.23 coins. Well, that was the worst-case scenario. But how? And how had this happened? Yes, he had been violated, but now was not the time to lose his head getting bogged down about how did this happen and how did that happen. He had to think clearly and see if some solution would present itself.

Selling everything in the apartment was one option. Another was to try to refinance the loan. He could go somewhere else and perhaps get a loan for twenty-two coins, but that would only make things worse. It would buy him time and a different master, if things didn't work. The list of things he could sell he didn't think added up to enough. One's furniture, one's jewelry, isn't worth much to anyone other than yourself. Upon cold examination, the sum total of his life's possessions didn't add up to very much.

Brian looked at his list of options. Many of them were unpleasant, and he wasn't going to like them, but he kept them on the list. Better to have an option than not. One good thing was that he had a bit of time. As far as he understood, he couldn't be foreclosed on until thirty days after the friendly review at the courthouse. It was called it an arbitration for a reason; they were quite arbitrary. Perhaps it would be best if he went down to the clinic. It seemed like the next best thing to do.

Brian summoned his car and made his way to the stairs. It was true, stairs were getting easier and easier. It wasn't like the days when he was small, and he would go running up the stairs to the arms of his father, but he was able to go down them quickly and not feel dizzy. There was a gentle mist when he stepped out the door, striding to the curb. The car was still two minutes away, but the rain was fine and cool enough to be refreshing without causing him to feel uncomfortably wet.

The car pulled up. He got in, the door slid shut behind him and off he went.

Clinic 14 was quiet and that was just fine with Brian. He approached the reception staff.

"Good morning sir, how may I be of assistance today?" the staff said happily.

"Hi, I'm Brian Agarwal, please call me King. I have come to pick up a copy of the medical records for one of my staff." Brian looked at his mobile. "686381KAA418," he read.

"Very good. One moment please." The staff paused for a moment, almost fifteen seconds, then smiled. "Would you like this sent to your mobile?"

"No," Brian answered, "I'd like a paper copy."

"Very good sir, please wait here." Then, "Feel free to be seated. This may take a few moments." The staff got up and went into a back room. Brian heard an old-style printer start-up, and page after page being printed.

The printer stopped, and Brian heard the papers being straightened. The staff reappeared with a folder marked in red letters 'Classified Medical Records.' Holding the folder out for Brian the staff prompted, "here you go."

"Thanks," Brian said, taking the folder. Without another word, he turned and walked out the door.

Back at his office, Brian sorted through the stack of papers. There was far more of it than he had imagined. He carefully wrote numbers on the top corners of the pages so that if something happened, he could put them back in order without having to figure out which document came before which.

There was documentation going all the way back to 418's birth. There was 418's pediatric doctor at the nursery. There were his vaccination records. Nutritional records, records of physical activity, there wasn't much of his life that wasn't recorded before his education. Well, they had to make sure that it was going to be a healthy and productive staff.

Brian found the papers on his education, and there was a lot of that. The readouts and reports that had been filed automatically by the med-techs who had implanted the cerebral interface…that wasn't what Brian was looking for. It was the bit about the exception, and there it was.

Leafing through the pages, Brian pulled them out of the file and placed them in a different folder that did not have the words *Classified Medical Records* printed in large red letters on its cover.

That evening, Brian discussed with Imelda what some of their options where. There was selling just about everything that they had, and that wasn't going to come up with nearly enough.

"I could get a job," Imelda said cheerfully.

Brian scoffed and Imelda looked hurt. "I'm sorry, I didn't mean that."

"What's wrong with it? I could work."

This was perhaps the worst thing about it. She could have a job, but in order to work you had to have someone who is willing to hire you, and if you didn't get paid, it was called volunteering. How could he put this nicely? "It's kind of you to think about that, and while I'd like that you never had to lift a finger. I don't think it's that simple."

Imelda squinted at him.

"Okay, what kind of work could you do?"

She shrugged. "I don't know, whatever."

"No." Brian shook his head. He'd married Imelda young, and she had moved from her mother's into their place. "It doesn't work like that anymore."

"What do you mean?"

"It's the staff. Anything that was simple, anything that was low paying, they do it, because they do it for less."

"But there must be something?" Her husband had listed their assets, and her jewelry was on the list. She'd not like to part with any of that, or the china, for that matter.

Brian grinned and started to laugh. The big problem was that staff was now getting paid so little—or, he was getting paid so little to manage his staff—that he was the reason they were he was in this position. And, because of the widespread use of staff, his wife couldn't get a job to help them get out of this situation. It made his head spin. If he didn't do something, they would both be getting jobs, the ones they wouldn't remember. "No, the staff have taken all the jobs that no one wanted to do. We need to think differently."

"Well, maybe it's a mistake? Maybe the judge will see this is all an error."

Brian didn't like putting his faith in judges who didn't care about anything but being judges. "I'm sure we will find something," he tried to soothe. It wasn't going to be good. But if he was going to sell everything, he had better make sure there wasn't anything left of his. This was going to hurt, a lot. "I have no doubt a solution will come to me, and everything is going to be all right." Brian tried to sound like he was confident, manly.

Imelda bit her lip. "This can't be real," she said.

"No, you are right, it's probably just a mistake."

Imelda smiled, but Brian didn't, and despite her best smile, she knew when Brian didn't want to talk further. She tried to look convincing.

The two of them went about the nightly routine, though there was something thin and cold in the air. Brian kept imagining the door was about to burst down. He imagined law enforcement staff knocking everything over—this was done to confuse and aid in the apprehension of the wanted—the shouting, the lights going out, the stomping of feet and finally the feeling of a boot on the center of his back as he was pinned chest first to the floor. Prince was now old enough for education; he would spend the rest of his days as staff.

Brian quietly slipped out to the washroom, turned on the shower and the sink, then flushed the toilet to hide the sound of his vomiting.

Sleep was thin, sharp and cut him a hundred times as he tossed in his bed. Brian didn't think Imelda was asleep, but she was pretending not to notice he was awake and saying nothing was better than saying some of the things that might have to come to pass. When the thin gray rays of early morning started to melt their way through the dirty panes of plastic glass that kept the rain out, Brian was glad. Lying in bed, tossing and turning, benefited no man, but getting up and ensuring you weren't going to sleep was certain to provide no rest. But now that morning was breaking, the torment of trying, or pretending, to sleep was over; to be replaced with the dark specter of being pushed into receivership.

Silently, Brian dressed, then stopped by Prince's room. Prince was sleeping so peacefully that King had to lean over him to make sure he was still breathing. How gentle and sweetly the innocent sleep, he thought, as he crept back out of the tiny bedroom and closed the cartoon plastered door. He felt sadness welling up in his eyes as he rooted around in the closet for his shoes. Prince must have played in here last night, for the shoes were all mixed up and nothing was where any adult would have put it. Brian had to wipe away a tear. This wasn't fair. Why did they always apply bankruptcies to families?

Finally finding his shoes, Brian sat down on a small bench that looked big enough for two people but only ever fit one, and felt more tears trickle down his face. His hands were in his shoes and he tried to wipe his face. This is a sad mess, he thought. The image of Prince restrained to a bed, his veins full of anesthetic, being prepped by two staff to be taken to the operating theater for "schooling", which was what they called it when they did it to children. This thought made first his hand clench, then his arm twitch and muscles he didn't know he had pushed back from under the leathery soft skin of his forearm. Soon his arms were both stiff and he felt anger rising up from his shoes. "No!" he whispered as loud as he could without waking anyone, "no, I shall not let this happen."

With anger and force, Brian managed to put his shoes on, almost snapping the laces as he cranked against them. In his mind, he stomped out the door, letting it slam—to go with his mood— but in the quiet of the apartment, he stood, struck the floor hard with one heel. He almost forgot about the file folder he'd put on the top of the fridge, and he had to quietly go get it. Yes, he was going to do this.

I walked into the café. Today King was sitting there, but he didn't have his usual air of comfort around him. He smiled at me and quickly looked around. I picked my way through the tables. Most of them were empty. It seemed darker outside. We must have gotten here earlier. "Hey King," I said casually, as I approached his booth.

"Hello," he stopped. "What is your name?"

I stopped. "My name," I could feel myself smiling, "my name is George."

King smiled. "George." He started nodding, then started shaking his head. "I never pictured you for a George."

I sat down. "Well, what did you think I called myself?"

King shrugged. He moved like someone who had been tense for a long time. "I don't know. I didn't know if you called yourself anything."

I shook my head at him. "Why would you think that?"

King reached down beside himself. "Well, it's not in here." He lifted onto the table a green folder with loose paper stuck into it. "I want you to read this."

I don't think I had ever seen so much paper in my whole life. "What makes you think that I can read?"

King's jaw dropped open.

"Ah, just kidding, but I've never seen so much paper in one place. I guess all that garbage that I used to take care of had to come from somewhere." I opened the cover. "Shit!"

"Shh." King crouched down over the table and held his finger in front of his "Shhing" lips. "We have to keep this quiet. Okay?"

"Okay," I said. I hadn't said 'shit,' all that loudly. "This is all about me."

"Yes." The wait staff appeared as King was speaking, and he transitioned into ordering without missing a beat. "We would like two super sampler breakfasts, make my eggs over hard, and do whatever you would like to the other eggs."

"Very good sir," said the wait staff, its hand moving as if it were writing over an empty booklet. "Would you like coffee and juice with that?"

"I will have coffee, and I think orange juice for my friend here." He motioned to me, but the staff took no notice.

"And would you like a fresh apple turnover to add on to the end of your meal?"

"No, that will be everything." King tried to be dismissive and it worked. The staff made a quarter turn and headed on to the next table to see if there was anything that they could get them, or perhaps inquire if the meal was everything that they had hoped and dreamed it would be.

The pages were all about me, how I had been involved in an exception involving a motor vehicle. The exception involved a loss of connectivity resulting in a run-time exception which created a crash for the vehicle and those in close proximity. In all, four single passenger vehicles had been involved in the exception before traffic could be brought to a stop.

From what I knew about medicine, I could tell I was fairly lucky. Most of the impact I had been exposed to had been absorbed in the fracturing of my left cheek. I had not been punctured like the occupants of two of the other vehicles. Because of this, I was transported to the nearest clinic. Hey, how about that? I was actually given the highest probability of surviving, even though initial prognosis was that I would likely no longer be functional. Hmmm.

I turned the page. At the clinic, I was stabilized and held for review. The review was done by some adjuster named Andrea Dover, but the signed review was by someone named Bolt Greene. The programmatically generated recommendation was that I should have pain medications only, and that I be recommended for retirement. But this had been overridden by the adjuster.

"Hey King," I said. I hadn't even noticed the food arriving, but it was there, and I was nibbling at it as I flipped through the pages. "I've met adjusters. Why did they override the recommendation for retirement?"

King shrugged and continued to work on his breakfast, "that is something that I don't know."

"Huh, that's odd, isn't it?"

"Very."

"That would mean that I would..." I stopped talking.

King nodded. "Yes, you would be retired."

"And?"

"You would be dead, that's true."

I didn't know what to think about this. I wanted to ask him if he would have been okay with that, but I didn't want to hear the answer.

"Just keep reading," King encouraged me.

I continued to read about how I had to be sent for "re-education," and that my cerebral interface appeared to be functional, although there was some voltage loss across the synapses. I knew that normally wasn't a good thing.

The re-education summary stated that I had suffered some brain damage and should be recommended for retirement. Again, there was a signature of Bolt Greene overriding the recommendation.

"Who is Bolt Greene?" I asked finally. "Is he or she some sort of God?"

King was sipping his coffee which he sprayed all over the table. "Oh, goodness, I'm sorry, but no. Bolt Greene is not a God, he's a paper pusher over at the insurance company that cover's your medical expenses."

"But he overrode the RFR recommendation. I've never seen any adjuster do that."

"Neither have I."

"In fact." I flipped back to the first page where the programming recommended that I be referred for retirement. "He did it twice."

King rolled his eyes. "Three times, actually."

My jaw opened.

"Keep reading."

The next page was an auto-generated page that said I had spent three weeks in the clinic and, by doing this, I now qualified for statutory retirement. Again, this was overridden by Bolt Greene.

"Wow! What is statutory retirement?" I had no idea any of this had happened.

"Statutory retirement is when you don't recover in twenty-one days and you're sent to the retirement facility so we can close your case. I will get paid for the work you don't do, and you move on."

"What?" There was a lot there. "Close the case? You get paid?"

King looked down like he'd been caught doing something awful. "You work for me," he said it quietly, "that's why I can change what you do." King looked up, stared me straight in the eye. "I hope that you are not mad?"

I had to look away. I threw my hands up and let them fall back onto my lap. "I don't even know what most of that stuff means."

"I don't want you to think of it like that." He squirmed a little. "It's just that everyone works for someone."

"You? Who do you work for?"

King smiled. "Um, I guess you could say that I work for myself or my family."

I didn't point out to him that I didn't have a family.

"Yes." King looked as serious and genuine as he ever had. "About the whole statutory retirement. See, Bolt wasn't supposed to override that. It's sort of like an alarm clock. To keep expenses down. When it goes off, your online life is deleted. At that time, your wife and kids were probably told you died."

I nodded. "Yeah, I've seen the results. That was awful."

King sliced off and took a bite of his mushy undercooked eggs. "It's the cheapest way to dispose of someone."

"Huh?" My head was reeling.

"I think you are going to need some time to take this all in," King told me, "it's a lot, what I wanted you to know was, I had nothing to do with you losing your wife. Okay, I moved her out of her job as the receptionist, but you needed a place to sit because you couldn't walk, and it seemed to matter to you."

"You did what?"

King smiled, as if he had said something that he had not intended to say. "Um, hehe, um, you know she worked for me, right?"

I rolled my eyes. "Yes," it did seem right. "Yes, that seems about right, sure."

"She had to do something? Everyone has to do something."

I nodded.

"And that is what she did."

"So, wait." It dawned on me. "That could have, that should have, been me?"

"You what?"

"Me that died, when the garbage fell on Belinda."

King looked like he wanted to crawl away and hide. "Um, I suppose."

"Damn."

King was right. I did need more time to absorb that. As it turns out, this life that I had, whatever I did have, was a gift. I got to think about it all day. I should have been retired; I should have been dead. How messed up is that?

The next meeting with King was rather cold. I didn't know what to say. I slid into the booth and food appeared.

"Hello King," I said, as I took my place. "Thank you."

"Thank you?"

"Yes."

We looked at each other for a while. Then he said, "It was nothing."

"It means something to me."

King looked visibly irritated, as if I had just said something wrong. "Look, how are you doing today?"

"Fine."

"I mean." He looked around again. "After I showed you all that stuff, what did you do?"

I blinked at him. "I'm not sure what you mean, I went to work."

"And?"

I didn't know what he wanted me to say. "And I did work things."

He looked at me out of the corner of his eye, as if I was going to look any different. "And how did you feel?"

"Pretty shitty, pretty special, I don't know. Weird."

King sat back, observing. He asked, "Did you want to scream or run or break anything?"

"I don't know what it is that you are getting at," I said, starting to get annoyed with him. "I went to work, it was boring, I thought a lot about what you showed me. I went home, I went for a walk in some mockup of a city park that may or may not have ever existed. But I went to sleep, and nothing happened that doesn't happen on every other day."

"Whew," King sighed out loud. "That's good."

"What did you think might happen?"

Brian shrugged, raised one hand. "I don't know, you saw how nutty staff goes when you confront them with the real-world. I was afraid that you couldn't handle it."

"That I might snap?"

Brian snapped his fingers and two heads turned to look at us. He pretended there was a fly buzzing around. "Yes, precisely."

"Well, I didn't."

"Good."

We sat for a few moments. He was being weird.

"So?" I said after a long pause.

King looked around. Cautiously, he leaned over the table. "I think I'm going to need you to help me."

41

JUSTICE

"BCPL LLP vs Brian Agarwal et al.," the law enforcement staff called into the packed hallway. Brian got up, and four other people dressed in suits got up. Brian looked at the suits as they filed in through the door that the staff was holding open. The first three didn't look at him. The last one did—it was a young woman, with blonde hair, tied up nicely so that her hair looked silky and smooth, and wearing nice clothes that had even been pressed, a white blouse and a red skirt suit. She gave him a smirk as she passed him, rolling her eyes to the ceiling as if to make a point.

Inside the courtroom, Brian was directed by the law enforcement staff to sit at the table to the left. He had brought everything he could think of, which was to say, nothing. He had never received any papers from BCPL, and he didn't have a relationship with the Seventh National Bank. So what was he to bring, his summons?

On the other side, they had lots of papers and forms. They seemed busy.

"All rise," the law enforcement staff said. "County clerk Susan K. Woland, presiding."

A short woman walked in, dressed in black robes and wearing her salt and pepper colored hair up in a tight bun. What was remarkable about her was that she had no makeup on. None, as if it hadn't been invented. Not even the obligatory smear of red on her lips, or a thin splash of black on the edges of the eyelids. It made her face look pale, weak colored, but Brian wasn't fooled. Judges could do anything in their courtroom.

She took her seat, and Brian took his. She scowled at Brian and banged her gavel. Everyone else in the courtroom who wasn't staff sat down.

"Very good," she looked down at her desk, "what do we have here, BCPL LLP vs Brian Agarwal et al."

As soon as she was done, the young woman in red stood up. "Good Morning Madam Arbitrator, I am Sheila Grantner, junior counsel for BCPL, it is a pleasure to be standing in front of you this morning." There was no sign of the smirk she had slipped Brian just moments ago. She was smiling sweetly.

"Thank you." The Arbitrator smiled down at the finely dressed woman. "It's always a pleasure to see you." Brian remained seated. "Would the party of the first part stand up?" She glared down at Brian. Brian stood up. "Good, would you introduce yourself to the tribunal?"

"Brian Agarwal." He was amazed how weak and thin his voice sounded. Despite all the wood paneling in this room, he sounded like vapor in the mist.

The woman on the bench raised her eyebrows.

"Madam. Arbitraire," Brian added.

"Humph," Madam Arbitrator snorted, "well, I suppose that will do." Brian didn't feel this was going well.

"Okay, let's get on with things, would the petitioner please read their complaint?"

Again, the pretty young woman—Brian hated that he found her pretty—rose and began speaking. "Thank you, Madam Arbitrator, If it would please the tribunal, we would like to state that on the 9th of March we did lend the party of the first part the sum of twenty crypto coins, which was to be repaid at a rate of 24.49% APR, with monthly payments. The payments were to include no principle, the principle to be due at the end of a hundred and twenty monthly periods. The payments that were to be made were 0.4082 crypto coins per month." She paused to take in a breath. Brian could see the Arbitrator following along.

"Very good. I do believe that you have established that you have a debt repayment contract, please continue," directed the Arbitrator.

Brian kept looking at the young woman. What was wrong with him? She was probably the most evil and nasty thing, the most threatening and dangerous beast he had ever had the misfortune to come across, and yet, he kept thinking how attractive, how immaculate, how fantastic she looked. Brian shook his head as the woman continued to speak.

"Should it please the tribunal, we would like to assert that the party of the first part has failed on two occasions to make the prescribed payments. We would like you to refer to article A, which we have submitted electronically with our petition, which is a duly signed loan and debt repayment agreement which states that in the event of two failures to pay the amount due for two consecutive monthly periods, that the loan can be accelerated at our discretion to make the entire amount, outstanding payments and principle due immediately."

"Uh, huh," said the Arbitrator. "What evidence do you provide that the party of the first part has not made the required payments?"

"If it should please the tribunal, I would like to refer this to Ms. Gerrard of Seventh National Bank."

Another woman, perhaps she was as old as she looked tired, like she needed a smoke, got to her feet, walked forward and stood in front of the desk where Ms. Grantner had resumed her seat. She spoke as if it was irritating for her to have to be there. "I'm Olivia Gerrard of Seventh National Bank, and it is a pleasure to appear before you, Madam Arbitrator." It didn't sound like she meant it.

"Thank you," the Arbitrator replied, "please continue." The Arbitrator flashed Brian a smile. Brian felt his flesh crawl.

"If it pleases the tribunal, I can swear and state that Brian Agarwal, the party of the first part, has failed to make any payments under this agreement." She said it like it was routine. She didn't even look at Brian.

"I see," said the Arbitrator, "and you have no payment records?"

The woman nodded. "Correct, I have no records, because there are no records."

"Very good," the Arbitrator said. "I will make that note." She appeared to be writing something. "Mr. Agarwal." She looked at Brian. "Would you please stand?" She waived her hand as if she was lifting Brian out of his seat. Brian stood. "Have you made any payments to BCPL or to Seventh National?"

The words didn't want to come out. "No," was the only thing that came out.

"Why not?"

"I was unaware of any obligations."

The Arbitrator raised her eyebrow. "You were unaware?"

"Yes," Brian replied.

"Is this your e-signature?" She held up a mobile tablet and pointed at it.

Brian couldn't see it from where he was standing. He tossed his hands up. "I can't see that from here."

"It says Brian Agarwal, is that you?"

"I am Brian Agarwal, but I didn't sign that." Brian replied, trying to stay calm.

"It says you did?"

"No, I didn't." Frustration was growing, even though he knew it would not be a good idea to let it boil over.

"Are you lying to this tribunal?"

"No!"

"Well, the signature says you signed it. These people say they sent you money and you haven't repaid it. What do you say about that?" She was clearly getting annoyed.

"But I didn't."

The Arbitrator sat back, "You come to this tribunal with not a shred of evidence to support your claims and you expect me to believe and turn aside hard evidence and sworn testimony of these good folks just because you say so?"

"No," Brian said, brimming with frustration, "I, that's not what I mean." How do you prove the absence of something that isn't there?

"I've heard enough," she said finally, "let's stop wasting the tribunal's time, Mr. Agarwal you have thirty days to repay the balance and three monthly payments to be deposited before five p.m. at Seventh National Bank, or to be tendered to this tribunal, in order to make good your debts, or you will be declared bankrupt and placed in receivership for the purposes of reclaiming losses incurred by the party of the second part." She banged her gavel.

There was no jumping for joy, and there was no shouting or exclamations. Everyone just went on their way, put their papers away and filed out of the tribunal room. It was just business. Brian stood there, his jaw hanging open. It was as awful as he believed.

42

HOME IS WHERE
THE HEART IS

The arbitration hearing, trial or whatever it was, was over so quickly that if Brian hadn't been there, he might not have thought it actually happened. Maybe just the brief intermission of a dream, something that bubbled up from the murk of the subconscious, because a piece of chicken got stuck in his intestine; meaning little more than a passing gas bubble.

Who had he been kidding? Had he expected this to be fair? Everyone knew it was a scam, but that's the game. If someone could get you to a tribunal, you had to pay, it's not set up for you to get a fair shake, it's set up to keep labor costs down. This kind of thing was supposed to happen to other people, yet here it was, happening to him; it made him shiver.

It would have been easy to think that, sitting at his desk again, waiting for something interesting like the garbage truck to show up and the staff to chase papers all around the parking lot. If he just kept his head down, he could enjoy the next thirty days and pretend to be surprised when the law enforcement staff came to break down his door and take him away. It would be nicer, he wouldn't have to bother Imelda. He'd not even have to explain it to her.

"No!" Brian said to himself, "no, that was not going to happen." He would not allow that to happen to Prince. Prince deserved better. He didn't deserve to be lobotomized and turned into a robot just because someone said his dad didn't pay his bills. Even if that last bit wasn't true, no one would care, and Prince deserved better.

Brian pulled out the paper he had been writing down his options. He crossed out the idea that he could just claim he hadn't got that money, and that wasn't his e-signature. The list of what he could do just got smaller. He felt sick again.

"Hello, Brian, is that you?" Suresh yelled into his phone.

Brian felt low doing this. "Yes, Suresh, this is Brian, how are you?"

"One minute, it's noisy out here." Suresh was walking across the plant floor, yelling into his phone, not at all certain Brian had heard him. But if Brian wanted to alk, he was going to have to wait until he got back to his office. The door slammed shut behind him, but it sounded like a curtain of silence fell. Suresh plucked the earplug from his ear. "Hey, King, can you hear me now?"

"Yeah," Brian answered, "How are you doing my old friend?"

"King." Suresh took a seat behind his desk, smiling from ear to ear. "You know I know that you are in some sort of trouble when you start calling me your old friend. What's up?"

"Hey, you know me, we go way back."

"I know, we've been going way back since always."

"But it isn't like that," Brian tried to explain.

Suresh sighed. "Okay, okay, what is it?"

"Look, I wouldn't be calling you unless it was important."

Suresh took advantage of the fact that Brian couldn't see him and made a nodding 'sure, sure' type gesture. "I know, you wouldn't be calling at all if you didn't need something."

"Ha, ha," Brian replied, "no, my brother, this is serious."

Brian told Suresh all about what had happened. In the end, Suresh replied, "Wow, that's horrible."

"Yeah, it is." Brian tried to keep the conversation going. "Do you think you could help me out?"

"Hey, my brother, you know how it is," Suresh began to explain, "money is tight and Mindy is looking at going to college soon, and I have to make sure that that all gets done. You know how it is. I just don't have anything left over. I'm tapped."

Brian felt his spirits fall. "Yeah, I know, thanks." He hung up the phone—Brian was pretty sure Suresh's daughter was only seven. What could he have expected? He wouldn't have loaned anyone the money either; you needed it to keep yourself safe. Quietly, Brian took his pen out and crossed another idea off his list.

The idea of going to another lender to pay back whoever this BCPL was, was probably not a good one. He had looked up some of the websites of lenders. It was possible, but with the 25% rollover fee they charged for setting up a new loan and paying off your existing one, owing 25 cc with three months to pay wasn't much better than owing 20 cc with only one month to pay. But if he had to, it would buy him another sixty to ninety days.

Both Brian's parents had passed, and Imelda's mother had passed shortly after they got married—it had been convenient Imelda had married him just before she became aware of her mother's stage four cancer. The honeymoon was short, and thankfully the palliative care was also short or that could have drained them of money. Imelda's father had run off just before Imelda was born, probably too chicken to be a dad. Though right now, Brian wasn't too proud to take money, even from him.

There were not a lot of options left. He could sell his car, it wasn't worth much, and he could shut down his office. That wouldn't get him anything, but the expense could keep him out of debt if he could get through the next month. If he sold everything, he was going to be short about 8cc, plus the 1.2243cc of interest, which he was going to have to come up with out of nowhere.

Brian sighed. He looked out over the parking lot. There were still paper and plastic bags blowing around, the garbage staff hadn't got everything. The idea he would have complained about them if they had not have worked for him made him smile. Then the idea he could soon be one of the staff wandering around picking up bits of garbage while in a complete stupor hit him, and the smile wiped itself from his face.

Okay, time for plan B, Brian thought. *Action must be taken,* He went to get another cappuccino from the kitchen area. A cappuccino is a small thing, but he might as well enjoy it. There might not be many more.

That night, when Brian got home and Imelda asked him how things had gone, he decided he didn't want a fight. He knew what she would say, there must be some other way. Instead, he said, "It went okay."

"Did they believe you that you didn't take out that loan?"

"Nope," he answered, "they did not."

"What happened?"

"I made a deal. I think if we can sell the car, we can refinance the loan, and now that we know about it, we can pay a penalty and start making payments on it."

"Payments! On a loan we didn't get?"

"Sure," Brian assured his wife. "It won't be that bad, you will see."

She looked at him suspiciously, and Brian could see her trying to do the math in her head. "I will put up and ad for the car tomorrow. We will sell it in no time."

That had been enough to distract her, before she could figure out the numbers didn't even come close to adding up. "Okay, but you make sure you get a proper receipt when you do make that payment."

"Of course, my little olive, I think we have this all worked out."

Brian didn't sleep well that night. He had George awakened an hour and a half earlier the next morning. This served three purposes: first, it saved him ninety minutes of not sleeping. Secondly, it meant there were dramatically fewer people at Jazmin's cafe. Finally, it meant he and George would have longer to discuss this plan.

43

ACROSS THE RIVER

I was going through a phase where I hated my concierge. It would pass. In two weeks or so, I'd be over it, but for now, the sight of his happy face was making my lip curl into a sneer. "Good morning Samuel, how nice to see you, again," I said. I had noticed concierges didn't have a good grasp of sarcasm. It didn't matter how you said it, it was what you said that mattered.

"Hello George, ready for another great day at work?"

"Why yes, that sounds lovely." If only once he would say that it would be a tedious or needlessly dangerous or remarkably disgusting day at work, the honesty would have been refreshing.

When I got woken, I didn't think anything other than it was another day, and I was likely going to see King and go to work. There was nothing different in the way I was dressed, the way I walked down the hall. The wait at the elevator was just the same, empty, which meant I was meeting King. The traffic was the same, but when I was let out, and after I made my way through the kitchen, which was buzzing in its own right, I was dumbstruck. The cafe was almost empty.

King sat in a booth. He had ordered food and it had just arrived, but there wasn't another diner within twenty feet of him in any direction. It was like we had the whole place to ourselves. Just like it would have been if we had met at a restaurant online.

I smiled at him, "good morning, King."

"Good morning George, did you sleep well?"

I beamed at him. "You called me George, thank you."

"Yeah, yeah." King waived his hand dismissively.

"Yes, I did sleep well," I answered his question, "or at least I think it was sleep. Maybe it's just resting."

"Yeah, I'm not sure if you do sleep, but you feel good?"

"As good as I ever feel, how about you?"

"Horrible, didn't sleep a wink."

"I'm sorry." I had heard myself say this a million times when I was selling shoes, but this time I actually meant to say it, and it sounded a bit odd.

"Okay, so listen up," King said. This time he didn't have to hunch over the table. "This is what we are going to do."

King laid out his plan. Any time I would open my mouth to say something, he would put his hand up and tell me to shut up and listen. "Just listen, let me explain, questions can come afterward. Shut up for now." I did what I was told, but it was an awful plan, though simple.

"So," I said finally, when he had finished and allowed me to speak. "You are sure you want to do this."

"No, not at all."

I rolled my eyes, looking for the next question.

"I have to do it." He broke the silence. "Do you have a better idea? I'm all ears."

I sighed. "No, but this seems...Not right."

"Look, it's part of me, or all of me."

I wanted to stall for time and think of something. "What's wrong with being staff?" Thinking of nothing else to ask.

King snorted. "Even you don't want to be staff."

He was right.

"This is why I need you. I just want to make sure it's done right."

"But I don't control my hands," I said, hoping to poke a hole in this idea of his.

"Maybe, but you can watch."

"Yes." This was true. "But it's not always pretty, and I'd rather not."

King shook his head. "You don't get it. I want you to watch so they don't take anything else."

"And what if you die? I get to watch that?"

King sat back, looking for an answer. He leaned forward again. "I would, even more than you, be sorry for that. But you see, I don't have a choice. I have to try this."

"King, you know what you are saying: being staff is a fate worse than possible death."

King looked down, ashamed. "I'd say it was a fate worse than possible death. I'm sorry."

"Thank you," I said dryly. "Good to know. Okay, what about me? How do I get out?"

"Get me out and I'll tell you," he added, "if you still need me to tell you."

We ate the rest of our breakfasts in silence. The restaurant was beginning to fill up. King and I were staring at each other.

"Well," King said finally, "I guess it is about time to get to work."

"I'll be pretty early," I added.

"I guess," he replied, "but we can't sit around here."

"I suppose." We got up, and he paid the check. We stepped outside; he called his car on his mobile. I tapped the side of my head and had Samuel call me a car to get to work. Without any more words, I opened the door of the cafe, walked through it, through the kitchen and into the back alley to wait for my car.

When I got to the clinic, the car stopped in the carport. I was early, thirty-five minutes early. I asked Samuel the time, that's how I knew. The car stopped and sat there, locked, with me inside of it. I waited the thirty-five minutes until the car unlocked itself and let me out. I didn't want to do that again, ever.

It was an uneventful day: I watched myself carry out my duties. I was fast and efficient. I didn't slip, and I didn't make mistakes that were not intended. I was perfect engineering. The day passed as all the other days, duly recorded, with nothing of any note to make it stand out from all the others.

The next morning, I got up early again. I hoped not as early as I had the day before, but I didn't have a way to tell, not without asking Samuel. It just felt best I not say anything unusual to Samuel. The walk was the same, the elevator was the same, empty. The queue at the carport was the same, non-existent. The traffic felt the same, but when I stepped out of the kitchen, I could tell it was later, thank goodness. I didn't want to spend any more time sitting in a non-moving car than I had do. That is a special kind of torment.

"Hello King," I said, as I slid down into my seat.

"Hello George," he replied, "it is nice to see you."

We both addressed our breakfasts. They were good. I was amazed at how I could eat now, without the pushback from inside. Food felt good. Food tasted better than a bag of drip.

Unexpectedly, King broke the silence. "You should try to stop eating or eat less at night. Stop using the feedbag."

Puzzled, I stopped eating and looked at him. He was serious.

"You want to get out, right?"

"Yes."

"If you get out, you won't be able to get feedbags."

I nodded. "Okay, maybe you have a point, but you know, that's my food."

"Well, just try to stop, with all you've been eating here, perhaps it's best." King smiled warmly.

"You haven't been feeding me to make me fat?"

King smiled again, "No, I wanted to see if you could do it?"

"Why?" I just had to know.

"Because if you can, I can."

"Can what?"

"Get out."

We continued to eat our breakfasts. We both finished everything on our plates. When we were done, King got up from the table. He held out his hand as if to help me up. "You ready for this?"

I took his hand and he pulled me to my feet. I nodded slowly and looked him in the eye. "Yes."

44

STEAK AND KIDNEY PIE

Around mid-morning, according to the file at 9:45, Brian Agarwal walked into Clinic 14. He walked in the front door after dismissing his car, which he told to go home, but to take two hours to get there, by any route possible. He further instructed the car to notify his wife's mobile when it got there, but no sooner than two hours from now. He stepped into the clinic and messaged his wife he was having great pains in his side and he had gone to Clinic 14. He said that he had sent the car home, that it should be there shortly to pick her up so she could come. He ended the message and turned off the mobile before Imelda could read and respond. Brian stood up, with all the resolve he could, and strode forward to the reception and checked in.

What Brian didn't tell George about the feedbag was that they put lots of other fun stuff into it: tranquilizers to keep staff calm, antipsychotics to keep them sane, some other stuff to keep them from becoming infected. There was another chemical that keeps staff well-preserved and makes the skin tough and hair fall out in a natural way that effectively solves the lice problem. There was growth hormone for obvious reasons, painkillers, anti-inflammatory agents, and things to make anyone heal quicker with no medical interaction. Really magic stuff that feed bag was, but after years of eating and living on just that, it turned the body toxic. Everyone in the business knew it. No one talked about it, because no one cared, and because no one cared, why not minimize total cost?

Brian presented the reception staff with a copy of a contract he had made. It gave instructions on what to do and who to notify when the procedure had been completed. The staff obediently took the contract. "I will add this to your file," the staff said, and went off to scan the document into the system so it could be added to Brian's file. When the staff returned, they handed the hard copy back to Brian. "Please wait here, medical technicians will be here shortly to assist you."

I was summoned to the white area of the clinic. I knew what it was. King had told me he was going to be coming in, this was his plan. This would allow him to clear his debt, and he wouldn't be staff. The logic of it was sound. If he didn't do this, it was a matter of time until he was here for a different procedure. I and the other tech stepped into white area with a restraining bed. It was King. He smiled ruefully, holding his arms out to either side with his palms open and exposed, as if he had nothing to hide. "I am here, please be gentle."

The file flashed before my eyes. Brian Agarwal was the name on the file, not King. I wanted to say something, why had he never told me his name, his real name? What kind of a pant load? Instead, I heard myself say, "Hello sir, we will take good care of you and be as gentle as possible." Not what I would have said, but I suppose it wasn't out of place.

"Please come with us," the other med-tech said to Brian. No, I still couldn't do it. He was still King to me. "You will need to get into a gown for this procedure."

King walked—slowly but quickly, considering what he was about to do—with us to a cubicle in the white area of the clinic. I produced a gown from a rack of folded gowns and King undressed. The other med-tech took his clothes away and secured them in a sanitary bag for storage.

I wanted to tell King everything was going to be okay, that he should not be worried. He looked scared, though, his dark coffee skin looked grayish and he was sweating. But I couldn't say anything of my own discretion. King looked at me, trying to see if he could see inside me. "Your eyes are not gray," he said. "Though, even though they do not focus, I know you are in there."

I didn't move and I didn't say anything. I don't think Samuel, or whatever was responding, was programmed to answer that. Finally, I said something surprising. "Do not be afraid. I am just staff which is here to be helpful. My eyes do not indicate a problem."

King straightened and took a half step back. "That is a weird thing to say." Then he smiled. "I bet we laugh about that later."

I wanted to say, yes, for sure, instead, "There is no laughing matter here, we are here to help you."

King nodded. My arm extended, holding out a thin dressing gown. "Please put this on for your own comfort and sanitation."

Taking the gown, King said softly, "Yes, thank you, my friend."

Was I glad the other med-tech staff returned.

King got on the bed and I told him, "Please make yourself comfortable while we secure you to the bed."

King tried to look relaxed. The other med-tech activated the bed, which swelled and firmed around him, holding him in place.

"Now we are going to place a mask over your face. This mask will provide oxygen and anesthetic so we can complete this procedure without causing you undue discomfort." King tried to nod. I could see his face push against the foam. I relaxed the foam so I could attach the mask. He laid back and closed his eyes, the mask instantly fogging with the heat of his breath.

"I am going to add the general anesthetic to the oxygen flow. Please try to count backwards from one hundred."

King opened his eyes, looked right at me and closed them. "One hundred, ninety-nine, ninety-eight," and he was down.

We wheeled King from one cubicle down a short pristine white hallway to the operating theater in the white clinic. I was glad I was being guided because the room was so white, I couldn't see anything but the patient, my tools and my hands.

Quickly and efficiently, we deflated the restraining foam and went to work. Cleaning the site of the incision. I got my scalpel out and, with precision I could not have imagined, plunged it into the side of my friend and started cutting fine strokes through his flesh to open a window through which I could work. I could see I was going to have to remove a bone. King wasn't going to like that when he came around, but my hands were doing it because it had to be done.

I got out the saw quickly, before I could take in what I was doing. I had the blade spinning and was cutting through bone in order to get a clear passage toward the right kidney. The bone cut cleanly and snapped off with a satisfying plonk, landing in the palm of my hand. I put it aside and continued with my work.

Expertly, I reached in and lifted the kidney out of its resting place. It felt all warm and soft, and I clamped it so that I could cut it out without damaging it. Again, with speed that made it hard for me to follow, I was in, out and sewing up the place where the kidney used to be attached to the man I called King. I glanced at his vitals. I knew by the way I was behaving that I'd either killed him—and there was no way I could save him—or I was done, and it was over.

I wanted to slow down as I sterilized the wound area. I wanted to make sure I'd done it right, but Samuel or some programmer was driving, and I cleaned it up as quickly as I had opened it up. We wiped down the operating room. We would come back later to sterilize, and I bagged the bit of rib I had removed, sealed it and put it aside with King's clothes and possessions. In what seemed like no time, we were both out of the operating room, pushing King into a recovery cubicle.

As we were leaving, we were summoned to the front of the clinic. A woman about King's age, with the same dark color of skin and much smoother black hair, had rushed into the reception. She was accompanied by a small boy who looked like a miniature version of King. The woman was virtually dragging the boy, and she was trying to talk to the receptionist as soon as she had burst through the front doors.

"Where is my husband?" she asked. There was clear and present panic in her voice. I guessed King had not explained this little plan of his to her. Even though I had only experienced marriage online, there were things that were so deeply rooted in the human nervous system that it was unmistakable. I tried to walk faster. Best to let someone else handle this. I hit the doors and felt a wave of relief. I didn't want to explain this to her.

The reception staff did their job too. Well, I suppose there wasn't much to it. Confirm that this woman belonged to that man, or that man belonged to this woman. I took five strides into the gray area and turned right around in mid-stride and headed straight back out into the white area.

"Hello madam," I heard myself say, "how can I be of assistance to you?" I was already pulling up the file in my mind.

"What happened? Tell me what happened!" I thought she was going to grab me and shake me. Maybe she was, but she saw that I was still covered in blood, so she pulled back. She looked with horror at the red all over my hands, arms and a few splatters on my chest.

"We have removed your husband's right kidney. The surgery, at this point in time, has been successful. The kidney is en route to its recipient and the patient is sedated, resting and expected to make a full recovery. We expect, if there are no complications, that he will be fit for release in forty-eight hours." Well, that seemed pretty straight forward, I thought.

"What do you mean you took out his kidney?"

"The kidney has been removed in accordance with a donorship contract that had been signed and is being executed." I was a little surprised at the sharpness with which I said this. There wasn't a lot of feel good in the way that came out.

"How could you?" She seemed to be searching for questions.

I would have told her it was going to be all right, and I had witnessed everything, and that everything went according to plan and that we didn't have to do any emergency extra anything other than take out some rib, which wasn't that unexpected. I would have told her that he did this for you, and he was going to be just fine. I would have even told her I would personally watch over him, but that's not what I said. "We simply executed a private contract that has been put into force involving your husband."

She blinked at me; her mouth open, like she wanted me to clarify something astounding.

"He asked us to," I heard myself say. An amazingly concise statement for the talking program that I am. I was surprised I'd said it.

She staggered back. I reached out to hold her in place, so she didn't fall. I smeared blood on her arms where I grabbed her. "Please come this way. You may sit with the patient as long as you like." I walked her over to his cubicle. She tried to throw herself on him, but I grabbed her—I'm sure it hurt her, but she was full of adrenaline—and held her back. "You should be careful, and do not touch the torso or put weight on the patient, as you could trigger internal hemorrhaging." When I felt her relax, and she started to sob, I let her go. "I will now get you a chair so you may be more comfortable." Against my better judgment, I went to fetch a chair from the waiting room.

45

POST OP

The next morning, I got to sleep in. I didn't feel any different when I woke up, I didn't feel like I had slept longer. I only knew it because as I stepped into the hallway, I had to join the herd heading to the elevator.

We did do the elevator in rounds, coordinated so that we all moved at once into the lift. We wedged ourselves as tightly as we could, so the doors would just slide shut without hitting anyone, without having to pop open or slice something off because something was sticking out.

Up we went, and I shuffled along with everyone else, waiting my turn to get into the car that had been arranged just for me to take me to work. King would still be in the hospital. It would be good to get there and check in on him. There was a chilling thought: what if I found him dead? Other than the displeasure I would feel, placing his body out for the removal teams, what would I do? What would become of me? Would I still work? Would I just be retired? Would I just cease to be?

As I stepped into the car, it occurred to me that everything that I was, what little that was, was entirely at the behest and the whim of King. If King should have so decided, I would have been off to retirement. If King had not decided, I'd never have tried food, I'd be stuck in this internet not knowing anything else other than what every staff dimly knew: that there was an outside world and it wasn't as much fun, and, it wasn't worth much as it was hard and confusing. Oh, I sure hope King was okay. I went through it in my mind again, I'd done everything right, and there were no surprises. He'd be fine. He had to be.

Traffic seemed bad that day, and I didn't feel like we were taking the normal route. Something must have happened, in which case there was a chance I'd be dealing with exceptions where I got in. No, King would take priority over staff. It always worked that way, and I'd be able to find out that he was fine.

Eventually, I managed to make it to work. And what I thought was going to happen, was happening. Because King was in the clinic overnight, I had to go and check on whether he was still alive, first. Well, at least I was going to check, that was a good sign. I strode into the white area of the clinic, walked right past the reception staff who paid no attention to me, and opened the curtain.

To my great relief, the sound startled King. He smiled at me. I didn't smile at him. I went about preparing to check his heart rate and take his blood pressure.

"Good morning George," King said. He was smiling at me, but I was not smiling at him. "I am glad to see you," he continued. He looked like he'd been beaten. He also had the look of a man who has some relief after a long time of being under great strain.

I'm glad to see you,—and boy, was I ever—was what I would have said, but instead, "Good morning sir, how are you feeling today?" came the mechanical words with my voice.

King laughed, immediately wincing, choking back his laughter. Tears were forming at the corner of his eyes. I took his arm to wrap it in a canvass cuff. "This will not hurt," I said, as I started to pump the bulb to take King's blood pressure.

"Well, when we can, we will chat," he said, "I think everything went well."

"Your procedure seems to have been completed properly." I was surprised to hear myself say this. It was just what I wanted to tell him, something along the lines of everything will be all right. "We do not foresee any complications at this time, but we are going to keep you here for another twenty-eight hours to ensure there are not any." Well, that was nice.

King smiled at me, like he did at the café. "Thank you, George, I appreciate that."

I went about taking his temperature. Suddenly, the curtain was ripped open again.

"Hello, my petunia," King said, his voice weak, but he got it out before she could say anything. "How are you this morning?"

She was stymied, "I," she started. I could see clouds come across her face and her eyebrows tilted down in the middle. "Just what do you think you were doing?" The five seconds that it took for the thermometer to take a reading was too long.

"Your temperature appears to be normal. This is a good sign; you appear to be healing properly." I put the thermometer away, quickly folded the blood pressure cuff. "If you need anything, please ring, there is a buzzer on the side of your bed."

"Yes, thank you," King said he smiled at me.

As I turned to go, she said, "What is wrong with you? Talking to staff? Donating kidneys, have you lost your mind?" I was glad I was walking away from that conversation.

When I got back to the gray area, there were five cars waiting in the carport. There had been an exception: I had been right; the trip took too long. The other med-tech was waiting for me so that we could lift the bodies onto beds and roll them off to the incinerator. I was just glad King was alright.

Throughout the day, I was scheduled to step in every two hours to verify that King was still alive. We only checked the staff patients once every shift, but I looked in on King an additional five times. He slept a lot. His wife would come and go, the chairs we provided were not comfortable, and I suppose she had to go eat.

Each time that I checked in on King, he was looking better and better, though I still didn't know how he was going to get up in less than twenty-four hours.

The last time I came to check in on King, his wife and his son were back. King smiled as he saw me. He addressed his son. "Prince, you are the best son that a father ever had." I wanted to smile. It was nice he was introducing me to his son.

"Daddy, why did you let them do this?" the boy asked.

"Well, someday you will understand, when you have a family of your own." King looked up at me again. "But a man has to sometimes make sacrifices, even painful sacrifices, for his family."

I did my checks. "Mr. Agarwal, you are getting better. You are on track for release tomorrow," I heard myself say.

"See, Prince," King said to his son, "everything is going to be okay."

Prince was busy playing with a screen. I wanted to take it from him, put it down, look him in the eye, and tell him his father is talking to him. But these things are often lost on small boys.

Sadly, it was the end of my shift. I went home feeling better I hadn't killed King. He would make it. I think.

The next morning was more of the same. The same grind, the same group of people headed to work. But this time I was missing real food, my stomach was rumbling, and I wanted to eat something, anything. It didn't feel right to have nothing in my stomach, and I found myself feeling a little angry, edgy, agitated. Something was amiss.

At the clinic, my first stop was King. He was awake, alone, and waiting for me with a broad smile.

"Good morning Mr. Agarwal," I said, mechanically, politely, as I opened the curtains.

"Good morning George, how is the stomach?"

I turned to look at him. Quickly, I reached under his gown and gave him a quick check. "There does not appear to be any abnormality in your abdominal area. Are you suffering any specific discomfort or pains in any specific location?"

King smiled, almost laughed, stopped by a painful wince. "No," he answered, "I am fine. I figure you might not be feeling right."

"Do not worry about me. I am here to provide services and to look after you while you are a guest at this clinic," I almost shot back.

"Well, that's nice to know."

"You are welcome." I loved how I was stiff, but always polite.

"We will talk later," he added.

"Yes, I will give you an update the next time that I come to check in on you," I added with flat matter of fact.

King nodded. "Help me sit up."

"Certainly," before I knew it, I was adjusting his bed with the foot pedals and had my arms around King lifting him up so that he could sit in bed. "Is that better?"

"Yes," he said, "could you get my mobile?"

"Certainly, sir." I went out to where we kept patients' personal effects. I grabbed his mobile—How nice, we had even charged it for him—and brought it to him.

"Thank you." He started poking around, and I turned to leave. "No, wait," he said. I stopped. "Just one second, and, um, let me see. Yes! Thank you, George, you've saved me, the payment has posted. I can rest now."

I turned, "You will not be needing me any further?"

King reopened his eyes. "No, you are needed. I just wanted you to know it worked. I'm tired and need to rest. Please come back later."

"Very good." I felt myself smile. I hope I had. I turned and went about my business. I hoped he would be asleep when I came back in two hours.

46

THE MORNING AFTER

Like always, the sun did, indeed, come up. What was good was I knew that I was going to the café, because there were fewer feet plodding along in the hallway toward the elevator. I was glad, very glad. Maybe things would be as they were before.

The trip was quick but seemed long. When I got out in the alley behind the café, it was raining a thin but greasy rain from the leaden sky, which managed only a crack between the buildings. I hurried in the back door, in order to not get any greasier than necessary. I was clumsy as I picked my way through the kitchen and burst out into the cafe.

I was hoping to see King sitting there, smiling, looking as he always did; a little smug, slightly pleased with himself, two breakfasts, a sheepish grin across his face. And sure enough, there he was. Though the grin wasn't sheepish, it was more of relief, as if he wondered if I would show up.

"Hello King," I said, as I picked my way across the dining room. "How are you feeling?"

"I don't know," he said, contemplating putting sugar in his coffee. "I'm not sure if it's thanks to you or no thanks to you, but I feel tired and weak. Other than that, I feel like a weight has been lifted off my back."

I crinkled my brow as I sat down.

"I don't have to sell my car. That's one nice thing. I don't have to worry about being declared bankrupt, not this month anyway." He breathed heavily. "That's a relief."

I nodded. "I imagine it is." The food looked so good, my stomach was growling and raging. It had missed its usual fix. I didn't know what I wanted to eat first, all of it, if I could.

"I am glad you did that. How did it go? I'm guessing it's all right. I'm not dead and I'm out of the clinic."

I smiled at him. "I was only a spectator, but it looked as it should to me."

"Did they take anything they were not supposed to?" He was quite serious in asking, "I have all the other organs I should have."

"Well." I drew it to out play with him. "We did." I took a sip of juice, smacked my lips. "Man, that's good juice," I put the glass down and stared at it, as if I'd never seen one before.

"You did, what?"

"Huh, I'm sorry, what were we talking about?"

"Oh, shut up." He pretended to slam his hands down, and it caught him in the side again, causing him to move in slow motion.

"It's going to be a while until you feel like yourself. Take your pain killers if you need them," I told him, "and don't overdo it. You don't want a broken suture. Re-bleeds are a bitch." I told him flatly.

"Hrmph."

"We didn't take anything extra, but we did have to take out part of your rib. It was in the way. Sorry."

King smiled. "So nothing else, okay. I found the rib in my things."

"I thought that was weird. Keeping it."

"I asked for any extra parts to be returned to me."

I winced.

"Like I said, I didn't want them to help themselves to anything extra."

"Why would they do that?" I asked.

"Because they can."

We ate for a while. It was good to see King again. He was eating and he'd be okay. Though I did see that he had a cane. He tried to slide it out of sight after he caught me looking at it. After a long while, I had to ask, "So, what do I do?"

King raised his eyebrows.

I waited. I thought he was formulating words, but he didn't respond. "So how do we fix me?"

King nodded. "First, you come for breakfast every day."

"I can do this." I smiled. I liked real food. It was always slightly different, not like online when it was always precisely the same.

"Do you have a tap for water in wherever you live?" King looked me in the eye.

"Yeah, it's tiny," I answered.

"No problem, can you do this?" King held out his hands, making a cup. I held out my hands, making a cup. "Good, now you take the water and you fill the cup, and you hold it up like so." He lifted his hands to his face, so his palms were against his lips. "Then you drink."

I did the same.

"Good, good," he said. He took a sip of his coffee. "Don't plug in your feedbag at night."

"Yeah, about that...you know it's food, right?"

"There are all sorts of stuff in it, all you need from it is the water, and if you drink real water, you should be fine. You need to learn to drink water. There is stuff in your feed bag that when you stop taking it, you are going to be sick."

"I know there are antibiotics, so I don't get infected."

King waved. "Don't worry about that. There are antipsychotics and tranquilizers to keep you from losing your mind. I was looking into it when it looked like I might become staff."

"What?"

"Yep. Try not hooking up tonight."

"What's going to happen to me?" I asked. This didn't seem like such a good idea.

"Hopefully, nothing." King smiled. He raised his fork with a hunk of sausage on it and saluted me. "You will have breakfast here, in the morning, every morning."

47

DETOX

I had already detoxed once. When I had stopped spending my nights at Dr Pong's. I thought that was bad. But now I worked in the clinic and knew this was going to be the physical side of addiction. Dr. Pong's was mental addiction, a habit that had no other replacement. This was a chemical that had no habit but needed to be removed.

That night, I did what King had told me. I got home, and I drank as much water as I could. I sat down in my chair and I plugged myself in but didn't hook up the feed bag.

"Hello Samuel," I said as I came online in full immersion. "How are you this evening?"

Samuel assembled himself out of the dots. "Hello George, what would you like to do this evening?"

Smiling, I said I would like to go to McDonald's, and my wish was his command and the world started to swirl into dots and re-assemble into the outline of the same McDonald's I wasn't able to order anything from after the exception.

"Thanks Samuel," I said as I strode into the restaurant leaving him behind on the street. I walked right up to the counter. "I would like three Big Macs, a double quarter pounder, extra fries, a chocolate shake, apple pie and, hmm, how about forty nuggets?"

"Very good sir." The girl behind the counter quickly entered it onto the counter, and the counter went green when she pressed the payment button. "Please be seated, and your meal will be delivered to you."

"Thank you, and may I have a smile."

The girl behind the counter flashed me a broad smile.

"Thank you again."

I found a spot where I could look out over the street. Samuel was down there lurking around like a man in a trench coat. As soon as I sat down, food started appearing on the table, first as a swarm of dots and then as things more solid. The smell hit me all at once as soon as the last dots found their assigned place.

I tore open polystyrene containers and started munching into big macs. You know, funny thing, it felt like I was eating, in every way. I kept eating and the taste and feeling kept coming, even though I wasn't hooked up to a feed bag. The act of eating and the act of feeding where two different things. Huh. Go figure.

I ate everything. I even used my finger to get the last grains of salt out of the bottom of my fry package. It was good, so very good. I wondered what it tasted like in real life. Could it possibly be this good? I even let out an appreciative burp as I pushed myself away from the table. My stomach felt heavy, like I had just eaten. But I didn't have the same sort of sleepy feeling I had when I ate too much at Jazmin's. Funny that. They recreated everything, but I suppose it wouldn't do to have people just eat and go to sleep. Folks need to party.

The next morning, I woke up to the familiar greeting of Samuel: "Good morning George. Time to get up." I felt groggy, which was weird. I didn't go crazy last night, but I felt like I was stuck to my clothes, like somehow they had melted into the upper layer of my skin. "Samuel," I said to my ever-attentive concierge, "Could you help me up and get me washed up?"

Expecting the sensation of a band-aid being ripped off my body, or the skin on my back peeling off in a perfect husk, I was surprised when none of that happened. Easily, my clothes fell to the floor and into the waste bin as I stepped into the shower. The water, while colder, always colder than I liked it, did not sting, but rather felt like water being shot against my skin, making my flesh move out of the way as the blade of cleaning fluid scrubbed up and down my body. It was a little discomforting to think I felt like I'd melted into my clothes, but good to get the sweat off.

Once washed, dried, we dressed. But even with Samuel taking control, I felt weird, like I was taller than I should be. My neck felt like it had been stretched. As we walked through the hallway, I was in constant fear of striking my forehead on the fluorescent lights.

The elevator was fun. It felt like the floor was soft. When I stepped in, the elevator gave a little, but I couldn't help but think that maybe the floor was rubber, and if the elevator moved too fast or I got too heavy, I might just rip through it and go plunging to my death. Thankfully the elevator was empty, but for me, I wanted to put my hands out and try to hold myself, so I wouldn't put any pressure on the floor.

A great gasp escaped me when the doors slid open. Cautiously, I stepped out onto the carport. For some reason I had been holding my breath. I didn't understand that, but all of a sudden, I didn't like the elevator shaft anymore. It was long and deep and who knows what I would find at the bottom once I spat into the springs and mechanisms that lay wait there.

Obediently, a car pulled up. It opened and I got in, but I didn't seem to fit anymore, my legs were too long and didn't seem to bend in the right places. Somehow, Samuel made me fit into the car, and as the lid slid down and the darkness of the car enveloped me, I started to feel cramped. I'd experienced darkness like this before, all around me, where I could, if I fell out of my chair and through the wall of darkness that was enclosing around me, simply disappear. I didn't want to disappear, so I held on for dear life as the car started moving. I couldn't handle this. "Samuel, can I play solitaire?" I heard myself shout.

"Why certainly you can," he said, pleased to be of service. But he was ever watching. I knew he was watching, and no doubt making reports. "What type of solitaire?"

"What do you mean? Who cares? Any type, whatever I played last."

"Very good." I could hear the smile in his voice.

The ride was nauseating, more than normal, and I felt itchy when I got out of the car. I turned Samuel off. I'd take it from here. Normally I just walked in. Today I had to get my bearings. I didn't feel right. My arms now seemed the wrong size. I reached for the door. It seemed far away, and I smacked my hand into it. Shaking my hand out, I inspected it—no damage. I looked at the door again, it was normal again. This time I was able to open it. Cautiously I entered the kitchen.

There was staff running this way and that way. Some of them with hot things, some with pointy things. It occurred to me that they might not see me. What if one turned and plunged a pointy thing or spilled a hot thing on me? I gathered myself, held my breath and, perhaps closing my eyes, dashed through the ever-moving, scissoring, bodies of the staff hard at work. What a relief it was to make it through the kitchen.

Just as cautiously, I stepped into the dining room. A waitress blew past me and I had to catch myself against the wall. I saw King sitting over in a booth, two large plates of food waiting. Okay, I could do this. I wound my way through the maze of tables. There was sweat on my brow and I could feel my pants sticking to my backside in an unpleasant way. With a great sigh, I threw myself down into the booth.

"How are you feeling today?" King asked me. "Did you do what I asked you to do?"

I looked around, wondering if someone was listening. I was about to answer.

"I see you did." King mused out loud.

"I don't feel good," I blurted out. It was louder than I wanted, and I felt like someone was pressing down on my neck.

King nodded. "Yes, I thought this kind of thing might happen." He reached into his pocket and pulled out a little yellow bottle. He opened it, shook out a tablet and handed it to me.

"What is it?"

King smiled. "Why do you care all of a sudden?"

"I like to know what I'm taking."

"But you didn't know what you were taking before."

I felt annoyed. "That was different."

"Don't worry about it. It's something to calm your nerves, a mild sedative, so you don't feel so rough." He said it as if it was nothing.

I popped it into my mouth, washed it down with juice.

"Might take a while to kick in, there might be a pain killer in it. It should make you feel pretty good."

I knew exactly what he had done. These were his after-surgery pills. "You know you are not supposed to do that." I remembered the man who got his stomach pumped. I was pretty certain that any uncontrolled use of any medication was supposed to be reported. But to whom? And wouldn't I just be reporting myself?

"Don't tell anyone," King smiled. He thought about it. "Or tell someone. They'd take me away; do you want that?"

I shook my head.

"You knew all that before you took the pill?"

I smiled in spite of myself. "Sure, I did."

"You still took the pill."

"I sure did." I thought about it. "What were you going to do to me, now after all this?"

King nodded. "It gets better, but it might be worse tomorrow, try to keep busy, if you need, message me."

"You need to rest," I commented.

"No," King replied. "I have to get to work. I have to make sure I have my court. I mean, tribunal dates straightened out. I have things to do."

I was busy loading my toast with marmalade. I liked it because it had stuff in it. It wasn't liquid. Perhaps food shouldn't be liquid?

He took a deep breath. He clearly wasn't feeling perfect. "You keep yourself busy, that's the best way to deal with this. Whatever you do, if you get any nutty ideas, don't act on them."

I nodded. "Addiction withdrawal."

"Yes," King replied, "but this is just the physical side. You just need to deal with it."

"I guess I'm lucky," I stated flatly.

Mercifully, work took the edge off of everything. Okay, that's not true, but by being at work I could turn my bodily functions over to Samuel, and I didn't have to worry about not being able to fit my head through the door or how far it was to the door handle. Samuel took care of everything for me. And if I wasn't well, he would have sent me to the clinic after my shift so I could be put right. All I had to do was somehow make busy and while away the time. Solitaire, slots, whatever would pass the time. Nothing serious, nothing that required thought. I just simply let Samuel drive. I wasn't well. But that's the beauty of staff, they don't take sick days unless they are infected or broken.

The next morning was worse. I woke in the early hours because I actually was sick. Why I should feel sick was something I couldn't understand. It wasn't like I ate the drugs they had been putting in my feed bags. But my stomach was turning over and I got up, rolled around the chair knocking things around, made it to the sink and threw up.

"Are you not well?" Samuel asked me when I reconnected.

"Oh, hey Samuel, no, I think I just, I thought my hands were sticky and I had to wash them."

I wasn't sure what Samuel was doing, but evidently, when I slept, he slept.

"Are you sure?"

"Yes, I just knocked the connector off my head."

"It's magnetic."

He sounded like he didn't buy it. "Like I said, I must have moved my hands. They were feeling sticky, I got up to wash them. I'm sleepy, can I go back to sleep now?"

"Sure," Samuel said soothingly, "pleasant dreams."

I didn't sleep and Samuel stayed up with me. "Are you certain you are not unwell?" he asked.

"I'm fine," I said, and I rolled to my side, even though I was in my chair. I could move a little. I twisted my head to make the connector pop off. I tapped the side of my head and went offline altogether. No sense staying up with my babysitter all night.

Trying to make myself comfortable, I closed my eyes. I could hear myself breathe. I could hear the water running in the pipes. I could hear how small my condo was, every breath seemed to be right in my ear. In the darkness I felt like the walls were just inches away from either side of my head. Like I'd been decapitated, my head put in a box, and I hadn't actually moved in years, maybe not ever. I lived here, a head, stuck in a tiny box.

I wanted to turn on the lights. I had to get up to do that. But I didn't think I was alone in the room. I heard something scurrying, shuffling, behind the walls. A bump, and I thought I heard my drawers opening. There was someone in here. I got up, the lights came on and I blinked. There was no one here. The sounds had come from the far end of my condo and the right wall where I had my drawers. I opened the drawer where I dumped my uniform—it was empty. I opened the drawer where every day I took a fresh uniform, leaving none. It now contained one full, neatly folded uniform. Quickly I opened my food cabinet. There were three feed bags neatly stacked one on top of the other. I suddenly felt like my condo wasn't private, like nothing I did couldn't be seen. I grabbed the three feedbags and took them over to my sink. I gouged at them with my fingernails until they burst open and I squeezed the contents out and into the sink.

The walls felt like they were closing in on me. But the best thing to do was to get back into the chair and re-connect. That way I wouldn't have to listen to all the rustling in the walls. They sounded like footsteps, tiny little footsteps.

"Hi Samuel," I interjected before he could ask how I was. "I dropped something, I had to pick it up."

"Oh goodness, is anything broken, do you need maintenance?"

"No, my feeding tower fell over, I guess I knocked it over again."

"Is it broken, it's important you eat."

"No, it's not broken, I just knocked it over." I tried to sound confident.

"Good."

"If it's all the same to you, I'd just like to get back to sleep."

"Sure." I could hear the smile in his voice again. "Nighty, night."

"Good morning George," Samuel woke me once again. Somehow, I was back in the hotel, even though I hadn't done anything to get there. I felt awful, my throat was dry and I smelled like aluminum and dirt.

"Good morning Samuel, thank you for waking me." Not sure what possessed me to say that.

"You are welcome, it is always a pleasure to wake you," he replied. Interesting, it almost sounded genuine.

"Well," I said, "let's get going. You drive." The truth was I felt horrible, like a hot iron bar had been shoved through the front of my head. My cheeks were hot. My skin was itchy, I smelled awful and the room was shifting on me. I'm not sure I could have stood on my own. Getting through the kitchen was going to be fun, but maybe it would wear off.

Samuel took care of everything. I just went along for the ride. Afraid of everything, but wise enough to keep my mouth shut. Before I knew it, I was standing in the warm mist behind the cafe. I sighed. I can do this, I thought. I would just have to dash through the kitchen. I used two hands to open the door. The kitchen was a beehive of action. I closed my eyes. I could do this. *Just do this*! I felt myself moving. *That's it.* Perhaps I should have opened my eyes, because I ran straight into a staff with a flat of eggs. The eggs went flying. I bounced off a prep table and knocked over a waitress. I was more like a bowling ball than a person. Somehow, I managed to stay on my feet, my hands flailing and knocking over bowls. I heard dishes crash somewhere behind me, and I felt myself step on a sausage patty, but I made it.

There was no rush of people to confront me for what I had done. Staff don't work like that. They simply pick themselves up, clean up the mess and continue about their business. I pushed the door open to the dining room. The corner of it hit a wait staff who was bringing in an order.

I heard someone laughing, not a hearty full laugh, but a laugh nonetheless coming from the corner. It was King, and he was getting up from his booth. "You wait there." His voice just made it across the dining room. "I'll come and help you." He slowly picked his way through the obstacle course of chairs, tables, elbows and backsides. "This damn cane," he waved it, used it to smack chairs as he pushed through the obstructions. Finally, eventually, made it to me. He held out his arm like a railing. "Here. Grab my arm. I heard you in the kitchen, I can only imagine the mess, it sounded like an elephant had been let loose back there."

I took his arm. It was easier to let him steer.

"All that crashing and banging, I knew it must be you. Come, sit, eat; have something to put you right." He smiled as he led me. I felt exhausted, and I'd just gotten up. My legs felt cramped. He seemed to be enjoying this, helping me, like I didn't know how to walk.

We attracted some dirty looks as we shuffled across the room but otherwise made it without incident. No more plates broken, and no more coffee spilled. I flopped into the seat. I thought I could hear people whispering all around.

King sat down in front of me. "You look like shit," he said, and smiled broadly.

I looked around, had anyone heard that? Had he just given me away?

"Relax, now you look like you just stole a chocolate bar," King chided me.

"What?" I could feel something cold running down my back.

"Here, take one of these, no take two." He handed me two tablets from his yellow plastic container.

I took them and quickly popped them in my mouth. "But you need these," I said as I reached for something to help swallow them.

"Maybe, but you need them more." King unwrapped his cutlery. "I have some good news if you can get through today. I was reading, tomorrow will be better."

"Huh?" I wasn't sure that these were eggs, I was busy poking them with my finger, just in case they would start trying to slither off my plate.

"You will be calmer tomorrow, so I've read."

"Read?"

"Yes, you know, articles, online, about withdrawal."

I looked up. "Oh that, it can take a few days. Tends to get worse then better."

King smiled. "Yes, why don't you enjoy your breakfast? We are safe here, no one knows, and no one cares who we are." He paused for a second, just to see if I was listening and make it sink in. "Relax, everything is good."

"Right," I said, not at all sure. But I knew he was right. I think I had come across that too. Though I wasn't sure about the old man two tables to our left. He was wearing hearing aids—could they be listening devices?"

King snapped his fingers. "You need to trust me." He pointed at my breakfast. "Just do what I say, and things will be all right."

I smiled. He smiled, we smiled together. I hated this feeling, wanting to jump up and run, but not knowing where to go. Everyone was watching.

"Eat, you'll feel better."

Tentatively, I lifted a triangle of soggy white bread to my mouth. He was right. As soon as the oil, fat and salt hit my tongue, I started to feel better.

The food made a big difference. I felt so much better, and King ordered some extra sausages for me. "The fat will help you feel more relaxed," he told me, and he was right. By the time we were done, I felt much better. "Just keep things quiet today," was his only advice, "I'll see you tomorrow." And we were off. I put Samuel back in charge, and he led me through the kitchen with agility that I'd been sadly lacking on my own.

"Hello Samuel," I said, "let's play poker today."

"Very good George, here is a list of the online casinos you can play in, which one would you like."

"*Casino! Casino! Casino!* Sounds good to me," I told me. In truth, they were all the same, just the color of the screen was different when you looked at the cards on the table. It didn't matter, but it was as good as anything to pass the time.

I can tell you this: it can be painful to spend the day playing games just to make the time pass. I was doing horribly, but I made sure I was at a limited bet table. I didn't care; occasionally, I would win some outrageously impossible hand, but generally I lost. The day just seemed to go on and on. I didn't want to look; I didn't want to do anything. I just wanted the day to end. The pills King gave me had really worked, but I still felt paranoid, like someone was watching, and I knew Samuel was, but at least I didn't feel my skin shaking and sliding over my bones and I'd stopped sweating. The cards kept getting dealt, again and again and again, always the same. How could people do this day after day without going mad?

48

REST

The day of the tribunal came, as it said it would on the registered letter that had been delivered to Brian's office. The letter had told him he had to pay 21.64cc, which was point four more crypto coins than Brian had thought. There was also a surprise charge of $500 for tribunal administrative fees. *How nice,* Brian thought. *Bad enough to be ripped off by the banks, but the courts too?* But what are you going to do? Five hundred dollars was nothing compared to 21.64 crypto coins, but still, it is five hundred dollars, which he would miss and would rather have had.

The night before, Brian couldn't sleep. His wife was still angry with him, and he tossed and turned on the sofa. At about two in the morning, Prince came out of his room, two hands clutching a stuffed giraffe in front of him.

"Hi Daddy," he said, "is mommy still mad at you?"

"Yes, little buddy, she is." Brian didn't like lying to his son. Even the type of lies that most parents gave their kids which just allowed them not to have to explain everything.

"Daddy," Prince asked, "is everything going to be all right?"

"Why, of course." To Brian, as a father, the thought his son at this age should even worry about anything tweaked him with fear.

"Is that why you went to the clinic? Were you sick?"

Brian sat up, turning the couch from a bed to a sofa again. "No, Prince, I wasn't sick."

"Mommy says you had an operation."

Brian had hoped not to have to explain it to him, not yet. Maybe in a few years, maybe when he was back sleeping in his own bed again. "Yes, that is true." He didn't say anything more, hoping Prince would leave it.

"I asked mommy why you had the operation," Prince volunteered, "she said it's because you are a pig-headed idiot." Being called that by his wife he would have understood, but he felt a pain in his chest hearing that from his son. "She also said you did it so we could get some money."

Brian nodded. "She is right." He realized being specific would help. "About the money part."

"She said you did this so we wouldn't have to become staff."

Well, that degree of bluntness wasn't something that Brian was ready for. "Um, well, yes, that's true too."

Prince looked down at his foot as he swept it back and forth on the floor. "I don't want to be staff."

Brian sighed. What a relief! The way they talk about it, staff have all the fun. Staff don't have to work because they don't notice it. Staff never feel pain. Staff play and party all the time. Staff get to experience the immersive internet. Staff don't have to worry about money as every one of them is rich beyond their dreams in the online world. Staff get to take any drug they want with no ill-effects. Staff can't catch STDs. Staff don't have to think, and probably the most attractive aspect of being staff: they get to play all day and don't have to go to school. "Oh, hey cowboy, that isn't going to happen to you or me or mommy or anyone?"

Prince smiled. "Is everything is going to be all right?"

"Yes, yes, it is." Brian felt a wave of relief wash over him and lift him up. His son was old enough to understand, not stupid enough to fall for any of the stuff they said about staff. Best of all, Prince understood that what he had done was for him too. Warmth within his heart, Brian held his hands out to his son.

Prince stepped in and let his dad give him a hug. "Then, daddy?"

"Hmm," Brian mumbled, enjoying this hug like he had no other.

Prince stepped back. "Why aren't you sleeping?"

"Oh, that, um, you know, I don't know."

Prince held out his stuffed giraffe. "Take Charlie, he's good at helping me get to sleep."

It had been a long time, Brian reached out and took the giraffe. Perhaps he'd been a bad dad. He hadn't known his son had named his stuffed animal, but he was going to get a second chance. Brian took the stuffed giraffe. "Thank you, Prince. I think this is exactly what I was missing."

Prince grinned and gave him a big thumbs up. "Okay daddy, I need to go back to bed." *So much like a little man,* Brian thought. Before he could say anything, Prince was gone.

Brian rolled over holding the giraffe close. He'd done well. He wasn't perfect, but he had done better than he thought. He tried closing his eyes, but they would not yield to sleep. Tomorrow was too big a day.

49

FORECLOSURE

Brian was getting better. When he rolled off the couch, there were no shooting pains. His head was full of sleep, but his heart was already pounding. This was a big day. The fear he would sleep through the day, to be woken by the sound of boots busting down his door and law enforcement staff, taking himself, his wife and son captive, had been avoided for now. His mobile was sitting on the table beside the couch. He dropped the giraffe that Prince had given him as he grabbed for the mobile. No, he must pick up the giraffe and put it somewhere nice, perhaps at the kitchen table. Seated, like it was waiting for breakfast. Brian zigzagged over to the kitchen. His feet reminded him of his age.

He sat the giraffe down at his place at the breakfast table. He'd have to get going. He opened his mobile. "Wake 418 and have him meet me at Jazmin's cafe in forty minutes." He told the mobile. There was a beep, and the order became listed in his history.

Creeping back into his bedroom, he quietly got dressed. Imelda slept soundly. Wryly, Brian wondered if she would wake up if the law enforcement staff busted down the door. His bet was on no. He kissed her on the forehead and slipped out the door. This would be a good day if he just made it to where he had to go.

Brian used the stairs again. This time, he felt so much better about them. He knew before he was just staving off death, and today he was also just staving off death of a slightly different kind. But this more symbolic death left him feeling much more appreciative of life. Now he wanted to take the stairs, not just to try to keep his medical costs down. With agility he didn't know he had, he bounded down the stairs. At the bottom, and only once he reached the bottom, did he call for his car.

The door made a hideous creak—it probably always had, he'd just not noticed—as he pushed it open and stepped into the early morning humidity. Within moments his clothes were sticking to his skin, and his shorts were trying to crawl up his legs. He breathed deeply the sweet humid air and tried to let it fill his lungs. It was a little gritty, but it had been a long time since he had felt free. The sky to the east was starting to brighten. It was going to be a great day, and the sun was going to come up and tomorrow it would come up again, and he'd be able to see it.

The car pulled up, the door opened, and Brian got in. "I'd like to go to Jazmin's cafe," he told the car.

The car took a moment to calculate the route. "I have selected the fastest..."

Brian interrupted the car. "Confirmed." And with that, the car belted him in, and he was on his way.

At Jazmin's, Brian ordered two Big Ben All Out Samplers, the largest breakfast platters he could find on the menu. One with coffee and the other with orange juice. Perhaps he should mix it up sometime and order tomato juice and see if it threw George off. Nah, best not. It was surprising what decades of taking anti-psychotic drugs, even in small amounts, could do to a fellow. He decided it was best not to mess with the poor guy too much.

He'd gotten good at timing this. If he was going to have a greasy breakfast, he at least wanted to have it hot, but he didn't want it not to be on the table when George got here. The nice thing about staff was they do things the same way all the time. They couldn't help it; it always took six minutes from the time he orders for the food to appear on his table. Never, seven and not five, but six, always six. Right on schedule, the food appeared on his table.

Yesterday it sounded like a bull crashing around in a china shop. He wondered how many dishes had been broken. Thankfully staff knew their station and they hadn't added it to his bill. Today there was only a little bit of crashing: something metal. A large bowl crashed on the floor, but there was no breaking glass or smashing of china. George appeared, glancing back at the kitchen as he freed himself from the kitchen and the oblivious staff. Evidently, he was feeling a bit better than he did yesterday.

"Good morning George," Brian said, without looking up from his breakfast at the figure that was working his way through the largely empty restaurant.

"Good morning King," George said back. "Why are we here so early?"

"I have a busy day," Brian responded. "I don't want to be late for anything. I've decided to be early for everything."

"Hmm," George replied, taking a seat opposite of Brian. "Thank you for ordering breakfast. I feel much better today."

"I thought you would." Brian reached into his pocket and took out his magic yellow canister. "Have one," he said as he opened it. "You look much better. You don't look like someone who is being followed." He placed the pill on the table between them.

George looked around. No one was looking, and he smiled at Brian. "No thank you. It's getting better."

The truth of the matter was, I had stopped hearing things—or, stopped paying attention to things I always heard but usually didn't notice. The sweat, which was much like thick goo, was greatly reduced, and I didn't feel like my skin wasn't quite attached to my body. I felt tired, and kind of dizzy, but with a little effort I could navigate the kitchen with only the knocking over of one large metal bowl full of sliced green stuff.

It was nice of King to think of me, and even offer the pill. Now that I was getting better, I knew they had helped, and if they didn't, they put me in a good frame of mind for the day. I pushed it back across the table. "No thank you, I'm getting better," I told King.

"Well, I am glad."

"What do you have to do today that you can't be late for?"

King smiled. "You remember that surgery that you did? Today, I have to pay the lender."

"Can't you do that online?"

King smiled. "You know technology. If I pay online, I'm worried that they will say I didn't pay because some record wasn't updated somewhere."

"That doesn't sound fair."

"Life isn't fair, you know that." He was doing that thing with his coffee cup again.

I smiled. And we ate. Today the food tasted much better, and my head didn't feel funny. "So King, tell me, today you are going to solve your problem, how about me?"

King smiled. "One more day, I want to make sure this goes okay."

How was I supposed to argue?

Brian and George went their separate ways. George took a car to the clinic and sat there for fifty minutes in the carport before the car would let him out. Brian didn't go to his office; he went to the courthouse. He put his car on 'make busy' and went inside. It was still early when he passed through the metal detectors, made it to the elevator and up to the third floor where the tribunal's hearing room was located. He was the first one there. Which was good, he hadn't missed it. He checked his mobile, it was working. He logged into the bank. He had twenty-five cc in his account, more than enough to pay his debts—not enough to maybe help him start a new business or find an income stream which might lead to a better life—but enough for now.

Brian knew if he had been late, everything would have happened on time. As it was, he wasn't, and therefore there was some rainstorm which caused a number of traffic exceptions, and everyone else was late. Brian didn't care. He smiled as he watched people hurrying in, their hands filled with papers. Their hair and clothes looked a little rumpled from having been stuck in traffic.

The team from BCPL showed up, and they sat across from him. When they didn't think he was looking, they stared at him. When he looked, they smiled and looked away. Brian felt his blood starting to heat. He'd love to go over there and sort this out in a physical way, but if he did, he would miss the tribunal. That would never do. He tried to calm himself and think of how good it was going to be when he paid them off. He made a note to himself that he must not give away how he had managed to find the money and act as if it was no big thing. He thought to himself: don't give them the satisfaction.

The time for the tribunal arrived, but the adjudicator had not, so they continued to sit there, playing eye games. Twenty minutes passed. Other rooms were letting people in, but not Brian's. Thirty minutes, still no change. Finally, forty-two minutes late, Susan K. Woland, county clerk and bankruptcy adjudicator shuffled down the hallway. "I'm sorry I am late," she called to everyone seated. A law enforcement staff opened the door for her. Brian stood to go in, but the staff told him to be seated until the tribunal was called to order. Brian sat and waited some more. The woman from BCPL smiled thinly at him.

Twenty minutes later, the door opened again, and the law enforcement staff stepped back into the hallway and invited everyone in. Brian tried not to look at the crowd that had tried to railroad him into bankruptcy. Brian sat by himself to the left as the opposition sat on the right and arranged their bags, papers and arguments.

"All rise," the staff said, "madam Arbitrator Susan K Woland, presiding." The Arbitrator woman walked in with a pleasant smile on her face.

"Good morning," she addressed the room in general. "What is first on the agenda?"

A clerical staff standing behind her stepped forward. "The petition of declaration of bankruptcy, second tribunal meeting, BCPL LLP vs Brian Agarwal et al."

"Very good," the adjudicator announced. "Would the complainant rise?" The woman from BCPL was wearing a red tartan suit that made Brian's eyes want to bleed just a bit. But he didn't want to look at her anyway.

"Yes, madam adjudicator, I am Sheila Grantner of BCPL. It is a pleasure to see you this morning." Brian wanted to go over and pop her one in the mouth. No one should be that happy to be in a courtroom.

"Thank you. Does the complainant wish to continue to pursue the petition?"

"Why yes." She cleared her throat so she would not be misheard. "BCPL would like to pursue the petition."

"Very good." The adjudicator made a note on her desk. "How much of the debt is outstanding?"

"Yes, if it pleases the tribunal, we would like to state we have not received any of the payments from the party of the first part." She nodded in the direction of Brian.

"Would you please rise, Mr. Agarwal?" the adjudicator ordered. Brian stood up, his heart pounding. "Mr. Agarwal, have you made any or all of the payments on this debt?"

Brian started to speak, "If it would please the tribunal," but his voice came out weak and strangled, and he repeated, "If it would please the tribunal, I have the means to make the payment in full now."

"Oh," the adjudicator said with some surprise. It was normal that the defendant would throw themselves on the mercy of the tribunal. "Payment in full? How novel."

"Yes." Brian held up his mobile. "I can transfer the money right now, if the nice lady from the Seventh National Bank would give me the wallet number. I would be happy to do this for everyone to witness."

"Oh, well that's very good," the adjudicator said. "Would the 'nice lady from the Seventh National Bank' please rise?"

The court was still and silent, and Brian could hear his heart beating.

"Mr. Agarwal," the adjudicator addressed him slowly, savoring this, "you seem to have failed to make arrangements to make payment."

"But, wait," Brian tried to explain. How was he to know the bank lady would forget to show up, or she wouldn't show up? The walls of the courtroom seemed to be closing in as fast as the air seemed to be sucked out of the room. He had hoped to avoid a situation where he made payment to the bank, but delays posting it to some account would have had them testify that it hadn't been received. The fact that it popped up one day late after some silly bureaucratic clearing wouldn't undo the surgeries once started. The room started to swoon, a swarm of black dots seemed to be surging out of the walls, the adjudicator's bench, the ceiling, the floor.

"Mr. Agarwal. It states clearly that payment must be received today or may be made at the tribunal hearing. Nowhere does it say you will be excused if you can make payment, but for whatever reason, you do not. You are responsible for getting payment executed, or else the petition will get executed." The adjudicator was enjoying this. Brian thought he was going to faint. Her voice was coming from someplace high above him, and he felt like the whirling dots of reality were digging a hole beneath him and that he was going to fall through the floor. "It has always been your responsibility to tender payment and..."

The door opened. "I'm sorry, I got stuck in traffic, and my heel broke." The older washed-out woman from the bank entered the courtroom.

"I see." The adjudicator seemed disappointed. "Ms. Gerrard,"

"Yes, madam adjudicator," she said as she wobbled past the desks.

"If Mr. Agarwal can make payment, can you provide him with the address to which it should be made?"

"Yes madam, I can."

Brian heaved a sigh of relief. "Thank you," he whispered under his breath. *That was close.*

50

IT'S OKAY

Brian had thought he was going to have a celebration after the tribunal. He had staved off a major threat to himself and his family. He should be pleased; he should be happy. But that was a closer shave than he ever anticipated. It was clear to him now that as long as he continued to live this way, he would be subject to this kind of thing again. If the bank lady had just called in sick, he would be sedated by now, not back at his office.

He still had goosebumps on his arms, and he didn't feel like he could get warm again. He'd spent a lot of time in the washroom, trying to feel clean, trying to feel all right again. He looked at himself in the mirror, both hands on the sink. His eyes were red, his skin was worn. The rich brown cheeks of his youth were now graying with bad diet and aging. It's okay when it isn't you, Brian said to himself. Can't let that happen again. It occurred to him he only had one more kidney left, and you weren't allowed to live very long without any kidneys.

"Right." Brian grabbed some rough brown paper towels, rubbed them on his face. They didn't absorb anything, but the friction made the water go away. The feeling of his face reminded him that, because of today, he still had his own body to himself. "I start from here." He crumpled the useless paper, stuffed it into the trash bin, and strode out of the washroom.

It still was a good day.

51

DAMAGED

"Good morning, George," King said as I worked my way across the dining room of the cafe. He was smiling, and there was a glow about him I'd not seen before.

"Good morning King. You are looking pleased with yourself. I guess it went well."

King smiled warmly. "Yes, though it was scarier than I thought it would be."

"You? Scared?" It didn't seem possible.

"Yeah." King started in on an egg.

The idea of King being afraid of anything seemed absurd. I tried to wrap my head around it as I chewed on my toast. I wanted to ask how. "Why?" is what came out instead.

"I had a lot to lose," he added.

"Hmm," I took a sip of orange juice, "must be awful."

"So..." King broke into a broad smile. "How about you?"

"Me?"

King glanced around quickly, maybe what he was about to say wasn't allowed. "Yeah, let's get you out of here."

I had thought of how I didn't like how I lived. I wanted something better, but I didn't know what. "I don't know isn't that sort of quick?"

"Nonsense, what are you waiting for?" There was a look in his eye, something shiny I'd never seen it before.

"How? What am I going to do? Where am I going to go? How am I going to survive?" It never occurred to me I could actually stop just being staff.

King shrugged with his face. "I don't know. You seem to know something about being a medical technician."

"Oh no! That's only when I'm at work, I don't remember any of that."

"Yes, you do."

"No, when I'm not at work I don't know how to go take out an appendix," I argued.

King sat back, leaning against the back of the booth. He shook his head gently from side to side. "If I cut myself, could you put a band-aid on my cut?"

"Yes, but you should put some antibiotic cream on it first. It should be cleaned and disinfected, or else you will be sorry. And then you will be back, that's if you don't need stitches." It blurted out of me.

"And if I needed stitches, should I do it?"

"No, let me, you will infect the wound and I've seen it done."

King nodded. "See you do know stuff, you can help."

I knew he was trying to trick me. "But I can't take out your appendix."

"No, perhaps not. Maybe someday. You learn quickly, you know that?"

"I do?" That sounded wonderful. Momentarily, I forgot what we were talking about.

"Yes, so you can do that. Be a doctor or a nurse, no. A medic."

"Where do I go?" I was still intrigued about being a fast learner.

"Don't worry about that, but you have to be ready to leave all of this, all of whatever you have in your condo, all of whatever you have online behind."

The very matter of fact way he said it made it sound like no big thing. I had to think about it. I'd never be able to go to Dr. Pong's; I'd never go to the casino. I'd never pass my day playing solitaire or exchanging messages with people I'd never meet or people who might not even be real. There was so much to leave behind, like feed bags that contained drugs that made you sick if you stopped taking them. "Okay, how do I do this?"

King smiled. There was a shine to his eyes. "Now we are talking! First thing is, you must trust me."

I shrugged.

"Do whatever I say, do it the way I tell you."

"Sure."

"Don't get sidetracked by any well-meaning staff or concierge or anything you might have heard before."

"Okay, I got it."

"No, I need you to promise, do I like I tell you, promise?" He was deadly serious.

"Okay," I said, it was hard to keep eye contact with him, I'd never seen him this intense. "I promise."

"Good, here's exactly what you do..."

King explained the plan. There wasn't anything for him to do, just sit back and watch and hope that everything was going to work out. I had to do everything. I told him I couldn't do it. I mean, as long as I stayed here, I was good. I could go to work. It was boring, but it was life.

King laughed at me. "This isn't life, this is existence." Then he seemed to get mad at me. "Do you want out or not? You are going to have to let go of whatever you thought you had."

"Yes," I answered. "But what if it goes wrong? I'd be dead."

"And if you stay? You know, I have a family too, I can't keep coming here for breakfast every day. If you stay, you're as good as dead; remember Belinda? We just have to wait a bit longer until your body gets disposed of." He sat back. "You have nothing to lose, so why wouldn't today be a good day?"

"But I won't see you again." It sounded pathetic, and King shot me a look like what I had just said wasn't true. I tried to think of an answer. King was the only real person in my life. Otherwise, my existence was completely empty. No wonder they put stuff in the feed bags. "Right, let's do this."

"Samuel," I called out from the security of my car. "Hey, Samuel,"

Samuel appeared in front of the card game I was playing. "Yes George, what may I do for you?"

"My head hurts," I told him.

"Really?"

"Yes, there is a grittiness behind my eyes."

"How long has this been going on?" Samuel asked, with absolutely genuine concern.

"Hmm," I said, "I don't know. A long time." I wanted to say weeks, three or so, but that would mean I knew what weeks were. "It's getting worse. It started as slight discomfort, but I can't stand the pain anymore. It hurts all the time."

"Really?"

"Yes, it's no fun. It's getting worse."

"I think we should check you into the clinic for examination. I think that would be best. It could help make the pain in your head go away. Shall I arrange this?"

"Oh, yes, Samuel, anything to make this pain go away."

I continued riding just as I always had. But when we got to the clinic, I didn't get out of the car. I had to wait. There was only one med-tech that day—the other must be sick—and he would have to do his rounds before he would come and let me out of the car. Well, I'd done it now. As I sat there, I started to become very cold with fear. King had told me everything would be all right, just don't press any buttons, don't flip any switches. Just follow along and wait. Right now, I was waiting. Whatever happened, even if I died, I wouldn't miss being jammed into these little metal eggs.

Finally, the car opened. There was one med-tech standing there, the one I usually worked with. He looked at me with no expression on his face. He reached down and pulled me out of the car. Since there was only one of him, he dug his hands into my ribs as he pulled me up. I wanted to say something, but Samuel was still driving, until I got strapped into the restraining bed. Samuel was in charge, though it hurt, I couldn't do anything.

It was not at all reassuring when Samuel told me, "Now that you are safely secured, I am going to turn control of your body back to you."

"Okay," I said.

"You might find this very disorienting, but we are going to have to take you offline for a while so we can do an examination."

I knew what Samuel was talking about, the way Belinda had flipped out when King took her offline. "Yeah, I guess that has to happen."

"I am glad you understand," Samuel said, "but as soon as you have finished being examined, I can assure you that you will be back online again."

"Okay, do what you have to." It wasn't being offline that worried me, it was the testing that worried me. But King said it would be all right. I just hope I wasn't cooked by the time we were done.

First came the easy stuff. But here I had a chance to blow it. I could just say I was fine, and nothing bothered me. And, because it didn't require any tests and because no one had seen me behaving erratically, I would have been able to go home at the end of the day. No, it couldn't go on this way...

"Yes, my head hurts at the end of the day." I answered a question I had asked another staff a few weeks ago.

"You have headaches?" the med-tech asked me. He looked at me but didn't focus.

"Yes, they are awful," I added.

"Could you describe these headaches?" And for some reason that seemed out of place, the med-tech added, "Please."

"Well," I tried to imagine how to get this right, "I get them in the top of my head. My eyes are sore, and my head hurts like I just don't want to look at anything anymore."

The med-tech took out a flashlight. "This is a retinoscope," the staff told me, "please keep your eyes open, and tell me if there is any discomfort when I activate the light." The light turned on. It was bright. I couldn't see anything but light and I wanted to pull away. "Did you feel any discomfort?" the med-tech asked.

"No." I saw the med-tech's hands start to move to another instrument. "It only happens when I am at work," I added quickly. I'd hate to talk myself into needless eye surgery.

"It does?" the med-tech asked me for confirmation.

I had to think about this. I was pretty sure that, after this, there would be no return. I took a deep breath. "Yes," I answered. "When I get home, I find that I have to take off some of my clothes, soak them, and put them on my forehead as rags to cool things down and make me feel better."

"Do you close your eyes?"

"Why of course," I responded, like it was obvious.

"And when you close your eyes, what do you see?"

"Oh," I remembered what to say. "I see all the things that I do at work." I said this convincingly. It was easy when it wasn't a lie. I loved that.

"What do you do?"

"I work with you..." I wanted to add 'knucklehead,' but I had to remember that this staff likely had no idea I was the other staff it worked with. "I work as a med-tech," I corrected.

"And you remember this?" The questions were just as programmed, and I was stepping through a sorting maze of triage. I tried not to think too much about it, but it was interesting to go down this path again.

"Oh yes, I don't want to, but I do."

"So, you are online, and you remember your duties as a med-tech. Do you remember how to be a med-tech?"

"As much as I can." Whoops, too much truth. "I mean, I don't want to, but I do. I close my eyes at night, and I remember setting bones and stitching up cuts. You know I don't want to remember these things. I just want a normal life." Funny that, the truth, a lie, the truth, a lie and finally the truth. *Nothing disguises lies better than the truth.*

"We can help you. Do not worry, you are in the right place and everything will be all right." The tech said it so flatly, with such mechanical monotony, that it was obviously a lie.

Because I had arrived early, and because there were no surprise visits, even though the med-tech staff was alone, I was prepared and taken off to the operating theater. With great effort, I tried to keep my breath under control and not completely freak out. It was worse when you know what was going to happen. We entered the operating theater. I looked up at the ceiling, nothing else for me to see. I saw the computer come into view. I felt my bed shudder, as it was anchored into place. The snap of a cable being fixed to the side of my head was like a great iron door being shut with a rusty clang. In the echo of the snap, I heard the med-tech walk away.

At first it felt like a gentle buzz. I knew the staff was behind the counter, pressing that load button. Is that was it was like when they uploaded instructions to my head? Then there was a similar buzz, and a gentle feeling of sucking. My eyes wanted to push together as the knowledge was pulled out of my head. You know, I'd always thought it was painless, feelingless, but it wasn't, there was still friction. *Uh-oh,* I remembered how the staff I had examined, the clerical staff, had suffered and writhed on his examination bed at the touch of my hands on that control panel. And we were just beginning.

It didn't take long for the surge of data—in and out, in and out—to start to heat up. There was friction, and the more times that it loaded the hotter the wire on the side of my head seemed, the hotter the interface behind my forehead seemed to get. It was heating, swelling and pushing back against the data. Making it harder for it to flow in, making it sticky and harder to suck out. In moments I'd gone from breathing to gasping to moaning. Now it was becoming like a knife, dull and rusty, being plunged into my temple. My eyes felt like they were bleeding. Each pulse caused my body to twitch. Liquid streamed from my eyes. My heart pounded in my head. The interface was getting hot, burning, and I imagined my brain starting to smoke. King had told me I had to do this. I hope I survived. I didn't think I was going to. It was too hot. The interface would simply sear its way through my brain and leave a dark scorch mark on the back of my skull. I started to scream.

How long this went on, I couldn't know. Every muscle in my body was writhing, contracting, tearing, and my mind was sizzling. Not with thought, but with a hot square of lead pressing down on my brain, simple, hot, pain! A square of red-hot metal cauterizing my frontal lobe. The torture did come to an end. I don't remember much of it. I was in a puddle of sweat and blood, and as soon as the cable was disconnected from my head, I collapsed and fell into deep, dreamless sleep.

Bolt Greene read his messages. *Oh no,* he thought. He could see the claim for 686381KAA418. It clearly said a diagnosis had been made. That staff was now suffering from data bleed. *Shoot!* He would have to go down to the clinic. *This was a damned inconvenient time for Andrea Dover to go on vacation. She should be happy to have a job.* Bolt shook his head. "Fuck. I hate going to clinics." He looked at the clock in the corner of his computer screen. It was almost lunchtime. If he pretended he didn't see this message and just went for lunch, could he put it off until tomorrow? He must have some important meeting this afternoon, though he couldn't remember, but maybe it would take care of itself and he wouldn't have to go. Nah, he'd still have to go and document the body, but at least it would be cleaned up. Dang it, sometimes life wasn't fair.

I lay in the hallway, offline. I dozed, my head feeling like someone had ripped it open. If I died, I wouldn't have cared. It would have been mercy.

Sometime in the afternoon, King came to see me. I felt cooked. He walked in, accompanied by the med-tech staff. "This is the staff?" King asked, as he approached me.

"Yes," said the med-tech.

King smiled at me. My eyes tried to focus on him. I felt scrambled. I tried to make words come out, but none would. "What is the prognosis?" King asked.

"This staff has data bleed, and as such, we have recommended that it be retired."

King turned and looked at the staff. "It looks pretty clear to me, what are we waiting for?"

The staff answered directly, "The recommendation has not been confirmed by the adjuster."

"That bastard!" King did a good job of pretending that he was mad. "I want my money, when can we get this moving?"

The staff answered, "We have put in a request an adjuster be sent."

"Okay, okay." King turned to face me. I managed to make my eyes focus on him. "Well, this one looks pretty busted up. Hello, is there anyone in there? Could you make me some coffee?"

I managed a smile. I opened my mouth to say something, but all that came out was a hoarse whisper. "Sorry, I am a tea pot!"

King smiled back at me, nodding warmly. "Very good."

The staff paused for a moment. "What you are seeing is disorientation, which is a byproduct of neural interface testing. This will wear off. I can administer a stimulant if you wish?"

"No, that won't be necessary, just as long as he gets his senses back." King referred to me as a *he.* I could have jumped up off the bed, except I was restrained.

"The stupor will wear off in about five hours," the staff added.

"Well, that's good," King said, "I see everything is going to plan, I hear this staff has been suffering and if he just remembers to trust, things will be all right."

The med-tech seemed to struggle to find a context to answer King. "This staff is suffering from data bleed and it is recommended that it be sent for retirement. Trust is not required."

"Okay, I have seen enough, could you lead me out of here?" King asked.

"Certainly," I heard the voice of the med-tech say, "please follow me."

King did not follow. He leaned over and whispered, "Remember the plan, don't press any buttons, stay calm." I blinked. King straightened, loudly pronouncing, "Oh, what a shame to lose a valuable staff!" He made a wide sweeping gesture with his arms, and I felt a pulling on my right arm as something was knocked out of my catheter. I heard King's footsteps receding into the darkness.

52

RETIREMENT

I was hungry the next morning. Sometime in the evening, I had woken, coming back to my senses. I never wanted to go through anything like that again. No wonder they had to get you when you were a kid. If anyone knew what this was like, no sane person would want this!

But here I was, offline again, and trapped. Stuck to my bed. I knew King was out there and it gave me hope. Perhaps he would come and see me this morning. If it were morning. I stared up at the ceiling; the lights were as they always were. Nothing moved, everything looked dank and dreary. I wanted to go back online, just so I could talk to anyone. Even Samuel, who wasn't real.

I only knew it was morning, because the med-techs were switched off. The new morning crew would come and check to see if I were alive. I saw briefly a face before my eyes, and I felt someone re-attach my feed bag. I imagined the poison slowly starting to seep into my veins through my arm. I told myself it took a couple of hours for the feed bag to finish. It was sustained exposure to the anti-psyches that made them work. I wanted to rip the plug right out of my arm. If only I was free. Until then, though, I had to wait.

"Right this way, Mr. Greene," I heard the med-tech say. It wasn't the voice of the med-tech that I usually worked with, it was a different voice. I'd been replaced. But more importantly than that, I'd get to meet Bolt Greene. The Bolt Greene! I wanted to get up. I wanted a good look at him. I wanted to thank this Bolt Greene for allowing me to be a man and not a walking automaton. It was like meeting a superhero.

"Here we are," the staff said.

I saw the top of his head, curly hair, and glasses. He peered over me. Instead of being radiant and having an ethereal glow around his head, he had pimples and, from my angle, a few hairs growing out of his nose. He looked at me with complete disgust, his face twisted like a child's looking at a box that didn't contain chocolates but rather mashed-up frogs. "Eich," Bolt Greene said, "this one looks pretty sickly. What is the diagnosis?"

"Data Bleed," replied the staff.

"What is the prognosis?" Bolt Greene asked.

"Bleed will continue. Recommendation for retirement."

Bolt Greene stepped away. I would never see him again, but I heard him say, "I second that. You know, it's too bad I can't just e-sign something from the office and skip all this. Things like that are disgusting. It ruins my lunch."

I heard him walking away. I imagined how long it would take for him to walk the distance that I thought that he would walk. He would have to tick a box and press his finger to a pad, and he would walk out the entrance of the white clinic and be gone. Never to think of me again. It was a pretty good guess. Within moments, the med-techs were back, unhooking me as they wheeled me around. I could see that the majority of the bag of poison that they were feeding me was still in the bag. Good, I thought. Maybe I wouldn't have to go through that again.

As they started to push me, Samuel appeared in my vision again. "Good news!" He chimed cheerfully, "you have reached retirement!"

"Hello Samuel, nice to see you," I lied, "What happened to me?"

"Well, I am afraid that you are too sick to work," he said with convincing sincerity. "But the good news is that your lifetime of hard work as paid off."

"Oh?"

"Yes! You are going to retire." The usually blue screen behind him start to shimmer and disappear into a bunch of dots. Behind him appeared a long beach with rolling surf, palm trees and, I swear, a huge fish that jumped out of the water. "Just think of all the fun that you will have. You no longer have to work, you have earned the right to sit back, relax and enjoy the best that life has to offer."

I could feel a puff of air as a car entered the carport. But the visual display was all the things that I could do and experience in retirement. There were pictures of men and women together. Everyone looked so young and vital. I could go surfing, rock climbing. Apparently, there were even real roller coasters. I wondered how they would stack up to the ones online. After you've been on a roller coaster that has gaps in the tracks online, what could the real-world possibly offer?

The video show continued: there was, food too, and pictures of rows of men and women laughing, lounging and doing recreational chemicals. All chemicals were on the table for retirees. That's one of the best things about being retired, everyone knows that. You can do just about anything that you like because you have earned it!

I felt myself being loaded into a car, the seat snugging around me. Anything that I had ever wanted. All I had to do was ask a staff for it, and they would get it for me, cheerfully. This was the prime of my life, and now all I had to do was sit back and enjoy. The car started moving, but the video display took my mind off the motion. If I hadn't had brain damage, I think I would have liked the idea of retirement, but instead I felt afraid. *Why, after all this time, should anyone give anything like that to me? I know, lifetime of service, but no one cared before.*

The ride was fairly short. The video slide show, which had me swimming with sea turtles, ended abruptly. Samuel stepped back in front of the display, which had swizzled back to blue screen.

"Good news," he claimed, enthusiastic as ever, not a hint of insincerity. "We have arrived at your new retirement home. Now, I should let you know, it's not like your condo. You are now going to be sharing common areas, where you can interact with other staff who have also been retired. It should be fun!"

I felt arms pick me up and I was immediately transferred into a restraining chair. Well, this wasn't walking around free. "Hey Samuel," I cried out in my own head, "minimize yourself."

"I'm sorry, no can do," he said with a smile, "it's all part of the experience." The video display continued. I found myself strolling through a large glass-roofed atrium. There were tropical flowers and fountains. There were porters and attendants dressed in nice suits, crisp white linen, everyone was nodding at me as I wandered in. "Welcome to retirement, the world is your oyster, simply for you to choose what you want, when you want, whatever you want." We cut away to another tropical setting, one with a long dock, at the end of which a chair sat beside a table, where a round yellow drink with an umbrella and a straw sat waiting. The ocean water was still, and you could see the clouds at sunset, reflected pink, blue and white off the perfect mirror surface of the ocean.

I felt the foam encircling me. I was being taken somewhere, but what I saw was the trees all around me, the smell of pine in my nose, a fresh forest—smelling like newly-mopped floors—early in the morning. I was hiking up a mountain path. "You can have and experience anything that you want. This is the ultimate. This is everything that you wanted," I heard Samuel's voice tell me. I strode the last few steps up the mountain path. The air cleared, there was mist everywhere around me, leading me, parting in front as me as I stepped out on a mountain top. Looking down I could see a river running through a gorge a thousand feet below. "And all of it is the real thing," Samuel added. "Just sit back and enjoy the fruits of your labor. You have earned it."

I felt something cold on the side of my head, and there was a tremendous buzzing in my ear and *Whack!* a bolt of lightning shot through my head. My eyes rolled. Samuel didn't disappear in a swarm of black dots, he was just gone—the room, gray, drab, spun before me and I felt my head hit my chest.

When I awoke, I wasn't in a restraining chair. I was simply seated in a regular chair. Maybe someone had taken the chair out of my condo.

The room was gray, gloomy. There was a window, but it had bars on it, and it was dirty enough that I couldn't see anything out of it. It was sometime around noon. My guess was that I had been out for an hour or so. My head was throbbing like I'd been hit. I tapped the side of my head. Nothing.

"Hey," I yelled. I was retired now. People were supposed to come and serve me. "Hey, is there anybody out there?"

A light went on above my chair. It was fixed into the ceiling. I heard footsteps coming.

"Hello." Medical staff, in a clean orange outfit, stepped into the room and greeted me. "How are you today?"

"I'm, I, I don't know, what's going on here?"

"Retirement."

"Retirement?" I asked incredulously, "What do you mean?" The staff seemed unfazed, by this. "What about the beach? What about mountain climbing?"

The staff responded evenly. "It's entirely possible for you to go to the beach or to climb a mountain."

"Oh, good," I answered. "Let's do that."

The staff ignored my question. "First, I need to explain this to you. If at any time you need assistance, please press the small red button under the left side of your chair. To your right, we have hooked up a feeding station. This will feed you while you enjoy your retirement."

"What about the internet?" I asked.

"Immersive internet is reserved for full-time working staff," the staff explained. "Now that you have retired, you no longer qualify."

"So, what? Like I'm not allowed on the internet?"

The staff responded dryly. "No, you are not able to go on the internet. For security reasons we have had to reset the firmware of your cerebral interface. Therefore, you have no means to interface with the internet. We hope you understand this inconvenience."

"Wow, this is a pretty crappy retirement."

The staff was undeterred by my comment. "You may also notice that on the right there is another button, attached to your feeding line, which splices in some of your favorite recreational substances. Please feel free to partake in those at your leisure, and to whatever degree you wish."

I looked at the button. It was so small and red, confusingly identical to the assistance button, but I had expected it to be large and red. I bet if I pushed it, there would be no sirens, there would be no lights going off, no confetti, no trumpets blaring. It would simply go *click*.

"Each time you press the button, an additional dose of your substance of choice, in your case it is opium, will be dispensed into your bloodstream. Please enjoy." The staff was as mechanical and stiff as all the other staff. But I could see how this worked. Knowing how Belinda had come offline, likely everyone freaked and started jamming away at the button.

"If you need anything else, remember the button on your left-hand side rings for me. Or just call out, as you have." The staff turned and left.

I was left there all alone. Complete silence. Sitting in a chair. Staring at a wall. No idea where I was. I remembered what King had told me: don't press the button.

"No one can make you accept a fate that you didn't choose. The problem is, you don't know that you have a choice." I remembered the urgency in his face. "I just realized this, when I was up against the tribunal. No one can make you do this, you have to accept this. When you get to the retirement home, don't press the button. If you press the button, you will never get up. If you keep pressing, the button it will kill you."

Then the thought occurred to me: food was so much better in real life. Wouldn't real opium also be better? I could press the button once. I could enjoy a good hit. It would be, dare I say, a once, no, a first, in-a-lifetime experience. My hand reached for the button. It was smooth and red, like a little pill. The bliss I would feel as the opium hit my brain...it would be wonderful. It would make this dull headache go away.

"Just get yourself up. It's easy," King had corrected himself. "No, it is hard, but you have to do it, get up."

The button felt good. I could feel the chemicals warming me from the inside out, my brain dissolving into nothing. Yes, this would be good, this would be fine. I didn't need anything; material things were irrelevant. Helping people: overrated. A black velvet cloak was swirling around and would soon envelope me. And after I had dreamed that dream, I could dream it again...

"George, trust me, do as I say."

I found myself on my feet, walking past the med-tech station. It was very similar to my own clinic, but fewer people. Everyone here was hooked up to a feeding tower with a second bag of recreation juice added to it. The med-tech looked at me but did not focus. I waved, walked down the hallway and stepped through the door that said, "Danger! Alarm! Exit!" It was a lie, there was no alarm.

Finally, I was free.

EPILOGUE

The fact that the door didn't scream surprised me. It was unreal, stepping into a dream. The day was hot and the light was blinding. I almost fell down the stairs, catching myself on a railing as I headed toward the street.

"Hey! Hey George!" I heard a familiar voice yelling at me. My eyes were still adjusting to so much light. I tried to wave back in the direction of the sound. "George, let me come and get you." A moment later, King was there. "Hey, hey! You did it!"

"I did?"

"Yes, you did." I could feel his hands on me. He was giving me half a hug and half shaking me.

I felt disoriented. "I, I'm not sure." I didn't know what I was trying to say.

"Never mind," King said enthusiastically, "let's go have breakfast."

"Really?"

"Yes, really. I bet you are hungry."

It all seemed like a dream. The restaurant was right across the street from the door I had come out of. We managed to cross the street in a fortunate break in the traffic and entered the restaurant. The wait staff didn't move and didn't greet King. He led me to a table by a window, where he could see the door of the building I'd just come out of. There were already dirty dishes on the table.

"Hey, I was hungry," King explained. "Let's order something for you." He snapped his fingers, pointed to me as a wait staff appeared.

"Yes sir, what may I get for you?"

My jaw dropped open. I'd never been asked. Staff had never talked to me like this. I was real. I felt like my heart wasn't beating any more. Words didn't come out; this was absolutely euphorically divine.

"Never mind," King interrupted—pulling the staffs gaze away from me—"my friend here, he's new in town. I think I know what

336

he likes, I think he'll have..." King ordered for me, which was good because I was still getting over being treated as a real person; we were on the level.

This was a much smaller café. We might have been the only ones in it, but it smelled just as good. The food seemed to arrive instantly. We ate, and it tasted good. Maybe because it was the first food I'd had in a long time, or maybe because it was real food. "Were you scared?" he asked me.

"Yeah."

King smiled. "But now you see, it all didn't matter anyway. It was all nothing."

"Yeah." It was so weird knowing I didn't have to go to work. We had all the time in the world. "What now?" I asked.

King smiled. I didn't know he had a gold tooth.

The zap to my head must have knocked me out. The next thing I knew, I was riding in King's car. It was a very different car. It wasn't like a metal egg that you couldn't see out of. He still had computer screens, but he also had windows. Once we got moving, he reached forward. "Check this out," he said, just before he pulled open the curtains.

"Oh my gosh!" All I could see was the back of a car, just like ours. I could see the back of their head as clearly as if they were sitting in the booth behind King at Jazmin's cafe.

"I bet you've never seen what goes on outside a car."

Actually, I had, in the garbage truck. But being this low, my heart had immediately started pounding. From this perspective, I could see why some exceptions were so dangerous. There was no distance between vehicles. "If I didn't know better, I'd say we were touching that other car." It had seemed so much safer, sitting high up in the garbage truck.

"Nah, don't worry, I'm not driving. Sit back and relax."

It took a while for me to relax. The sun began to lose its intensity as we left the city and the cars started to space out. There was a clock in the dash, and King was busy teaching me to read it. It was fairly simple, but I'd never seen a round one before, always digital, and it took some time for me to get the hang of it. King laughed and we had a great time.

He started to pull things up on his computer. It was weird looking at the internet with only such a small, two-dimensional window. It was like watching those old-time television shows, before the immersive technology. He showed me some pages about settlements. I was going to a settlement—many settlements didn't have things like the internet, or if they did, it would look like it did here in King's car—but they would have need for someone who could fix cuts and set bones. Skills like that, practical things, are hard to find. *Knowledge is carefully hoarded.* "It turns out not many people know how to do these things anymore," King commented as I read the page. "You are going to be a popular man." I'm not sure I ever remember being called a man.

We left the highway and headed out onto a different road, a smaller road, one you could turn in any direction from, onto any other roads. We headed along for a while and I saw fields planted in orderly rows. We had been driving for hours. The sun was going down and the sky was becoming more orange and less blue.

"Okay my friend," King said, as the car pulled off a long dirt road and into a parking lot. At one end of the lot there was a path leading into the trees. I could see lights. The trees were just a veil to obscure the road. "In there is a settlement that needs a medic. Are you ready for this?"

I wasn't. "Sure, I guess," I lied. "But what about you?"

King smiled. "Don't worry about me. I have to find my own way."

I didn't like this. My only friend in the world, and I had to accept that he just had to *find his own way?* "I, so, I." I didn't know what to say, "I'm not going to see you again?" I blurted out.

King laughed, nodded. "No." Then he thought about it. "I mean yes, I mean, I'm sure we will meet again."

"How?"

King put his head back on the seat and took a deep breath. "You see, that's the problem, I don't know how." He looked at me, serious all of a sudden. "The how doesn't matter. If I want to see you, I will." I shook my head at him, trying to understand.

"I have to thank you," he added, confusing me more.

I blinked at him. "Why? For what?"

"I had got all stuck in the minor things in life. I wasn't growing. I was too worried about how to do this or how to not do that. Too many hows, no intention, not enough doing." He was very serious with me, didn't seem to worry if I didn't get what he was saying. "You can immobilize yourself trying to figure out how to do something, and life will pass you by."

For the first time, my head was starting to hurt, and it wasn't caused by online stimulus. "So?" I asked, not knowing how to respond.

"So," he answered, "If you want something: first, you need to decide what you want, and intend to get it. Next, do something about it. Take action. Then, see if you are any closer to what you intend, and, decide what you need to do next."

"Huh?"

King smiled, as if he suddenly understood what he, himself, was getting at. "See? That's how I'll find you. And if not, you will find me."

"I have no idea what you are talking about?"

King grinned. "Yeah, isn't it great? It seems random, like life." He smiled widely.

"So, what am I supposed to do?"

King shook his head, "I haven't the foggiest, but I'd suggest you go in there and introduce yourself as a medic. I bet they need your help."

I looked at the lights. I could see there was a large structure, with big windows, tents, several smaller wooden buildings. "I don't know how."

"Trust me, do as I say. And stop asking how. It leads to paralysis. You will be fine, you'll be great." He smiled at me. His eyes had a faraway look, like he was remembering something, something warm. I felt better. I knew he was right.

I smiled. "Okay," I turned to the door, but it didn't open. "But how do I get out of this tin can?"

"Here," King pressed a button on the dash, "some buttons can be pressed." He smiled. The door started to slide open. I got out, and it felt good to feel my legs unfold again. The air was different here. There was a sharpness, a cleanness.

I turned back to the car. "Hey, King," I said through the open door. "I *will* see you again."

King laughed. "That's the spirit. You bet!" Then he leaned over the empty chair and shooed me with his hand, as if I was a small boy. "Now go. Be happy!"

The door started to slide down. Through the window of the car, I could see him smiling, content. The car started to roll. I could see his mouth move, and I thought he said, *See you later, my friend.* Then he was gone.

I turned, looked down the path. It was getting dark, and there were figures and shapes moving in the distant shadows of flickering lights. I was alone now, no-one controlled me. I felt no fear, no worry, no pain. I started to move, for the first time in my life I was walking, freely, on my own; my first steps, toward the light.

DISCUSSION QUESTIONS

Does this story have a happy ending?

What does rebirth mean in an electronic age?

Is all work the same? Should it be?

Why can't Andrea Dover get promoted? Or can she? What must she do?

How many people die in this novel? Do the main characters? Is metaphoric death required in order to be reborn, or is rebirth simply a choice?

There comes a point where 418/George refers to his wife as an "it." Is this the end of his marriage? Is this necessary for George to rehumanize himself?

Is gender identity unimportant, a human right, or somewhere in between?

Technology atrophies and breaks in this world—why?

Businesses that embrace cheap commodity labor are more profitable than those that invest in manufacturing capital (machinery). Is this really possible?

The creation of the staff class has imploded the wage structure and wiped out lesser-paid economic classes. Brian, who is a business owner, is evidence of the indirect effect toward the next-higher income brackets. Discuss Brian's reaction to it. How can he avoid being pulled into the staff class?

There are four sources of new staff:
  – Voluntary
  – Birth
  – Debtors
  – Corrections

Discuss the implications of each subclass of staff.

Brian and George are both paralyzed by the class system. Is Brian complicit? And how can they become free?

Both Brian and George are very isolated, neither having a significant group of friends or family to assist them. But Brian and George must cooperate in order to avoid disaster. Are we in danger of becoming as insular as George and Brian? What is preventing that?

Do Brian and George attain freedom?

Is life fair? Should it be?

Brian has his identity stolen and no-one cares, not even himself. Would we have more or less privacy in an immersive internet world?

Self-driving cars always turn right—left, in left-hand driving jurisdictions—which is somewhat different than what occurs when people drive cars. This changed the way roads are planned. What else would self-driving cars do to the way we live?

Are exceptions inevitable within a program or network of programs? If they are inevitable, are they really exceptions or simply edge cases that need to be handled?

There are several examples of programming artifacts—such as typing at a keyboard that doesn't exist—within the novel. Is there anybody writing new programming, or has cheap, commodity-like labor killed off the incentive to innovate?

Would you want to live in this world?

What would you do if you were confronted with this world?